THE HITCH-HIKER

Also by the Meg Hutchinson

Abel's Daughter

For the Sake of Her Child

A Handful of Silver

No Place of Angels

A Promise Given

Bitter Seed

Pit Bank Wench

Child of Sin

No Place for a Woman

The Judas Touch

THE
HITCH-HIKER

Meg Hutchinson writing as
Margaret Astbury

CORONET BOOKS
Hodder & Stoughton

Copyright © 2001 by Meg Hutchinson

First published in Great Britain in 2001 by Hodder and Stoughton
A division of Hodder Headline
First published in paperback in 2001 by Hodder and Stoughton
A Coronet paperback

A CIP catalogue record for this title is available from the British Library.

ISBN 0 340 79294 9

Typeset in Centaur by Phoenix Typesetting, Ilkley, West Yorkshire

Printed and bound in Great Britain by
Mackays of Chatham plc, Chatham, Kent

Hodder and Stoughton
A division of Hodder Headline
338 Euston Road
London NW1 3BH

With thanks to WPC 5072 Sam Kirk and
to PC 9839 Barry Fitzgerald for the pleasant way
they answered my questions one rainy
afternoon in Wednesbury Town Centre

The Hitch-Hiker

Following the murder of Anna, Richard Torrey injures three men leaving them half dead in the yard of a pub. No charge being laid, he gets a job as chauffeur to a local businessman, going to live on his estate in Shropshire. There he has an encounter with some unseen force in the ancient church, and the priest subsequently commits suicide.

There follows a series of murders all of which seem to have some connection with a hitch-hiker.

Martha Sim, an old inhabitant of Monkswell, implies the deaths have something to do with Richard Torrey; an evil has come with him to the village.

Following a drugs raid on the store owned by his employer, Torrey and Kate Mallory, a journalist, see the man drop to his death. Deciding he must now leave Monkswell, Torrey sees the figure of the dead Anna. The haunting continues until he at last admits to its presence and joins with Martha Sim to exorcise it.

Chapter One

It came as before; brushing his face, fingering his body held tense beneath the black clerical gown. He didn't want to move, he didn't want to breathe. The Reverend Peter Darley shuddered, holding the moan between tight lips, conscious of every orifice being an entry for . . .

'Our Father which art in Heaven . . .'

He tried to pray, but as they had been on the previous occasion the words were lost in that terrible silent laughter.

'. . . hallowed be Thy name . . .'

He tried again, lungs tight, burning, pressing up into his throat. He had to breathe! Oh God, he had to breathe!

Fingers clenching into fists he struck at empty space as his lips broke apart and he sucked at rain-washed air.

'No! I won't . . . I won't, you can't make me!'

But the cry was useless. The Reverend Darley knew it was already inside him, curled into his mouth, his nostrils, invading his brain. Sleep-starved eyes closed, their bruise-dark lids stark against pallid cheeks, his lips moving in prayer.

'Holy Mother, not here . . . please, not here.'

On each side the walls of the ancient church seemed to watch and listen.

'Our Father,' the words whispered between lips stiff with fear but at once that same soundless laughter swirled inside his head, voluptuous drowning laughter that subdued his efforts to resist, that overwhelmed his mind with its own creeping malignance before slipping away.

It knew it was the stronger, it knew he had no power against it. Peter Darley, vicar of the church of St James the Apostle, opened eyes ringed with dark circles, eyes that reflected inner fear, inner revulsion. The evil that had plagued him was not gone, it would come again. His glance flicked over the ancient walls pocked with shadowed alcoves.

Though it no longer caressed his body he could feel the pulse of its being, of its waiting in the screening of gloom, waiting for him.

At his sides his hands clenched more tightly, forcing the knuckles into small mounds, while beads of perspiration trailed over his cheeks like so many tired tears. Blinking the worst of them away he looked along the length of the nave to where the high altar stood bathed in a soft glow of muted colours, blues, reds and yellows, and high up on the grey walls fingers of cool sunlight dipped into the palette of medieval windows to paint a brilliant homage around the tall golden cross at its centre.

In the stillness it came again.

A sob caught in his throat, the fine hairs on the back of his neck stiffened and his whole body trembled.

This was what it wanted. It was here with him in the church, the evil that haunted him, here was where it sought fulfilment; here, before the high altar, the place where it would take its reckoning. But it couldn't, it must not perform its sacrilege in the house of God!

'Help me,' he whispered into the silence, 'help me, Lord.'

Amid the cloistered shadows a soft sultry laugh seemed to echo from the stillness and a hint of perfume, illusive yet definite, filled his nose and throat, the delicate yet spicy aroma flicking memories locked in the deep recesses of his mind, stirring sludgy depths, filtering, refining, then halting mockingly just beyond the edge of conscious recall.

Peter Darley's hands came together in the attitude of prayer. Along shafts of light dust motes swam like tiny goldfish trapped for all eternity in rivers of sunlight that washed over the brass plates of centuries-old tombs set in the stone floor.

'Help me.'

He whispered again but as before his prayer went unanswered except by the touch of malignant fingers. His breath catching in his throat he watched the snake-like streams of shadow slide over the cold grey walls. That evil had come again and it would go on coming, taking advantage of his naïvety about life. And he was naïve, he knew that now . . . now that it was too late. What experience had he had? An only child smotheringly protected by a mother's love. Yes, both parents have loved him and his father had loved his mother, loved her too much to risk hurting her by breaking the stranglehold he knew she had on their son, loved her too much to release the lad he could see collapsing beneath the strain; so, young as he was, Peter Darley had taken refuge in the church. He had attended every service, his mother at his side; he had been a diligent attendant at the sessions of Sunday school, when every moment of each lesson was filled with guilt for the relief he felt at being free of her if only for a short while.

Then at seventeen he had left his all-male church school for a post as clerk in the office of a newly opened store but that had been for him a kind of purgatory, being laughed at for his unrealistic views of life by men and women alike until he had broken under the stress.

A vocation in the priesthood. The old priest who had helped him over the hurdles of childhood advised his parents and they had willingly seen their son enter the Seminary.

It had been so peaceful there, so quiet. The loss of it flooded over him in a wave of grief that left him trembling. In the gentle atmosphere of the cloisters, the companionship of men intent on training to serve God as he was, the dedication and understanding of his tutors, all had helped heal his heart and his mind until at the time of his ordination into the priesthood he wanted only to stay in that quiet peace that was the Seminary, to teach as he himself was taught; but that had been denied him. The Lord had other work for him to do. The Bishop had smiled as he had said it, and though he must have seen the old fear flash in his eyes he had moved on to congratulate the other newly ordained, Peter Darley already forgotten in his mind.

Had the Lord too forgotten him?

From the shadowed pews of the empty church a sound disturbed the silence, a rustling like that of a breeze among dried leaves and beneath it that soul-deadening silent laughter that seemed to answer his thought.

'Our Father . . .'

Keeping his eyes on the far altar he began that prayer for salvation but even as the first words trembled on his lips the laughter increased, filling his head with the malevolence of a sound only he could hear while unseen fingers touched again at his body.

'Lord of Heaven, Lord of truth and goodness, forget not thy servant . . .'

Desperately the young priest tried to hold on to his flagging courage.

But where had been his own truth, his own goodness? Was the torment he was living now a retribution, a punishment for his failures? And he had failed the cloth in so many ways: in the hours spent praying to be transferred from his appointment as assistant priest at the church of St Lawrence in that smoked-grimed little Black Country town of Darlaston; in lying to himself and God when pretending not to notice the unusual interest Philip Bartley showed in the local boy scouts. He had told himself the mercy of Heaven was being shown when that longed-for transfer had come and he was positioned here at Monkswell, with Bartley as a friend who gave unlimited access to his meadows for the scout jamborees. A friend! He held the sob in his throat. Bartley had not been a friend sent of the Lord of Heaven, but one who had led the way to the Devil!

Breath coming now in audible sobs Peter Darley stared along the path he must follow, along the nave to where the high altar stood; to where that terrible evil waited. Drawn by hands he could not see and a power he could not resist he began the long walk down that shadowed nave. The altar was the place he must honour the God he served, the God he had defiled . . . the place where waited his own destruction.

'Another bloody water lily!'

Police Inspector Bruce Daniels glanced at the first few lines of a closely typed page.

Why the hell land this on his desk, was he the only bloody copper on the force?

Irritation fanning the bile already burning in his throat he slammed the file shut, skimming it across an already well-littered desk.

Why give him the case? So they'd found another one floatin' in the cut, that was nothing new, and neither was the fact the investigatin' of it had been ladled on to his plate! Well, it would be a bloody long time afore that plate were emptied!

Swallowing the acid collecting in his mouth he reached into the pocket of his worn tweed jacket, taking out a slim yellow packet. He ate more of these things than was good for him. He slipped a round white tablet into his mouth. Bloody stomach! One day he'd have it seen to.

One day! Slipping the pack back into his pocket he glared again at the buff-coloured file spewing half of its contents on to the desk. With an irritation as raw as the acid on his tongue he pushed at the tide of paper, sending various files falling to the floor. That day would be like his promotion, a bloody long time in coming!

'Tea, sir.'

Daniels glanced at the young officer who, having set a mug of tea in the few inches of clear space on his desk, now bent to retrieve the fallen files. Sandy hair brushed smartly back from a fresh face, every button gleaming like a miniature beacon on a well-pressed uniform. He had looked like that twenty years ago.

'I've put you a couple of biscuits, sir, chocolate digestive, the sergeant said you like digestive.'

Nodding his thanks, Daniels glanced bad-temperedly at the small flowered plate as the younger man left. Biscuits . . . ! Christ, that was all his stomach needed!

With bismuth a thick coating on his tongue he took a mouthful of tea, cursing under his breath as the unexpected heat of it stung the back of his throat.

. . . unlawful killing by person or persons unknown . . .

The words he had read a moment ago, already printed as clearly on his mind as they were on that page, returned as he sipped the hot drink. It was only one more body fished from the canal, some other bloody smart alec got too big for his patent leathers, so somebody had taken him out. So what! He took a bigger mouthful of tea, playing it over his tongue, rinsing the residue of the indigestion tablet from his mouth. Somebody had picked one more scab off the arse of society, well done for them. But Inspector Bruce Daniels wouldn't be investigating that little crime. Retrieving the file he placed it in a tray marked 'pending'. He had a bigger fish on his line, one that would bring promotion . . . yes, this time the top brass would have to give him his dues.

Leaning backwards in his chair he pressed his spine against it, relishing the fierce contact.

This was what he had waited all these years for and he wasn't going to throw away his chance by enquiring into the killing of some little shit of a back-alley tart.

Bruce Daniels was on his way up. He would make Divisional Inspector before Christmas and then . . . he wiped his tongue over the roof of his mouth to clear the last sticky trace of bismuth . . . it would be upwards all the way; he had no intention of spending any more years on a poky little force, he was going to the top no matter whose head he trod in the shit on his way.

He leaned harder against the chair, tilting it on to its back legs and rocking back and forth, his mind already in a different sphere.

'Done, Inspector?'

Letting the chair drop back on to all four feet, Daniels glanced at his watch as the same young constable returned to pick up his empty mug.

'Biscuits not to your taste, sir?'

'Spoil what the wife has waiting for me.'

That one would give the whole bloody lot of 'em a

laugh. Daniels watched the door close. The entire station knew the situation between him and Marjorie: he wasn't interested and she couldn't care less. A home where a fingerprint on a table or a crease in the bedcover was a criminal act was all that mattered to Marjorie.

Had it really been eighteen years they'd been married? Was the Marjorie of now the same girl that had asked him for directions that summer day? He had been appointed to the Darlaston force straight from the police college and the town had seemed dirty and unwelcoming after Sedgeton where he had lived with his grandparents. And that was a dirty little town. Daniels closed his throat against the surge of acid that refused to be calmed by the bismuth tablet. What else could you expect with the heavy industry it boasted then? But it boasted no longer, the place was dying on its feet and the children of those earlier workers stood on street corners listening to its last breath. As for welcoming, who truly welcomed a copper?

But Marjorie's parents had, or at least that was the way it had seemed then.

In the outer office a phone screamed for attention.

He had thought they had welcomed him for himself but it was a husband for their daughter they really welcomed. PC Bruce Daniels or Jack bloody Sprat, they weren't bothered either way just so long as Marjorie was off their hands. They had courted for two years and in all that time he hadn't had enough sense to realise which way the wind was blowing, too half soaked to see Marjorie was more interested in what was in her bottom drawer than she was in him.

He glanced at the door as the duty sergeant's voice spoke into the phone.

To be fair to Marjorie it had to be admitted that she had tried in those first years, always a meal ready despite never really knowing when he was free of the station, and the food was still there whenever he went back to their two-up two-down in King Edward Street, but a man needed more than food; and following the death of their only child that particular need had gone unsatisfied for longer and longer until now it never even reared its head.

Rearing its head! Staring down into his lap Inspector Daniels almost smiled. If Marjorie saw that rear its head she'd like to throw one of her precious cushions at it . . . but she would smooth the cushion afterwards!

With his face screwed up against the fire in his throat, he glanced again at his watch. Eight twenty-five. He could go home to a wife who bored the balls off him or he could go for a drink. Pushing to his feet he tapped his jacket pocket with that habitual move of checking he had car keys and stomach tablets. There was no contest!

Acknowledging the goodnight of the duty sergeant he walked outside to the car park, lifting his shoulders against the unexpected bite of night air. Right now he would appreciate a stiff whisky, not to mention a friendly little chat with Sounder. He slipped a key into the door of the tobacco-coloured car. Yes, a chat with Sounder might prove very propitious.

Settling behind the wheel he stared for several seconds through the dirt-streaked windscreen. Some might call it a bit of luck his meeting a bloke like Sounder. Inspector

Daniels's top lip flickered precariously near a smile.

'You make your own bloody luck . . .' He turned the key to bring the engine to life. 'It's called using your head . . . and anybody else's arse that happens to be around!'

A white-robed attendant danced a few quick nervous steps, wisely widening the gap between himself and the man with ice in his eyes and death on his mind.

Behind them the door of the mortuary closed on soft silent hinges. Light, brilliant and harshly white, knuckled his eyes like the fist of an attacker and he stood a moment unmoving, hardly breathing yet every nerve vitally, painfully alive, transmitting to his brain the cold impersonal atmosphere of death. He blinked once against the glare. Why the bloody hell was the place lit up like a beacon? The dead were not going to need it, not going to get up and walk! The only journey they would be taking would be in a wooden box.

'It's this way, Mr Torrey . . .'

The mortician flashed a well-rehearsed dental advert his way.

'We thought you might prefer to view the deceased in our Chapel of Rest, it's very tasteful.'

Tasteful! Richard Torrey laughed but no sound came from his tight throat. What did a bloody corpse know about tasteful surroundings? Luxury estate or council refuse dump, it was all the same when you were lying on a slab!

Irony mixing with the anger that had throbbed in him

these last weeks turned the ice in his eyes to poison-tipped darts. Why had it happened . . . they had been so happy?

Glancing at the man who stood a head taller than himself, the slim-shouldered mortuary technician showed the anxiety that had gripped him with this man's arrival. He looked as if he hated the world and wouldn't be satisfied until he had kicked the life out of it. It was usual for the bereaved to show emotion, the emotion of grief, yet this man seemed to have no grief, only a cold, grinding bitterness.

'You're sure you are going to be all right, Mr Torrey?'

Richard Torrey looked down at the narrow face, seeing none of the anxiety in the rabbit eyes. He wanted only to lash out, to kick this suave little man in his too-perfect teeth. Instead he nodded, elbowing the blank-faced door blocking his path, his six-foot frame slamming it hard against an inside wall.

It had been five days!

He swallowed the half gallon of saliva suddenly filling his mouth, the contraction of his throat loud in his ears.

Five days since the police had called. He hadn't seen Anna for weeks before that, yet call it instinct, call it second sight, give it any bloody name you like, he had known why they had come.

There had been two of them. He followed behind the dapper little figure in white jacket and trousers, white rubber-soled shoes making no sound on the rubber-tiled floor. They had both been uniformed constables. Torrey smiled grimly at the memory. Neither had looked old enough to be out without his mother. What was it folk said? When the coppers begin to look no more than kids it was you who were getting old.

They'd asked the usual questions. Was he Mr Richard Torrey, was this his usual abode? Where the hell did they think he usually abode? A cosy self-contained flat on the first floor of Buckingham Palace? One of them had written his replies in a slim black-bound notebook, the sort you could buy in any branch of Woolworth's, and Torrey had found himself wondering did they buy their own or did it come with the truncheon.

Would you take a look at this, sir?

The constable who wasn't writing had a voice deep and resonant which belied the pimply youth of his face. It had been a black and white pencil sketch, a drawing, an artist's impression not a photo-fit, not one of those cut-and-fit jobs, a piecing together of individual features that always finished up dead ringers for Frankenstein's monster.

That was fortunate for those two constables. Torrey's lips tightened. Had they given him that sort of picture of Anna he would have shoved it so far up their arses they would have needed a throat surgeon to get it out!

He had looked at the sketch then asked himself why . . . why had Anna left . . . why go off without a word . . . hadn't they been happy together?

The official questioning had gone on.

Torrey continued to follow the attendant, who kept a short distance between them as he led the way along a faceless white-walled corridor.

Did he know the person in that sketch . . . had the person resided at this address . . . for how long . . . when had this person left . . . for what reason . . . had he had any contact with that person during that time?

He'd cracked a little then, allowing an uncertain fear of that of which he was only too certain get to him. The feeling that had ripped through him then returned now, a cold certain fear that sliced every vein.

That person had a bloody name! He'd shouted, skimming the carefully drawn sketch at the nearest police officer, a perverse sort of satisfaction cooling the flames of temper as the young man grabbed for it and the cap he had secured beneath his arm followed his notebook to the floor.

We must ask you not to leave the district without first informing the station . . .

The second constable had sounded nervous as his colleague bent to retrieve cap and notebook. It hadn't been an unfounded nervousness. Torrey followed as his guide turned left. At that moment he could have gone for the two of them, snapped at least one neck before a truncheon found its mark.

You understand sir . . .

The pimple-faced one had almost run for the door as he spoke, followed arse-close by the other.

. . . you are not to leave the area unless informing us first, you may be required for further questioning should the need arise . . .

He had suddenly wanted to laugh. Fear and hurt mixing like a drug, he had simply wanted to laugh. Even now, following along the cold antiseptic corridors of the council morgue he felt the same wild irrational urge. Christ, who taught those bloody kids? Was that what they were sent to training colleges to learn, or had those two been something special?

'*I'm not about to take off for bloody Rio . . .*' he'd snapped, close at their well-polished heels as they reached the door. '*You've asked your questions, now how about answering one of mine? Why a pencil sketch, why not a photograph?*'

His blood had curdled as he'd watched them squirm for an answer, curdled as it was doing now.

'The deceased, Mr Torrey . . . you are a relative?'

Blinking more in an effort to clear his thoughts than against the brilliant whiteness of the corridor he didn't remember walking along, Torrey looked at the mortuary attendant. This time teeth were invisible behind the discretionary cover of full, rather pink, lips; it was as well! His fingers curled into compacted balls of dynamite. One more of those media-conscious smiles and he wouldn't be able to prevent himself performing a quick, though very painful, extraction!

'Yes.' He spoke the lie quietly. Let this little runt ask for identification and it would be the last thing he'd ever ask.

'I'm sorry to have to ask, but we have our jobs to do, you understand.'

Oh, he understood all right! He understood; constables, mortuary attendants, detectives, they all had their bloody jobs to do, only some bastards took such a bloody delight!

He turned away, the desire to smash that fact into somebody's face almost too much to hold. It wasn't this man's fault, so whose fault was it that his life was in shreds!

*

The lighting inside the Chapel of Rest was softer, more subdued, easier on the eyes but harder on the nerves. Christ, he'd never thought to feel like this, like a child terrified to move in case something unseen and unnamed grabbed him; but unlike a child he couldn't scream until someone came to take away his fear. He had to move, to go forward, to walk to the low glass-enclosed dais in the centre of this silent watching room, an overhead beam spotlighting the plain deal box set on it.

Torrey's nostrils widened, gulping in air, taking his lungs to overfill. Squeamishness was not one of his short-comings, dead bodies didn't worry him, not any more. He'd seen enough of them during his tour of duty in Northern Ireland, men and women chewed by bombs into twisted lumps of flesh which bore no resemblance to human beings, guns ripping people apart. Reprisals! Jesus, that was an overworked word.

It seemed his whole life had been bound up with re-prisals. As a kid he'd beaten those who had laughed at his secondhand clothes, at brightly polished shoes they knew had no bottoms in. Oh yes, the wonderful Welfare State! It was supposed to ensure no one lived a life of poverty, that everything in the garden stayed lovely . . . until you asked for help, like his mother had when his father had walked out on them. That had been his biggest cause for taking reprisals but not once had he told his mother the reasons for the almost permanent black eye, the never-ending bruises.

'Fighting again, Torrey!'

Christ, he could hear the words of the headmaster that had become an almost daily chant.

'We must see if we can do something about that!'

But what could that headmaster do? Could he ease the pain of his mother, wipe the tears a young boy saw in her eyes every night and morning?

In the end nobody had done anything. She was still young enough to work was the verdict of that so-supportive state, she must get a job; and that was what she had done, she had worked her life away for pennies while he had fought his way to St Bartholomew's school every morning then back to Dangerfield Lane every afternoon, lashing out at the lads who sneered behind his back.

He had joined the Army the moment he was old enough. That way he could ease her burden, take away the responsibility for feeding and clothing him, his pay sent home. But it hadn't gone home for long, twelve months after his signing up his mother had died.

Reprisals! Richard Torrey drew a long slow breath. How did you take reprisal for that!

Perhaps he had thought that the Army would put an end to all that, that at last the reprisals would stop. But in Ireland he had learned how wrong that hope was.

He breathed again, unable to check the thoughts that spiralled in his mind. There had been faults on both sides, but too many murders had been crowded under the umbrella of reprisal; too many kids without brain enough to think for themselves found it easy to take the gun others shoved into their hands, easy to mark a target, easy to pick off some poor sod, squeeze the trigger and watch him fall apart, so easy to claim they did it for their God.

He'd joined the Army with the intention of becoming permanent after the initial three years, of making the service his lifetime career, but Ireland had changed all that; sectarian murder? Slaughter in the name of religion was the way he'd seen it and it had sickened him; the Army could do without him and he could do without religion!

Suddenly aware his temples were drumming a tattoo he released the air from bursting lungs only to drag in more, equally deeply. No, dead bodies had come to mean less than nothing to him, one more or less, where was the difference? But this time . . . he felt the sweat on the palms of his hands, the taste of moisture oozing from his top lip into his mouth . . . this time it was Anna, *his* Anna.

Lifting the back of his hand he wiped it beneath his nostrils like a kid dashing away snot, but he was wiping away evidence of his own fear; fear of what he knew waited for him there in its gleaming nest, in that box carefully draped with red cloth. They might as well have left the blood!

'Would you rather leave now, Mr Torrey?'

'No!' He did not look at the figure who moved to stand beside him. With his fingers dug deep into sweat-soaked palms he walked slowly forward, fear of what he would see pressing hard on his throat, what he knew he might see, yet in a thousand years would never have guessed.

Chapter Two

Sounder was already well lubricated.

Daniels collected drinks from the bar, nodding with satisfaction to himself as he carried them to a table already littered with empty glasses, a lining of froth attesting to their previous contents, each standing in its own tiny puddle of Banks's best bitter. The Frying Pan wasn't exactly known for its captivating interior but then he wasn't here for the home comforts, he was here for the floor show.

Placing the drinks on the table he took one of the hard wooden chairs, noting the other man's subtle choice of location as he sat. Not near enough to the bar to be obvious, but then Sounder did not need to be close in order to overhear a conversation even in a room where everybody seemed to be competing for voice of the year; with ears as keen as a bat's radar, Sounder could pick up the drop of a wet fart from a mile away.

Taking a pull from his glass Inspector Daniels sent a

casual, no-movement glance cutting through the fog of tobacco smoke. A new face at the bar! It had not gone unnoticed as he had waited to be served, now he took in the expensive suit and leather shoes. Neither Rubery Owen nor any of the other factories in Darlaston had ever paid that sort of wage! Letting his seemingly non-enquiring glance slide to the left he watched a cloth-capped figure weave through a door marked 'Toilets'. He knew it gave on to a passage that led to a tumble-down yard housing the usual offices; not that the 'Gents' was used overmuch, the local clientele usually directing their jet against the wall. The women? He couldn't vouch for the inside of their piss parlour but if it was anything like the other stinking hole then they would surely bottle up their water 'til they found a cleaner place to pour it!

The other man's nod acknowledged the double whisky, no ice no water, placed beside his elbow but he said nothing as Daniels lowered himself on to his own chair, so placed as not to obstruct the view of the bar.

'Been anything good on the box lately?'

Daniels's glance lifted to the television angled on the wall behind the bar, the sound turned too low for anyone to hear, the re-run of the afternoon's horse racing events going mainly unwatched.

'Might 'ave bin.'

A line of creamy froth adorning his upper lip, the small round-shouldered man seemed less than interested in conversation.

'Had any winners?' Taking another swallow of his own

neat whisky the inspector's glance seemed non-committal.

'A few.'

'You've done a bloody sight better than me then.'

Reaching into the pocket of his shabby tweed jacket Daniels drew out a full packet of Royals. Smoking didn't help his stomach but it helped his concentration. Offering the pack to the other man he watched dirt-lined fingers extract a cigarette, place one between cracked lips then slip the rest of the pack into his pocket before leaning towards the lighted match.

'I could do with a winner.' Daniels held the match to his own cigarette before extinguishing it with a long smoke-filled breath.

'We could all do with them, most times betting is like wiping your arse on money.' His eyes on the television screen the other man twisted his lips, angling the cigarette into the corner of his mouth.

'Well I've had enough of the non-starters.' Daniels's voice dropped a few octaves but not so low his companion did not catch the hint of warning. 'I want to know what's going on, who's brought those men on to my patch and why.'

'You 'as to follow form . . .'

'No, Sounder, I don't!' Daniels snapped. 'And I don't 'ave to listen to your racing jargon, leave that for the tipsters. I'll 'ave what I pay for in language that can 'ave no two ways about it.'

The mouse-brown head rose and fell following the lift of horses over the fences, the screwed-up mouth tightening.

Catching the displeasure flick across the narrow ferret-like face Inspector Daniels delivered the ultimatum he had often relished. Sounder must know that this time he meant business.

'How do you feel about getting a job, Sounder, say a bricklayer's labourer . . . ? I hear they are taking on new hands on that housing site up along Katherine's Cross, a bit more tiring than signing on the dole once a week but then you won't mind a bit of manual labour, will you?'

Watching the look that flashed into the other man's eyes, Daniels felt himself teetering on the brink of a smile but he continued to speak without falling over the edge.

'Well, Sounder, what's it to be . . . do I hear what's going on or do you hear goodbye from the dole office?'

Tipping his glass to his mouth in a final effort to collect the last drops of moisture, Echo Sounder placed it back on the table, edging it slightly nearer to Daniels's elbow than it had been before. Daniels was a bastard. The threat of shopping him to the dole hadn't been said just to make conversation, he'd do it and revel in it.

'Another one?' Daniels picked up both glasses, the calves of his legs pushing his chair backwards. He would give what he had said time to sink in, not that there was much danger of it not doing so!

At the crowded bar he waited to be served, his eyes raking the room while appearing to look at nothing and no one in particular. Years of practice had brought this illusion to a fine art and by the time he had paid the barmaid a cheeky compliment and received his change in kind he had registered every face in the noisy, smoky room.

Placing the double whisky strategically beside the fresh pint of best bitter he had also bought – another few quid on his bloody expense sheet – he hooked a foot around one leg of his chair bringing it smartly beneath him. His tongue already savouring his own Glen Malt he sat down, not moving his head as the door to the street swung open and a draught of night air stirred the banks of low-lying tobacco smoke into thick grey swirls.

Beside him Sounder's quick little eyes never moved from the silent horses racing across the television screen but Daniels knew he had also noted the smart grey-suited figure go to stand beside the other newcomer at the bar, one foot resting on the brass rail that ran the length of it, an elbow propped on the beer-soaked counter. That wouldn't do a lot for his smart clobber.

Reaching for the brimming pint, dirt-ingrained fingers closing claw-like about the glass, Sounder drank noisily, wiping froth from his lips with the back of his hand. The inspector wouldn't take kindly to evasion, but then a free tongue could prove a missing tongue.

'Them two been brought in from York,' he murmured, attentively studying his glass. 'Stables 'ere . . .'

'I said cut the racing jargon! If I want it like that I'll buy the *Sporting Pink!*'

His hand reaching irritably to his pocket for cigarettes Daniels remembered what had happened to the previous pack. He'd wait until he was back in the car. His glance following black-etched fingers transfer beer foam to trouser leg, Daniels digested the information titbit, at the same time wondering whether his informant's racing profits ever stretched to buying a bar of soap or his conversation was carried on in any other than racing terms. Living most of his life hanging around the tracks he fitted everything into the style of language peculiar to the racing fraternity and talked of people as just so much horseflesh.

'So what 'ave you got on those two?' he spoke again. 'And don't say you 'ave nothing, for a dog don't take a pee in this town without you knowin' about it.'

The question hanging in smoke-hazed air, Daniels waited. Had his words been too much for the little nark to decipher? He watched the narrow face, brown and weather-lined. It looked like an oversized walnut, except walnuts didn't have eyes or ears and Sounder had both, and it was certain they were trained on the two strangers standing at the bar.

Resisting the urge to look in their direction the inspector took a swallow from his glass. The gear those men were wearing didn't come from Burtons; Darlaston had never seen clobber like that and here in the Frying Pan it was about as invisible as a boil on the end of the nose.

'Word 'as it they've been brought in by Philip Bartley. Seems he has a shipment of summat special bein' brought to that new place he's built across at the Leys, summat as'll sell for more than a fiver.'

Jargon or not Daniels understood. This was going to cost him plenty, Sounder meant to rake off as much as he could before letting his tongue loose. His hand touched again to his pocket and again withdrew leaving the packet untouched inside it. Bloody cigarettes! He couldn't really afford to smoke at all on his pittance of a salary, let alone get through sixty a day, but even trying to kick the habit would be like cutting his own throat; how could a man think without a fag between his lips?

The movement of Daniels's hand had not gone unnoticed and Sounder touched a finger to his own well-drained glass, continuing reluctantly when his companion remained blind to the unspoken request.

'You knows of Bartley?' he muttered.

Daniels's memory clicked into gear. Bartley owned a chain of supermarkets springing up in every town in the Black Country. But it was all a bit too much too soon for the money to have come from wages that had once been earned in the steel mill; question was, just where had it come from? Shoving the thought to the back of his mind he cast a sideways glance at the bar before answering.

'I've heard of him. So what's he up to that needs new talent?'

'I can't tell you that, Mr Daniels.' The beady little eyes fastened once more on the empty glass.

'You can and you will, or spend a few nights in the nick while you ponder which horse to back next, not that you'll have much chance of laying bets, Winson Green prison is no bloody holiday hotel. So . . . do you want to go over that one again?'

Wiping a hand beneath damp nostrils before stroking it along his trouser leg, Sounder shook his head.

'I ain't heard no more . . .'

'Stop negotiating, Sounder!' Daniels's voice cracked like a pistol shot. 'Try messing me about and I'll have you inside quicker than you can fart!'

'It . . . it be nowt more'n a guess.' Beady eyes watched a tablet being placed on the inspector's tongue.

'Then make sure you give it your best go, the beds at the Green ain't what you might call luxurious.'

'There's word of a meeting . . .' Catching the frown Sounder remembered the order to speak in plain English. Bloody coppers! He stared irately at his empty glass. Daniels understood all right, saying otherwise was no more than bloody-mindedness. Maybe he was in a foul mood because he'd sat his arse on one of his wife's fancy cushions and had his balls chewed off for doin' it!

'. . . there's word of summat big goin' on,' he went on, a smile at his own thoughts hidden, along with his nose as he searched for the last drop in an empty glass, 'and it 'pears that Bartley be at back of it.'

'Where and when?'

'That big new building of Bartley's out along of the Leys be where I 'ear, but as for when . . .'

Inspector Bruce Daniels leaned back hard on the chair, lifting two of its legs clear of the bare wooden floor. 'Echo, you know quite a lot about horse racing but I wonder how much do you know of the law? For example, did you know that claiming money from Her Majesty's Treasury on false pretences carries a severe penalty, or that failure to declare income – however it be got – to the Inland Revenue can result in being locked away so long that nobody remembers you exist?'

At the bar the two men tossed off the last of their drinks, their departure followed by more than one pair of curious eyes.

'It be set for Wednesday,' Sounder returned grudgingly. 'But don't tek that as gospel, it be . . .'

'I know, a guess. But a guess is sometimes better than nothing, let's hope this is one of those times.' Daniels watched the sudden swirl of tobacco smoke churned by the rush of air from the closing door reassemble, settling like grey clouds at just above head height. 'Now how about making it a double and guessing at what time Bartley will make a move?'

'Two thirty a.m.' Sounder nudged his empty glass.

'Helped by who?'

The obvious once more ignored, the grimy hand lifted again to damp nostrils. Daniels missed nothing. It would pay nowt to try putting one over on 'im; pity he weren't so bloody quick in going to the bar!

The inspector watched his informant in silence, drawing in deep breaths of secondary smoke which did little to alleviate his desire for a cigarette. Ferret-thin, brown hair thick and mane-like, eyes green yet at the same time gold with pupils split like a cat's, a mouth that seemed to grudge opening to let out quickly spurted words, the shoulder pads of his too-large jacket hanging well past the edge of his shoulders, Echo Sounder toyed with an empty glass.

'Doc Walker.'

Heavy eyelids lifted fractionally and as those cat-like eyes touched his, Daniels felt as though a barbed instrument suddenly pierced his eyeballs. Then the lids dropped again and the sensation was gone.

'An' he's lettin' nobody close enough to get to see what it is they've cooked up between 'em; it be my bet there be too much ridin' on this little venture for Bartley to tek any chances.'

Acid surging up violently from his stomach washed into Daniels's mouth, the fire of it causing his eyes to water.

Doc Walker!

He blinked, forcing the moisture gathered in his eyes to spill like tears on to his cheeks. Walker had been struck off by the General Medical Council for improper practice; he'd done five years for supplying drugs, would have done a bloody sight longer if it hadn't been for that smart-arsed London lawyer! He swallowed and sent the stinging liquid back down his suffering throat. If Doc Walker was involved then the 'race' was crooked, and if Bartley was in on it . . . He swallowed again, reaching for another BiSoDol tablet. He'd wanted that particular pigeon for some time; if he could take them both . . . !

'Anything I should know of, any handicap?'

Beneath the hooded lids Sounder's eyes gleamed the hint of a smile at the use of the word; for somebody not understanding tipsters' terms, Daniels wasn't doing so badly.

'Not any *I* know of . . .'

Taking a cigarette from the pack he had slipped with apparent forgetfulness into his own pocket, and now slipped back without offering them to their previous owner, he struck a match, inhaling deeply as the tip of the tobacco turned a dull red. Closing one eye as the drift of smoke curled into it he held the burning match, seeming to study its rate of burn as Daniels waited.

'. . . but don't let that throw you,' he said as the match burned down to his fingers and he dropped it into a pool of beer slopped on to the centre of the table. 'Bartley has had runners in the field afore, he be no novice at the game and he's out for the cup at this meeting.'

Why the hell did Sounder have to talk like a bloody horse-race commentator? Renewed irritation stirred the acid in Daniels's throat. He wanted to slam the little shit into a cell and let him roast for a week, but to come down on him at this point would mean him drying up altogether and things were too promising to give up now. Bartley had pulled off drug trafficking before, that he would bet his pension on, but catching him at it . . . that had been tried and had failed. Christ, what were the chances of getting him this time . . . do that and promotion would be a certain follow up.

Picking up the other man's glass he resigned himself to buying another round. If he hoped to get Sounder to do a canary then he must be prepared to feed him, and the particular brand of seed was labelled Glenfiddich.

Exchanging another savoury comment with the barmaid he passed a five-pound note across the counter, his glance on the high, pushed-together breasts and the low-cut neckline designed to keep the punters' eyes off the measure in their glasses. A look was the closest he was likely to get to any such delectable fruit, the closest he'd got these many years; in fact he sometimes found himself trying to remember whether Marjorie had tits.

Pocketing his change he glanced again at longed-for territory. Banks's best bitter was good but there were other attractions that helped keep the Frying Pan the most frequented tavern in Darlaston.

Setting the Scotch in front of the man whose eyes might as well have been glued to the television screen, Daniels looked around briefly and saw there had been no fresh comings or goings, the low-lying cloud of smoke hanging undisturbed over the room.

'You better make that worth it,' he grunted, already feeling the dent in his expense allowance.

Grimed fingers closed possessively about the smaller glass; drink before answering, that way Daniels couldn't take the Scotch back. Running a tongue over dry lips, gathering the last tiny golden drop, Echo Sounder answered quietly.

'Nobody seems to know much about that pair who stood at the bar, or if they does then they ain't sayin'. Bartley has ears everywhere and his justice be dished out quicker than that of the law; a man talks and he finishes up in the cut with his innards dragged out . . .'

Was that what had happened to the latest water lily? Daniels kept the question to himself as Sounder muttered on.

'. . . they both matches word of a couple that gied the coppers the slip a few weeks back, that drugs haul up York way. Your lot got the stuff but they d'ain't get the runners . . .'

He flicked his eyes sideways, a mocking laugh in the cat-like green depths.

'. . . you could always phone for a description, Mr Daniels, I'm sure them up at York'd be glad to 'elp.'

And even more glad to muscle in! One word of heroin being Philip Bartley's game and he could kiss goodbye to the case and to his promotion.

Sounder smiled into his glass. That bit about contacting York coppers had the inspector riled.

'Cut the comedy!' Daniels's voice was as sharp as the acid in his stomach. 'Where are they staying?'

'Not in Darlaston, that's fer sure. I did 'ear summat about a 'otel in Brummagem . . .'

Birmingham! Daniels winced. Should that lot get wind of what was going on they'd be all over the place like blue-arsed flies.

'. . . the Weston was mentioned,' Sounder carried on, 'big posh place close by the Rotunda, but Bartley ain't one to count the pennies if a thing be worth the 'aving so you can bet yer prick that place be where them two be holed up.'

Bet his prick . . . and lose it? Daniels almost smiled. Why not? He'd used it for nothing other than to piss through for longer than even he could remember.

'Anything else?' He watched the narrow face intently. He had to be sure, had to get everything he could on this one. Sounder had been making no joke when he'd said Philip Bartley was no novice at this game.

'Ain't nuthin' I've heard of . . .'

Daniels watched Sounder's fingers grind the last

half inch of cigarette into an ashtray whose lion logo was already lost beneath layers of crushed tobacco, smoke folding the rest of his words in a grey embrace. '. . . Bartley keeps things close to 'is chest, but 'e needn't be appryensive, there be none hereabout can play in his league.'

Could be the going might get tough, prove a little too hard for the runners! Daniels shoved his chair back, the feet scraping on the wooden floor. Christ, he was getting to think in Sounder's jargon!

'Mr Daniels . . .'

It was spoken so quietly that anyone more than half a yard away would have no chance of hearing.

'. . . 'ow about a packet o' fags afore you leaves?'

Reaching into the pocket he had fondled several times while talking, Inspector Bruce Daniels dropped a second carton of Royals cigarettes on to the stained table. It wasn't quite filled with tobacco but there was enough money in it to keep the scruffy little songbird happy.

'An' Mr Daniels' – the voice was lower, quieter still but the inspector caught it – 'if it be you should manage to get into the winner's enclosure, then 'ave yourself a look up their arse, could be you'll find more'n shit!'

Tapping his pocket and feeling the outline of car keys, his frame disturbed the pall of smoke as Daniels opened the door that gave on to the street, the sudden draught of air sending the smoke scurrying into demented swirls, each coiling into the other and seeking protection from being sucked out into the night.

'. . . *could be you'll find more'n shit.*'

Lighting up a cigarette he breathed in deeply, relishing the bite of smoke against his lungs. Then slipping a key into the lock he opened the car, a hint, faint yet nevertheless a hint, of a smile damaging the straight line of his mouth.

Chapter Three

'Into Thy hand, O Lord, we commend the spirit . . .'

Dark red curtains parted soundlessly and the coffin with its solitary wreath of purple and white irises, a small white card edged with black and bearing the single word 'Torrey', glided slowly and silently from sight.

From his place in the front pew of Ryecroft Crematorium Torrey watched. He could have chosen to sit anywhere in the tiny chapel, in any one of the rows of well-polished pews. Apart from the vicar, he was the only one there; no family, and today at least Anna had no other friend.

'. . . in the sure and certain knowledge of the resurrection to eternal life . . .'

His black clerical gown relieved by a white silk stole about his shoulders the priest closed the prayer book, intoning the final words of the funeral service from memory. Then turning to Torrey he raised one hand, making the sign of the cross as he spoke the benediction.

'May the blessing of Almighty God . . .'

Where the bloody hell had God been as Anna was being murdered! Stamping from the pew he brushed past the priest to stand before the closed curtains. Who had done this, killed the one person in the world he loved? He didn't know. But he would, yes, by Christ he would! And when he did they would die as Anna had died.

Standing in the doorway, the vicar waited. He had officiated at the crematorium and at cemeteries many times, reciting prayers for the dead and comforting the bereaved; but this man seemed to want no comfort, no word of sympathy. Fidgeting with the stole he glanced at the man standing staring at the closed curtains. One mourner, one single solitary mourner; it was no business of his, but nevertheless it was unusual.

In the dimness of the tiny, all-denominational chapel, Torrey turned to take in the bareness of it all. No colourful stained glass, no statues of the heavenly hierarchy, no hymns or organ swelling away the silence; just bare walls and that small raised platform that had held the coffin. Now that too was gone. But this wasn't the end. He turned back to the red velvet closing off all that had meant anything to him. An eye for an eye, wasn't that what the Good Book said? The Bible! The laugh remained trapped in his throat. Since when had the Bible done his sort any good! It was nothing but a placebo, an opiate trotted out to the working classes through the centuries. Whenever the likes of Richard Torrey had questioned the fairness of the system the words were preached: it was easier for a camel to pass through the needle's eye . . . as you sow in this world, so you reap in the next . . . He knew them all off by heart! But where did that leave Anna?

Automatically his hand moved towards his brow as it so often had when he was a boy at St Bartholomew's. They'd spent as much time in church praying and making the sign of the cross as they had doing all the rest of the school work put together. And for what! His hand dropped before the signing was done. It had been nothing but crap and he'd finished with it. An eye for an eye . . . ! That wasn't enough; it couldn't even begin to make up for what he'd lost. An eye for an eye! He laughed aloud, pushing past the waiting priest. It was going to take more than that, much more to atone for Anna's death.

Changing down through the gears Inspector Daniels eased the Ford around a tight bend. Marjorie didn't like him using the car for anything other than the short run to her sister's on a Sunday afternoon; Marjorie would like to keep it polished, where the neighbours could see it. Marjorie would keep it in a bloody glass case!

The little finger of his left hand moved to flick a switch just beneath the steering wheel and wiper blades whispered across the windscreen clearing fast-accumulating spots of rain.

Bloody weather! He took a right, checking his mirror for following traffic. Railway Street! He snorted. What sort of bloody name was that! Darlaston had no railway;

that had gone, wiped away by some smart-arsed git who'd never been to the town.

His foot came down on the accelerator, sending the car shooting forwards. A shadow, black on grey, just cleared his wheels as, tyres screaming, he turned left too sharply. Ahead of him a solitary street lamp, the only one with an unbroken head, grudgingly shed a pool of tubercular yellow light. Why leave that one? His eyes were already beyond the sickly smudge. Perishing vandals! Nothing was safe from them; bloody kids getting their kicks from smashing everything in view.

Acid boiling up from his stomach adding to his irritation, he pressed harder on the pedal. It wasn't just lamp posts either, nothing and nobody was safe from them. But they must not be punished, what they did was a cry for help. Cry for help! That was some trite shit dreamed up by do-gooders out to make a name for themselves and arseholes to the public. Too bad the cat was no longer legal, lay that across their backs a time or two and they wouldn't feel so clever; lay it on like Jack Daniels, with all the strength of a foundry man's arm.

The belt across his backside had been part of Bruce Daniels's growing up as had the regular beatings his mother had suffered.

Acid surged higher, burning the length of his gullet before settling like a pool of flame in his throat.

He'd become used to seeing his mother's face swollen and bruised, her eyes almost closed by those huge iron fists; yes, he'd got used to it but never forgiven it. His father beating him to rid himself of the devil riding his back was one thing, but beating his mother . . . He swallowed but the acid remained, just as the memory of that night remained.

She had tried to shield him that night as she always had. He wrenched the car around a bend, the scream of tyres echoing the scream in his heart.

Just sixteen he'd been then. Sixteen and working a nine-hour shift at Lloyd's steelworks, then attending the local Institute evening classes from seven thirty to nine thirty Monday to Friday. The benefit of that had been twofold. He could study for a City and Guilds certificate in engineering while at the same time it took him out of the drab two-up two-down council house in Barfield Road.

Jabbing a foot on the brake he swore vehemently at the dog darting across his path.

His mother had done her best, scrubbing and cleaning that house after scrubbing and polishing her heart out for folk who paid her in pennies, but it did no good. What bits of furniture she possessed had come from the ragman's cart, their days of presenting a decent front long gone. She had cleaned the house that last night. Daniels blinked, feeling the moisture gather behind his eyelids. She was putting his tea on the table when his father had staggered into the kitchen. Reeking of whisky, eyes bloodshot, he had swept one arm across the table, sending the bowl of hot broth hurtling against the wall.

'*That'sh right,*' he'd slurred, '*feed your whelp, you no-good bloody bitch, feed the runt, never mind me!*'

Hands locked on the wheel, Daniels felt the shiver run down his back as he remembered the thick fingers going to that broad leather belt, releasing the buckle with a dexterity only regular use could give and no amount of booze could take away.

'. . . never mind me . . .'

The belt had swung in a singing arc, its heavy metal buckle crashing on to the scrubbed wooden table.

'. . . well I'll gie 'im a taste o' summat more'n broth, 'e won't feel like eatin' when I be done wi' 'im!'

Daniels squeezed his eyes tight shut for a second as memory showed him the thin worn-out figure of his mother pushing him off the chair and placing her own body between him and the mindless drunken brute that had fathered him.

Ahead of him the road stretched away, its darkness peopled by shadows.

He had run then. God forgive him, he'd run that time as he always had. Knowing his mother was in for a belting he'd been too afraid to even try shielding her. He'd run! Oh Christ . . . he'd run!

The patter of rain on the roof brought the memory to life the same way it did on those nights he lay awake beside Marjorie, her hair done up in curlers.

The evening class had finished without his hearing one word of the lecture. He'd taken the long route home, along the canal and across the back of the chemical works. His father would be out, gone back to drinking with his cronies in the Struggler public house. But that hadn't been the reason for taking the scenic route home, it was reluctance to face his mother's bruises. Only his mother had not been there!

The house had been silent. That in itself was not unusual. They hardly ever had money for food let alone the luxury of a wireless set. The unusual thing had been seeing his father sitting alone. He glanced sideways as if looking again at the cheap enamel clock stood on the rickety sideboard. It hadn't been much after ten and his father never staggered in until after midnight, yet there he was sitting alone at the kitchen table.

Taking care to stand with the door still open at his back he had asked where his mother was. Jack Daniels had not looked up as he answered.

The hospital! Daniels felt again the sick despair he had felt as that answer had come. He remembered the cry he had been unable to hold inside, remembered running as though his arse were afire. She was already dead when he got there. He had not asked the cause . . . he had no need, he had known already.

He breathed hard, the pain as raw and biting as it had been thirty years ago.

His father had still been sitting at the table when he'd walked slowly back into the silent kitchen but his head had jerked quickly on its bull neck when told his wife was dead.

'An' where was yoh?'

In his mind's eye Inspector Bruce Daniels saw the bloodshot eyes fill with a new blood lust as his father had pushed to his feet.

'*Where was yoh when yer mother tumbled over that chair? I'll tell yer where yer was, paradin' yer prick in front o' them wenches down along the canal . . . that be where yoh was!*'

48

Parading his prick. Daniels swung the car hard right. It would have been funny if it hadn't been so pathetic; fat chance he'd had of pulling any wench, him in trousers that shone brighter than a harvest moon and a jacket that hadn't fitted properly since he was fourteen.

He'd watched the massive hands go to the buckle of the wide black leather belt.

He glanced at his own hands gripped too tight about the steering wheel.

That was when he had lashed out. He'd grabbed the heavy flat iron from the kitchen range and struck at the drunken face, then struck again as Jack Daniels had staggered backwards; he had kept on striking until no vestige of flesh was visible beneath the blood.

He had felt none of the fury that had always driven his father, none of that compulsion to hurt, only a sweet soul-cleansing. Had that been the sweetness of revenge?

Jack Daniels had been a big-boned man, large framed and heavy, but almost as if aided by powers other than his own he had managed to get him to that part of the canal overlooked by old coal workings, those heaps of pit waste piled into black hills. Dragging the still form to the top he had rolled it on to its back, then scooping handfuls of that rough slag he had rubbed it into the bleeding face, repeating the process several times before sending the body rolling into a pit of slime-filled water. If he were found before he rotted it would seem Jack Daniels had slipped while in one of his regular drunken stupors and slithered to his death.

He had never been back to that house since. From that

time on he had lived with his grandparents at Sedgeton until being appointed to the Darlaston police force.

A car flashed past and Daniels blinked against the glare, snapping back from his childhood. The headlights of the Ford were following a line of tiny Victorian houses fronting straight on to the pavement; houses that would benefit more from a bulldozer than from renovation.

Right foot switching from accelerator to brake pedal he pressed gently, changing gear and turning the car more carefully as he took another corner. With his eyes screwed up to peer at the dark smudge of the houses he found what he was looking for. Dropping to a crawl he eased the nose of the vehicle over the lip of the pavement, bumping it cautiously on to the patch of derelict ground, watching intently the headlights picking out shadowed, uneven mounds that were the remains of long-demolished buildings. The last thing he needed was a bloody puncture! Why the hell did the council never finish a job!

Killing the engine he sat staring through the windscreen. Jesus, what a dump Darlaston was, as much a dump as Sedgeton had been. But then he had little intention of remaining here; Bruce Daniels wasn't going to be kept down for ever, and this business with Bartley would provide just the lift he needed.

Reaching into the glove compartment he drew out a slim blue and yellow carton, flicking up the top and extracting a white tablet. Placing the BiSoDol on the back of his tongue he sucked hard. Christ, he really would have to see a doctor!

Mint-flavoured saliva making no inroad into the acid

burning his throat, he swore softly. It had been like this since that phone call. So a stiff had been pulled from the cut! What was mind-blowing about that? That stretch of water held all kinds of filth, so why should a corpse create such a stir?

But it had, and the ripples had reached the top.

'Play it down,' the Chief Constable had ordered in a phone call direct to him. Had he thought that would cut out any talk? It had only set tongues wagging at the station; why did the top brass want to speak personally to an inspector on some shitty little insignificant force? 'Keep this from the press,' he'd been told, 'this one isn't for broadcasting.' There had been no why or wherefore, not even 'Do your best, Inspector'; just a flat order with an even flatter implication: keep this one quiet or it's your arse will feel the kick!

Well he'd managed that, helped by a local teenager being picked to try for Albion. That had grabbed the headline of the *Star* and the nationals had no column space for some back-alley suicide.

Only it hadn't been a suicide! Daniels watched raindrops gather into rivulets that streamed down the windscreen. He had seen the body. No one sane or insane did that to themselves. But why that phone call, what was it had set the cat among those particular pigeons? The answers were there and this could be his chance to play with the big boys. Bartley and this . . . together they must spell promotion!

Flicking a second tablet into his mouth he tossed the carton back into the glove compartment. Echo would be here in the Frying Pan. Christ, somebody had a sense of humour to name a pub that, but then there were more deals cooked inside that place . . .

Climbing from the car he locked the door, putting the keys into his jacket pocket. If anybody knew anything of that tart's murder it would be Echo Sounder, and a pint and a packet of Royals would set that little grass talking.

Torrey drew a long breath, seeing again the picture that haunted him, the picture of an attractive face framed with white-blonde hair, a generous mouth parted in a wide smile, laughing hyacinth-blue eyes filled with vivid promise.

He had tried pretending things were all right, but Anna wasn't there, Anna wasn't anywhere; but some murdering bastard was and he would find him.

The last dregs of beer dribbling down his chin he sent the glass crashing against the wall. He had been drinking since that funeral, but the brain he hoped to numb remained expensively clear. Flopping back on to the bed, one arm drooped loosely over the side, the other flung across his chest, fingers digging convulsively into hard flesh.

But it wasn't his own flesh he felt there. It was a firm supple flesh, arms and legs frosted with a dusting of fine white-gold hairs. Anna!

A cry breaking from him he flung both arms above his head, twin sets of knuckles cracking against the wooden headboard.

But Anna was dead . . . the body he had held so often here in this bed was gone, burned to ashes. His Anna, his beautiful golden Anna . . .

Teeth gritted together hard enough to press the roots against his skull, he searched his mind for answers he could not find. Why, why had Anna been murdered . . . why?

He had found neither rhyme nor reason, and those bastards at the police station had been no help. Anna was already written off as far as they were concerned.

'. . . We will of course continue with our enquiries, but given the information so far . . .'

Enquiries, fuck! Torrey's fingers tightened, caressing the life from some imagined throat. They'd got no more intention of proceeding with enquiries than they had of admitting to being the arseholes they were!

But maybe it wasn't all their fault, maybe the police really did have nothing to go on . . . but the looks on their faces when he'd been told the coroner had given permission for the body to be released for burial: no understanding of what he was feeling, no pity, no attempt made to soften the blow. They couldn't wet nurse, that much he recognised, but that one man . . . Christ, what was it made him enjoy ripping out another's entrails!

If only he had some idea who had murdered Anna, if only he could get his hands on that killer.

Fingers curling even tighter he pressed the hard knuckles against his eyes but it was just pain on pain, it did nothing to drive away the desire to kill or the desire for what he'd lost.

'I want him dead, Anna!' The words burst out in a torrent of hate and frustration. 'Whoever did that to you, whoever had a hand in it, I want him dead!'

With the swiftness of a hand wiping mist from a steamed mirror Torrey's mind suddenly cleared, and like a wisp of cloud forming on a far horizon a word edged silently into his consciousness. Lying still he allowed it to grow, offering no resistance, willing it to come until it filled his brain.

Ritchie . . .

Soft and golden as that beloved body, the one word echoed in his mind.

Anna! With eyes flying open he jumped from the bed. But Anna wasn't there.

Anna would never be there again.

Chapter Four

The thick-set man swaggered to the bar of the Bird-in-Hand, his size twelve boots sounding the charge.

Torrey watched him, noting the sweat gathered in tiny glistening globules on his heavy face; he was nervous, loud mouthed but nervous. He'd seen the type before but tonight he was in no mood for their brand of humour. The football season was over, the excuse for mouthing off at a referee a safe distance away was temporarily snatched away, leaving louts like this one to look for a fresh source of amusement. He ran his tongue over his lips. If the fool thought to have found that amusement here, with him, then the fellow had thought right; but the fun might not prove to his liking!

A snigger sliding between wet lips, the man turned to Torrey.

'Where's your girlfriend tonight . . . where's the little tart, found herself a bigger prick to play with?'

Clenching his fingers together Torrey forced himself

to stay put as a burst of laughter followed the words.

'Three pints,' the man turned away to give his order to the landlord, 'an' mek sure yoh fill the glasses, oh an' a gin and lemon.'

Scooping the glasses of beer together, thick fingers spanning all three, he swaggered back to his table; the two others sat there, erupting into fresh laughter as with some choice remark he set the drinks in front of them.

'Don't go forgetting this one.'

Jim Povey, landlord of the Bird-in-Hand, indicated the glass left on the counter as the heavy-set man lowered himself into a chair.

'That!' Tiny globules of moisture pushing together to form a minuscule stream running over his cheeks, the man enjoyed the moment. 'That be for his tart, reckon the little trull will be needin' it; who's the bitch suckin' off this time . . . ?'

Jim Povey had time to glance at Torrey, but time to grab the drink had gone. Like dynamite triggered to the hundredth of a second the glass was in Torrey's hand and he was already half-way across a room suddenly fallen silent.

Reaching the other man's table he stood looking at the grinning features of the three obviously out for trouble. Balancing the glass between loose fingers he smiled, an easy deceptive smile that hid his every instinct to smash it into those yellowed, gapped teeth.

'Thanks for the drink,' he raised the glass in salute, 'but the tart doesn't like gin, and neither do I.'

'No?' The heavy face smirked up at him. 'Well I bet we knows what yer does like, eh lads?'

Probably in his mid-twenties the second of the trio laughed widely, black fillings showing like a badly tarmaced road. 'Ar we does, we bets yoh likes being sucked off an' all.'

'Does yer shave it first?' The first of them glanced about his watching audience.

'Yeah, does you shave it or don't the bint mind 'avin' hairs in 'er mouth?'

'Let's 'ave a look!' The third member of the comedy act made a grab for Torrey's crotch. 'Let's see if he shaves it afore puttin' it in the whore's mouth.'

'Leave it out, Shafto!' Chair legs scraped noisily on bare floorboards and a metal-studded boot banged against Torrey's ankle as the thick-set man leaned quickly forwards, catching the other's wrist and bringing his knuckles hard down on the table. 'We don't want to go bringing 'im off in 'ere do we, we wants to play first.' He leered up at Torrey. 'The bloke likes to play . . . don't ya, mate?'

The answer was quiet and even, masking the desire to kill. 'There's a lot of things I like to do, the same as there are some things I dislike doing.' Torrey paused, his mouth curving in a laconic smile. 'But there is one thing I positively *never* do . . . and that is to drink with piss ants like you!'

Gin and then the glass slammed into the smirking face. Torrey caught the lapels of a greasy jacket, hauling the figure to its feet. His smile never wavering he brought the heavy face close to his own, his next words grit between his teeth. 'Now, if you still want to play I suggest we do it outside, but remember . . . I'm not into conversation!'

'Torrey!' Jim Povey leaned across the bar. 'Any rough stuff an' I'll 'ave the police 'ere.'

Eyes glinting like icebergs in the setting sun, Torrey held the figure clear of the floor. 'Better ring 'em now, Jim, or there'll be nothing left of our friends by the time they arrive!'

Flinging the surprised man back into his chair he turned away, shouldering open the door that led to a small yard, taking only seconds to put the eight-foot wall at his back. They would have to come at him from the front, one thing being certain: they would come together. Their kind attacked in packs, too shit-scared to face a man alone.

They came then, erupting through the door in a compact group, positioning themselves back to back like the cheap fairground ornament his mother had kept on the sideboard. Watching them, he would have laughed could he have squeezed it past the hate. They had seen too many movies, each one fancied himself as being James Cagney, but Cagney's back could break as easy as the next man's!

'There 'e is, Red, over by the wall.' The shortest of them pointed to where Torrey stood, a darker smudge in the shadows.

Tension that threatened to screw him to the floor of that yard held every muscle as Torrey waited.

'So that be where the lover boy went.' The one called Red swivelled to face Torrey. 'Found a good place for it, 'ave yer? That's nice, but don't go gettin' 'em off yet, I likes doin' that meself.'

His cohort laughed admiringly, following him across the yard; but he threw out an arm, halting their advance.

'Wait yer turn, lads, we don't want to frighten 'im, do we? One at a time, that be good manners . . .'

The dim glow of one low-watt bulb lighting the entrance to the 'Mens' showed the leer on Red's face. The bastard was really handsome, his face looked like he'd lost an argument with a bus.

'. . . 'sides, like I've told yer afore . . .' Red continued his oratory, 'it'll only tek one man to put this shit on 'is back.'

Arms coming protectively across his chest, his tone designed to strip flesh from bone, Torrey spat out his answer.

'That lets you out then!'

'Why you bloody whore-loving bastard!' The furious Red hurled himself at the figure standing against the wall, only Torrey wasn't there. Side-stepping at the last moment he scraped the winded man off the brickwork, twisting him tight into his own body, a forearm across the throat. One swift backward jerk, and Red's throat rattled softly in the shadows. Studded boots scraping the concrete the unconscious man slid to the floor, Torrey stepping over him with blood lust in his nostrils, the promise of death shining through the slits that were his eyes.

Arms held loose at his sides he waited, but the looseness was a lethal deception. The Army's unarmed combat training had given him a whiplash reaction as well as the ability to kill a man in seconds using nothing but his hands.

The remaining two were suddenly cautious, their shoulders touching as they advanced. Half of him wanted them to split and run but the other half, the half that wanted to kill, willed them on.

He wanted this; more than that, he *needed* it. P'raps smashing some bastard's face to a pulp would take away the bitterness, take away the pain.

No one else had followed from the pub, there was no sound of a police car. If Povey had carried out his threat and called the blues they were not here yet; that left more than enough time to see this pair off.

Just clear of his reach the two men separated, dancing nervously to each side of him. Torrey breathed slow and regular. Watch and wait, let them make the first move.

Overhead the moon quitted the scene, leaving the electric light bulb sole spectator to the coming offensive.

Wait . . . ! Torrey repulsed the urge to reach out . . . wait, they would come soon enough.

That was when the pot-bellied one lunged.

Every vestige of the years of Army training held Torrey ready. His muscles taut, he took the rush full on, the impact spreading evenly through him. Catching the surprised man in a grip of steel he carried him with him as he dropped to one knee, a lightening chop to the neck rendering him senseless.

That was when Shafto made his move.

A boot catching Torrey in the face kicked away the last

shadow of remorse, stamping the seal on the sentence he was already about to execute.

On his feet, anger subduing pain, one foot sent the last of his attackers sprawling backwards. He was still sliding when Torrey reached him. It took half of one second to whip him on to his front, the other half to press a knee into the backbone.

'I could kill you, you bastard, and Christ knows I want to!' Torrey pressured the knee harder against the spine, ignoring the man's cry of fear. 'But there's something I need you to tell your pals; if I meet with you again then you are three dead men!'

Holding his head beneath the stream of icy water, Richard Torrey tried to pull his thoughts together. He thought he'd heard a voice call his name, thought he'd heard Anna . . . but Anna was dead.

So what was it? He lifted his head, staring at himself in the cheap mirror above the basin. Imagination, stress causing his mind to play tricks, or just a longing so great to be with Anna again his mind had literally fulfilled that longing?

He touched a finger to the swelling that kick had caused to the bridge of his nose. Never one for vanity, the move was pure tension. Those bastards had been given the word all right! The elation that had flooded him as his assailants had fallen one by one flooded him now as he reached for a towel. They had walked tall, all three of them, only not quite tall enough!

He walked slowly from the bathroom into the living room. He'd been aware of them watching him for an hour or more. They hadn't rushed their fences; had it been from caution or the need to drink themselves brave?

But there was no time to dwell on that now. He ought not to have come back to the house, everybody in that pub had seen him, seen the men follow him out into the yard. It wouldn't take long for somebody to find them and then . . .

Throwing aside the wet towel he started for the stairs, then paused. He'd need no change of gear in prison and that was where he'd be when those men brought a charge of grievous bodily harm, and what a smirk that would bring to some copper's face.

Taking time only to grab his jacket he left the house. The rear gardens . . . that was his surest way. Separated only by a few rickety palings, the gardens of the council houses ran together in an almost unbroken line to the main Wolverhampton Road. But that was too near where he'd left three unconscious men . . . yet that might be the best way after all! He pulled on the jacket. Who would think of looking for him so close to that pub, and once clear he could hitch a lift anywhere.

Philip Bartley drew up to the traffic roundabout. It was a foul night, rain hammering on the roof of the car, wipers barely clearing the windscreen. Maybe he should have stayed the night in a hotel. Huh! He laughed softly. Where the hell did you find a decent hotel in Darlaston, even in this bloody new millennium? But there was a beneficial side to the rain; it would keep unwanted noses out of that business going on down at the new place, business it was best he stay clear of.

Holding the powerful Rover on the clutch he waited for an opening in the traffic, lights splintered by raindrops flashing by in quick succession.

He had left everything in Doc Walker's hands and this time there had better be no cock-up or the little one-time doctor would have no hands!

Impatient, he let the car drift forward a few yards then brought it back, repeating the manoeuvre as he watched his right for a gap in what seemed a never-ending flow. Christ, a dog shouldn't be out on such a night! He let the car drift again, fingers tapping the steering wheel, swearing aloud as a huge lorry threw greasy spray across his windshield.

Bloody foreign wagons! He flicked the wipers. Any country in the world could send their shit to the UK, flog their rubbish to the natives!

A slight lull in the stream of lights was long enough. He gunned the car forwards, two fingers raised as the sound of irate car horns followed. Firestones gripping the wet surface he smiled as he joined the traffic tearing along the M6.

He really shouldn't complain about imports, though; without his own particular sort he wouldn't be driving home to a hundred-acre estate holding a four-hundred-year-old manor house at its green heart.

It had been a dicey move on his part taking a voluntary

pay-off from Bilston steelworks, but he'd seen what was on the cards: the foundry would close no matter what and there would be hundreds in a job market that was rapidly fading into non-existence. So he'd taken the offer, been among the first to go, and risked the lot on what had been no more than a glorified corner shop in King Street. But beneath his nurturing hand it had grown. It seemed he had a particular charm that appealed to the ladies; he could persuade them that one packet of biscuits wasn't really enough, and their little darlings surely deserved chocolate rather than plain and perhaps a pound of sausages should really be a pound of best steak. Now the little shop had become a supermarket with replicas of itself in towns all over the Midlands. His shops offered a wide range, household requirements as well as food, but it was in poultry where the real profits lay; luckily those interfering gits in the Ministry of Agriculture hadn't damaged it too much.

'Salmonella my arse!' he grunted, tyres screeching as he flashed up to the Gailey roundabout. 'The virus is probably as old as mankind but it takes bloody politicians to stir it up!'

Painted road signs gleamed in the headlights but he ignored them. He'd travelled this way so often he knew it inside out. Taking the exit signposted A5, he turned off.

Christ, this road couldn't have been repaved twice since the Romans built it! He flinched, feeling the car ride the pitted surface. As for lighting, it must have fared better when it was still Watling Street.

He muttered softly as he peered ahead, the darkness

sudden after the garish overhead lighting of the motor-
way. Hitting the main beam he breathed sharply as it
picked out the wet figure, shoulders hunched against the
rain, thumb raised with the gesture of the hitch-hiker.
Even through the curtain of rain he could see long legs
encased in jeans, wet hair plastered to the neck. With any
luck it would be blond; with any luck he could be in with
a shout!

'God, it's one hell of a night!'

The rain-sodden figure slid into the car, pulling the
door closed quickly as if afraid of being ordered out again.
'Thanks for stopping, I thought I'd never get a lift.'

One hand flicked strands of wet hair back from the
face. 'The whole day has been a bitch.'

It sounded more than a complaint against the weather.
Bartley set the Rover in motion, endowing the road behind
with a shower of silver droplets.

'Where are you headed?' He pressed harder on the
accelerator, enjoying the feeling, the surge of speed the
three-litre engine afforded. That was another of his likes,
speed; fast cars, fast profits and fast women, they had their
uses, though the latter didn't rate too highly, his tastes lay
mostly in the opposite direction.

'Where would you like me to drop you?'

His long legs stretched towards the solace of the heater,
the other man gave a single shake of the head.

'I'll leave that to you.'

Bartley's foot depressed the pedal further and the

powerful car punched forwards. There was always the chance he'd get stopped by some cop nursemaiding a trap, and get done for exceeding the speed limit, but hell, it was worth it, and on a night like this it was a hundred to one chance anyway; to get a copper out of his vehicle tonight would take nothing short of the passing of the three wise men, each mounted on a camel.

'I'm heading for Monkswell.' He glanced sideways at the long legs. 'But I could easily run you on somewhere else if it would suit you better.'

'It's six and two threes to me!'

Bartley smiled inwardly. That meant his half-drowned passenger had nowhere to go. Pity there were no service stations on this stretch of road, now why hadn't the Romans thought of that! He smiled again. A good meal could just improve his chances. He glanced again at the long jeans-clad legs, the vee where they joined the torso. He'd like to see more but he was an old hand at this knight of the road game, he knew how to play, and rushing in wasn't the way. Let his hitch-hiker relax, let the warmth and luxury of leather do its part, it was an hour's drive home.

Chapter Five

'I was just about to give up, thank goodness I didn't.'

'And go back where?'

'That's just it, it was Hobson's choice; truth is I have nowhere to go back to.'

Philip Bartley's inner smile widened.

'Toss your jacket in the back. I'll stop at the first pub we come to, you can p'raps dry off a little.'

The hitch-hiker smiled briefly. 'Thanks, but there's no sense in drying off simply to get soaked again, this rain hasn't let up for days and I can't see it stopping tonight.'

Lights travelling fast came up to the Rover's tail. Lifting his eyes to the driving mirror Bartley breathed a sigh of relief. It wasn't a police car, just some maniac who either had one hell of a bit of stuff waiting for him or else was on a suicide bid.

'Kamikaze driver!' he snapped, watching the tail lights evaporate into the distance.

'He does seem in a bit of a hurry,' his passenger answered, twisting out of the wet jacket.

Imperial Leather? Bartley caught the fresh pleasant aroma. His hitch-hiker obviously rated personal hygiene high.

'We will be passing the Bell soon,' he glanced sideways, 'it's a decent little place and they do excellent meals; what say we stop?'

'No thanks. I don't think the landlord would welcome me in this state, his chairs definitely wouldn't benefit from my wet clothes; and talking of chairs, I feel terribly guilty about yours, your passenger seat, that is. It's going to be awfully damp.'

Bartley eased back his speed as the narrow country road twisted and turned; come face to face with another vehicle and they could all finish up decorating the hedge.

'Forget the car,' he smiled, 'a piece of damp upholstery isn't about to give me a heart attack; if I was worried about the car then I wouldn't have picked you up in the first place.'

Beside him his passenger smoothed a hand over a long lean thigh and Bartley's fingers tightened about the wheel. Christ, keep that up and it wouldn't need another vehicle to see him in the hedge!

'Maybe not,' the answer was soft, almost musical, 'but thanks anyway, I truly was thinking no one would ever stop.'

Ahead, the lights warned of an approaching vehicle and Bartley touched the brake, slowing for a tractor to pull into a farmyard.

'How long had you been standing there?' He picked up speed.

'A couple of hours.' The long-legged figure eased in the seat and a spicy tang, pleasant and fresh like a summer field under a veil of dew, filled the car.

Somewhere a half-forgotten memory stirred in Bartley's mind. Where had he smelled that aroma before?

'You must have had some place in mind.' Unable to place the memory he dismissed it. 'Some place you were headed for, to stand so long in this weather.'

A laugh, a light sound that didn't fool Bartley at all, lasted only a moment. 'I thought I'd just see where the road leads, though I could have chosen a better time.'

On the right of the road the cheerily lighted Bell public house passed without reference.

'If you mean the weather, it rains any time of year in this country.'

'What else would I refer to?'

Once again the light laugh. Once again Bartley was not deceived.

'Like a lover's tiff?'

Pushing damp hair back from a face turning towards the side window the hitch-hiker once again shook his head.

'My landlady couldn't wait any longer for my rent,' the slightly musical voice began. 'She said she was no bleeding Philanthropic Society. I hope this doesn't sound too awful but I found it strange she understood the term. There was another tenant for my room, she said, somebody who would pay up on time. She probably already held the poor sod's dole money.'

'Did she have yours?' Bartley's question was quick.

'No.' The face remained turned to the window as though the darkness beyond would take the words and hide them away in the blackness. 'Though she tried hard enough to get her paws on it.'

'So how come if you were receiving benefit you didn't pay your rent?'

It took time to answer and when it came the reply was with a shrug of the shoulders. 'It's a long story.'

'So what else do you have to do on a wet night unless it's to tell me to mind my own business?'

The head turned, fixing on a point beyond the windscreen. By the lighting of the instrument panel Bartley saw long tapering fingers stroke again along the thighs. He liked long fingers . . . he liked taut thighs more.

'I couldn't find work, everywhere the answer was the same, no more hands were needed.'

It sounded like a quote and probably was. Bartley negotiated a narrow bridge fording a stream invisible in night shadow. His own supervisors had said more or less the same many times.

His eyes riveted to the front, the hitch-hiker went on.

'After a week or two of that you get so you don't want to ask any more, you try to make do with the dole, only there is precious little of that and once your landlady has taken her share,' damp shoulders shrugged, 'I suppose I could have taken up the art of breaking and entering but that's not my style.'

The headlights of the car played over darkened lanes

and hedges bedecked with a million glistening raindrops, picking out a sign half hidden by growth.

'This is where I turn off. If you like I'll run you into the village. It's nothing to shout about but the pub has a couple of rooms it lets out in the summer. It's your last chance of a dry berth, there are no hotels and no more than a couple of farmhouses between here and Monkswell so, as the vicar said to the wedding guests, it's speak now or for ever hold your peace.'

Bringing the car to a halt, Bartley caught a whiff of the tangy fragrance as his passenger shifted position. Where the hell had he smelled that before? One of the staff in the office? He couldn't remember. Another hitch-hiker? Doubtful, they were usually the back-packer type, marijuana and sweat was their particular cologne, whereas this one . . . He glanced sideways but the face was turned from him. It wasn't the face stirring up those familiar feelings, though, not the face had him hard.

'A room sounds nice but with no money to pay . . . you'd better let me out here.'

An arm reaching for the jacket on the rear seat sent a waft of fragrance and Bartley's memory stirred again, kicking at the threshold of consciousness, but again it fell away unrecognised.

Why try to remember, whatever it was lay in the past; this was now and if he didn't move he'd lose whatever chance it might hold, and with any kind of luck it would be better than the last time. He'd picked a kid up last week but it had proved hardly worth the effort. Oh he'd been willing all right, but the kid had come much too quick, over before he'd got in. Pity, that! He liked his lovemaking to last, enjoying the buzz foreplay gave. Jesus, the thought of it was giving him a stand.

This one had said there was no money for a room. Bartley nursed the car engine. Christ, let it be true, don't let it blow away now.

'There's a room at my place for the night, at least it will give you a chance to dry your gear and get your act together.'

Bartley tried to keep his tone non-committal but it wasn't easy, there was something about this one had him horny as a ram.

'Tomorrow I can run you back to Walsall or you can go on to wherever it is you want to go, either way the choice is yours.'

'That's one offer I won't refuse.'

The face still did not turn his way but the answer, soft and musical, made him want to sigh with relief. Why, for Christ's sake! He sent the car surging into the darkness. This was just a pick-up, if he was lucky a one-night stand like those he'd had a hundred times before, so why were his pulses pounding like bloody sledgehammers?

'I really didn't fancy a night under the hedge . . .'

The hiker turned, tangy fragrance filling the car as their shoulders touched, the rest of the words a throaty whisper.

'. . . especially not alone.'

One hand touched along Bartley's shoulder, sliding into the nape of his neck, a moist tongue flicking the lobe of his ear.

'I really would like to thank you.'

A long-fingered hand touched high up on his thigh, the lips moved from his ear, trailing the side of his neck, their softness increasing the stiffness in his crotch. Christ, he'd picked a winner!

When he didn't knock it away the hand moved upwards and inwards, fingers spreading into his groin, stroking the throbbing fullness inside his trousers. He grabbed a sharp breath, the muscles of his stomach contracting as though he'd been kicked, and the car veered sharply.

'Keep that up and you'll have us in the hedge.'

He twisted the wheel, bringing them back on to the rough unsurfaced track.

'Don't you like it?'

Wrapped in that warm, spicy fragrance, its promise insinuated itself into Bartley's nostrils, drugging his brain, sharpening the desire, adding to the potent force that had him standing like a granite column.

'Course I bloody well do,' he gasped, 'but not while I'm driving.'

'You could stop . . .'

Fingers stroked his bulging crotch.

'. . . why wait? You don't have to drive home first . . . do you?'

Christ! Bartley drew another sharp breath. This one knew how to bring a man on, knew all the angles.

'Why not have what you want now?'

Lips touched his cheek then darted quickly to his mouth, a soft moist touch fermenting the need brewing between his legs.

'Why not here and again when you get home, there's no one to see so why not, you *can* make twice, can't you?'

'Yeah.' Bartley jerked as the fingers massaged testicles already swollen to the full. 'I can make it.'

Lips touched again into the fold of his neck and just below the waist fingers played with the fastening of his trousers.

'So then . . . let's stop.'

It was no more than a whisper yet it dinned into Bartley's brain, its perfumed promise infecting his reason.

'If a thing is pleasing then doing it twice is twice as pleasing.'

The zip came down and so did Bartley's foot, the brake slammed home so hard it brought the car screeching to a halt, slewing it side on into the hedge.

'In the back.' He croaked, hardly recognising the voice as his own.

'Later.' It was a soft whisper just above his mouth as he was pressed back against his seat. 'Have this one on me, you can make the next one yours.'

Trousers wide open now he lifted, allowing them to drop free of his hips, gasping with pleasure at the tanta-lising, deliberate brush of fingers against his thighs, trailing slowly into his groin, cupping the hard mass between his legs before circling the stem of his jerking flesh.

Breath coming in quick gasps, Bartley closed his eyes, every nerve in his body singing wildly as the hand stroked the length of him, then grabbing the wrist he held it hard against him.

'Not yet!' The slight laugh was low, teasingly remonstrative. 'You have to wait, you can't have all of it at once, the best comes later.'

The slender wrist twisted free, a tongue slipping sinuously into his mouth. Bartley dropped both hands to his sides. He wanted whatever this one had to give, whichever way the giving might go.

One by one he felt the buttons of his shirt slip free, felt it pushed from his chest and soft lips descend from his throat marking a line down the centre of his chest and stomach. At his navel they halted and, afraid it might end there, he pushed upwards with his hips, his stiffened flesh performing a wild Cossack leap as a wet tongue slowly baptised the swollen head.

Sweet Jesus! He hadn't had it like this for a long time, not since . . . but beneath the exquisite torture his mind refused the search. What did it matter who the other one had been, it was this one, the one mouthing his jerking flesh, sucking it deep into the throat. Throwing his hips upwards again he pushed deeper into the warm moist mouth.

'You like that, don't you, Philip?'

Moaning as the column of flesh was released, throbbing against his stomach, the word seemed to linger, trying to enter his mind: Philip . . . nobody called him Philip . . . but the tip of a tongue sliding down his pulsing length took the thought away.

Those hands were pushing now, spreading his legs apart. Christ, he wanted his legs open, wanted the mouth that was sucking his prick to swallow his balls!

In an agony of slowness the mouth drew free. Head dipping further, the smooth face pressed into the spread of his legs teasing, tormenting. Blood racing he twisted, wanting the mouth he knew was ready to take him, ready to bring the play to its conclusion, to suck out the fire burning in the pit of his stomach.

'Suck it,' he rasped, 'suck it . . . suck it!'

A quiet laugh rolling in the back of the throat, mouth closed about the rampant erection, a tongue caressed the swollen tip with long, gut-wrenching strokes. It was too much to bear; Bartley grabbed the damp hair, pulling the head closer into his groin, pushing with all his strength, grinding his throbbing member deeper and deeper into the throat until almost with a scream he exploded.

Sinking into the upholstery, eyes still screwed up against the emotions that had rocked him, he breathed hard, one hand resting on a perspiration-soaked chest.

'You like this, don't you, Philip?'

It was so soft, so seductive that despite his recent eruption Bartley felt an answering flicker. Jesus, he'd have to be careful, this one could have him hard again in two minutes!

A spicy aroma stirring his senses, his memory flashed an attractive face bending over his own, a wide generous mouth, vibrant blue eyes . . . but even as he sought to recognise it the memory was gone.

Opening his eyes he stared at those of the hitch-hiker who had just made love to him, eyes that glowed with an almost unreal luminosity. The full mouth smiled as it whispered.

'We'll do this again, Philip . . . I promise.'

His body heavy after the passion of a moment ago, Philip Bartley smiled. 'I look forward to it . . .' He paused. 'I forgot to ask your name, what do I call you?'

A soft laugh vibrated against the stillness of the car.

'Are you all right, sir . . . are you hurt?'

Senses still reeling, Philip Bartley turned to the beam of light aimed through the window.

'Looks like he's taken a bump, get the door open.'

Christ, the police! They were going to love this, the bloke up at the Abbey having it off in the car, a bloody hitch-hiker mouthing between his legs.

Lord, what did he say now! His brain clearing instantly he pulled at his shirt, but it was already together, every button fastened. Frowning, he glanced down towards his lap. His trousers were in place about his hips, the fastening closed.

'Take it easy, sir, you've had a bit of an accident.'

Bartley glanced at the seat beside his. There was no hitch-hiker, the seat was empty, the door wedged against the hedge still locked!

Richard Torrey watched the several lorries parked on a patch of waste ground opposite the café. Cartwright's was popular with long-distance drivers; if he could slip into the back of one of those lorries he could be well clear of Darlaston by morning.

He had reached the Bull Stake, going by way of the narrow Pinfold Alley so as not to be seen passing the

Bird-in-Hand, then continued by way of Kings Hill to Wednesbury.

But there was only spitting distance between the two towns, it wouldn't be wise to loiter.

Trying the first three lorries, he swore softly finding the tail gates locked. The next was an eight-wheeler, that would certainly be locked. The only other likely one was close to the street lamp. Torrey smiled acidly. Whenever you wanted a street lamp there was never one with a bulb that worked, yet right here, the very last place he needed a light, there was one . . . shining right over that bloody lorry!

Locked! He pulled at the rear door, every instinct wanting to kick it in. So what now . . . should he risk taking a bus at the White Horse and going into Brum? He could get a train there and go north or south, it wouldn't matter which.

'Looking for something, mate?'

Rounding the lorry he almost collided with a burly-looking man, one hand on the handle of the driver's door. There was no sense in lying, he didn't even want to.

Pushing wet hair away from his eyes he shook the lapels of his jacket.

'I thought I might get a ride.'

'Then why not ask?'

'I guessed these had been left for the night, I didn't think any of the drivers would be around to ask or I might have done. I just wanted to be out of this rain, and a lorry is your only bet when you're broke. But there's no damage done, I'm not after your load.'

'Wouldn't 'ave done you much good if you 'ad been.' The burly man swept a glance over the vehicle, 'I'm carryin' waste paper, no good for anythin' other than pulpin'.'

Pulling open the door he swung into the cab. 'If it's only a ride you're after then jump in.'

Chapter Six

By no stretch of the imagination could the inside of that cab be called comfortable but it was dry. Torrey settled into the seat. After some of the Army vehicles he'd been in this could be called luxury.

'So how come you're on the road on a night like this?'

Christ, the man wanted conversation! Eyes closed, Torrey grunted. 'No choice when you've been kicked out of your lodgings.'

'Why was that?' The driver eased the lorry around a bend in the road and when Torrey made no answer he added, 'Spent your money on the weed instead of paying your rent, I suppose. I get half a dozen of your sort every week, smoked their brains away, 'ave some of 'em. Got no more bloody sense, can't see they be killing theirselves.'

Eyes clamped together, Torrey made no answer. Breathing smooth and regular he feigned sleep.

'Another bloody crackhead!' Disgust loud in the words, the lorry driver reached on to the dashboard, fumbling a cigarette from a half-empty packet. If he had any sense he'd chuck this one back out into the rain. The cigarette lit and between his lips, he squinted at the figure partly slumped in the seat. But this was no kid, no junkie half out of his head on marijuana. This man looked fit, his body hard and well toned; he looked as though he knew how to handle himself. Twisting the cigarette to the opposite side of his mouth he turned back to the windscreen, peering through the slashing rain. On the other hand, it might make more sense just to let him sleep.

Torrey sensed the resolve of the driver and relaxed. He had not missed paying his rent; but that was the reason Anna had given the night they had first met. It had rained that night too. His thoughts drifting he remembered the rain-soaked figure, blonde shoulder-length hair plastered into the neck, vividly blue eyes blinking raindrops from long curling lashes.

'*It wasn't too bad the first time I missed paying . . .*'

The soft musical voice spoke the memories in his mind.

'*. . . my landlady understood, or so she told me. She said there were little things folk had to buy, of course I could pay a week and a half for the next two weeks. I thought that very fair and though it meant going without a few meals I paid her . . .*'

Behind closed eyes Torrey saw again the face that had looked at him, the half smile that even then had tugged at his insides.

'*. . . then come a week I simply had to buy a pair of shoes — you can only make do with cardboard insoles for so long — I got the cheapest I could find but even so they saw off a good slice of that week's dole . . .*'

He had looked at the shoes, cheap was right. Black plimsolls that had squelched with every move.

'. . . *then I saw an ad in the* Star, *it was a job restocking the shelves of one of the shops in King Street; it didn't exactly pay a fortune but it was more than I got from being on the dole, and it would mean being able to get out of that house without having to walk the streets or sit the whole day in the park going slowly out of my mind with boredom. Trouble was, I didn't think the manager would give me a second glance, seeing the clothes I wore . . .*'

Cheap as the canvas shoes, the coat was faring badly in the downpour. '*In here.*' Torrey remembered leading the way into Peoli's sweet shop cum ice-cream parlour and ordering two hot drinks.

Sipping one, Anna had continued her explanation. '*I mentioned the job to my landlady's son. He was all for my trying for it, suggesting I use what money I had to buy some clothes that would at least look presentable if I managed to land an interview; it would be all right about my rent, he said he would fix things with his mother.*'

Torrey looked back across the months that separated him now from that first fateful night, seeing again those long fingers tighten about each other, the anger that drew those full lips into a straight line.

'*I didn't get the job . . .*'

The words went on, quiet yet filling his head with their sound, drowning the noise of the lorry's horn and the driver's loud expletive as he twisted the wheel, swerving the heavy vehicle from the path of another.

'*. . . and when I couldn't pay my arrears the son came to my room. He was pleasant . . . at first.*' The musical voice had faltered. '*We could work something out. Then he touched my legs, trailed his* *fingers up over my thigh, and I knew what his idea of "something" was, and I told him I could do without it, that I wanted no old man stinking of pee pawing me. That was when he got nasty. His mother could do without things too, she could do without a lodger who couldn't pay the rent! Maybe she couldn't, but the real crunch was Herbie couldn't do without being serviced, an' if I wasn't prepared to oblige then I was out, so here I am . . . out!'*

What had followed seemed natural enough. There was a spare room in the house that had been his mother's and was now rented by him. Going by town council rules he should not have sub-let, but who gave a shit for council rules! He had offered the room to Anna. Torrey swallowed hard, a vision of that laughing face dancing beneath his closed lids. At twenty-four Anna had been ten years his junior and as widely different in temperament as in appearance. Five feet six inches tall, with blonde hair curling softly back from a wide forehead, eyes the colour of early hyacinths sparkling as if sprinkled with dew, while the mouth . . . Torrey felt the sudden tightening of his crotch . . . the mouth had been soft and generous.

Taking Anna to live with him had stirred up a hornet's nest. He had never been what was termed 'social', preferring to keep himself to himself, a loner, probably due to his childhood as the only child of over-possessive parents. Whatever the reason it had set the locals buzzing when 'that there Torrey' 'ad teken himself a lodger, a lodger 'andsome as a chocolate box! But it wasn't simply the fact he had taken a lodger that had set the whole of Darlaston talking, it was the lodger he had taken.

Tyres crunching the road surface being the only sound

in the warm cab, Richard Torrey let the memories wash over him.

It was a scandal . . . it shouldn't be allowed . . . he should be turned out . . . somebody should report it to the council, them two living together in the same 'ouse, it weren't decent. Thank the Lord 'is poor mother be dead, the shock would 'ave killed her! Nice woman her'd bin, kept that 'ouse smart as a new pin; and 'im, that lad o' hers, she'd tried 'er best forrim but 'e was allus strange, too quiet to be natural, an' now look at 'im!

The talk had gone on, vicious and condemning but he hadn't cared. Tittle-tattling over the back fence was what women in these parts thrived on and so long as they kept their comments to themselves he could live with it.

Anna had been at the house a month before they became lovers. Torrey had watched the graceful movements of the slender lissom form, listened to the husky voice, his own body responding in a way he fought to control. Sex had never held a great deal of interest for him, and now . . . ! The whole idea was ludicrous, laughable. Christ, the whole idea was unthinkable! But that was what he did think of, too long and too often. What that supple body would feel like in his arms, that soft mouth crushed beneath his own. The more he thought of it the stronger grew the desire, yet never once had he given way to it. Not until that night!

He still wasn't absolutely clear how it had happened. He'd cooked the evening meal, fish and chips, as he remembered – well money wasn't too plentiful just then and he was keeping both of them – then Anna had produced a bottle of wine and though he wondered how on earth such a minor miracle had been achieved, he hadn't asked. After they'd eaten he had offered to wash up while Anna took the bath first. It hadn't been easy holding on to wet dishes with the thought of that golden nakedness pulling out your brain and a prick that jumped like an untamed stallion with every sound from the bathroom.

'*Richard!*' The throaty sound of his name had come through the door to the right of the kitchen sink, from the bathroom which was downstairs, and his stomach had knotted. He should never have suggested that he do the washing up, he should have gone out, to the Regal to see the latest film or the Staffordshire Knot for a pint. Jesus! He should have done anything except stay in that house.

But he had, and when Anna called again he'd answered. God, where had his brain been! '*Sorry to be such a nuisance,*' Anna had apologised, '*but I've completely forgotten the towels. Would it be too much trouble for you to fetch them from the airing cupboard and pass them through? The door is open.*'

He'd fetched them of course — big blue fluffy ones, the sort Anna loved using — then, his mind screaming he was a bloody fool, he'd taken them into the bathroom.

Anna was already out of the bath, rivulets of water trickling down over chest and flat stomach, tracing silver pathways that merged and disappeared among the hair clustered thickly in a golden triangle. Torrey had stood there staring, his penis inside tight jeans bucking and jerking to be free, his fingers gripping the towels as a dying man clings to life. With curls clinging damply to that wide brow, supple body glistening with water, Anna had stood like a Raphaelesque angel. '*Ritchie, I'd like to say thank you . . . properly.*'

'*I don't want your bloody thanks.*' Richard's head had jerked upwards, eyes filled with anger he couldn't control, lips drawn back over his teeth in a snarl. '*How many times for Christ's sake . . . I don't want your bloody thanks.*'

'*Well if you won't take my thanks . . . take me.*'

It was simple and quiet, the smile a shadow about Anna's mouth.

Torrey never could remember much beyond that point; one moment they were standing there facing each other, the next they were locked together on the bathroom floor, his hands and mouth tasting every part of the body that intoxicated him.

Anna had stayed almost a year.

Every night their lovemaking found new heights, the element of love stronger for Torrey than the passion it followed. They fitted well together both as lovers and friends; Anna seemed happy enough enjoying the days they spent in each other's company, but more than that she seemed to enjoy their nights, holding each other naked in bed, trailing a hand along Torrey's thighs and stopping just short of his penis to nestle in his crotch, fingers drawing so lightly over his testicles and back along the swollen length it was like a drag lead drawing everything out of him.

Then Anna had left!

No row, no explanation, no nothing. Just gone. Torrey felt the pain he had felt then, a pain that almost ripped him in two. For weeks he had just hung about the house waiting for Anna to return, hoping for Anna to return, banging his fists against the wall when it didn't happen. At night he had walked the towns searching the pubs and cafés, they even let him into the night club once he'd cleaned himself up. But Anna wasn't in Darlaston, nor in Wednesbury or Walsall. Anna, it seemed, had disappeared from the face of the earth.

Only Anna hadn't!

It was just over a month later that the two constables had called. Five days more and he'd been told which mortuary the body was in.

Torrey pressed his eyelids down harder as the laughing face faded, giving way to the one he'd seen in that mortuary.

Now he understood why Anna had died, now he understood there being no report in the newspapers and the reluctance of the police to allow him to identify the body. Someone must have known the people Anna had got entangled with and the police had played along in keeping the murder under wraps.

Anna, his Anna was dead. He pushed upright, staring out through the windscreen. But Richard Torrey was very much alive. Slowly, in the silence of his mind, the words formed. Whoever had killed Anna, no matter if one or several, he wanted them dead . . . he wanted them dead!

'You have it all sorted and ready?'

Philip Bartley stood up as he asked the question.

Coming around an impressive desk he stared at the man standing a clear six inches below his own six feet.

'I want no slip-ups, there's near enough a king's ransom riding on this deal. You stay with it, you hear me, stay with it and leave the whisky bottle at home 'til it's done with.'

'You can leave everything to me.' The shorter man answered, his left cheek twitching nervously. 'It will all be done as you say.'

'It had better be!' Bartley's tone echoed the warning of his steel-hard eyes. 'Anything goes wrong, anything at all, Walker, and you can kiss your arse goodbye!'

Nervousness turning to truculence, Frederick 'Doc' Walker peered up over the rims of heavy horn-rimmed spectacles. 'Nothing can go wrong, I said I've seen to it all personally.'

A laugh grating the back of his throat, Philip Bartley walked to the door of his well-appointed office, one hand resting on the handle. 'I remember your seeing to that business five years ago, that was your personal doing as I recall.'

'I was shopped!' The little man's tight mouth clipped the words, his own grey eyes venomous behind their glass barrier. 'Stitched up, and you know by whom; but the bastard has paid for it, nobody'll be hearing from him again. Nobody gets a second go at putting one over on Doc Walker.'

'And you won't be getting a second go should you mess this up.' Bartley smiled, the cold calculating smile of a snake. 'I don't often have to pay for mistakes, but should one be made I settle the account in full . . . painfully . . . but in full. I hope I make myself clear.'

Jumped-up piece of shit! Frederick Walker, one-time FRCS, tugged angrily at the lapel of his coat as Bartley's pretty fair-haired secretary rose sinuously from her chair, skirt riding high over nylon-clad knees. Who the hell did Bartley think he was? Not so much as a letter after his name yet look at him, boss of a chain of supermarkets, with a bank account from here to eternity; not that half of it came from the shops, Bartley had fingers in richer cream pies than that!

'Take care how you go, Mr Walker,' the secretary's shrill voice piped, followed immediately by a high-pitched giggle that rubbed his nerves like sandpaper. What the hell did she care, what the hell did anyone care? Out in the street with its busy stream of traffic, he blinked owlishly. Truth was nobody cared for Frederick Walker, but get this little job over, get this business with Bartley finished successfully and then they'd care; then they'd know who it was they were dealing with, and they'd all pay. From that moment on the services of Doc Walker would no longer come cheap.

Inspector Bruce Daniels lit one more cigarette, checking the time on his watch as he blew out a cloud of grey smoke that settled in the car. That would be something else for Marjorie to carp about! The only bloody time they had a conversation of more than three words was when she went on about her precious furniture or the bloody car. Christ, what wouldn't he give to be able to turn the clock back, life wouldn't see him in the police force then.

'How much longer, sir?'

'As long as it bloody takes!' He blew another stream of smoke, ignoring the younger man's cough. Young coppers today wanted everything on a plate. They should have been on stake-outs twenty years ago; there were no squad cars to sit in then and coppers, even detective inspectors, couldn't afford their own on the pay they got then. Not that it was much more now, and without Marjorie's bit o' money from her old man's passing they wouldn't have this one.

Two thirty. He checked the time again. That was what Echo Sounder had told him but it was already nearer three; if that little runt had fed him wrong he wouldn't see the outside of Winson Green for a very long time. Bruce Daniels didn't sit in a car 'til his arse was numb for nothing.

But Echo had sense enough to know that. He dragged hard on the Royal, adding to the smoke hanging heavy on the still air trapped inside the car, turning a deaf ear to the appealing cough of the detective sergeant sitting in the seat beside him. What the hell was the hold up? Christ, if this didn't go down after he'd had most of the force put on to it . . . !

Acid curdled sharp in his gut. P'raps he should have passed this one on, let somebody else take it . . . and take the glory if it did turn out to be what he thought? Not bloody likely! This one was his, this would be his promotion.

'Reckon we've bin had, sir?'

'Why should I?' Daniels released smoke on a long slow breath.

'Well,' the young officer shifted uncomfortably, 'time's getting on, it'll be light soon.'

'So what! Don't lorries run in the light?'

'I only meant . . .'

'I know what you meant!' Flicking the rest of the cigarette through a window he opened only fractionally, Daniels felt in his pocket for an indigestion tablet. 'But there be time yet, probably the weather has 'em running late.'

He didn't really believe that and from the way the other man turned his head he knew he didn't either. But it didn't matter what they believed, here they were and here they stayed no matter how long.

Bartley had bought well. Sucking on the tablet, Daniels gazed out at the houses lining each side of the street like little black boxes. The old bolt and nut works along the back of the Leys had been derelict for years, no doubt Bartley had bought that and the surrounding land for loose change. It had taken less than three months to demolish the factory and put one of his new-fangled supermarkets on the site. Putting it there was good for custom from the housing estates beginning to spring up like weeds, but it was also good for tonight's operation. Close enough to the town for lorries passing in the early hours to draw no particular attention; Darlaston had long been used to that.

Glancing again at his watch, Daniels tutted irritably. A

sudden bank of cloud meant he couldn't see the time and he wouldn't risk lighting up again. The flare of a match could catch the attention of a possible night-owler, somebody who didn't know when it was best to be in bed.

Yes, Bartley had bought well, he thought again, but not well enough. With the junctions of Baulk Street and Alma Street blocked by police cars there would be no way out other than going by way of the waste ground behind that store and that would be suicide. The whole area was a patchwork of old gin pits and was littered with shafts, some of them flooded, the rest ready to cave in beneath the weight of a kid's trolley cart let alone a fully loaded lorry.

'Lorry passing St Lawrence church,' – Daniels stared at the two-way radio crackling into life – 'proceeding north along Church Street.'

Grabbing the microphone he hissed into it. 'All cars remain where you are, I repeat remain where you are, nobody move!'

At the bend of the road powerful lights shattered the darkness. Shouting for the sergeant to do the same, Daniels bent low in his seat as a lorry trundled past.

'Shouldn't we follow him, sir?'

The sudden movement having sent acid gushing into his throat, Daniels straightened, feeling for the tablets in his pocket.

'And put the bloody wind up him! That'll be all I need, that'll put me nicely in the Super's good books . . . I don't think! Give him time, let him start to unload then we'll go take a look, see if Echo sang the right song.'

Somewhere among the night shadows the clock of St Lawrence church chimed three. Daniels spoke again into the intercom.

'Five minutes, then you move into position. Parker, Davis, if so much as a fart gets past them road blocks you'll 'ave me to deal with. The rest of you follow me into that yard, and remember no bloody hooters, I don't want our bird flying the loft!'

Every second painful, Daniels counted them in his mind. This had to be what he thought, what he'd prayed for. There might never be another chance like this one. The half-finished tablet sliding down his throat, he slammed the car into gear.

'This is where you get your comeuppance, Bartley,' he muttered as the car surged forward, 'and Inspector Bruce Daniels gets his promotion.'

Chapter Seven

The Reverend Peter Darley's hands shook on the steering wheel of his small car. He needed sleep, but sleep no longer came without nightmares, and his days . . . they were often tormented by the evil that waited within his church. He could apply for sabbatical leave, go into retreat for a while, the Bishop would almost surely agree. But that would not cleanse away the evil that stalked him, only the forgiveness of the Church could do that, only the Church could absolve; and for him there would be no forgiveness, his sin would warrant no absolution.

'I be sorry to bother you, Reverend, but mother be askin' special for you to come.'

White apron swamping her thin figure, a grey-haired woman bustled along the path leading towards the gate of a small half-timbered cottage, smiling apologetically at the priest clambering from the car.

'It's no bother, Hilda.' He returned the smile, seeing the one on the woman's face change to a look of concern.

'I told mother we shouldn't go being of a nuisance.'

'Now who told you you would be a nuisance?'

'Nobody ain't needed to,' the woman answered, sweeping his face with a sharp speculative glance. 'Tis plain to see you don't be as well as might be. You've been looking peaky this last week or so and as such needs no more placed on your shoulders than needs be!'

'Just a little tired, Hilda.' Stooping, he followed through the low doorway into a room where every stick of furniture shone and the smell of home baking wafted from a kitchen he knew from past experience was scrubbed bright.

'Mother be in the parlour.' Hilda was already in the doorway, her brow creasing with worry. 'I ain't never knowed her to refuse to come to the rectory afore, not in all my fifty-five years . . . I tell you, Reverend, it has me right feared.'

'There you go again, Hilda, worrying over nothing. Like myself, your mother is just a little tired. I've no doubt it is simply a result of the weather we have been having, all those thunderstorms, they make the air feel so heavy.'

'You be right, they does.' The woman nodded. 'And for all the rain they brings it don't ease things none. But mother will be a waitin' of you so I'll just sit the tea leaves in the pot then I'll take you through.'

'Tea sounds wonderful, Hilda.' He smiled. 'But it will come more quickly if I find my own way to the parlour.'

'Well ain't no way you'll get lost.' She turned towards the kitchen. 'You go on and I'll fetch you in a buttered scone and some of mother's raspberry jam.'

'You come then, Reverend.' Martha Sim looked at the man drawing up a chair to sit beside her.

'Did you think I would not?'

Eyes blackberry-bright stared from the old woman's lined face. 'I held no doubts you would try, same as I holds none there be that would prevent it should it feel the need.'

'It?' The Reverend Darley tried a laugh but it died in his throat. 'Now what does that mean?'

As she rested against the back of the chair the woman's eyes remained unblinking. 'You be knowing full well the meaning of my words. I speak not lightly when I says I knows what it be has your skin pale as wax candles, what it be has you afraid to enter your own church.'

'Martha, that's nonsense!'

Every word steady, Martha Sim answered, 'Nonsense, is it . . . and is it nonsense I speak when I tells you it comes on a breath of sweet spice, that the robes you wear be no barrier to its touch, the cross on your breast no protection? Be it also nonsense when I says it walks with you along that nave, that it follows to the very steps of the high altar and there it waits, waits to take what you gave once before?'

How could she know? No one had been in the church, no one had seen, and neither of them would speak to another about what had taken place there. Peter Darley dropped his glance, his fingers going to the cross hanging from his neck.

'You be asking yourself how is it Martha Sim knows that of which no word has been spoken; now Martha Sim asks you, does what she speak be lies, do you deny the truth of her words?'

From the kitchen sounds of crockery being placed on a tray drifted into the silence that dropped between them. To answer . . . to own to knowing of the presence he felt each time he entered his own church . . . he could not, he could not admit to the terrible deed that had been done there. This woman could not know . . . nobody could!

'Silence speaks loud, Reverend.' The old woman nodded. 'It also speaks words the tongue finds too hard, but in that silence I hear the truth, that same truth you keeps hidden in your heart.'

'How?' Hazel eyes clouded with unhappiness lifted to the lined face. 'How do you know, Martha? The cards . . . the crystal? You know the teachings of the Church, such practices are unholy.'

'I knows the teachings!' The woman answered quickly. 'I knows that by visiting the witch of Endor, Saul were given a truth he hadn't thought to hear and so he pronounced the practice evil, and now the Church teaches the Lord will surely put from Him those who use the ancient powers. But it were not the Lord's word, it were the word of a king driven mad. We were made in the image of God, Reverend. We were given great powers in that once perfect world, powers of the mind that many have forgotten how to use, many but not all. I has no use for cards or crystal, I keeps to the ancient ways as did my mother and hers as far back as time stretches; yes, I knows the Church looks upon such practice as unholy, but there be other practices they sees the same way, some of which truly bring evil in their wake, and it be such an evil that follows behind you, one that will take your sanity unless you rids yourself of it.'

Unless he rid himself of it! Fingers curved about the cross, Peter Darley's eyelids pressed hard down. Hadn't he prayed, knelt before that altar for hours at a stretch? Hadn't he asked forgiveness a thousand times since it had happened? If the Lord did not forgive, how could he ever hope to be rid of that vile presence!

'There we be, a cup o' fresh tea and a scone straight from the oven. You'll enjoy that, Reverend.'

Opening his eyes the priest tried to smile. 'You are very kind, Hilda, but I'm afraid I'm not hungry.'

Martha Sim looked at the pale face. Hungry? Maybe not, but feared, yes the priest was feared, and he had every need to be!

Hilda's pleasant face smiled as she poured tea. 'Oh you don't need to be hungry to eat a fresh baked scone, Reverend, and what with a dollop of mother's raspberry jam it'll fair slide down. Now you gets to eatin' a couple while I goes look to the oven.'

My mother and hers.

That was what Martha had said. A family tradition that reached back through time. He took the tea, staring into the cup. Did her daughter too practise what she called the ancient ways, did Hilda also know of that terrible sin?

Taking her own cup as her daughter left the pin-neat room the old woman spoke again.

'You take mind of what Martha Sim be telling you. Evil walks at your side, an evil that laughs at your Church; it is strong, Reverend, very strong and you must . . .'

'No more, Martha!'

'Listen to me!' Her black eyes brilliant as jet, the woman caught at his sleeve as he replaced cup and saucer on the tray. 'This be no insect buzzing about you, you can't brush it away like some troublesome wasp; you has to deal with it as it deals with you, use the ancient ways.'

'No!' The priest stood up. 'I'll hear no more. What you speak of is against the Faith, it is as evil in its way as . . .'

'As the way of the Dark One?' The woman's hands dropped to her lap. 'It is one of his follows you, one that will take you into hell. You think those hours on your knees will save you? No, Reverend, they have given no protection nor will they. There be no hope, save the way I speaks of . . . you must fight fire with fire . . .'

The woman meant well, but to follow her path, to break faith with the teachings of the Church would damn his soul as surely as he himself had damned it that after-noon a year ago. Raising one hand he made the sign of benediction then smiled gently.

'Stay well, Martha, I hope to see you and Hilda in church on Sunday.'

Listening to her daughter chatting as she saw the priest to the gate, Martha Sim closed her eyes. 'He thinks the Church will save him,' she muttered, 'but it won't . . . it won't!'

'Was that body fished from the canal anything to do with the rumpus that happened in the yard of the Bird-in-Hand a few nights ago?'

Standing outside the police station in Crescent Road, Kate Mallory stepped forward as the tobacco-coloured Ford estate car drew to a halt. She had waited an hour for Daniels to show and this time he was going to talk to her!

How the bloody hell was it this woman got hold of everything that went down in this town? Inspector Daniels tried to brush past, irritation showing clearly on his face.

'You were given the information regarding the occurrence at the public house. I have no more to add.'

Oh but there was more to add! Kate Mallory's journalistic nose twitched. Problem was how to get it out of this tight-mouthed cop, but get it she would . . . somehow.

'What about the man, Torrey, wasn't it? Is there going to be an arrest?'

Daniels reached the first of the three steps that led up to the entrance of the red-brick police station but the quick-moving Kate was in front of him. Acid burning his gullet he stared at her.

'You are very well aware that no charge has been brought, no charge . . . no arrest.'

'Isn't it more true to say Torrey can't be found, that he disappeared the night he half killed those three men and that is the reason he has not been arrested?'

Who the hell had been talking? Was it Sounder? Had the little shit taken a pay-off from the *Star* as well as from him? What was more, had he supplied any information on that bloody water lily? Keep it under wraps had been the word from the top, let nobody know more about that corpse than that it had been taken from the canal and remained unidentified. That was what he had done but who could tell what a sewer rat like Sounder could dredge up? Truth or lies, the newspapers printed it and if they ran a story on that his arse would hit the streets. He had no idea why the top brass wanted that murder kept dark and he hadn't asked, but had Echo Sounder known? And had he sold the information? If so, he would find permanent lodgings in Winson Green. Teeth gritted together he looked at the girl barring his way. She was plain looking but a slight twist to the mouth lent interest to her face and the hair, rich sherry almost auburn, curled attractively around it. How old was she, twenty-five – twenty-six? Old enough to have enough sense to know there was no future for her in the job she was doing, she'd far better get herself a husband and a couple of kids.

'If, as you seem to think, Mr Torrey has disappeared,' he answered tiredly, 'then the reason is not one of imminent arrest.'

'Imminent . . . !' Kate's quick eyes fastened on his. 'Then you are thinking of making one in the future?'

'What I might or might not be thinking has nothing to do with you, now get out of my way before I have you run in for wasting police time.'

'Why did Torrey beat up those three men?'

The question hurling itself in his face Inspector Bruce Daniels hesitated, one foot on the next step.

'Look,' he said sourly, 'you've been given all there is to give on that, if you want any more why don't you go look for your disappeared Mr Torrey and ask him yourself, or better still why not go see those three louts; you won't need to give them a hiding to get them to talk, just wave your cheque book at 'em.'

'Thank you, Inspector.' Kate hitched her over-full bag higher on her shoulder. 'That should make quite an interesting headline: *Police Inspector tells journalist . . . pay lager louts for information.*'

Sitting at his desk, Daniels felt for the tablets. One day soon he would see a doctor, but not yet, there were things to do first, things like nailing Bartley . . . and he would, by God he would! Popping a tablet on his tongue he sucked viciously. Bloody journalists, they were enough to make any man's guts ache; them and Connor. He'd liked their attention all right, preening like a prize cock when giving interviews on that drugs haul, yet the snipe-nosed bugger had done sod all in any of it. It was him, Daniels, who'd had the Bartley building watched, noting the comings and goings, paying particular attention to the fact that the chestnut-haired stranger and his companion of the grey suit had made no appearance. That had been a bit of a set-back; why had Bartley had them fetched in if there was no deal in the offing? But he'd followed the tip Echo Sounder had given him. Given him! Daniels laughed sourly. That little shit wouldn't give a blind man a light! But in this he'd been right. That lorry had gone sweeping past the Ford, a stationary car had aroused no suspicion in that driver. They had had no way of knowing how long it would take to load, but this particular branch of Bartley Holdings dealt with the distribution of frozen poultry, and with that sort of cargo you didn't let the grass grow under your feet; yet rushing in could foul up the whole thing. So he'd waited, pulling in just as the doors of the container lorry were being closed.

He sucked the BiSoDol tablet on his tongue.

Doc Walker's face had been a picture as the warrant to search had been flashed under his nose: Christ, there couldn't have been a look like that since they'd scrapped the death penalty!

What were they looking for, what on earth did they expect to find in a factory unit freezing chickens? *'Surely there has been some mistake, if you will tell me what this is all in aid of, officer . . .'* The little shit! Daniels sucked hard, swallowing saliva that had no effect on the acid scorching his gut.

What was he looking for? The two heavies Bartley had probably spent a small fortune hiring had swaggered from the shadow of the building but the swagger had disappeared as several squad cars had roared into the yard, the two men running for the back fence. They were fast on the home stretch. That was how Sounder had described them, but a couple of his officers ran for the Tipton Harriers, and *they* were fast; Bartley's two hadn't even made the waste ground.

Walker had twittered all the time the place had been ripped apart, a smirk on his ferret face when the search remained negative, and all the time the two men he had seen in the bar of the Frying Pan stood a little to one side, his own harriers close enough to bring them to heel should they try to make another run for it.

His back pressing into the chair he lifted the front legs clear of the floor. Sounder had said the big money was on this one and Sounder hadn't been wrong. Even so he had almost missed it. It had been Sounder's last words as he'd made to leave that pub. They had pushed their way into his mind, forcing through the fog that had clouded his brain.

'. . . if it be you should manage to get into the winner's enclosure then 'ave yourself a look up their arse, could be you'll find more'n shit!'

That had been the final piece in the puzzle, that had given him the clue. He'd had the lorry unlocked, emptied and every one of five thousand chickens opened up. He'd found what he was looking for then all right. He'd found it there, stuffed tight up the arses of several boxes of frozen chickens, packed inside those plastic bags along with the giblets; found it just as Superintendent bloody James Connor had come driving into the yard. Half a million quids worth of pure heroin, found just in time for Connor to take over: 'I'll take things from here.'

Letting the chair legs bang to the floor, Daniels swiped a hand across the desk sending folders falling to the ground, the acid of those words burning more fiercely than that of his stomach. Connor had bided his time, waltzing in at the vital moment, taking over that which he'd sweated over. He hadn't dealt with Sounder, he hadn't sat for hours in a bloody car waiting for the thing to break; but that had made no difference, Connor was Superintendent, his was the say, his the decision and he'd made it. He had taken over the case and with it the glory. Detective Inspector Bruce Daniels was still just that, Detective Inspector . . . his promotion gone. Connor had the dope and he had those two runners who were overseeing the operation, he even had Doc Walker, but he didn't have the one that really mattered, the one behind the whole bloody set-up, he didn't have Bartley. That one had been too crafty, he wasn't going to get caught within fifty miles of the stuff.

Lighting a cigarette he grimaced. That tablet had done no good, his innards were still on fire. Marjorie said he should see the quack, but what would he do? He drew hard on the cigarette, taking smoke deep into his lungs. Would he write some marvellous prescription that would rid a man of a nagging wife, give him promotion, make his life sweet and rosy? Like bloody hell he would! Only men like Jim Connor had things all worked out and served up to 'em on a plate.

But Bartley hadn't been served up. Daniels felt a moment of elation, at least Connor couldn't add that to his list of triumphs. Oh, Bartley had known of the pick-up but his lawyers would make mincemeat of the force if they tried sticking that on him, but at least Doc Walker wouldn't be free again, not this side of fifteen years.

'You have helped keep the children of this town safe.'

That had been only a little of the crap spouted by the newspapers. Jim Connor wasn't bothered about that dope hitting the streets. Stupid bastards, he'd said; who cared what them kids turned themselves into, if they were daft enough to mess with that shit then they deserved all they got. Nabbing a couple of pushers and Walker hadn't landed the distributor, and so meant no more to an organised ring than a poke in the eye, but it had given Jim Connor a Deputy Commissioner's desk.

Daniels finished the cigarette, grinding the last of it into the ashtray. Christ, his gullet was like an inferno!

And for all the time and effort he'd put in, what had the arrests brought Bruce Daniels? Sweet bloody Fanny Adams, that's what it had brought him, zero, zilch, nothing except for an expense sheet.

Had Sounder known more than he'd spilled . . . had he known Bartley would go missing? Daniels's mouth slipped a little further on its perpetual downward slope. That nasty little trait of withholding information was liable to bring him a severe case of broken bones . . . or worse, if the right folk got to know what a sweet singing voice he had, he could finish up getting the same course of treatment as that tart they'd pulled from the cut.

But what the fuck did he care for Sounder! He'd paid the little runt and if those dope pedlars did the same, making it a once and final payment, it would cause Bruce Daniels no grief, same as that trash from the canal had caused him none; canaries like Sounder or some little screw got themselves bumped off, what did it matter? Neither had given him what he wanted, neither had brought him any nearer promotion. Bruce Daniels had been someone the brass could fart around with, a beano cop good for a laugh then used to wipe their arse on!

Resign, Marjorie has said, get out of it altogether. And do what? What else was there for a copper near retirement? Some bloody night-watchman's post in one of Darlaston's factories? P'raps he should ask Bartley, get set on as security guard at the place on the Leys, watching out for nosy coppers sniffing out dope! What a smile that would put on his face, it might be almost as big as the one that getting away without any charge of handling dope must have put on it. 'Leave it,' had been Connor's final word, 'the case warrants no further investigation, Bartley obviously had no knowledge of the crime being committed.'

No knowledge! Slamming from his office to the Ford parked in the yard, Daniels swore vehemently. Like hell Bartley had no knowledge! But why no more investigations?

Sitting behind the wheel he felt for the pack of antacid tablets. Why would Connor call in the hounds . . . why give up so easily? A tablet half-way to his mouth, Detective Inspector Bruce Daniels almost smiled. Could it be the new Deputy Commissioner had known of that pick-up, was he somehow involved?

'*Leave it!*'

He turned the key, listening to the contented purr of the engine.

'*The case warrants no further investigation.*'

Guiding the car out of Victoria Road he headed for Katherine's Cross. 'No further investigation,' he spat. 'Well, up yours, Mr Deputy Commissioner!'

'It's a lovely spot, though it be a bit quiet after Bilston; not that I misses the noise o' them steelworks but a chap misses a pint and a game o' darts wi' his mates.'

'What about the Jolly Abbot, don't they have a dart board?' Richard Torrey looked at the man offering him a glass of ale.

'Oh they'n gorra board.' George Barnes led the way to a wooden bench set close to a small pool, water from a stone fountain trickling softly on to the wide green pads of pink water lilies. 'And the folk there'm friendly enough, but it ain't the same, what they knows about the smeltin' and rollin' o' steel would be lost on a pin's 'ead, an' what I knows about cows and sheep be a good match.'

It was easy to see what he meant. Torrey took a long swallow of the refreshing drink. That lorry driver had set him down here a couple of weeks back and he'd sharp found there was nothing of interest to him. But he'd decided to stick it out for a while. Saying he was a writer and needed somewhere quiet to work he had rented a caravan. That had accounted for most of his money but at least it provided a reason for his being here and it not being a holiday season the site was unoccupied except for himself. That was one point in its favour, the other being he could rest up here, let the aftermath of that scuffle in the yard of the Bird-in-Hand die the death, and here maybe he would forget Anna; but not the promise he had made. Anyone involved in that murder would go the same way. He didn't know how he would find them, but somehow – somewhere, he would.

'Have you ever thought of going back?'

'To what?' George Barnes shook his head. 'I'm turned fifty-eight, who would set a bloke on at my age? They wants young kids, kids they can pay in tenners; besides, the missis likes it 'ere, though atween you an' me I know there be times when 'er misses Bilston, same as me. You would allus find 'er at the market on a Monday, liked a bargain, did the missis. But what about yourself, will you go back once that book o' yourn be finished?'

'I might have to go before that.'

'Oh, why be that then?'

'Money.' Torrey emptied his glass. 'Or rather the lack of it. I'll have to put the writing on hold until I can make some more. I have done a couple of bits here and there around the village but it didn't pay for more than a couple of meals at the Jolly Abbot.'

'Don't surprise me.' The other man answered flatly. 'Most folk hereabout would skin a fart and sell the peel for tuppence. They don't exactly take to spendin', but the bloke that owns this place ain't too bad, could be he might find you summat as'll tide you over. I ain't sayin' as he will but there again I ain't sayin' as he won't, all I do say is it be worth the tryin', if you wants to be 'ere a bit longer that is.'

It might be best at that. Thanks given for the drink Torrey walked on slowly along the narrow lane. Coming to where it joined the road through the village he paused, watching a small car come to a halt. He'd seen that car before, it had been parked beside the church he'd visited the first day he'd been here. Paying it no real mind he turned away as the door opened. Whoever the driver was he'd obviously picked up a friend.

Chapter Eight

The Reverend Peter Darley put the car into gear, easing it forwards as the figure he had picked up settled into the seat beside him.

'I'm going as far as the village if that's any good to you.'

'Thank you.' The answer was low, almost musical.

Thank heaven he had seen this person standing at the side of the road. That half hour spent at the Sim cottage had unsettled nerves already rubbed raw, it would help to hold a normal conversation. Peter Darley glanced at the figure in the passenger seat, the face turned away to watch the passing scenery.

'Are you staying in Monkswell?'

'Yes.'

The figure was not exactly talkative, but it was somehow reassuring to have someone there. The priest drove carefully, keeping the car well into the hedge, wary of tractors that came and went between farms and fields.

'It's a pretty village,' he tried again, 'I hope you enjoy it. Are you staying long?'

'A few days.'

It seemed there was a laugh in the voice. Peter Darley drew to a halt, allowing a herd of cows to cross the narrow lane, watching their slow procession to the farm's milking sheds.

'Afternoon, Reverend.' A ruddy-cheeked man holding a long stick smiled in at the car window. 'Sorry to 'old you up but old Marilyn there be a one to tek 'er time.'

'Not to worry, Amos,' the priest smiled, 'you can't expect the famous to hurry for ordinary folk like us, they are very temperamental.'

'Well I don't be knowin' about that, but the old girl won't tek no 'urrying; I says to my Carrie if that there cow 'ad the same shape as Marilyn Monroe and not just the same name I could sell 'er for a fortune, as it is I just 'as to wait on 'er tekin' 'er time.'

'You let her do that, I'm in no hurry and I'm certain my friend here won't mind a few minutes wait.'

'Well that be understandin', Reverend,' the farmer glanced to the passenger seat, the brows of his weather-beaten face drawing together, 'it . . . it be understandin' of you both.'

'Amos has the finest dairy herd in the district.' Peter Darley drove on. 'He swears it is all due to giving each cow the name of some famous film star, he says it makes them feel special so they act that way by increasing their milk yield. It's utter nonsense of course but Amos believes it.'

'Many things are labelled nonsense until they are proven to be true, wouldn't you agree?'

There was a laugh in that voice, but this time it was a mocking, cynical sound.

'You should see the church while you are here.' Peter Darley pushed the thought away, trying to bypass the awkwardness of the moment. 'It is very old and really quite beautiful.'

The seat beside him creaked as his passenger twisted around, a spicy fragrance filling the car.

'Oh I've seen the church . . .'

Peter Darley's fingers gripped the wheel, the hair on the back of his neck rising.

'. . . I've been there . . .'

A long-fingered hand reached out, stroking slowly over a thigh suddenly trembling beneath the covering robe.

'. . . we have both been there . . . together . . . you remember, Peter?'

'Please!' The priest's voice trembled on a sob, 'Please . . . I was wrong . . . it was wrong . . . !'

'Oh no, Peter!'

The figure beside him laughed again, the hand moving into the crotch of the trembling priest.

'When you want a thing as badly as you did how can it be wrong to take it? And you did take it, Peter, and you will again . . . I promise!'

'No!' The cry almost a scream, the Reverend Darley jammed a foot to the brake, staring at the seat beside him as the car swerved into the hedge, a seat that was empty.

There were only two places you would find Echo Sounder apart from the flea-ridden bed he had in that doss house where he rented a room, and that was one place he wasn't going to look.

Detective Inspector Bruce Daniels slammed the door of the Ford, turning the key in the lock and at the same time glancing the length of Willenhall Street. If Sounder wasn't here in the Frying Pan then he'd pay a visit to Harry Hodgkin in Pinfold Street, that one still took as many betting slips as ever he'd taken over the counter when he'd sold groceries, and Harry Hodgkin, like many another in Darlaston, wouldn't relish a visit from Bruce Daniels! Dropping the keys into his pocket he walked into the tap room, its air a constant smoke screen from the steady flow of workers coming and going on shift, or spending their dinner hour over a pint of best.

'Thought I'd find you here.'

Echo Sounder did not look up as the inspector slid into a chair but still he saw that only one glass was carried.

'I hear there was a bit of a shindig at the Bird-in-Hand the other night.' Daniels took a swallow of his beer. 'So who was it throwin' the punches?'

''Ow would I know, I never uses the Bird.'

So the little runt was playin' it that way. Daniels came near to a smile. Well, a game lightened the day a bit.

'You never use soap either but you know about it; you'll also know about the inside of a prison cell if you try pissin' me about! Those betting slips in your pocket'll give the magistrate some interesting reading and Harry Hodgkin won't be too pleased when he hears who it was got him sent down for running a book without a licence.'

'I only 'eard.' The little man swallowed nervously.

Daniels lit a cigarette and replaced the pack in his pocket. Royals might be the cheapest smokes on the market but they were still a drain on his pay; Sounder could buy his own this time around.

'So,' he blew smoke upwards in one smooth stream, 'what was it you 'eard?'

'It be worth a pint, Mr Daniels, tellin' you be worth a pint.'

Daniels felt the hot surge of acid bite in his chest. Christ, it was getting so he couldn't put anything past his throat! Feeling for the familiar packet he slipped a tablet into his mouth.

'Not telling me will be worth more than a pint,' he grated, 'it'll be worth a night in the cells plus a good few months as a guest of the Queen, Featherstone prison be my guess.'

Sounder decided against trying his luck again. Daniels had become even more of a bastard since that do along at Bartley's place, word had it the credit for them arrests 'ad bin snatched from under 'is nose, tekin' a certain bit o' promotion along with it. 'I d'ain't catch no name 'cept one were called Red, I don't know nothin' of the other pair.'

'I wouldn't keep anything back, Sounder.' Daniels sucked on the tablet, his eyes holding fast to the ferret face bent over a nearly empty glass. 'They don't serve beer in

Featherstone and the only bet you'll make is whether or not you reach your bunk with all your bones in one piece.'

'It's the truth, Mr Daniels, I d'ain't 'ear no other name spoke, I don't know who them three blokes was.'

It was a lie. Daniels reached for his glass then pushed it away as the flame burning in his chest flared into his throat. But he couldn't really blame Sounder for telling it. From what the investigating officer had been told they were three right bully boys; if they got wind of a canary singing the bird would soon be stuffed, balls pushed so far up his arse no doctor at the Sister Dora hospital would get 'em down.

'But you know who it was laid them out.'

He knew. Echo Sounder lowered his head nearer the glass. He knew who'd dropped Red and 'is mates, who it was 'ad left one with a broken collar bone and a fractured skull, the other with a dislocated backbone; he also knew the same would 'appen to 'im if word got around he'd sung. But Featherstone! Daniels wasn't the man he'd been a couple o' weeks back, he'd been a bastard then but 'e was more of a one now. Try pulling the wool over 'is eyes and the next bed you slept in would be in the nick!

'Word 'as it the one you be after backing 'ad a stable along of Dangerfield Lane.'

His temper not benefiting from the bile in his throat, Daniels snapped. 'Cut the bloody racetrack lingo, I'm in no mood to interpret that shit.'

'The bloke who done it, left them three sleeping in the yard o' the Bird, seems it were Torrey . . . Richard Torrey.'

'You said he *had* a place in Dangerfield Lane?' Daniels

waited as his informant took a sip of his remaining beer.

Sounder's eyes moved swiftly around the smoke-hazed room. Jesus, why couldn't Daniels bugger off! If 'e was seen talkin' to the blues . . .

'Still does.' He mumbled into the glass held tight between both hands. 'But 'e ain't bin seen nowheres near it since that night.'

There had been no formal complaint. Those three had laid no charge; whatever had caused that fight neither the combatants nor the landlord wanted the police involved. But it had been a good way of getting Sounder rattled. Satisfied his opening gambit had worked, Daniels lit another cigarette.

'And what of Bartley?' He asked the question quietly, letting the words out on a breath of smoke sent to merge with the haze settled like a cloud over the tap room.

Raising the glass to his mouth Echo Sounder tipped the last few dregs of beer into his mouth before pushing up from the table. Let this bastard arrest 'im! He banged the glass on to the bar, the landlord's glance following as he scuttled through the door. Let Daniels send 'im down, let 'im put 'im away, there'd be no more singing about Bartley, that was a horse that carried stakes too high for Echo Sounder. The word had gone out, the odds on winning were a thousand to one . . . and the pay-out was a swim in the canal with your throat cut!

'I wonder why I thought I might find you here?'

Easing her shoulder bag along her arm Kate Mallory

settled herself on the vacant half of the park bench. 'Has the Frying Pan stopped serving beer or is it the clientele . . . someone got a bit too nosy?'

'Bugger off!' Taking the *Sporting Pink* from his pocket, Echo Sounder held the pages in front of his face.

'Now, now! Your mother taught you better than that, she told you always to be polite to a lady.'

'So 'er did.' He turned a page. 'So bugger off . . . please.'

The sarcasm of the snapped answer rolling off her like water from a duck's back, Kate rummaged in the depths of a bag large enough to hold her grandmother's piano – except her grandmother had sold it and gone on a weekend trip to Brighton with the proceeds. Good old Granny, she never let the grass grow under her feet . . . and neither would her granddaughter. After finding the purse that had strategically withdrawn beneath a welter of chocolate wrappers and scrawled interview notes she made a drama out of opening it, knowing not all of the little man's attention was on his newspaper. Sounder liked to bet, he liked it a lot, but that particular pleasure needed money to support it. Taking out several notes she counted them, returning to the purse all but one. This she rolled, holding it between her fingers like a cigarette.

'I spoke to Inspector Daniels this morning . . .'

Beside her the newspaper rustled nervously.

'. . . he said to talk to you. He said you could tell me about that shindig at the Bird-in-Hand a few nights back.'

'What shindig?' The ferret eyes glanced at the rolled-up banknote. 'I ain't 'eard of no such.'

A sudden bout of deafness! Kate smiled internally. A

fiver would work wonders in the curing of that. Reaching again for her purse she gave a brief shrug.

'The inspector must have been mistaken . . . pity he was wrong for I hear from our sports desk there are a few good horses running today.'

'Hold on . . .'

Kate's inner smile widened at the note of near panic in the squeaky voice. Money put back in her purse was liable to give this man a seizure.

'. . . that scuffle, I seems to remember now.'

'I thought you would!' Kate rolled the note temptingly between her fingers. But he had to remember very clearly if he hoped to get his grimy claws on her money.

A swift glance encompassing the park telling him they were not watched, Echo Sounder rested the newspaper on his knees. You couldn't be careful enough in this town, even the bloody trees had eyes.

'Landlord along of the Bird reckons it were all over in a spit. Three blokes . . . a Red summat or other were the name of one of 'em . . .'

'I got all of that myself when I talked to the landlord, it's not the three who got turned over I want to know about, I want to know about the man who laid them in nice neat positions in that yard.'

'Don't know nuthin' about him . . . 'cept he done time in the Army!' The downward shift of the banknote towards the cavernous bag changed Sounder's mind. 'Served with the commandos in Northern Ireland so they says.'

'And what else do they say?'

Kate watched the ferret face. His eyeballs couldn't stick any closer to that fiver if she superglued them to it!

'He lives in Dangerfield Lane, in a council house that used to be rented by his mother; his old man buggered off while he was a lad, don't ask me why cos I don't know . . .'

The note still held dexterously between her fingers, Kate withdrew a couple of cigarettes from her bag, placing one between her lips and dropping the other on to the newspaper. She wouldn't ask, she wasn't interested in the parents, only in the son. Trying to keep her face far from the grime-covered hand that held the lighted match to her cigarette she listened as he went on.

'. . . but nobody ain't seen 'im there in that house since that fight, nor seen 'im around in Darlaston neither.'

All of this she knew already! Kate drew heavily on her cigarette, blowing a long stream of smoke into the air. Patience, she told herself as she watched the diaphanous grey veil thin and spread on the afternoon breeze; patience, Kate me lass, if the man don't cough he don't get the syrup.

Sensing his reward slipping away, Sounder glanced furtively about the open spaces of the park. Newspaper folk weren't like the blues, a copper's nark was sure of his pay-off but wi' bloody journalists you never knowed, they paid or they d'ain't, it were all according to which side of the bed they'd rolled from any day.

'His name be Torrey,' he hissed from the side of his screwed mouth, 'Richard Torrey.'

Not enough. Kate ground the stub of her half-smoked cigarette into the gravel beneath her feet, at the same time hitching her bag on to her shoulder. He had half a second to prove his nickname, to Echo every last syllable he'd heard or that fiver would be like the Dodo, gone for ever!

'One more thing . . .' Sounder twisted around on the seat, his hand half extended to take his prize '. . . word has it Torrey had a friend . . . the sort who lives in . . .'

'Lives in?' One finely arched brow — Kate's chief claim to facial beauty after her quite nice amber-coloured eyes — rose.

'Well . . . you knows . . .'

Was she being fair to him? Kate watched Sounder squirm beneath her steady gaze. The man might be all sorts of a toad but he obviously had difficulty in talking of sex; her fivers were hard earned, though, so let him work as hard for one of them.

'No,' she said, hiding the fact she knew his discomfort. 'I don't know, so tell me.'

For a moment Kate felt she had twanged the little man's strings a mite too hard. Damn! She clutched the strap of her bag. She never had known when to shout whoa!

'It were a tart he picked up off the streets . . .'

Kate thought her breath of relief must sound like a Cunard liner leaving the dock.

'. . . caused quite a stir in the Lane, set folks' tongues waggin' but med no difference. The tart stayed put until about a year ago then it seemed it was thanks Mr Torrey and off wi'out so much as a kiss me arse. Them as lived around him reckons he weren't the same man after that, he'd never bin what yer might call friendly afore but once that split come they say he'd cut yer throat as lief look at yer.'

'Were they lovers?'

For the first time the ferrety eyes left the banknote to rest disconcertedly on the newspaper.

'You meks yer own mind up about that.'

Ninety-nine per cent of it already made up, Kate rolled the banknote once more.

'And the name of Torrey's lover?'

'I don't know!'

He didn't know or wouldn't say? Kate's slightly off-level lips pursed thoughtfully. Echo wasn't a man to back off after coming this far, he wouldn't risk an afternoon's betting slips by withholding a name; it was safe to say that in this at least he was telling the truth.

'Was that fight anything to do with the body the police fished from the canal?' It was blunt and unexpected as she had meant it to be but the hoped-for reaction was typical of a lead balloon – it didn't rise.

Glancing again at the rolled-up note he had already bidden a sad farewell, Echo Sounder shook his unkempt head. 'Don't know that neither, d'ain't once hear it spoke, don't think anybody did. Whether you pays or whether you don't I can't tell you no more of that one; kept theirselves to theirselves, they did, 'ad nowt to do wi' neighbours.'

Sufficient unto themselves! Well . . . well! Dropping the banknote on to the newspaper Kate gathered her bag and walked slowly from the park, glancing at the red-brick police station as she passed. The cagey inspector hadn't mentioned any of this. But then a girl didn't find every egg in the hen house, she sometimes had to look under the hedge.

＊

The church of St James the Apostle had stood since Norman times. Set on a gentle rise it overlooked the village of Monkswell. It had somehow escaped the attentions of the minions of Henry VIII who had carried out that king's reformation, the riches of the Abbot's house interesting them far more. That had been stripped of any treasures it may once have held and the house sold into private hands, but the little church had remained untouched.

The Reverend Peter Darley stared out from the car at the grey stone walls. There had been a hitch-hiker standing at the side of the road, someone had climbed into the car; he had talked to them . . . someone *had* been there! So why had the passenger seat been empty even before the car had come to a halt? Imagination? He drew a trembling breath. It had been no trick of the mind.

His head swimming he climbed from the car and stood drawing in lungfuls of air, but the spicy fragrance remained stubbornly in his nostrils. He had not noticed it at first, but as that hand had touched him, as that voice had spoken his name, the aroma had become stronger, an aroma he remembered so well.

'. . . *you did take it, Peter, and you will again . . .*'

No. Please God, no! Staring at the church Peter Darley made the silent plea he had made so often these past few days, but even as he did so he knew it was useless. He should go back to the rectory, heaven knew he felt sick enough.

But then heaven knew many things concerning the Reverend Peter Darley. He caught the sob, holding it in his throat.

He had to go in, he had to observe the practices of the Church.

Fear clawed at his chest as he walked beneath the ancient lych gate and up to the age-blackened door. It would be waiting there inside, waiting as it did each time he came.

To one side a raven flapped heavy black wings, launching its body into the purpling sky, its harsh croak carrying on the hushed stillness of early evening.

There would be no one inside, the folk of Monkswell were too busy to come to Evensong. He could leave, nobody would know. But the Lord would know!

Releasing the sob caged in his throat he stepped into the shadowed church but the breath replacing the sob was a scented agony, a nausea that made him long to return outside; but to return was to replace one breath with another equally intoxicating draught. Standing at the entrance to the nave he closed his eyes, trying to centre his mind on physical reality, to rend a hole in the unreality filling his lungs and mind, trying to tear open some mental gap through which to draw the smells of wax polish, of old books.

Beside him in the shadows a pew creaked, its woodwork reacting to the cool of evening. Stretching out a hand he clutched at its lovingly polished frame, calling on its strength to hold him upright, but more to hold him here at the start of the aisle, to prevent his moving forwards, to forbid the strength of that power already beginning to call him.

Seated in a corner at the rear of the church Richard Torrey made to move. He hadn't reckoned on staying. He didn't really know what had drawn him to see inside the building, churches had never been on his agenda and he certainly wanted no part of their mumbo jumbo, not even as a passive observer. But catching sight of the priest's face as he stepped into the light streaming in through the windows, Torrey sat down sharply. God, the man looked like death!

The sound of Torrey's movement echoed in the quiet church but Peter Darley didn't hear. The sharp sweetness he had smelled in the car hung over him, thickening, intensifying in the silent stillness, resisting his efforts to dislodge it, increasing the desire spreading like some malignant growth, a perfumed cancer consuming his will, eclipsing his reason.

'Our Father . . .'

Torrey caught the quiet words. They sounded more as if the priest were crying than praying. Interest outstripping his antipathy towards the church he watched the black-robed figure move on slowly down the aisle and strained to catch the sobbing words.

'Our Father . . .' Peter Darley spoke again but a soundless mocking laugh stripped the prayer from his lips with lightening efficiency, leaving him gasping at the speed.

From his seat Richard Torrey caught the backward jerk of the priest's head. It was as though somebody had smacked the fellow in the mouth.

Halfway along the aisle Peter Darley hesitated. He had tried to resist the power that called on him, but it was too strong; he could not fight it alone, yet he was alone, deserted by all he had once held precious, a desertion bought at his own price. He had known what he was doing, known the sin he was committing.

He moved on, lips moving in prayer that would not be spoken, passing beneath the rood-screen with its central figure of a crucified Christ flanked by a weeping Virgin Mary and a mortified John the Beloved. The crimson carpet that began the approach to the high altar was soft beneath his tread, swallowing the sound of reluctant feet, taking into itself his last hope of recall from the nightmare that waited.

Three steps. He looked at the altar that stood a little way back from the rood-screen. Three steps and he would stand before it. Lifting his hand he tried to make the sign of the cross, to seek its protection from the evil that waited, but again the mocking laugh that was no laugh at all dashed the action from his struggling mind.

All of his Army training coming into play, Richard Torrey moved soundlessly towards the further end of the church. The priest moved like a man in a dream, or a man who was ill! Reaching the front pew he heard the quiet recitation begin. If the man was not ill then his offer of help could be viewed as interference. Slipping once more into a seat he watched the priest lift his face towards the altar. He would wait!

'Whoso dwelleth under the defence of the Most High shall abide under the shadow of the Almighty . . .'

The words croaked out, but who could say this priest didn't always talk like that? Torrey sat unmoving as the words dragged themselves out.

'. . . I will say unto the Lord, Thou art my hope, my stronghold: My God, in Him will I trust. For He shall deliver thee from the snare of the hunter . . .'

Behind him Peter Darley felt a touch against his neck; soft fingertips traced his hairline while all around the air thickened with the tangy scent of spice. It was here as he knew it would be, waiting for him, waiting to draw him into that same evil.

'Our Father . . .' Two words were all that came before those fingers transferred to the base of his stomach, before their sensual touch knocked the prayer from him with the force of a hammer blow.

No! Peter Darley's head jerked on his neck, his whole being in the cry that made no sound. It couldn't happen here, this was sanctified ground, this was a house of God. But it would happen, as it had already happened!

Torrey watched the priest slip to his knees. Was there always this much fervour? He tried thinking back to his school days but the memories, if he had any, were buried too far in the past.

Please! Peter Darley cried silently to the presence touching his body but the touching went on. Sexual, arousing, the touch of a lover, it played over his stomach, into his crotch, while something soft yet definite brushed his cheek. A shudder — half desire, half revulsion — recalled a temporary sanity and he tried to turn away, to break that delicious contact; but his body was no longer his own, it refused to answer his desperate request, emitting no response to his mental despair.

'Our Father . . .' He tried again but the will to pray was slipping away, melting before the hot tide of yearning washing up from the depths of him. The soft warmth, so like a breath, fanned across his face, the brush of one cheek against another.

Speechless now he snatched a breath, holding it in his throat, using it as defence to hold back a torment he knew would grow, accumulate into an agony of pleasure that would drain the last of his will to fight. A projection of a tired brain, imagined, unreal? Peter Darley could no longer define, he could only tremble with relief as he felt it leave him.

From the pew Richard Torrey watched the priest turn his head to look to where a screen of carved railing enclosed the Lady chapel. He had read the plaque set in the wall saying the chapel had been built more than four hundred years ago by a grateful Sir Henry Beddingley whose wife seemingly had benefited from the prayers of the clergy, recovering sufficiently from some obscure malady to bear him eleven children. Some cure! P'raps he should sign on with the priesthood instead of a doctor. What was the fellow looking at, there was nobody there! Glancing back to the priest he watched him rise to his feet, his head turning to face forwards. Was he imagining it or was the fellow acting like a Hollywood zombie?

The presence no longer touching him, Peter Darley stood at the foot of the chancel steps. It did not caress him yet he knew it was still there, sensed the vulpine laughter as the beckoning began again. It was a movement without movement, a speaking that had no voice, and he could do nothing but answer.

His feet, lifting of their own volition, carried him in the wake of that irresistible promise; his lips moved without any recognition on his part of the mumbled words trickling from them.

'He shall defend thee under His wings; Thou shalt not be afraid for any terror . . . nor for the sickness that destroyeth in the noon day.'

Still not knowing why he sat there Torrey remained motionless. The priest was moving up the steps leading to the altar. The guy was on his feet and moving, there was nothing wrong with him except maybe for a touch too much of religion. He should go, leave now before the sickness spread! But he did not go, instead he sat with his eyes on that black-robed figure.

'. . . not be afraid for any terror . . . nor for the sickness . . .'

On the first of the three steps the priest's words faded, becoming lost among the mellowed walls of the church, swallowed by the creeping shadows. Peter Darley no longer felt terror and his only sickness was that of desire.

It was on the third step it touched him again.

Torrey watched the priest come to a halt, saw him stiffen. What was with this man, why the drama?

Light from the beautiful east window playing over his waxen features, the Reverend Peter Darley tried to speak the words that might bring spiritual aid but as that soft breath-like touch played over him, sending his body rigid, contracting his stomach with tight breath-wrenching spasms, they were gone, obliterated by the wordless whisper insinuating into his mind. Giving himself over to it his body lost its rigidity, becoming pliant, moulding itself to that unspoken suggestion.

Fingers toyed sensuously with his neck and his knees folded slowly beneath the insistence of unseen hands. He raised his eyes to the altar, to the golden cross supporting the saviour of man and saw it drown in the wave of desire that engulfed him, delivering him a willing sacrifice to the thing he dreaded yet at the same time longed for. Fragrance subtle with the tangy freshness of an autumn morning filled nostrils flared wide to receive it. No longer trying to withhold the attack on his senses he sucked it in, hungry for it as an infant hungry for mother's milk, his memory no longer striving to recall its origin, the whole of him revelling in the touch of formless hands beneath his cleric's robe, beneath each stitch of clothing, stroking, fondling.

Torrey caught the faint moan as the priest slid to the ground before the altar. Perhaps he should to go see that the fellow wasn't sick or in pain, but even as he tried to rise he felt a heaviness on his shoulders, a pressing down that held him in his seat.

Stretched out at the top of the chancel steps Peter Darley felt no pain, only an exquisite sensuous touch that had him yearning for more. In the centre of his chest the invisible hands rested then began a slow descent over a stomach pulled tense, touching his navel, stopping at the fringe of pubic hair. Gasping, the priest pushed his body upwards, seeking to draw that sweet torture to where his swollen flesh throbbed. A low laugh, soundless and exultant, whispered against his temple then brushed his parted lips. Peter Darley's mouth widened and in the ecstasy that possessed him received a moist tongue.

Around Torrey the church dimmed as if the lovely afternoon had turned abruptly into night, and with the going of the sun's rays went all beauty from that chancel, from the graceful carved pews and the lovely little Lady chapel. The stone walls lost their mellowed look, standing grey and stark beneath a menacing shroud of silently deepening shadows.

Outside in the churchyard the returning raven flapped heavily into the sprawling oak but the gnarled branch offered no rest. Hopping as if the selected perch held a current of electricity the bird rose with a nervous croak, flapping across the quiet churchyard, skimming low over moss-covered headstones, its large black wings casting no shadow on the ground beneath.

Inside the church the two men heard nothing. The pressure on his shoulders still holding him, Torrey watched the priest spread his legs apart, watched his body arch upwards. What in the world was he doing?

Peter Darley moaned again, oblivious to all but that seeking, probing tongue and the hands that left every nerve a tingling pinpoint of flame as they caressed the insides of his thighs, each movement carrying up to his navel before sliding slowly downwards once more, each time coming tantalisingly nearer to his thrusting flesh but at the last second avoiding, denying that which the hands promised; and still that moist tongue played over his lips, delved expertly into the warm depths of his mouth.

The man must be having some kind of fit! And what the hell was *he* doing? Nothing except watching! The quick anger of impotence flushed through Torrey. He wasn't really being held back unless it was by his own imaginings and he wasn't given to those. Gripping the arm of the pew he tried to push to his feet but the force that held him was too strong. What was it, what was happening to him . . . and what was happening to that priest?

At the head of the Chancel steps Peter Darley's body jerked. The arc of movement over his stomach reduced its span and an unseen finger flicked against the tight hard mass of his testicles. The touch making him gasp, he breathed in spice-fragranced air that seemed to wrap him in its own scented cloud. The finger moved again and then again, touching, stroking, each erotic contact sending his body arching upwards, jerking like a marionette dancing to the dictates of a puppeteer. His breath, harsh and shallow, echoed from the shadow-draped walls, each gasp tumbling into the other in the effort to escape the confines of his throat, while his body ached from the unaccustomed pushing; but he was mindless of all save that exquisite teasing. Slowly, tormentingly, the fingers pushed through the mound of soft hair and he shuddered at the white hot flare that swept every nerve. Above his open mouth the mocking laugh was a warm sweet breath that rocked his senses further.

Then all movement ceased, holding in its own stillness his breath.

Torrey watched. Had the man blacked out, was he unconscious? He'd seen men suffer fits before, knew the medication they needed and what could happen if it wasn't administered; and that priest needed help. Christ, what was it with him, why couldn't he move! In a silence that seemed everlasting he stared at the figure stretched out on the ground, then breathed a sigh of relief when he heard the soft moan. But whatever had caused the priest to thrash about wasn't over, his body was jerking again.

The touch, gentle and slow, brushed the hardened flesh between the Reverend Darley's legs, tracing a lingering line over the tight stretched column, releasing his breath in a quivering gasp as he thrust upwards, eager for his own defilement; but the unseen hand dragged on, churning every nerve into a spiral of need that screamed for release yet yearned for the pleasure of it to go on.

'Please!' He moaned quietly. 'Please . . . please . . . !'

All around, that soft silent laughter echoed, growing, filling his ears with its mockery; but still the sweet torture went on, touching, drawing away, each delicate sensation ripping through him, the pleasure of it leaving him sucking in great gulps of tangy spice-filled air. His body taut, his mind lost to the pleasure of that touch, he gave a long juddering gasp that degenerated into a sobbing moan reverberating in his throat.

The sound of his own desecration.

Chapter Nine

Back at the station in Victoria Road Inspector Bruce Daniels glared around the poky office he shared with just about everybody else. He'd joined the police with great expectations; a local lad with a sad background, he was going to rise up through the force, become somebody; and where was he twenty years later? A bloody tuppenny copper still stuck in a tuppenny town! That business over at the Leys had been his one big chance, one! He pushed a hand along the littered desk. That was the only number they come in and his had been grabbed by Superintendent James bloody Connor. Only he wasn't Superintendent Connor any more, he was Deputy Commissioner Connor, a promotion he hadn't earned and didn't deserve. But wasn't that the way it always went? Let some other bugger do the work, then you snatch the reward! And Bartley, he was to be left alone, he warranted no investigation, why? There was more to that decision than met the eye.

He glanced at the enamel mug placed on the desk,

steam from it curling upwards, then at the young officer, his uniform pressed and neat, buttons shining like a row of medals.

Medals! He picked up the mug. There were no bloody medals in this game, least not for anybody on the Darlaston force.

'I went to thirty-three King Street, sir.'

Daniels looked up. 'King Street?'

'The breaking and entering sir. You said to go round there.'

'Did I?' Daniels frowned. 'So what did you get?'

'Not a lot, sir.' The young constable sounded apologetic. 'The woman said it were hard to say exactly what had been taken.'

'Huh!' The bark born of acid which the mouthful of tea brought bubbling into Daniels's throat had the constable clear his own with a nervous swallow.

'She said the shock had been too much, that she might remember later on.'

'And later on the tea leaf will be clear away and that'll be the last we'll be likely to see of him or number thirty-three's missing goods. Like Torrey they'll be clear away.'

'Like who, sir?'

Flicking a BiSoDol tablet into his mouth Inspector Bruce Daniels's brain clicked into gear.

No further investigation into Bartley's doings. No more follow-up of that tart pulled from the canal. Holding the tablet pressed against the roof of his mouth he sat upright. Two 'thou shalt nots' in as many days, could that mean the two were somehow connected? And Torrey, wasn't that the name of the only person to come forward to claim the body? He swallowed, bismuth dampening the fire beginning to lick his throat. Find Torrey and you find the identity of the corpse, find that and it just might lead to Bartley.

With a second whisky and soda in his hand Philip Bartley felt the shivers gradually decrease. Driving home alone unnerved him since that night, but he certainly wasn't picking up any more hitch-hikers. There *had* been someone standing there in the rain, he *had* climbed into the Rover and they *had* made love. Christ, you didn't imagine a thing like that! But he must have imagined it, there had been no other person in the car when those two coppers flashed their torch, no one sitting in the passenger seat, and there wasn't room between the car and the hedge for the door to have opened.

Had it been an illusion, a fantasy? He gulped at the drink. Whatever it had been, it had him jumping at shadows, shadows that filled his nostrils with that special fragrance.

Taking his drink he walked from the beautifully furnished sitting room through elegantly draped French windows into the garden, breathing the still air that heralded early evening. He'd been spooked, nothing more; the insistent drum of rain, a brain tired after the day's business; yes, a fantasy and no more.

Taking a long breath he looked back at the house, bathed now in a soft opalescent light. Monkswell Abbey with its tall, spiralled brick chimneys and deep-set mullioned windows sat like a jewel amid gently rolling land, his land.

He'd come a long way from the Bilston steelworks, a long way in every sense of the word, but it was a background he would never forget. It had taught him how to stand on his own two feet, to fight for himself whatever the odds and above all to make his decisions then stick to them. He'd had to learn fast; when he was tipping a crucible filled with molten steel no man had time for any other, no matter how young. You were expected to know your job, to know where to be and where not to be at any and every moment and take the consequences if you were wrong, and those consequences could be maiming or even death.

Like old Joe Turner. He sipped the whisky as memories returned. Sixty-four and with a lifetime of making steel, the old man had slipped, knocking himself out on the concrete-hard earthen floor as the overhead crucible tipped. There had been no time to drag him clear even if any of the men had reasoned it worth the trying, and no way to stop the ribbon of flaming metal, a myriad tiny sparks spitting from its bubbling mass as it flowed over the unconscious man.

He'd been just fifteen years old. He closed his eyes on the memory. Just days out of the classroom when he'd seen that old man devoured by molten steel; and in all the years between, the horror of that scene had never left him. And he had worked in that foundry. Christ, how he'd worked! Then after squeezing him dry the industry had begun to crack. Oh it had been well covered by the government, but papering over those cracks had not stopped the decay. Yet he had had the foresight to see where those cracks were headed and got out. He'd used every penny of the money he'd saved and every penny he could beg or borrow to buy on to the ladder that led up out of the overcrowded houses teeming with kids, away from the factories and canals; and from that first step he'd hauled himself up by the arse, building his food business little by little, store by store, first Darlaston then Wednesbury and so on, town by town until now he owned a Midlands-wide chain; and with them had come this.

He let his gaze wander over the expanse of greenery, over the perfectly kept gardens, then back to the house. Herringbone brickwork and low arched windows, many of their lozenge-shaped panes the original Tudor glass, gleamed in the lowering sun. Yes, his gamble had paid off and was still paying. Philip Bartley was a respected member of the community here and in the Black Country. From first buying the Abbey he'd set about ensuring that. A new roof for the village hall, a barn turned into a centre for the local youth with snooker, gym and soft drinks; then there was the Women's Institute, he'd helped finance several projects there, and of course the scout and guide rallies he allowed to take place on Abbey land. But all of this made no noticeable dents in an income funded by more than glorified grocery shops; dope was where the real money came from. Sipping from the glass that had quieted his nerves, he smiled. He was making more than sufficient for life's little pleasures, especially the ones he had usually found thumbing a lift.

'Telephone, Mr Bartley.'

Glad of the call that halted the memory of that last hitch-hiker he nodded towards the middle-aged woman who kept his house, and together with her husband saw to the running of the place. He had brought them in from Bilston and so far the arrangement had worked well. The couple seemed sufficient unto themselves, apart from hiring labour to help keep the grounds trim. Off duty they stayed in the cottage that went with the job and, more importantly, made no comment on the number of casual acquaintances he brought home.

'Philip Bartley.' He spoke abruptly into the telephone. 'Ah yes, Peter . . . no, I hadn't forgotten . . . yes fine, around eight then.'

'That was Father Darley.' He glanced at the woman he had signalled should wait. 'He's coming to see about the camping expedition that will be using the top meadow this weekend.' He paused, a smile touching the corners of his mouth. It never hurt to turn on the charm, charm had always proved his ace in the hand. 'Mrs Barnes, I know I say this every time we are invaded but I'm going to say it again: if you don't want them here they don't come. I won't have you or George tired out running around after a bunch of kids, you work hard enough as it is.'

The woman smiled and Philip Bartley kept his own expression even. Silly cow, what the hell did it matter what she wanted!

'We don't do nothin' as we don't get paid for,' the

woman answered. 'And George and me we don't 'ave to run around after them scouts nor them girl guides, they cooks their own food an' leaves no mess for others to clean up.'

'Well, if you're satisfied, Mrs Barnes, but don't ever feel you can't tell me should things prove too much.' The false smile curved a little more. 'Remember you wear the pants here.'

Well you certainly don't, not when you've got one of your fancy pieces 'ere, you don't! Maggie Barnes hid the thought behind her own forced smile.

'Me wear pants,' she shook her head as if amused, 'not with my bottom.'

'Go on with you.' Philip Bartley laughed. 'You know it drives your George wild.'

Turning for the kitchen Maggie lost the smile. At least her George preferred a woman's bottom, unlike some her could name . . . and not all of 'em in this house neither!

'Oh,' she hesitated. 'George says there be a man askin' to see you, seems he be after a job.'

Refilling his glass Bartley did not look up. 'Have George send him up after Reverend Darley leaves.'

There'd been something strange about that priest, about the way he'd carried on. Torrey closed the door of the caravan behind him. That had been no church service; no priest he'd ever seen had carried on like that, moaning and threshing, legs wide open. If he hadn't known better he would have said the fellow was being serviced by a very adept prostitute! Then there was that pressure on his own shoulders, something that held him in the pew. Had that been real . . . was that any less strange than the actions of the priest? Even when he had at last been able to move, had gone to the man's assistance, he had been brushed aside, thanked for his offer but told there was nothing wrong, the priest was not feeling ill, everything was perfectly all right.

Perfectly all right! Torrey set off across the field. Shit, he'd hate to be in that church if everything wasn't all right! That priest was hiding something, and judging by his face as they'd left the church it was something which, if not settled soon, might well prove his end.

But that wasn't *his* worry. Coming from the field into a narrow lane he walked on towards the Barnes's cottage. Why was he going there, why let the old man talk him into asking for a job? He wanted Anna's killer found, wanted him dead. That wouldn't happen here. He should go back to Darlaston and to hell with the police; if those three opened their mouths about who it was laid them out in the yard of the Bird-in-Hand then Richard Torrey would be guilty of GBH and put away for a couple of years, but so what, he was as good as dead anyway!

He would go to the cottage. Talk to the old man, make some excuse for not asking for any job.

Turning the bend of the lane he looked to where the gate of the little house stood white against a well-cut yew hedge. There was someone else there, a figure with a hand resting on the gate. A woman . . . or was it a man? He couldn't quite make out, the evening sun shining in his eyes made it difficult to distinguish. But he could see the hair; bright gold, it seemed to radiate, to shimmer as the head turned towards him. A rabbit scuttling across his path drew his attention and when he looked back the figure was gone.

This was the excuse he needed. The Barneses had a visitor, he would just say he'd changed his mind about asking for work and leave, they would be too taken up with their other caller to try talking him round.

'There you be, lad, I've a glass of ale ready for you.'

At the gate of the cottage Richard Torrey frowned. He would have thought the man to be inside with his visitor.

'No, George, no ale for me. I won't be staying.' He smiled. 'I don't want to take your time when you have a guest.'

'Guest?' George Barnes looked up from his seat on the wood bench. 'We don't 'ave no guest, why should you think we 'ad?'

'I saw him . . . or her . . . standing here by the gate.'

'Ain't bin nobody standin' at the gate. I been sittin' 'ere an hour an' more and ain't nobody been nigh. You be the first.'

'But I'd swear . . . I saw the hair, it was so bright it seemed to glow, and whoever it was turned and looked straight at me.'

George Barnes shook his head, a puzzled look creeping across his face. 'I knows my eyes ain't what they was when I worked in that steel mill, lad, but they ain't gone altogether. If'n anybody had been standin' agen that gate then I'd 'ave seen 'em clear, clear as I sees you, an' I tells you as I told you a minute gone, you be the first to pass this way.'

'It must have been a trick of the light.' Torrey glanced to where the evening sun sprinkled gold spots between the leaves of spreading trees.

'Ar, lad, the light.' George poured beer from a prettily patterned jug. 'It does that sometimes, plays tricks on folk.'

The same as that church! Torrey pushed open the gate. He would accept the drink the man was kind enough to offer, but he'd take no job.

Dangerfield Lane, that's what Echo had said. Torrey had a place in Dangerfield Lane. Inspector Daniels drove steadily along Pinfold Street. It had been easy enough to get the number of the house, Echo had his uses! But he would say no more of Bartley. The man was terrified of Bartley. Now why was that, do you suppose?

Glancing to the right he saw John Harris's shoe repairs shop. He'd got Marjorie to take his black leathers in, they could do with being soled and healed, and Harris was a decent chap, he did a good job.

Marjorie! He recalled their conversation at breakfast.

'Why can't I learn to drive?' she'd demanded. 'Other women drive, so why can't I learn now?'

Drive! All Marjorie could manage was a whist drive. Well, why shouldn't she learn now? Cos she hadn't the brain for it; put wheels on a bloody armchair and she might manage that, but a car . . . forget it! To his right the Regal cinema turned bingo hall announced its latest pay bonanza. Marjorie would be in there with the rest of 'em come the evening ... pity them places didn't play all night, that way he could have a couple of nights a week in his own house without constant warnings of 'Don't sit on the cushions, I've just straightened them ... don't you light that cigarette in here ... !'

The Duke of York public house looming large he indicated before turning right into Dangerfield Lane, sweeping past the squat line of council houses to one side, and what was left of Courts Farm on the other. Changes! His mind flashed to his boyhood. There had been so many changes; the goods line where a lad could jump on to a railway wagon and ride as far as he could walk back, the old Lodge Holes coal mine, the open ground that stretched to Kings Hill; or the other way across the grounds of the chemical works where many a deed went unseen, where a lad could take a body and roll it down a cinder bank into the canal!

It served him right ... it served him right!

Daniels breathed hard, pushing the memory of his father's death from him. That was the past, this was the present and he had a man to find.

Stopping the car a little way off from the house Echo Sounder had indicated, he glanced non-committally at its lace-curtained front. He could have applied for a warrant to search the place but then the Wednesbury force would have wanted in, this was their patch. No, he'd wait and Echo would listen, and if he wanted to stay on the street he'd sing of Torrey's return ... but only to Inspector Bruce Daniels.

Glancing at the house once more he noted no build up of newspapers poking from the letterbox and that no milk bottle, full or otherwise, decorated the doorstep. Had they been cancelled or did the man fetch them daily from a shop? At the next-door window a curtain twitched. He was drawing attention; probably the only car seen to park in this street was that of the 'visiting lady', employed to inspect council property. Huh! He snorted. She could put the wind up any of the folk here-about far more efficiently than any copper . . . including himself.

Across the street the curtain twitched again. Turning the key he put the car in gear, deciding it would be less conspicuous to return via Barfield and Margaret Roads than to make a three-point turn.

A pint in the Bird-in-Hand and a chat with Echo? No, his gut wouldn't take either. There had been no sign of activity at that house so it was a sure bet Torrey hadn't returned as yet, and Echo would let him know when it was otherwise. There had been no unusual activity at Bartley's place either but that didn't go to say there was nothing going on, just another sure bet Connor had warned Bartley to keep things on hold for a while.

Bringing the car to a halt outside the station he gazed idly across Victoria Park. But his brain was far from idle. Somewhere there was a link between Deputy Commissioner Jim Connor, Philip Bartley and Torrey, he could feel it in his water!

'*No further investigation.*'

He climbed from the car, patting the pocket he

dropped the keys into. There were ways and means of investigating . . . and Bruce Daniels knew more than one!

Unfortunate that the scouts had chosen this weekend for their rally. Glass in hand, Philip Bartley walked out on to a patio ornamented with tubs of brilliantly petalled flowers. He might have brought that new office junior down for the weekend; attractive, golden-haired . . . and blonds had always been a particular favourite: something about their fair skin? Whatever . . . they always turned him on, some more than others. Like the one he'd picked up the other night, the hitch-hiker soaked with rain . . . he wouldn't think about that. Bartley's hand shook, it had been an illusion . . . he'd been tired, it was no more than that! Yet even to think of it frightened the crap out of him.

Whisky chasing the shadows from his mind he ran a glance over the lovely old house. He'd had some good times here, had some active little playmates. Like the one he'd picked up some months back . . . Christ, they'd had some sessions together. The kid had liked it, liked it every way, mouth, arse, the lot. Pity there had been jealousy of the odd playmate in between; the way that one could fuck you'd have expected a welcome for the extra bit, but no. Instead the little shit had come down with a bad case of sanctimony; there oughtn't to be any casual affairs, he'd got one lover, hadn't he!

Yes, he'd had a lover. Bartley refilled the glass from the decanter he had carried outdoors with him then took a swallow, remembering an attractive face, a full laughing mouth and hyacinth eyes. Golden-haired, and who knows, they might have been together now if the kid hadn't turned so bloody awkward; to pout and sulk was one thing but to go off and shag ... still ... he turned to stare across the lawn to fields rolling away into the shadowing distance . . . what did a kid with a cabbage for a brain matter? Picking up a fresh piece every week might not have the convenience of a live-in lover but then neither did it hold any of the drawbacks; besides which – he took a mouthful of whisky, savouring it on his tongue – he liked the turnover.

She couldn't make copy out of this. Sitting in the busy newspaper office, Kate Mallory screwed the seventh sheet of paper in an hour into a ball and dropped it into the wastepaper basket beside her chair. There were too many ifs and maybes and not enough definites. Even the easiest editor would not go along with what she had gleaned, and hers wasn't the easiest.

'You trying to put my arse in court?' Kate smiled at the words she knew he would hurl at her. 'Print that and we'll have a libel case it'll take a year's sales to settle.'

And one that would see her out of a job. Lighting a cigarette she ignored the sign that said 'Thank you for not smoking'.

She had hoped the informative Mr Sounder would have furnished more information on the elusive Richard Torrey, but there ... a girl couldn't have everything.

'There's been a hold-up at the newsagent on Pinfold Street, gaffer says for you to go along there and see what you can get.'

'You mean Thompson's?' Kate blew an uninterested stream of smoke towards the ceiling. 'They must have got away with all of two pence, the place doesn't make more than that in a week.'

'Don't know about that,' her colleague smiled, 'all I know is the boss said to tell you to go there.'

Stubbing out the cigarette Kate rummaged in a bag almost as big as she was.

'Well, whoever it was tried their hand at robbery will still be there; old man Thompson has a face like Medusa, one look and it turns you to stone.'

'Shall I see if a photographer is free?'

'If you like, but I think our beloved editor is scrapin' the bottom of the barrel.'

'And our beloved editor thinks you won't have a barrel to scrape if you don't get out of here!'

Bent over her bag, Kate had not seen the figure of the editor stride from his tiny inner sanctum to come and stand at her desk. Looking up quickly she tried to smile.

'I was just . . .'

'I know what you was just! But you can get yourself to that shop, and those . . .' he pointed to the pack of Rothman's sitting on her desk, 'will finish up killing you!'

'And deprive you of the pleasure . . . they wouldn't dare.'

'Smart arse!' The editor turned back towards his office.

'You've seen Thompson's,' Kate called after him, 'it's

no bigger than a postage stamp, couldn't a junior cover the story . . . supposing there is a story.'

'There's always a story, Kate, all you have to do is find it. Oh and Kate . . .' he paused to grin back at her, 'you are the junior!'

His own grin as wide as that of his editor, the sports reporter leaned both hands on the cluttered desk.

'You can do it, cowboy, go get 'em!'

Christ, with that pair she need never buy a ticket for a comedy show! Disgruntled, Kate scooped her bag to her shoulder. Bloody pissy little stories, a break-in here, a lost cat there, when was she going to be given something worthwhile? Comedy . . . Yes, it was that all right, her job had become a Comedy of Errors. But there *was* something out there and as the big boss said, 'all you have to do is find it'.

Chapter Ten

He was cold, cold from the same terror that had turned the morning Mass into an ordeal of horror haunted with the memory of what had happened during the service of Evensong. He had thanked that stranger for his solicitude but had wanted no help; for all his kind offer the man could not have helped . . . no one could.

Although the summer evening was warm the Reverend Peter Darley shuddered: despite the fear that still ran in him he had to go back inside the church. He wanted to tear off his vestments, leave them here on the ground and run, but he knew he couldn't; he must behave as if everything in his world were neat and in its place, as if everything were normal.

'Have mercy on me, O God . . .'

His lips moving in whispered prayer he stepped into the church, seeing the shadows move along the grey walls, feeling them reach out to wrap dark tentacles about him as he began to pass down a nave that seemed to go on into infinity.

'. . . have mercy upon me, after Thy great goodness . . .'

High up in the walls evening sunlight touched the lofty arched windows but the shadows did not retreat.

'. . . according to the multitude of Thy mercies . . .'

From the carved rood-screen the figures of the Virgin, Christ and John looked down, their painted tears almost real in that subdued light. But the tears were not for him.

'. . . do away mine offences . . .'

He knew his offences were too great.

'. . . cleanse me from my wickedness and sin . . .'

And that sin had been too vile.

'. . . for I acknowledge my faults . . .'

He reached the sacristy.

'. . . my sin is ever before me . . .'

Passing into the small cluttered sacristy he caught the faint fragrance, elusive, delicate, yet touched with spice. The priest leaned heavily against the door, a sob heaving up from his chest.

It was a fragrance he recognised.

'Peter!'

Philip Bartley smiled at the young clergyman following his housekeeper out to the patio.

'How nice to see you, you don't come up to the Abbey nearly often enough. Drink?' He lifted the crystal decanter and as the priest shook his head, added, 'Coffee then.'

A brief nod his answer, the Reverend Darley dropped

in to one of the wicker armchairs as the housekeeper turned back towards the kitchen.

'Are you all right, you look ill. I'll call . . .'

'No.' Peter Darley looked up quickly. 'I'm all right, please . . . don't call anyone.'

'You don't look it.' Bartley took another of the chairs. 'In fact you look shit scared . . . I might say you look as though you've seen a ghost . . .' He laughed briefly. 'You haven't, have you?'

Peter Darley shook his head but as he looked at the other man his eyes were dark shafts of misery. How could he say it wasn't something seen but felt? He had felt that touch the moment the sacristy door had closed, felt that something waiting there as if it knew he must come to remove the garment of church service.

He let his glance fall, unable to look into another's eyes, wanting to hide the revulsion in his own. Those lips had brushed his, a tongue thrusting into his mouth even as he lifted the surplice over his head. A finger-like touch had caressed his cheek and neck, touched an ear lobe, and all the time that hint of fragrance. He had tried to turn away, to open the door and run from the church but hands he could not see had held him . . . his own desire had held him. The feathery stroking dropping to his navel had fanned across his stomach, creeping to the crevices between his thighs, and the exquisite torture had become too much. He had snatched off his clothing, standing naked before that invisible abuse, pushing backwards and forwards as a warm liquid mouth had taken his hardened flesh. Moaning with the dreadful pleasure he had slid to the stone floor, his body arching, lifting towards that final consummation. But how could he tell Bartley this . . . how could he tell anyone?

'Well, something is wrong,' Bartley answered. 'That's plain to see; look, let me call a doctor . . .'

'No . . . no!' It was quick, jerky. 'I don't need a doctor. It's nothing, a late night working on a sermon, it . . . it's quite a fault of mine leaving that task 'til the last minute, then I have to knock myself out getting it done; I'll be fine after a night's rest.'

'Well I can't force you to see a doctor, if you won't you won't, but that doesn't stop me thinking you are a bloody fool.'

'That's your prerogative, Phil.' The priest smiled up at the housekeeper, glad her arrival put a temporary end to the need for further answer.

'I've brought a plate of ham and cucumber sandwiches.' She glanced at the priest. 'Excuse me sayin', Reverend, but you look as if a good hot meal be more like what you be needin'.'

'My sentiments exactly, Mrs Barnes, so he will be staying to dinner, and if you have any objections, Peter, you can take them up with Mrs Barnes.'

A fleeting smile tensing his mouth Peter Darley shook his head. 'I wouldn't dare.'

'Neither would I, it would take a braver man than me.'

Maggie Barnes watched the smile she knew to be as false as the man. She was grateful to Philip Bartley for giving her George a job that got him away from the grind of the steel mill but she was under no illusion about him or the bits of trash he often brought to this house.

'The man George spoke of, he be at the cottage.'

Sipping at his drink Philip Bartley glanced at his guest. 'Someone looking for a job; if you don't mind being left alone for a few minutes I could see him now and it will be done with.'

'I'll bring him to the study then.' Maggie Barnes turned away. She had seen corpses looking healthier than that there priest.

He hadn't intended to take the job. Richard Torrey walked slowly along the twisting darkening lanes that led to the caravan. He had intended to apologise to the man for taking his time then leave, so why hadn't he? Yes, why hadn't he? There was nothing here in this backwater for him, but then there was nothing anywhere for him, not without Anna. He'd said nothing of that business to Bartley, in fact he'd told him hardly anything apart from his Army service; it hadn't bothered him that the man might tell him to get lost, that was what he wanted; yet when he'd been offered the position of chauffeur cum bodyguard it almost felt as if something outside of himself had pressed him into accepting. But why would Bartley want a bodyguard?

A horse trotted across a field, its head coming over a rusted gate in hopeful search. Torrey reached a hand to its muzzle, apologising for the lack of an apple.

'What do you think, lad?' he murmured, stroking the

animal's nose. 'A bit Chicago-gangster style? Yeah, me too!' But the money was good and here was the same as Dangerfield Lane . . . without Anna both were empty for him.

Why had Anna left him, why go off without saying anything . . . hadn't they had it good together? It had caused a rash of talking in Darlaston, heads turning as they passed but gossip had never bothered them, they had lived life for themselves . . . then it had ended, Anna had gone and there had been no word, no sign until that police photograph he'd seen posted outside the station, the photograph of a tattoo, a tiny mermaid sittting on a rock. He'd gone back to look at it half a dozen times before going inside and asking was that mark on the inner right hip. The nightmare had started there with that photo, and the end . . . ?

He patted the velvety nose and turned away along the lane. Who was to say it would ever end? There had been nothing of Anna's left behind, nothing to give a clue as to who or why. It might have been that nobody but Torrey himself had ever lived in that house. Then almost as soon as they started the police enquiries had ceased. 'Yes, of course they were investigating . . .' Reaching the caravan Torrey stood for a moment staring at the last of the sun falling over the rim of the horizon.

Like bloody hell they were investigating!

'I want them dead, Anna!' He snatched open the door. 'The one that did the killing and the bloody copper that's covering for him, I want them dead, I want them all dead!'

Slamming the door shut behind him he stood in half

darkness, his senses flaring as a delicate spicy fragrance filled his nostrils.

Pouring coffee from a silver pot into petal-thin Spode china cups Philip Bartley felt a rush of pleasure. He liked the best — of living, that was — and that was what he had now and what he would go on having, nothing but the best; and his little pick-ups on those journeys home? He would have those too now he had a chauffeur to make the journeys with him.

'So, Peter,' he smiled at the priest across the table, 'about how many of these scouts of yours can I expect to be invaded by this time?'

Peter Darley stirred demerara sugar into his coffee. 'Around thirty and four scout masters.' He swallowed some of the hot liquid, feeling it sting his throat. 'It is a few more than I was first told but if it's too many I will . . .'

'Don't worry about numbers.' Bartley took his own coffee without sugar, he kept an eye on his weight, fat was one thing he didn't intend to acquire. 'The top field is large enough to take them, they are bringing their own tents I take it?'

Peter Darley nodded. 'Tents, cooking equipment, everything they are likely to need except for water.'

'Well, the brook is clear enough but it might be better if they used that for swimming and take their drinking water from the taps up at the old stables. Barnes tells me they still function.'

'Thanks . . . I'll tell them.'

'Where are they from . . . London?'

Finishing his coffee the priest shook his head again. 'Not this time, they are from somewhere nearer to the Midlands, a place called Wednesfield. I'm afraid I can't tell you any more than that, I don't know the place at all.'

But he did! Bartley stared into his cup. He'd lived just a few miles from that town almost all of his life, maybe some of the blokes he'd worked with in the steel mill would have kids in that troop. This was one weekend he would not visit the top field. Looking up he said, 'Well, if the weather holds they should enjoy themselves; I suppose we'll be hearing "gin gan goolie" again.'

'Afraid so, a good old sing-song around the camp fire before bed is an integral part of scouting, Phil, you must remember.'

'I was never in the scouts.' Philip Bartley's mind flashed back to his boyhood. There had always been too much to do helping to keep the family, selling firewood from door to door after school, then round again with a basket of pikelets that was almost as big as he was; he was lucky if he got a swim in the canal on a Sunday afternoon let alone take off for days with a group of scouts, and he was in the steel mill by the time he'd turned fifteen.

'As a matter of fact neither was I, as a youngster I preferred my own company. I suppose you think that strange.'

Leaving the memory to slide silently back into the deep reaches of his mind, Bartley answered, 'Not unless I think myself strange. Truth to tell I was a loner as a kid, but then there was never the time for anything other than helping Mother make ends meet . . . anyway I always seemed to make out better on my own, liked my own company, I suppose.'

Refusing more coffee, Peter Darley looked genuinely surprised. 'Really! Nobody would ever guess seeing the easy way you have with people, the way you get stuck in when the scouts or the guides are here or when the village fête is on; I would have said you'd been used to that sort of thing all your life.'

Getting up from the table and going to a beautiful Regency sideboard set against one wall, Bartley picked up a brandy decanter. 'Ah, you see how easy it is to be mistaken about people.'

It was only too easy. Peter Darley refused the offered brandy. He would never have believed what was happening in that church, never have believed such evil could enter a House of God . . . but it had.

'Phil,' he rose from his chair, 'could we talk outside, it . . . it's still warm.'

Taking the decanter with him, Bartley followed. What the hell was wrong with the man, he'd been jumpy ever since he got here!

Standing on the patio Peter Darley stared at a line of copper beeches standing sentinel where the garden gave on to open land.

'Phil,' he asked quietly, 'do you remember a guest you first brought here to the house some twelve months back?'

'You'll have to be a bit more specific than that,' Bartley laughed, 'I have a lot of folk stay here.'

'Yes, and most of your guests stay just a few days,

but this one was here longer, for several months in fact.'

Waiting while the other man refilled his glass the priest went on. 'This one was young, early twenties I think, golden hair, but it was the eyes . . . they were particularly attractive, a rather striking shade of blue, like early hyacinths I always thought.'

'Could fit any amount of guests I've had at the Abbey,' Bartley answered, 'I like young people, I like having them around, I shall encounter old age soon enough without going out of my way to meet it.'

'This one stayed here quite some time,' the priest persisted, a film of moisture glinting above his top lip, 'I was sure you would remember.'

'Well, a name has been known to help.' Bartley took a hefty swallow of brandy. He needed no name to help him remember, he knew only too well who it was Darley was talking about, but why now? The stupid cunt was . . .

Wiping a hand across the lower half of his face and simply spreading the moisture, the priest murmured, 'The name . . . the name was Anna.'

Bartley filled his mouth with brandy, holding it on his tongue, swishing it around his teeth, taking a long time to swallow. It was too much of a coincidence. There was that business in the car the other night, he hadn't imagined that for all he'd tried to convince himself he had; he'd felt those hands, that mouth, he'd heard that voice and smelled that fragrance, he *had* picked up a goddamn hitch-hiker! But there had been no one with him when the police had opened the car. Could something of the same nature have happened to Darley? Christ, look at the man, something had happened that was scaring the shit out of him!

'Anna.' He pursued his lips, giving himself more time. He had to go on, refusing to say any more would look suspicious. 'Yes, now I come to think I do remember, very attractive, but why ask?'

Peter Darley's breath trembled, tumbling the lie together. 'I . . . I don't know really . . . just . . . just thinking. It's strange how people you had forgotten suddenly spring to mind.'

Like my arse you'd forgotten! Bartley filled his glass from the decanter, his shaking hand rattling the stopper in its neck. From the look of you I'd say you've been reminded . . . and quite recently! Filling his mouth with the rich velvet liquid he let it lie, trying to wash away the sour taste suddenly invading his throat, giving the thought time to fade.

'The last I heard was when the stupid bugger took off from here like a bat out of hell . . . and I haven't given the piece of trash a thought since!'

Darley glanced at the man whose face turned now towards the moonlit garden. Had he really forgotten so completely, after all he and Anna had been . . . he forced the thought back, afraid of the emotions that had always ripped him apart whenever he'd thought of the two of them together.

'Do you?' Bartley's question came quietly. 'Do you ever think of Anna?'

'No . . . no.' His head dropping into his hands, the priest's whole body shook. 'To tell the truth . . .'

What was the truth? Bartley turned, watching the figure bent forwards in the chair. Something had this man dancing with the moon and that something was to do with that golden-haired whore!

He retook his chair, leaning towards the priest but not touching him. 'Look,' he said quietly, 'I hate bloody clichés and I hate this one most of all, but it does often help to talk if something's bothering you.' He could add that he knew what that something was, that it had happened to him a few nights ago, and he too had been shaken rigid by his own imaginings, only he hadn't imagined it. And by the look of Darley neither had he.

'I don't know how to begin.' The priest lifted his head to look at the other man, his eyes tortured with fear. 'It . . . it will sound so ridiculous.'

Despite himself Bartley stood up, moving to stand at the edge of the patio, his own gaze losing itself among the moon-chased shadows of beech trees. The poor bloke looked as if he'd gone through hell. He couldn't look into those eyes again, not for some moments.

'How do you know unless you try?' He kept his back turned. 'And even if it should sound that way who's to know? I don't go spreading a confidence, Peter.'

'It began a few days ago, I was alone in the church . . . at least I thought I was until . . .'

'Until?' Bartley stood in silence as the priest hesitated. Until the touch of soft hands, a mouth pressed against your crotch, until you couldn't breathe . . . was that what 'until' meant? But it couldn't be, not the priest, not even Anna would go that far.

'Something . . . something seemed to follow me along the nave . . .'

Bartley waited for the other man's long trembling breath to subside.

'. . . I . . . I thought someone else was in the church but when I looked around I could see no one. It was fairly dark and the shadows . . .' he laughed self-consciously '. . . they seem to move with you, they can give you the jitters sometimes.'

Shadows had given everybody the jitters at some time or another but it wasn't shadows had Darley's face the colour of a week-old corpse! Watching him now, the nuances of emotions and fear flicking constantly over that fine-boned face, Bartley could sense the terror in the man. It took more than shadows to cause that.

'I told myself it was nonsense.' Peter Darley's hands twisted in his lap. 'That there was nothing there. But then . . .'

'Then?' Bartley urged.

'I felt it, I felt . . . hands, it was as if hands touched my face, the back of my neck . . . ! You know me, Phil, we've been friends a long time, have you ever known me given to flights of fancy?'

Bartley smiled as the ashen face lifted to him. 'No, Peter, no I haven't but shadows . . .'

'You can't *feel* shadows.' It tore from the priest's throat. 'I *felt* it, Phil, I felt something touch me but there was nothing there.'

'You didn't see anything . . . anything at all?'

Hesitating, as if unwilling to commit his fear to words,

Peter Darley lowered his head and when he at last spoke his voice trembled.

'I . . . at the end of the nave, the steps up to the high altar . . . I thought I heard . . . it was a laugh but a laugh such as I never heard before, I can only describe it as evil . . . and that touch, it went on and on, never leaving me . . . then above the cross on the altar, a light like a flame and at its centre was a face. I thought it was . . . it looked like . . . Oh, I don't know, Phil, I don't know!'

'You thought the face was that of Anna?'

Silence telling him he was correct, Bartley nodded. 'Has it happened since?'

'Several times.'

'Always in the same place?'

His slight shoulders heaving, the priest tried to control the tremble that shook his reply. 'Always in the church though not every time at the same spot. The . . . the last was in the sacristy just before I came here . . . it hasn't happened anywhere except in the church and I don't believe it will.'

Something other than shadows in the dark pulsed in that voice. Philip Bartley stared quizzically at the pale face.

'Because . . .'

The answer was quiet. Bartley's spine suddenly tingled. Quiet and hopeless, the answer of a man condemned!

'. . . because it was in the church Anna and I made love.'

In the church! Bartley listened to the sobbing breaths, this man had been taken in his own church. His fingers tightened, crushing the glass. That little arsehole Anna had been capable of a great deal of spite but this, to take a priest in his own church! Why . . . for what reason, what good had it done? But then had Anna ever needed a reason for doing anything . . . and good? The little trollop had never known the meaning of the word!

Turning away he set the glass on the patio table. He didn't know yet what had happened to him that night in the car or what was certainly happening to Peter Darley, but he had no doubt that at the back of it all he would find that bitch Anna.

So Darley and Anna had had something going together. He couldn't blame him for that, priests had the same feelings other men had, the same needs. But Anna could have left him alone . . . Anna! He swore savagely beneath his breath. That bloody tart was too pretty for any man's safety!

'Does anybody else know about this?' He turned to the priest hunched in the chair, saw his fingers threading constantly in and out of each other.

'No,' Darley whispered. 'No, I'm sure of that, we were always so careful . . . at least I thought we were until . . .'

'Until?'

The question rested on silence until Bartley took an impatient step forwards.

'Look, Peter, we've been friends a long time and I want to help but if you feel you can't tell me, then use the church. From the look of you I'd say you are already three parts licked by this thing and unless you get help from somebody you're gonna go under altogether. What about speaking to the Bishop, or whoever your immediate boss is? Surely he can help sort this thing.'

'No!' The cry that set out as a shout became strangled. 'You don't understand, Phil, how could you? How could anyone who hasn't experienced it? I'm sorry.' The twisting hands became still. 'I apologise for my rudeness but to say anything to the Bishop would mean losing my church.'

His eyes almost lost in the bruise-dark hollows, Peter Darley had the look of a man staring at his own damnation.

'I couldn't face that,' he murmured, 'I couldn't face that.'

Chapter Eleven

'And to say nothing could mean losing your bloody mind!' Bartley lowered into the chair he had recently vacated. 'So okay, you don't want to talk to the Bishop, but like it or not you're gonna have to talk to somebody.'

'And tell them what?' The priest's mouth twisted as if he were about to cry. 'How can I tell anyone I made love in the house of God and that now I think I am being haunted. Lord, Phil!' He lifted a hand, spreading the thumb and fingers across his brow. 'I don't even know if any of this has taken place, whether I have been truly subjected to some form of visitation or whether the whole thing is merely hallucination, a product of my own guilt.'

Bartley could tell him he wasn't hallucinating. He could tell him that what had happened in that church was real enough. He could tell him that whatever had happened wasn't happening to him alone. He could tell him that one night he had picked up a young hitch-hiker at a junction off the M6, that it was pissing down with rain and that he'd felt sorry for the figure standing there soaked to the skin; that by the time they had hit Monkswell the kid had him harder than a ram and that the kid was sucking him off when a couple of coppers had interrupted. He could tell him that by the time one of the coppers tapped the window his hitch-hiker was gone and the passenger door of the Rover was still locked. He could tell him he'd smelled that fragrance . . . he could tell him . . . but he wouldn't!

Instead, he said, 'You say that you and Anna were always so careful whenever you were together until . . . until what, Peter? Could somebody have seen the pair of you? Could what's happening now be blackmail?'

How the bloody hell could it? He answered himself even as he asked. How can somebody arrange for invisible hands to stroke you to screaming pitch, for an invisible mouth to suck your balls dry? It needed solid flesh to do that and there had been nothing solid in Peter Darley's partner and he wasn't so sure about his own.

'I suppose we might have been seen yet I don't think we were.'

Darley stood up, going to stand at the edge of the slabbed patio where it dropped down several mellow stone steps to the lush green of a meticulously kept lawn. 'Could we walk in the garden a little?' he asked over his shoulder.

Bartley walked beside him, their footfalls soundless on the cushioning turf, the sharp cut of wood smoke drifting across on almost still air. Barnes was burning branches lopped from trees up along Monks Walk where his property bordered church lands. He should have left them for the scouts; still, he supposed there were more than enough for a couple of days' camp fires.

'It was one weekday evening when it happened for the first time.' Peter Darley kept his glance on the gardens, their well-stocked flowerbeds tiny jewelled islands in a sea of jade. 'Evensong, the last service of the day, we don't get many coming to Evensong,' he smiled ruefully, 'truth to tell, we don't get many worshippers at all during the week but then farmers and their wives are busy people, somehow I think the Lord understands. Anyway,' his smile faded, 'I was in the vestry checking that all was in readiness for the wedding that was being held the following day...' he paused, looking towards Bartley, 'young Robbie Partridge and Mellie Briers, you know Mellie, pretty girl, daughter of Sam and Amelia Briers. Their cottage stands on your land.'

'Yes of course I know Mellie; like you say, a pretty girl.' Bartley did remember. Well built, attractive, young. He felt the involuntary twitch inside his trousers, he wouldn't have minded a few turns around the bed with that one himself.

'It only took a moment to see Summers, our church-warden, had everything prepared and I was about to leave the vestry when Anna came in, wearing a pair of denims, the legs cut off making them into shorts that barely reached to the top of the legs.' The priest turned his face back towards the flower-filled borders, but couldn't eliminate the throb that crept into his voice. 'The

... the T-shirt was off ... it was a hot evening, Anna was flushed from jogging.'

Yes, Anna liked jogging, but liked showing off that superb body more! Bartley stayed silent.

'I said one shouldn't run so far in that sort of heat,' Darley went on, 'but Anna laughed and said it wasn't the sun causing this kind of heat, then before I realised it we were both naked and ...' he hesitated '... I thought I heard a noise from the sacristy like someone was in there and I stopped but Anna moaned, pulling me to the floor, rolling close into me, and I no longer cared if anyone else was there or not.'

It took a special kind of courage to talk about yourself in this way, a courage Bartley recognised he hadn't got and he waited until the priest controlled the anguish that shook his hands and voice.

'It was afterwards, we were both dressed and coming out of the vestry when I saw Summers. He looked at me as we passed the sacristy — the door was open — then he looked at Anna. I've never known to this day if he heard us in the vestry.'

'He couldn't have seen anything?' Bartley questioned quietly.

'No.' Darley shook his head. 'There is no window between the two rooms and I remember Anna closing the vestry door after coming in, and leaning against it. But there was nothing to say Summers didn't hear us, after all I heard him.'

'That's nothing to go on.' Overhead a plane zoomed across the evening sky. Bartley watched the lights of its wing tips. Get all this behind him and he would take a holiday abroad somewhere, Brazil or the Far East, somewhere exotic. He might take that office junior. 'It could have been anything Summers was hearing, as long as he didn't see he's got no proof. You say you were dressed and on your feet so there's nothing to worry over.'

'I think we both knew weeks before there was an attraction between us,' Darley went on. 'We had what I take it is the usual approach between lovers, Anna would touch my hand when no one was watching, then came snatched moments in the rectory when our hands explored each other, but that evening in the church was the first time we made love in the full sexual sense.'

'And afterwards?'

'It didn't seem to matter after that, the place, I mean.' The priest bent to pick a flower, tearing off its daisy-like petals and dropping them one by one to lie on the soft grass. 'We made love whenever and wherever we could, even . . . even before the high altar. I hadn't wanted it to happen there but Anna laughed me down as always. It was an act of love and God had created us to love one another. I knew it was wrong but I was too infatuated to argue, it only took the feel of that mouth on my body to blot out any objection I might have.'

Anna was always good at that, Bartley thought, not that he'd ever had any objections. The twitch flicked again inside his trousers. Christ, just remembering made him hard. In fact he hadn't been really comfortable since that night; his hitch-hiker, real or imaginary, had been too bloody good, he needed the same again and was going to have to arrange it soon. Pity the scouts were from Wednesfield, he usually dropped lucky with those, but he couldn't risk it this time, he would have to go elsewhere.

'I'm not ashamed!'

Bartley reluctantly pushed aside the mental image of the junior new to his office.

'No, I'm not ashamed.' Darley rushed on as the flood-gates of guilt pushed wide apart. 'I realise now that what I felt for Anna was infatuation, a delayed schoolboy crush, but at the time it felt like love and my regret now is not for what we did but for where we did it. Do you condemn me for that?'

Bartley watched the rays of the rising moon glitter on leaves, turning them to silver fire. 'I'm not in the business of condemning, Peter,' he said quietly, 'to each his own. From what you have said no one else was involved and neither of you had any other partner so no one got hurt; that being so I advise you to try to forget about it.'

'We hurt you didn't we, Phil?'

Bartley walked a little way across the lawn then turned to look at the lovely old Abbey that was now his home. The glow of the huge full moon turning the small lozenge panes to diamonds, playing over herringbone brickwork, lighting the great stone chimneys. How much had that little shithead told the priest standing beside him waiting for his answer, how much did he know? 'Hurt me?' he prevaricated.

'You loved Anna too, didn't you? Don't be angry, Phil, Anna told me of your relationship; said there were to be no secrets between us.'

I'll bet the bloody whore did! Bartley felt his anger build into a tidal wave. If only he had the loud-mouthed little shit here right now!

'You said you loved Anna,' he forced himself to be calm, 'to me it was nothing more than a means to an end. I wanted something, Anna got extremely well paid for supplying it. Ours was a business arrangement, nothing more.'

Despite his fears the priest smiled. He knew why this man did not condemn him, they were two of a kind.

As he led the way back to the house Bartley's mind raced. If Darley did go to the Bishop would that involve him? Damn that bloody whore, he'd worked too hard for what he'd got to lose it because of some randy little tramp who'd let any man have a ride for a quid!

'What does it all mean, Phil?' Despair was written heavy on the priest's face. 'Anna is dead, we both know that. Is this revenge for what we did, for what *I* did? That night . . . I said there was no place at the rectory, I couldn't take the risk of Anna's staying there, it would upset the parishioners; one night, I said, one night was all Anna could stay. I gave her what money I had, then locked myself in my bedroom; you see, that was another risk I could not take, I knew if Anna came into my room we would end up making love and I wouldn't have the strength to end it. When I came down to breakfast Anna had already left.'

He had thought it happening only to him, but the weird goings on, they were happening to Darley as well! Bartley swallowed the nervous spit collecting in his mouth. Could it be revenge, could the dead reach back to strike the living? He wouldn't put it past that little shit-head, but the dead were dead, there was no way back. Yet those hallucinations, they were close enough to be almost identical. The touch, the teasing, the perfume: it all added up to Anna! Could it be some kind of thought transfer-ence, some sharing of a guilt complex? But what did he have to feel guilty over, that bloody prima donna hadn't been exactly chucked out of the Abbey, in fact the little trollop had done all right out of the whole affair so why should he feel guilty?

'Phil.' Back in the living room Peter Darley looked at his host. 'Maybe, as you say, I should speak to the Bishop.'

What the bloody hell had he been thinking of to suggest that! Bartley swung round.

'I was wrong,' he said quickly. 'Speak of this to the Bishop or to anyone else and that robe you are wearing will be no protection. You must keep your mouth closed, Darley. Anna is dead, we know why and we know by whom. Open your mouth now and we'll both be dead men!'

Richard Torrey drew the car to a halt. Take your time, Philip Bartley had told him, get yourself sorted. Sorted! He smiled acidly. That had been done already, somebody had sorted Richard Torrey's life for him when they killed Anna. If only he had some clue, some lead as to who or why but there was no rhyme or reason, nothing . . . absolutely nothing. That was almost as bad as losing

Anna, this feeling of being tied, of being unable to do anything about it while all the time some bastard some-where was laughing! But he could bide his time and somewhere along the line that bastard would make a slip and when he did . . . Torrey's fingers tightened on the wheel . . . when he did there would be no holding back, no last-minute reprieve like there'd been for those three in the yard of the Bird-in-Hand, that one would die!

He glanced at the house. They'd been so happy here, or would it be truer to say *he'd* been happy here? Had it all been a blind on Anna's part . . . a pretence? Had the real intention been to use him until something better, someone with money to spend came along and then to leave? No! He banged a closed fist against the steering wheel. Anna hadn't been like that! So why had Anna left him, why go without a word?

A twitch of curtain at the next window bringing his mind to the business in hand, Torrey climbed from the car and walked steadily up the path to the house. In five minutes it would be all over Darlaston: 'Torrey was back, he was in the house.' One thing for sure, he thought as he closed the door behind him, nobody in Dangerfield Lane would ever need a telephone in the house, the bloody grapevine was cheaper and every bit as efficient!

Sort out what you want and I'll have a van pick it up. Bartley had been helpful but what had this house got that he wanted, what did it hold for him now Anna was no longer there?

'Sorry to be such a nuisance . . . the door is open.'

Standing in the kitchen Torrey stared at the bathroom

door, that voice echoing in his mind. Was that really where it had all started? No, for him it had begun long before that, it had begun that first moment he'd seen Anna, rain trickling from golden hair, blue eyes sparkling despite being drenched.

'Ritchie . . .'

Soft as velvet it came from the other side of the bathroom door, a door that somehow stood ajar. It had been closed when he came into the kitchen, he could swear . . .

'Ritchie . . .'

It was whisper-soft but it struck like a hammer. Anna . . . Anna was in the bathroom, Anna wasn't dead, Anna was here!

The gentle voice filling his mind like music, one stride took him across the poky little room. 'Anna!' Slamming the door wide back on its hinges he reached for that supple golden figure, the music becoming a long low moan when he saw the bathroom empty.

He was still standing, dry sobs rattling his throat when the knocker on the front door was banged. Stay where he was, ignore it and whoever it was would go away. But it came again, loud and insistent, a 'here I am and here I stay 'til you answer' kind of knock. Christ! Torrey's hands folded. If that was the bloody Kleeneasy bloke he'd stuff his tins and brushes up his arse!

'Richard Torrey?'

Torrey glanced at the man standing on the doorstep, one hand touching the pocket of a shabby tweed jacket which even from this distance smelled of tobacco.

'Richard Torrey?'

The question was asked again. Despair born of disappointment had already reached full-grown anger and Torrey's answer was a snarl. 'The man himself, and who the bloody hell are you?'

'I'm Detective Inspector Daniels, perhaps I could have a word.'

'P'raps you could . . . some time . . . but right now you can piss off!'

The door was almost closed when the hand that held an identification card came against it.

'It has to do with a body pulled from the canal, a body I believe you identified, Mr Torrey, one you claimed for burial.'

'Who . . . ?'

Stepping into the two-yard-square hall as Torrey's hand fell away from the door, Daniels answered. 'That's what I want to ask you, Mr Torrey.'

So Torrey was moving out, handing the house back to the council. Sitting in the Ford the inspector drew heavily on his second Royal. Sod Marjorie and her moaning about the car stinking of cigarette smoke, he could think better sitting here than in the station with everything and everybody circling round him. Torrey was moving, interesting that, but even more interesting was where he was moving to, and who with.

Bartley! He blew a stream of smoke that sought freedom through the window then, finding its escape route cut off, hung above Daniels's head in a depressed cloud. First that corpse in the canal, Torrey alone had stepped forward for that. Then Bartley's little venture with drugs followed by Torrey being taken on as chauffeur and given a place of his own on Bartley's estate. Bartley, Torrey and that tart. He finished the cigarette, flicking the butt from a window he closed as soon as the fragment of tobacco had fallen from it. That was no coincidence; he was no betting man but he'd stake a month's pay on that. Somehow the three were connected and Torrey was the link. But how?

The hour spent in that house had brought nothing, nothing except a smell in his nose. Daniels blew air down his nostrils. It had hit him as soon as he'd stepped inside that house and he could still smell it. It wasn't over-scented like that furniture polish Marjorie used, it had a spicy touch to it; strange that, he wouldn't have expected a bloke like Torrey to go in for perfumed stuff. But then there was a lot you might not expect of Torrey, like three men left concussed or with broken bones and not one of 'em laying a charge, not one owning to know who it was had attacked them; or like claiming that tart they'd pulled from the cut. A sudden surge of acid bit Daniels's throat and he reached the pack of BiSoDol from his pocket, slipping one of the tablets on to his tongue. This bloody stomach was giving him more gyp every day, maybe he would go see a quack.

Bartley, Torrey and that tart! Daniels sucked on the tablet, dragging its relief deep into his throat. A tart, he'd seen that for himself. Even then it had been hard to tell, one half of the face purple and distorted from a beating it had taken, the other half blown away by a shotgun. But the hush job that had been done. Was Torrey in on that too? Maybe, but he'd guess the other way. The look on the man's face whenever the tart had been mentioned said otherwise. That was something else you wouldn't expect of a man like that, what that corpse had been to him; somebody special, that much Torrey didn't need to say, his face said it for him.

Somebody special! Daniels climbed from the car, dropping the keys into his pocket. Could the little screw have been Torrey's lover . . .

'No further investigation.'

Daniels almost smiled. Fuck you, Mr Deputy Commissioner!

Chapter Twelve

'We would like you to come and 'ave lunch with us, Reverend, oi've got a lovely leg o' lamb in the oven, roast tatties an' mint sauce just the way oi knows you likes it, an' there's 'ome-made apple pie for afters; fresh it be, Tom just picked them Bramleys off the tree this mornin'.'

'That's an offer any man would find hard to refuse, Mrs Harper, much less one who mostly cooks for himself, but today I must do just that.'

Peter Darley ran a tired hand unconsciously through his hair. His face was pallid, tinged with the grey of exhaustion, his cheeks sunk in on themselves. His eyes, usually bright and alert, seemed too deeply set, ringed as they were with dark circles and filled now with something the woman saw as fear.

'Unfortunately I have some letters that must get off to the Ecclesiastical Board today, I must get them written before . . .' He stumbled as though afraid of adding 'before the evening service'.

He tried to smile, relying on the Lord to forgive his deliberate lie but he was in no state for socialising. It had taken every ounce of determination and a great deal of physical strength to get through the Sunday Mass.

Hardly able to control the convulsive shivers that still rocked him he took Tom Harper's hand. 'Thank you both.' The smile still wouldn't come and he saw the concern in the woman's observant eyes. Don't let her ask questions – he left the prayer open to any beneficient power that might yet have some pity left for him – just let them go, let them all go.

The handshake done, his arm dropped listlessly to his side. He must get away soon, away from the church, from the malignant evil that had tormented and teased all through the service, laughing at his efforts to dismiss it, fragmenting his nerves, destroying his resistance and tearing down the mental barrier he had erected about himself before venturing inside those walls. He had tried to free his mind of the force that had clamped it the moment Mass had begun, but it was too strong, it knew too well his failings, invisible hands caressing his genitals and arousing a desire he could do nothing to deny, bringing on an erection he was powerless to prevent; touching, stroking, the feel of a warm wet mouth bringing him to the very edge of ejaculation only to withdraw, leaving him sweating, yearning for it to begin all over again.

'I 'opes you're not going down with one o' them viruses doctor always seems to be goin' on about these days, you look awful poorly!' Rosie Harper's eyes narrowed. 'You really should come and 'ave a bite o' lunch an' leave those letters to another day . . . ain't nuthin' as won't keep, oi'll be bound.'

'Don't go on so, Rosie.' The grin Tom Harper gave his parish priest was apologetic. 'Reckon the lad knows 'is own business best. Women! They do go on a bit I reckon, Reverend, 'specially my Rosie; it's since kids 'ave grown an' gone . . . she don't 'ave no one to fuss on no more. Still, like 'er says, there do seem to be a whole lot o' they 'igh fallutin' viruses things about, so a bit o' care, eh?' His wink brought wrinkles folding in on each other. 'P'raps next Sunday?'

'Thanks, Tom, next Sunday it is.'

Peter Darley watched the couple walk away. Both in their mid-seventies, both still working the farm Tom had been born on, solid down-to-earth people; he wouldn't be able to fool them or any other of his parishioners for much longer, as it was there had already been several expressions of concern for his health.

Until today the evil that preyed upon him had done so only when there had been no one of the village attending service, the man offering help the other evening had not been a parishioner. But this morning had been different, today the tantalising assault had begun during Mass. He had felt the brush of lips against his own as he led the congregation in the Credo, felt the touch of hands between his thighs, fingers drawing along his penis until he had almost cried out the pleasure and the anguish; heard the silent laughter as the unseeable had stepped away leaving him trembling before the altar, the terror inside him greater for knowing his desire for physical fulfilment had been stronger than the desire for the withdrawal of the obscenity that was using him for its own evil ends.

Late summer sunshine was warm on his body but he was deathly cold, cold with a fear of that he felt was yet to come. He should see the Bishop, tell him of the dreadful visitations, but that would mean telling all. It would have to come out about him and Anna, what had happened between them there in the church. That would be seen as the cause of the evil now present there, he would lose his parish, he would be defrocked, at best it would be suggested he go into retreat for a year or two, for his own good. The church itself would have to be exorcised and rededicated . . . and if the evil did not respond? If it refused to leave? He shuddered, his eyes closing against the next thought: the church of St James would be abandoned, it would no longer exist as a house of God and it would be his fault! He couldn't take the risk. If he left the priesthood of his own volition then perhaps the evil would leave too, perhaps it was only himself it wanted and not the church.

He turned to face the open doorway. Whatever his ultimate decision he had to go in there now, he had to walk the length of the nave as far as the communion rail before he could enter the sacristy and there remove the yellow and white robes of Sunday Mass. Hands balling into tight fists in an effort to control the spasm of trembling that seized him, the Reverend Peter Darley stepped through the shadowed doorway.

*

'These flowers still 'as a lot o' life in 'em, it be a pity to throw 'em away.'

'They do certainly have a lot of scent left in them, a very pleasant smell, almost spicy.' Marcia James, president of the local Women's Institute, draped her coat neatly over the back of a pew. 'But they'll probably be droopy by morning, far better we replace them as usual.'

'I suppose you be right, they 'ave bin 'ere since Saturday, that be three days.' Rosie Harper picked up two of the vases. 'But they don't be so far gone we couldn't put 'em on one or two of they older graves, it be a pity the way some of 'em be so neglected. It be quite awful the way some folk turns their back on the dead.'

'A sign of the times, I'm afraid, Mrs Harper. Young people today seem to have little respect for anything and positively no thought for any other than themselves.'

'Ar.' Rosie Harper nodded. 'That be the way of the world, still it be a pity. I dread to think what future days might 'old for the church, even with our menfolk 'elping out whenever they can the grounds ain't what they was; seems when we be gone there'll be none to care what 'appens to the place.'

She unzipped the brown leather bag she had dropped on to a small offerings table, extracting perfectly laundered yellow dusters and a canister of spray polish. 'People ought to be made to face up to their responsibilities, not leave everything in the 'ands of others, flogging a willing 'orse be all it is . . . flogging a willing 'orse.'

'Some of those graves, especially those along the back wall, do go back a long way.' Marcia James took her own immaculate dusters and jar of Antique Wax polish, drawing them from their leather container with an air that was little short of a flourish; Rosie Harper wasn't going to put one over on her. 'Some of them are centuries old, you can no longer read the inscriptions on them.'

'Most of the families in the village go back just as far.' Rosie Harper had not missed the one-up-manship of the Antique Wax and fastened her frilly apron with a tighter pull than usual. 'If they looked after their own the church-yard would be a 'undred times more appealing.'

Marcia fastened her own apron about her waist, satisfied the glint in the other woman's eye was not due to the state of the churchyard. Taking her prize she started down the aisle heading for the communion rail, a pleased smile hovering about her lips. How could anyone describe a churchyard as appealing!

A low moan halted her and for a moment a cold hand seemed to press her chest, holding her back. 'Father Darley?' Alarm evident in her voice she called to the stooped figure hunched on the top chancel step.

'What is it?' Rosie Harper turned from the pew she was dusting.

'It's . . . it's Father Darley . . .' The answer floated backwards on a sea of sun-drenched dust as the light surged with sudden brilliance through the arched windows. She had not noticed until this moment how dark the church had been, but the sunlight brought no warmth with it. Marcia James shivered. Why was the church so cold?

Leaving her duster where it was, Rosie Harper shuffled

from the restricting space of the pew and ran down the aisle pushing aside the other woman, forgetting the awesome proximity of the high altar as she knelt beside the hunched figure whose black robe spread like a dark stain against the bright carpet. 'Father Darley, are you all right?'

He could feel the woman's hands beneath his arm trying to lift him and he could return no help. He didn't want to stand, he didn't want to face that altar.

'Mrs Harper.' The voice of the president of the Women's Institute took on the crisp command she assumed when delegating jobs to members she knew would derive no joy from them, her tone a barrier against any resistance. 'Mrs Harper, get help . . . Father Darley is ill.'

'No . . . no, I'm all right.' The priest pushed himself upwards as Rosie ignored the other woman. 'A giddy spell, that's all . . . really . . . I . . . I was up rather late last night . . . I'm still a little tired, nothing more.'

'You work far too hard, I'm always telling the ladies at the Institute so, aren't I, Mrs Harper?' Marcia James looked at the older woman whose face mirrored the alarm she herself had felt moments before when a hand seemed to press against her chest, almost as if some force had not wanted her to help the priest. 'Father Darley works too hard I tell them, and he can only push himself so far.'

The last was an admonishment as the young man rose unsteadily to his feet, one hand coming up to his brow and shielding his sight from the altar.

'All those boys' clubs,' Marcia's voice lost none of its challenge, 'outward-bound adventure holidays for deprived children, besides the scouts do's and the fund-raising fêtes at the village hall and up at the Manor . . .' She clucked impatiently around him like a blue-rinsed hen marshalling her erring chick, smoothing his rumpled cassock before taking his arm and shooing him gently down the steps and across the short expanse of red carpet.

The women had hold of him on either side but Peter Darley was only vaguely aware of their ministrations. His nostrils were filled with the cloying smell of his own body juices, underwear damp and sticky against his flesh, his mind numbed by the totality of his seduction.

'You pay far too much attention to others and not enough to yourself, isn't that so, Mrs Harper?'

The righteous voice clucked on but at least it gave him something to centre on. Using it as a level he forced the last remaining mists of passion from his mind. It had happened as he knew it would. The evil that had wrapped itself around him had not followed him here, it had waited for him, knowing he must come to it even as he told himself he came to worship. A shudder ran through him and he heard the solicitous voice of Marcia James, felt his rescuers' hands tighten supportively around his arms but there was no sensation of walking; his tread, no longer suffused by carpet, made no sound for him as he stepped on to the diamond-patterned black and white tiled flooring of the aisle, walked past the statue of the Virgin weeping at the feet of her crucified son. There was only the prickling at his back, the certainty that whatever was slowly destroying his life was still present, still hovering in the chancel recess.

'You must take more care of yourself . . .' they were passing the last of the dozen rows of ancient oak pews '. . . we can't have you being ill . . .' the hands released him, reaching for coats draped across redolent wood, '. . . and that's exactly what will happen, we've proved that this afternoon, haven't we?' Busy fingers did up the last of the coat buttons. 'Now we are going to see that you go right back to the rectory, Mrs Harper and myself are going to make you a hot meal and some strong coffee.'

'I can't . . . I have to see Jos.' His words sluggish, Peter Darley fought against the shadows not yet ejected from his mind, struggling like an opium addict to reach the surface of reality.

'You really should go 'ome, Reverend.' Rosie Harper spoke for the first time since that frightened call. She wanted to be out of the church, something, she didn't know what, wasn't quite right. She might almost say there was a presence, an unpleasant aura, a malicious unholiness, if she had the courage to say anything at all; as it was she said nothing.

From the periphery of his vision the priest saw the woman dip her fingers into the small basin of holy water, reverently making the sign of the cross, hand shaking as she touched damp fingertips to the centre of her forehead, above her heart, then the area above each thin breast.

Now it was his turn. He must dip his fingers into the water that had received the blessing, he must turn and make the sign of the Faith, he must acknowledge the altar.

'Old Jos Hampton can wait!' Marcia James's voice resumed the 'challenge me at your peril' ring of authority.

'That old man has blackmailed everyone for long enough, especially you . . .' she glanced at the young priest, his shoulders sagging, a hand hovering over the basin of holy water, '. . . you pander to the old blackguard far too much; threatening it will be too late if you don't go to him immediately he thinks you should. Huh!' She snorted indignantly. 'I reckon that when he does finally go to meet his maker the good Lord will tell him there's no place for the likes of him there.'

Peter Darley's hand fell, sending the china basin crashing to the floor, shattering it into a thousand tiny fragments, its sanctified contents seeping away into the cracks of the stone floor while his eyes lifted their agonised glance the length of the narrow aisle and across the chancel to the high altar. Sunlight pouring through crimson stained glass turned the white cloth to blood; lancets of red and gold streamed from the huge gold cross at its centre, spewing up then curling back on themselves, licking outwards once more, turning the area above the cross into a pool of dancing flickering flames, and at their centre . . .

A sob catching in his throat Peter Darley raised a hand in a desperate attempt to block out the mocking silent malevolence that smiled from the flames, a face that was foreign to him, yet a face he knew so well.

Chapter Thirteen

Standing outside the Town Hall, Kate Mallory relished the last few puffs on her cigarette. This would be the last she would be able to smoke for the next couple of hours . . . the next boring couple of hours listening to a politician lying his balls off. They were all the same. She dropped the stub of cigarette on to the ground, covering it with her foot. Promise the punters anything until their arse was on a government back bench, then it became a different story altogether.

Story! She hitched the cavernous brown leather bag on to her shoulder. What sort of a story did his holiness the editor expect her to dredge up out of this claptrap? A breaking and entering that proved to be a woman who had left her door key on the table so broke her own window to get into the house . . . a hold-up at the newsagent that had turned out to be no more than a couple of under-aged kids lifting a girlie magazine they didn't have money to pay for . . . and now this, a bloody political meeting; when was he going to give her a break? She had asked, but it was at that precise moment he seemed to undergo another bout of deafness.

Resigned to her fate, Kate joined the people drifting in ones and twos into the building.

Another bloody political meeting! His thoughts unknowingly matching those of the woman journalist taking a seat on the front row, Bruce Daniels glanced about the largest room of Darlaston Town Hall. They used to hold dances in here on Saturday nights, now it was all discos and fancy named night clubs. Dances! Huh, more like bloody physical jerks, kids today wouldn't know a waltz or a quickstep if they tumbled over one! And this crap, a rally on behalf of the Conservative Party. How many of the men and women in this town did they expect to vote Conservative? They were more like to chuck the Honourable Member into the Tame than vote forrim. That was why *he* was here, him and the uniformed coppers, it would take their brightly polished buttons to hold this lot in check should they turn nasty.

'. . . that is the aim of the Conservative Party . . .'

The smart down-the-nose voice droned on. From the corner of her eye Kate watched the man in a shabby tweed jacket fish a pack of cigarettes from his pocket then drop them back unopened. She knew how he felt, bored and dying for a smoke.

His fingers reluctantly leaving the packet of Royals, Inspector Daniels swore under his breath. Christ, these

MP blokes might be shit at running the country but they could talk. This one sounded like he'd been vaccinated with a gramophone needle; Lord, he could give an Aspro a headache!

He could slip outside. Eyes moving restlessly over the sparse audience, Daniels played with the idea. He could go next door into the Swan, have a pint and a smoke, who was to say he'd left . . . the young copper on the door? Would you have reported a detective inspector slipping out when supposedly on duty? Daniels smiled internally. Neither would that lad, but then he wouldn't be called upon to pass the test. Here Daniels was stuck and here he'd be 'til the whole bloody bore-your-balls-off meeting was finished.

'. . . our manifesto makes it clear . . .'

The only thing clear was the fact that that bloke standing at the microphone had the same bloody cushy number as all the rest of the government; Conservative or Labour, they knew which side their bread was buttered and come election times they each fought like hell to hang on to it. But there'd come a time they'd make a slip, just like Bartley would make a slip. But Torrey . . . Torrey was a different kettle of fish. Daniels's mind gradually lost its fragile hold on the speaker. Torrey had answered every question put to him in that house in Dangerfield Lane, not pleasantly and not, as Daniels's every instinct told him, truthfully, but he'd answered; yet he'd given no name to that corpse.

So how come Torrey knew about the mermaid, how did he know about that tattoo?

With a movement that had long ago become second nature the inspector reached for his cigarettes, replacing them as he saw a young woman's sherry-coloured head shake, her smile sympathetically understanding as she caught his eye.

'*I've only ever seen one like that.*'

The young woman's glance returning to the dais, Daniels's mind drifted back to Dangerfield Lane. Torrey had made that answer while looking him straight in the eye. It was an unusual tattoo and it had led him to believe he might recognise the dead person. A bloke he'd served with in Ireland had a similar mark on the inner right thigh, the other men were always pulling his leg over it. Name of O'Malley, came from Liverpool though his parents had been born Irish. So, had Torrey known the victim or hadn't he? Daniels pushed the question around. He couldn't be certain, a body with half a face bruised and battered beyond recognition, the other half blown away, how could he be sure?

Well, that bit was feasible enough . . . but the bit about the Irishman? That was a lie, Daniels had needed no National Health specs to see that one! But then if Torrey wasn't sure he knew the identity of that water lily, why claim the corpse for burial?

'. . . a vote for the Conservative Party is a vote for . . .'

The rest passed Daniels by, his mind already back with Torrey.

'*I wouldn't leave shit to be buried by the Council,*' the man had snapped; a person . . . any person whether known to him or not didn't deserve a pauper's grave.

'We promise you . . .'

'You promise . . . what bloody good be that, promises don't bring a man a wage!'

At the front of the audience Kate Mallory twisted around to get a view of the heckler who had constantly interrupted the proceedings much to the public's delight and her own thankfulness that something . . . anything . . . was happening to lift the evening.

'We promise you . . .'

'You'd promise the bloody moon to get votes!'

The shout, louder this time, brought a wave of restlessness to the listeners and Kate, sensing their dissent, was suddenly attentive.

'. . . you have our solemn promise,' the nasal voice droned on, trying valiantly to appear unflustered, 'there will be jobs for all.'

To one side of the room a heavily built man stood up, the legs of his chair scraping noisily on the wood floor.

'Ar, mate, jobs for all . . .'

His clenched fist rose, jabbing the air. This was more like it. Kate Mallory craned her neck. There might be a story in this after all.

'. . . but them cushy jobs, the sort that pays the money, them jobs goes to the likes o' yoh while the likes o' we . . . we 'as the sort that kills 'osses!'

Rummaging in her bag for pen and paper Kate forgot them as a second man jumped to his feet. This was too good to miss.

'Ar,' the voice rang out irately, 'we gets the shit, the jobs the like o' yoh in parliament know bugger all about an' doh intend to learn, we gets them jobs an' gets paid bloody pennies for the doin' of 'em!'

Snapped back to the present by the din of the hecklers' assenting peers, Daniels glanced at the uniformed constable standing by the door, then at the other standing halfway down the room. Two men, one of whom was no more than twenty if he was a day, two men and himself, what chance would they have if this lot let loose!

'I tell yer what . . .' a woman's shout rose over the scrabble of voices, 'yoh let my old mon 'ave yoh're job an' he'll let yoh 'ave his'n!'

A burst of laughter filling the room, Daniels breathed more easily. Get this lot riled up and anything could happen.

'. . . the government recognises . . .'

'Let's see if the government recognises this.'

Daniels was on the move even as the arm lifted. Launching himself forwards he knocked the man off balance and the missile, almost half a house brick, bounced on to the platform just a yard short of the speaker. One hand catching the shoulder of the man still stumbling about Daniels spun him round, one knee fitting nicely into the groin. It was doubtful any case of police cruelty would be brought by that bastard! Daniels straightened his jacket. And the possibility that his future chances of fatherhood were now probably zero would help reduce population growth! Glancing at the dais a near smile touched his mouth as he caught the look on that MP's face. Judging by his colour he'd either shit himself or had a heart attack!

Watching the pale-faced politician being shepherded from the dais, Kate Mallory gave a satisfied grin. Wait until she dropped this little item on to the desk of the almighty. But first, a word with the hero.

'I tells you, Martha, he weren't ill, it were not sickness 'ad 'im lying on the ground afore the altar . . .'

Rosie Harper took the tea Martha Sim offered, stirring it vigorously. '. . . 'E was a moaning and a cryin' out like 'e was in torment; I tell you it give the two o' we a fair turn.'

Taking her own cup Martha Sim looked over it at the woman sitting in her tiny kitchen. Born the same week they had grown together, friends for nigh on seventy-five years and one never having lied to the other. It could be relied upon, whatsoever Rosie Harper told was told true.

'There were no other body in the church?'

Rosie shook her head. 'None as I knowed of and none as I could see, savin' Marcia James.'

'Mrs James, did she see the same?' Martha Sim carried her cup to a seat set beneath a small window draped prettily with blue cotton curtains sprinkled with white daisies.

''T'were her heard it first, the Reverend moanin' like 'e 'ad a bad case o' the gripe.'

'What did her do?' asked Hilda.

'You knows Marcia James, fusses like a turkey cock, dishin' out orders an' all the while doin' nuthin'. Her went on about him doin' too much but it be my thinkin' as it ain't no parish work, no, nor no boys' clubs neither as brought that priest to his knees.'

Sipping her tea Martha sat quiet, the talk of her daughter and her friend making little impression on the thoughts that were no newcomers to her mind. She had seen the change come over Peter Darley, seen him go from a smiling cheerful lad to a pale quiet figure seemingly feared of its own shadow . . . and she knew the reason behind it.

'The Reverend said 'e were feelin' a mite tired that last time 'e called, said it were no more'n that. But there be tired an' there be exhausted an' I thinks 'e be nearer the last than 'e be to the first.'

'That be my thinkin' an' all.' Rosie nodded as Hilda finished speaking. 'Question is, will 'e tek help?'

'He'll ask none of the church for 'e knows they'll give none.' Martha spoke quietly.

Rosie Harper frowned, anxiety deepening the lines age had set on her face. 'But the lad be 'alf out of 'is mind with worry and it won't call for many weeks to tek the rest. Summat 'as to be done.'

'Meanin' what?' Blackberry eyes rested steadily on Rosie's face.

'You knows my meanin'!'

Yes, she knew the meaning. Martha drank her tea

slowly. There was only one way to help Peter Darley, one way to banish the evil that walked in his path, but he had refused that help.

'I told the Reverend what the three of us knows.' She returned her cup to the tray her daughter had laid with a hand-embroidered cloth. 'Though I said naught of you two holdin' that knowledge. I spoke of what the ancient ways have shown, what it is that follows after him, the evil that robes itself in sweet-smelling spice, a malignance that will eat away at his mind 'til his senses be gone and even then would not be satisfied, would not stop until it dragged him after it into hell.'

'You offered 'elp?'

Martha's bright eyes stayed on her friend. 'You knows the answer to that, Rosie Harper, same as you knows it were refused. Nonsense was what he called the words I spoke, said it were nonsense that he be afeared to enter his own church, but his eyes told different. He would take none of my help saying it were against the Faith, he would lift no hand against the Lord.'

'But this don't be any doin' of the Lord.'

'No,' Martha answered. 'It be the doin' of Satan, and mine is the hand that must be lifted against him.'

'Drive straight past, drive on, don't stop!'

Lying in the bed that came with the cottage placed at his disposal, Richard Torrey gazed into the darkness. He'd seen no hitch-hiker on the road but Bartley had sworn to seeing one. *'A young person,'* he'd said, *'fair hair and wearing jeans.*' He'd twisted round in the passenger seat, staring behind the car and Torrey had felt the shivers running through him. What the hell had this man so scared? What was it about a hitch-hiker that had him trembling like a leaf? Whatever it was he hadn't let on, the rest of the ride home passing in silence. But Torrey had his own worries, if you could call that inspector's visit to Dangerfield Lane a worry. He'd asked his questions and received his answers. Much good may they do him! Torrey smiled cynically. The police would get as much help from him as they had given, which was none at all.

Daniels . . . had that been the name? Daniels had seemed less than comfortable as they stood in the house – he'd had no intention of asking the bastard to sit down – and kept blowing through his nostrils, short sharp snippets of air as if he were trying to rid them of a smell. *Had* the man smelled any faint aroma? Shakira had been Anna's favourite but it had not been used since . . . no, there was no smell of that in the house any more, nothing reminiscent of that time.

Anna! Torrey felt his stomach tighten with longing. Christ, who would have thought! Who would have *ever* thought that he, Torrey, a bloke as tough as any commando in the unit, a man who'd fought and killed with the worst of them, would turn into a bloody love-sick fool? He'd had women, of course he had, how many men of his age hadn't . . . but he'd felt nothing for any of them, they'd served a purpose, a need, and that was all. He had wanted no attachments, no tied strings. Then he'd met Anna and his strong well-structured world had collapsed about his feet. He had fallen wonderfully, hopelessly in love, his life had suddenly filled with colour and laughter, had suddenly taken on a meaning it had never held before. Anna, his Anna; it was insane, ludicrous! Jesus, if it were any funnier he might laugh. But he wasn't laughing . . . it seemed more like he was dying.

It hadn't taken long. He stared at moon-cast shadows flickering on the walls. Silent shadows that appeared to still as he looked at them. Just as those vicious tongues had stilled whenever he walked past. Oh he knew what they said, the talk that had gone on, but he hadn't cared. He loved Anna and to hell with Darlaston, to hell with the world. No, it hadn't taken long, there might be no geniuses in that town but then it hadn't needed the brain of an Einstein to put that particular two and two together, and they'd come up with the answer. Torrey and his lodger were lovers, a pair of fornicators! But as long as Anna had been with him talk like that hadn't mattered, nothing had mattered so long as they were together. But after Anna had left, then the talk had hurt, then it stung like it had that night in the Bird-in-Hand, the night three men had come near to paying for it with their lives. Perhaps it was providence that had brought him here, providence prompted Philip Bartley to take him on as chauffeur; but whatever had prompted the move, one thing was certain . . . it had saved some man's life!

'I wanted to thank you again for your help,' Langford Wyndham MP doodled with his free hand on the memo pad lying on his desk, 'the West Midlands is never an easy venue . . .' there was a pause as the person on the other end of the line answered. 'Nevertheless,' Wyndham began again, the conversation switching to him, 'it was a bit of a bloody sharp move on your part and I'm grateful for it. It would have turned into a nasty moment. Most that get to our meetings are decent sorts, but some!' He snorted down the line, 'Some of 'em think the whole bloody country should revolve around them, they lay the sins of our Victorian Fathers at our feet, I'm afraid.' The silver Parker traced involved patterns on the memo pad. 'Yes, I'm inclined to agree,' Wyndham laughed, 'only don't tell anyone I said so. Well, I'm pretty grateful anyway and I won't forget what you did and neither will the PM, I'm certain. But listen, the reason I'm ringing is I'm having a few drinks on Thursday – my birthday – my wife is in a nursing home . . . What? Oh no . . . no, nothing serious just a little overtired, it's a hell of a job running the place in London and then of course there's our house in Surrey, and with her mother dying suddenly a month ago it's all got a bit on top of her so I insisted she stay a few days where she can relax completely. So, as I was saying, with my wife not being able to be present it's just a few drinks with some friends and I'd like you to come, if you're free, that is.'

A few more seconds, the contorted shapes on the memo pad twisted sinuously into one another then, 'That's great, so don't let anything get in the way, I'll see you Thursday evening . . . Evening suit? No. The whole thing is totally informal . . . Where? A friend has fixed the honours,

Benenden House at Brackley, following the A423 out of Coventry down the Ronshaw Gap . . . you can't miss it, then take the turning for Brackley. Right . . . right, about nine.'

Bruce Daniels put down the receiver and reached into his pocket. Extracting a white tablet from a blue and yellow carton he flicked it into his mouth. He was having to buy larger sizes these days; he patted the outline of the carton as he replaced it in the pocket of his jacket. He should get to a bloody quack . . . only not yet. He looked at the address written in his scrawling hand, Benenden House, Brackley. Bit of bloody luck that bloke running amok at the Town Hall, that politician had nearly shit himself. Daniels almost smiled. A bit of shit never hurt nobody and it certainly hadn't hurt him. Langford Wyndham wouldn't forget and neither would the PM so there was another chance of promotion coming up in the none-too-distant future. He flicked open his desk diary at the page for Thursday of this week, running his finger down the scrawled entries.

Invited for a birthday drink with the Secretary of State for Foreign Affairs. Daniels sucked on the tablet. He was back on the ladder and this time nobody was going to kick it from under him. Oh, Bartley was still placing the stuff somewhere, he knew that without being told, he wouldn't let a lucrative number like shifting drugs slip away because of one small-town police raid. No, Bartley would have the band playing somewhere else, he liked money too much to let the balloon drop out of a market like drugs; he had his chain of supermarkets but that couldn't account for the almost overnight fortune he'd acquired. Daniels burped loudly, stomach gas bringing a rush of burning acid into his throat. Bartley was smart but he was greedy and one day he was going to get too greedy, and when that day came Daniels would be the hero of the town a second time.

Chapter Fourteen

'It was a bloody daft thing to do. I warned you not to have it done anywhere near the Midlands.' Philip Bartley stared at the man sitting in his office. Lean and distinguished, looking impeccably tailored in a dark-blue cashmere suit, a same-coloured tie touching perfectly against an ice-white silk shirt, his visitor raised both eyebrows.

'Really, Bartley, don't you think you are overdoing the drama just a tiny bit?'

'No I bloody well don't!' Bartley wasn't overawed by public-school manners and this one was ready to piss into anybody's pot provided it suited him. 'The police have already raided this place and been sniffing about on the trail of some corpse!'

'Have they done that?' The eyebrows remained raised. 'Sniffed about on the trail of a corpse?'

Bartley threw the pen he was holding on to a desk polished to a blinding gleam. 'Not this place, no, but . . .'

'Then you have nothing to worry about.' The eyebrows lowered to their accustomed place. 'There was no identi-fication, the police files have been closed, nothing else will be heard of our attractive Anna. You should forget about it . . . I have.'

Forget about it, forget about that hitch-hiker who hadn't been real, forget about the hitch-hiker Darley had picked up yet hadn't been in the car when it stopped, forget the fact that the priest was being torn apart by something he couldn't see! That was easier said than done.

'There is a shipment coming in from South America on the twelfth, you will distribute it along the usual channels.'

'Not from here. I can't have any go through the Leys, it's too soon after that raid and the police will be watching.'

Rising to his feet Clifton Mather sauntered to the wide window through which could be seen factories with their attendants of box-like houses, his lip curling with distaste. Bartley had got the jumps but he'd take that shipment of narcotics and he'd get them passed to the buyers even supposing he had bubonic plague.

'I don't know how.' Mather turned. 'But it *will* get done. After all,' he smiled showing teeth it cost a fortune to maintain, 'we don't want the police to find another body floating in the canal.'

'I don't know how!' Bartley repeated the words as the door closed behind the tall blue-suited man, spitting each one out as though it were poison. He wasn't the one had the blues breathing down his neck, he wasn't the one would carry the can if that stuff were found here. Mather kept his hands clean by getting others to do the dirty work, like he'd done with Anna, like he might try doing with him. Bartley clamped his teeth together. That was another reason for taking on Torrey, the man could use his head as well as his hands. He'd told him about a fight in the yard of the Bird-in-Hand and three gob-happy yobbos left unconscious. He hadn't said what the fight was in aid of but then there wouldn't be too much mystery there, blokes with beer for a mouth shooting it off; what was of real interest was the way Torrey had handled them. Quick, clean, efficient. Yes, he felt better with Torrey at his side, felt good enough to p'raps take the new fair-haired employee, the one from dispatch, down to Monkswell next weekend.

'Shit!' Daniels swore loudly, feeling the judder of the car as he depressed the accelerator. He should have driven the Ford after all. He'd hired this from a garage. *It will look better you going in a bigger car,* Marjorie had insisted. *You don't want it to look like we've got nothing.* What the bloody hell had they got?

He muttered, slowing as he approached a road sign half-hidden by overhanging trees. Pressing the accelerator again he swore at the shudder that rippled the smooth ride. 'Can't be spark plugs,' he thought aloud, 'I was told the bloody thing was only serviced last week, anyway it feels more like the steering, a bloody Friday afternoon job no doubt; Christ, the British have a lot to learn! They still think it's enough to slap a British Made sticker on a bladder with a hole in it for it to sell.'

Taking a bend too wide he jerked the powerful car back to the left at the crown of the hill, swearing again as an oncoming driver blasted his horn. He was in the wrong but knowing it didn't help. He'd been irritable all day, might have been better not to have questioned those bloody little tykes about lead stripped from the roof of the factory being put up along of Booth Street, he should have let one of the constables do it, but if he'd bawled them out the way he had yesterday, there would have been a second Exodus and he wouldn't have been Moses leading the people to freedom.

Ronshaw Gap. The painted sign loomed in his head-lights like a giant white-winged moth. A few miles should see a right turn for Brackley. He glanced at the piece of paper he had propped on the dash – yes, the B4027 should take him right through the village, about five miles and Benenden House was on the left.

He eased his body sideways, his right hand fishing the carton from his pocket; it would help if he could get rid of this bloody acid. Juggling with the flip top he extricated a tablet and flicked it into his mouth, his hand sending the rest sliding to the floor when he went to close the box.

'Shit!' He spat irritably, he had no more and he couldn't risk going the entire evening without them. He would just have to pick some up when he arrived. But it wasn't just acid making him irritable. He checked a passing road sign, he was still on route. It was more that bloody scent in his nostrils; Christ, he could taste it with every swallow! He really was going to have to see a doctor, perhaps if he got this next promotion . . .

'Daniels, glad you could come.' Langford Wyndham, Secretary of State for Foreign Affairs, smiled the vacuous smile used for canvassing, his mind assessing the man shaking his hand. Still in the sticks, but shrewd. Bartley was right, it would be best to keep him sweet. 'Come and meet the others.'

Whisky in hand, Daniels worked hard at polite conversation; this wasn't his field, he was outclassed and felt it.

'I said ten years ago they were lending too much,' Clifton Mather was saying, 'it's one thing lending money to third-world countries and quite another getting it back. It had to happen.' He swallowed a gin and tonic. 'The interest has outstripped the repaying power. Take Brazil, for instance, the bloody country is bankrupt, we've lost millions writing off their loans, and there are several other countries following that lead. The banks have chopped off their own balls, and God knows what other part of the anatomy will go once the final calculations are made, don't you agree, Mr er . . . Daniels?'

'I don't know much about international banking, it's pretty much a closed book to me.'

'Now if it were bank robbers you were talking about we would both be more at home, eh Daniels?' James Connor, Deputy Commissioner of Police, smiled. 'That's much more our subject.'

'It *is* bloody robbery!' Maxwell Seton, another of the guests, exploded. 'And the bloody fools of banks helped load the money in the truck. Brazil and all the others have made a clean getaway with millions and what can be done about it? Fuck all, that's what we can do about it.'

'It'll be the investors that pay.' Daniels watched the banker through narrow eyes. 'The little man with sod all to begin with; the big wigs will be protected. The directors have too much to lose to let the big boys feel the sting.'

'What do you mean?' Seton swivelled an angry stare, aware of the amusement on the faces of the others. What the fuck did a bloody back-street policeman know about international money matters? It was a question if he made enough in a year to buy a bloody decent case of Bollinger.

'I should have thought you knew only too well.' Suddenly Daniels was back in the interview room facing a suspect across the table, very much in control, very much his own man. 'The government couldn't dole out public money to underdeveloped nations on the scale it was needed so the major banks were coerced into handing over, Christ only knows with what promises. The directors then pulled the wool over the eyes of their investors, promising millions in interest over the next ten years and the ordinary man in the street believed it; the directors were the men with the top jobs, they must have known what they were talking about.' Daniels almost smiled. 'Funny, isn't it, how often they turn out to be wrong? Especially when it's not their money they're playing with.'

'Don't argue with him, Seton,' Clifton Mather laughed at the embarrassed flush sweeping into Seton's face. 'The man is a detective, remember, we don't want you run in on a charge of conspiracy to embezzle the public.'

'That's not bloody funny, Mather,' Seton rounded angrily.

It might have developed into a slanging match, Daniels thought, disappointed at the disrupting arrival of late-comers, you nearly always learned something to advantage from a professional set-to. He turned as Langford Wyndham brought his additional guests into the room. One was short, a portly figure emphasising his lack of height, thinning grey hair losing the battle to cover his pinkish dome. Give him a bloody fishing rod, thought Daniels, and you've got the perfect garden gnome. He nodded into the un-gnomelike sharpness of the eyes with the uncomfortable feeling the man knew exactly what he'd been thinking.

'And Richard . . . Richard Torrey.'

Daniels's hand paused in mid-shake. Torrey . . . him again, the bloke who had claimed that corpse they'd pulled out of the Tame, the one with half a face missing. Connor had ordered a close down on that one, probably covering for one or two here assembled.

'Good evening.'

Torrey extended his hand and Daniels took it, acid suddenly belting into his throat.

'Good evening, Torrey.' He didn't voice the conver-sational additive 'we've met before', it was superfluous and superfluity wasn't Daniels's style. Besides, he preferred the others not to have the advantage of realising the two of them were old adversaries, anything they didn't know was an ace in his hand.

'Strohm!'

Maxwell Seton claimed the portly man's attention and Daniels took the opportunity to break away. He didn't want to talk to Torrey, what was between them was best left unsaid, no use in raising the dead. He swallowed a mouthful of whisky in an attempt to douse the fire in his throat. They'd have a bloody job raising one corpse in particular, those ashes had spread on the wind long since.

'One of my contacts is in the market for a consignment of ground to air.' Strohm and Seton gravitated towards the drinks, making no attempt to conceal what they were saying. The half of Daniels that was police trained an automatic ear on the conversation, the other half dealing with the mystery of Torrey's sudden appearance. What had he to do with the Secretary of State for Foreign Affairs or his entourage?

'You know we can't do business with Iran or Iraq.' Strohm's answer was an octave lower than Seton's but Daniels picked it up without trouble.

'Who said anything about Iran or Iraq?' Seton answered. 'My contact is interested in a different theatre altogether.'

'Like?'

'China!'

'And the shipping line?'

'Benson.'

'Under the Liberian flag?'

'Uh huh.' Seton nodded.

How bloody convenient! Daniels swallowed the re-
surgence of acid. These bastards knew every bloody angle
of the game. A shipment of arms supposedly for China
gets mistakenly unloaded in the Middle East, finishing in
Iran or Iraq or maybe Israel. War was these merchants'
living and they didn't care who died so long as the pick-
ings were fruitful.

'Give me a ring later, say next week some time.'
Strohm's back was towards Daniels. 'Could be we can do
business but this isn't the place to discuss it.'

'And now gentlemen,' across the room Bartley raised
his glass, 'let's all wish Langford a happy birthday and
many more of the same.'

'Happy birthday . . . many happy returns.'

Daniels glanced towards the group now clustering
around their host. Only Torrey remained on the outside,
his the only voice not adding to the chorus.

'Now for your present.'

Daniels almost puked at the grin stretching the men's
liberal mouths, at the covert 'all chaps together' look that
passed from each to the other. Bloody arsehole creepers
the lot of 'em!

'You must have a present on your birthday.'

It was all such a bloody sham. Daniels put his glass
down at the politician's polite, 'You shouldn't have.'
There probably wasn't a shit among the lot of them would
lift a finger if the bloke got kicked out of the Cabinet
tomorrow.

'In here.'

Bartley turned, leading the way towards tall mahogany double doors. Daniels followed reluctantly. He'd like to run the whole bloody parade into the nearest station, they were all as bent as a five-bob note. But if he wanted to dance he had to pay the piper.

Chapter Fifteen

Detective Inspector Bruce Daniels stared through the window of the car. Large and spacious, it gave him a feeling of unease. He would have been more comfortable in the Ford, in fact if he'd taken time to think after that phone call he might have been more comfortable not coming at all. '*How will it look, you refusing an invite from a Member of Parliament?*' Marjorie had harped after that invitation card had arrived. '*You have to go, you want to go up in the world, don't you?*' In the end he'd have gone up in a bloody hot-air balloon if it kept her quiet.

She'd propped the card on the shelf above the new-fangled tiled fireplace she'd insisted should replace the shiny black polished cast iron. '*You don't have the blackleading of it every week,*' she'd said with that self-righteous hard-done-by look on her face. '*Oh no, leave that for Marjorie, same as everything else be left for me to clean.*' He'd faced the brick wall of her determination again and turned away without attempting to scale it, and the card had rested against the clock that had been her mother's, the only thing she had wanted after the old woman died. They didn't want no old-fashioned stuff she'd said, they wanted modern furniture, contemporary this, contemporary that. Contemporary shit! He continued to stare out of the window, at the rain beginning to glide like silver worms along the glass. How long would crap like that last! He'd tried to tell Marjorie that, but talking to that woman was like talking to a stone.

Familiar acid rising to his throat he reached for one of the tablets he'd accidentally dropped on the floor earlier.

That card, the invitation for drinks being given by Langford Wyndham MP, whose head he'd saved from being cracked by half a house brick had hidden the clock-face for almost a week, only being lifted aside for the duster to pass behind it, Marjorie treating it like gold. Lord, it was a bloody invitation to drinks not a Knighthood from the Queen!

It might have been less tedious if it had been a summons to Buck House, at least that would have been over with quicker. It was just an informal get-together, his host had informed him, a more pleasant way of saying thanks than simply sending a letter.

A letter would have suited him better. He sucked on the tablet he'd needed all night. This sort of do might suit the likes of Bartley and that little arsehole of a Deputy Commissioner but Bruce Daniels preferred his company as he preferred his booze . . . genuine, and that lot tonight had been anything but. The only one among them he'd say came anywhere near the real thing had been Torrey.

Now why had he been there? Licking the sticky remains of the indigestion tablet from around his teeth, Daniels pondered the question he'd dwelt on for most of the previous two hours. They had talked when he'd gone to the toilet. Bartley he could understand, this get together of the businessmen of the constituency would include him, but Torrey, where had he fitted in?

'I'm Bartley's chauffeur, what's your excuse!' Torrey had answered the question, a smile touching his mouth while his eyes were forged steel.

His chauffeur or his cover? There had been no one else in those toilets, no one to hear what was asked: *'Was Bartley in on the murder of your friend, did you share the little screw, take turn and turn about? Was one getting more than the other so one of you got jealous and committed murder, wiped half of the pretty face with a shotgun?'*

Climbing from the car Daniels walked into the hotel, going straight to his room.

Torrey's steel-hard look had disappeared then and death had stared back, but Daniels had pressed his point.

'You could have done it, Torrey,' he'd said, *'with your Army training you know how to handle a gun, or was it Bartley . . . did he have your little bedfellow tucked up for good and put to bed in the cut?'*

There might have been a punch-up then; no, there *would* have been a punch-up then except the cloakroom attendant had walked in at that precise moment.

'*You two are mixed up in something.*' Daniels remembered the look in Torrey's eyes as he turned to dry his hands. '*I don't know what yet but I will, and when I do the next little venue you two will share won't be no hotel.*'

A heel kicking the door of his room closed behind him, he blew through his nose. The stuff used to clean those toilets had stayed with him the whole evening, a spicy scenty smell that at first hadn't seemed unpleasant, but it had stayed with him in his nostrils and in his throat until he'd wanted to puke; even the glass of whisky he'd allowed himself had done nothing to wash it away. If it clung to his clothes like it clung his throat, Marjorie would think he'd had himself a whore. A whore! He snorted again, the aroma of that washroom a taste on his tongue. It had been that long he wouldn't know what to do if he were given one free!

Opening the dark-blue overnight case he'd left on a chair — no use unpacking when he was leaving again the next morning — he rummaged among the shirts and underwear Marjorie had insisted on him bringing. Christ, they took less on a bloody safari!

Thank God the evening was over, listening to a politician lie through his teeth was bad enough at any time, but tonight with that smell in his nostrils! He fished a bottle from the case, swallowing whisky straight from it. Drinks here were too bloody expensive for his pocket. Taking another liberal swallow he set the bottle on a table next to the bed then picked up his blue striped pyjamas, p'raps brushing his teeth would get rid of the smell in his nose and a little more ferreting could get rid of Bartley . . . and Torrey? He brushed Colgate over his teeth. Christ, he'd get that sorted if it was the last thing he did!

Leaving his glass untouched and keeping his distance from the rest, Torrey followed the guests as they trooped across the room for the birthday surprise. Reaching the door after the others had passed inside he took in the room with one glance. Equal to the hall and the room they had just left, it breathed money. Silk-lined walls provided a perfect background for the paintings that lined it. He was no art connoisseur but he'd put his last penny on their being originals. Underfoot the parquet floor gleamed like sheened satin, reflecting light from smoked quartz chandeliers. The centre of the room was covered with one huge carpet a foot thick and on this stood a large oval double-pedestal walnut table.

Torrey brought his attention back to the group of guests. Which, if any, owned this costly little pile?

'What is it?' Langford Wyndham stood beside the table, his eyes on the large wicker container at its heart. From the periphery of the assembly Torrey watched the men, their dark lounge suits, collars and ties more suited to a business meeting than drinks with the boys; ordinary enough it seemed, so why wouldn't he trust any one of them as far as he could throw him?

'Yes,' Maxwell Seton called, 'what do you get for the man who has everything?'

Clifton Mather, designer-styled hair combed into

careful perfection, stepped forward, a bronzed and perfectly manicured hand touching Wyndham's sleeve. 'It's a picnic basket.'

Bloody picnic basket! Torrey watched Seton's teeth reflect as much light as the well-polished floors. He could feed the bloody five thousand with that.

'. . . now every time you take the family on a picnic you will remember our little get together this evening.' Seton finished almost on a giggle.

'Well go on, Langford,' Eric Strohm urged, 'open it.'

Torrey peered over the heads of the men gathered about the table. Even from this distance he could feel the tension. What bloody part *was* Bartley playing in all this? He switched back to the central scene. The Secretary of State for Foreign Affairs was releasing the catch that held the lid of the basket but he didn't lift the lid. That opened of its own accord.

Bartley momentarily forgotten, Torrey manoeuvred to see the basket more clearly. The lid was rising, now it was thrown back completely. Two golden arms twined upwards, wrists twisted across each other to bring the palms of long-fingered hands together in a frame for the raven-dark head. A spine twisting sinuously as the body pushed itself upwards, small perfect shoulders were followed by slim rounded hips. Smooth well-contoured legs stretched and the form was standing perfectly upright. With its arms lifted above the head it remained perfectly still, light gleaming on the lightly oiled limbs turning it into a golden statue.

Richard Torrey flicked a quick glance at the men, their

attention riveted to the scene in front of them. Maxwell Seton was leaning across the table, one hand part raised as if to stroke the creamy gold buttocks, Mather's mouth was slack, his tongue caressing the inside edge of his lower lip in a sweeping sensuous movement, while beside him Bartley's hot eyes stroked the perfect form. Torrey could almost see the saliva collecting at the corners of his mouth. Only Strohm displayed no emotion.

One delicate step, toes elegantly pointed, and the body was out of the basket; another titillating five seconds and it began to turn.

Perhaps it was a defence action, perhaps subconsciously he had no appetite for what was going on, but Torrey looked away. Daniels had left the room and he'd like to leave too, this kind of entertainment wasn't his idea of a good time, but as long as Bartley stayed then he must. He saw him now refilling a glass with more booze, keep that up and he'd be seeing another phantom hitch-hiker on the drive home. Daniels's surprise at seeing him here had been as marked as his own . . . so why was that copper here, why had he been invited to this boys' own shindig? Himself, yes, Bartley was reluctant to go as far as the toilet on his own, but how come Daniels had been invited . . . what part was he playing? Bartley and the rest were a load of crooks, that was a safe enough bet, but Daniels . . . no, the man might be an arsehole like the rest of the blues at that station but he was no crook.

Time would tell, it told all things eventually, but then he was in no hurry. Keep your head down and your eyes open had been the approach taken by his commando officers and it had always served him well, just as it had served him in the yard of the Bird-in-Hand.

An appreciative gasp brought him back. The figure on the table, arms still entwined above the head, now faced its audience. Dark hair curled down across a clear brow, large brown eyes lowered a fringe of lashes seductively withdrawing their invitation, while the slight parting of a full soft mouth re-offered it.

No dark shadows in the armpit, Torrey noted, and none at the base of that flat stomach; all body hair had been removed, allowing nothing to detract from the beauty of that golden body, nothing to draw the attention from the sizeable penis already reaching upwards.

'Happy birthday,' Clifton Mather clapped a hand to the shoulder of the politician, 'and after you've had your teeth into that we reckon you will have had one.'

Disgust thick in his throat Richard Torrey turned away.

This lot were a bunch of homos, nothing but a load of perverts.

Needing an excuse to get away he returned to the toilet then discovered he needed that office after all. Langford Wyndham and his fancy well-heeled friends were homosexuals! Hands held under the tap he rested his forehead against the huge mirror above the magnolia hand basin. 'The whole bloody bunch of them,' he could almost hear what Daniels would be saying, 'screaming bloody perverts, arse pokers, they don't want locking up, they need putting down, filthy dirty buggers!'

But Inspector Bruce Daniels was the sort who

condemned any couple making love before marriage. To his kind they were all seen as filthy dirty buggers. He and Anna, they had not been married . . . but their love had not been dirty, there had been nothing filthy in their relationship. He had loved Anna as deeply and truly as any man ever loved, but in the eyes of the copper their kind of love was despised, it would always be despised!

Daniels jerked awake, taking a minute to adjust to the fact that this wasn't his own bedroom, that he was in a hotel in the centre of Coventry, and the second fact that he wasn't alone. Lying for several seconds he listened to the low hum of the air conditioning system, swallowing as acid burned along his gut. That must be what had woken him, so why were the hairs on the back of his neck standing like guards on a parade ground?

The room still and silent yet charged like an electric battery, he reached for the lamp, at the same time rolling from the bed to crouch low against one wall. It was swift and soundless. Daniels had been schooled hard and early, his childhood teaching him to move fast and think the same way. With only his eyes moving, he took in the room. It was empty. Christ, if only that scent would clear from his nostrils! Pushing himself to his feet he crossed cautiously to the bathroom, one foot kicking the door back on its hinges, his eyes jerking to every corner. Empty! He slumped against the wall, beads of nervous sweat pricking his skin. Something had woken him and it wasn't the acid eating away his gut or the taste of that bloody hotel washroom that seemed permanently lodged in his throat.

Pulling in a long breath, a hand pressing to the fire burning below his ribcage, he crossed to the overnight bag and took out the BiSoDol. He was taking too many of these things. He threw the pack down, not bothering to close it. He really would see a medic, he would see one as soon as he got home. Picking up the bottle he'd left open beside the bed he took a swallow. He was fully awake. Chances were he wouldn't sleep again tonight and whisky would help him think.

He was half-way to stretching out on the bed when those same small hairs on the nape of his neck rose, every nerve screaming with sudden tension. There had been no sound, no movement, but some inner sense warned he was being watched. There was no one in the bathroom, he'd just come from there; and the window? Though they were seven storeys into the sky it was locked and barred with an ornate iron-work grille. Daniels's eyes did a quick recce. The lock on the door was in the closed position, heavy curtains shut out the night. There was nothing amiss, so why were his nerves singing like the Orpheus Male Voice Choir?

He shivered. The room was cold yet the heating was on, he could just hear the select murmur; but the temperature had fallen and was still sliding. P'raps a window was open after all . . . one of the cleaners . . . so why was no draught moving the curtains?

He'd check anyway, an intruder might choose to risk his neck coming in that way, it wasn't unknown even this high up; from one balcony to another, a quick jump, a firm hold and they were in. Leaving the bottle on the table he crossed to the window, he was no mite yet he moved as soundlessly as a cat, hardly disturbing the air that now crackled with cold. Grabbing the drapes he swung them open, the sound of metal rings scraping the rail harsh in the throbbing silence. The window was closed, the lock secure, the rain pattering against its reinforced glass. Nobody had come in that way.

Breath he hadn't realised he was holding slid between his teeth. 'You're letting this job get to you, Daniels,' he muttered, coughing against the smell in his nostrils, the taste scoring his tongue, peeling his teeth, 'you'll be seeing bloody ghosts next!'

Going to the bathroom he leant over the basin. Christ, the taste in his throat was poisoning him. Tomorrow he would see a doctor.

'It isn't acid you can taste.'

It was soft, no more than a whisper against his ear. Daniels whirled round, the whisper coming again even as he saw the bathroom was empty.

'You are tasting what I can do, you are tasting the flesh of a corpse left to rot in a canal.'

Straightening, Daniels whipped around to face the door, bile flaring in his chest and burning upwards into his throat as he stared at the figure standing in the doorway, a figure with pale gold hair and wide blue eyes.

'You remember that corpse, don't you, Inspector . . . ?'

The sound echoed in his head though the attractive smiling mouth didn't move.

'You should, it remembers you.'

The smile still on its lips, blue eyes reflecting the light, the figure faded into nothingness.

Chapter Sixteen

'*You are tasting what I can do . . .*'

The words ringing in his mind Inspector Bruce Daniels thrust the keys of his hotel room at the startled night clerk.

Where the hell had it come from? It hadn't been imagination, he knew that; and it hadn't been any dream, not with his head over that bathroom basin and his gut floating in acid. Throwing the overnight bag into the car he slid behind the wheel. He was no coward but he wanted out of that hotel. Pulling a handkerchief from his pocket he wiped the spread of moisture from his brow. There had been no one but him in that bedroom, he'd searched every inch of it; yet he'd heard those words as if the speaker stood next to him.

He slipped the handkerchief back into his pocket and turned the key in the ignition. It was still only half five but then an early start wouldn't hurt.

'*You are tasting what I can do . . .*'

Daniels's foot jerked down on the accelerator as the

words whispered again, but they were not in his mind this time. His glance going to the driving mirror, he saw the figure in the back seat. A golden-haired figure, the features indistinguishable in the uncertain light of dawn. That was it, the light was playing tricks. He glanced in the mirror again, breath sputtering in jerky rasps as he saw the rear of the car was empty. He should have had more sense, the bloody car had been locked, it was still locked when he picked it up ten minutes ago.

Releasing one hand from the wheel he fumbled in his pocket for the carton of BiSoDol. Finding what he wanted he slipped a tablet into his mouth. Christ, his mouth had all the flavour of rat droppings! He should never have accepted that invitation. Regardless of how much Marjorie moaned he should have turned it down. His foot touching down on the accelerator he chased his headlights through the greyness. Fuck Marjorie . . . 'and fuck you!' He shouted the last aloud as an oncoming farm wagon grated its horn.

Surging forwards the powerful car sliced into the shadowed narrowness between high hedges. Daniels's right foot pressed down, the steering rippled.

Ronshaw Gap. He pulled on to the traffic island, taking the exit for Birmingham. The trunk road was well lit, now he could really put the accelerator to the floor and any smart-arsed cop that pulled him over for speeding would get a nasty shock when he found a warrant card sticking out of his nostrils.

The car shot forwards answering the demand of his foot and Daniels swore as the steering rippled more pronouncedly. This heap of bloody junk would be returned and a vehicle inspector would follow soon after.

Overhead lamps lit this stretch of road, their reflections dancing like fireflies across the windscreen. Daniels coughed, trying to rid his mouth and throat of the vileness that turned his stomach. He lowered a window and the inrush of wind stirred the still air of the car, pushing the foetid taste further into his throat, filling his windpipe with its putridness. Waves of bile swelled upwards and he turned his head sideways, spitting through the window.

Just ahead a car screamed an oncoming warning. Daniels swore sickly then closed the window. No use in sucking more tablets, they were doing no good. There was some chewing gum in the glove compartment: that might help. Reaching into the tiny space he gasped as his fingers touched against something cold and slimy. A slug! He pulled his hand away sharply. One of those bloody jokers at that house, probably Seton, thought it quite a caper to put a slug in his car. Bloody know-it-all Mr International Banker hadn't liked being told a few home truths about his own particular trade and thought this a way of returning the compliment. He'd like to wring Seton's bloody neck!

It hadn't been like that with Anna, what they'd shared together hadn't been filthy.

Richard Torrey stood in the shower of his room, the hot water stinging his skin.

He had loved Anna, he still loved Anna.

He lifted his face to the spray, wanting the bite of the water, needing it to drive away the misery.

He had lain awake long after Bartley had finished his reverie and he had been free to get away to the room given him at the back of the lovely house.

He had wanted Anna, wanted to feel that supple body in his arms, that mouth pressed against his own. But even as his soul cried out for it he knew it could not happen, Anna was gone, Anna was dead, he would never hear that voice again.

But he had heard it! He struck a fist hard against the tiles. He *had* heard it. That night in the house, after he'd laid out those three louts. Only Anna called him Ritchie. He had been so sure, but if it had come once, if it had been Anna somehow reaching back to him, why wouldn't it come in the hours he'd lain awake? He'd tried. Although every part of his brain, every fibre of him said he was being a fool still he'd tried to hear that voice again, have it whisper in his mind, but it had been no good. In the end he had got up, to lie any longer was just to prolong the agony.

Turning off the shower he dried and dressed. Outside the sky was still that nebulous uncertain shade of grey, the moment when nature wasn't sure whether to make the next minute day or leave it as night. There would be no one about yet, judging by the amount of booze those men had put away it could be hours before they surfaced. A jog around the grounds would help clear the shadows from his mind. His hand closing on his jacket hanging in the wardrobe he rejected it. A jacket wasn't the best wear for a brisk run. Choosing a sweater he paused, fingering the soft wool. This had been Anna's favourite. It had often been chosen instead of a jacket when they had gone for walks together; *'It picks out those sexy hazel tints in your eyes,'* Anna had said and always smiled when he wore it. Slipping it now over his head, Torrey caught a hint of fragrance, but it was not the soap he had used in the shower. He breathed deeply, taking the fragrance into his nose, his throat, his heart. The fragrance of Shakira.

Daniels breathed short shallow breaths trying to keep the pungent rancid taste out of his throat. Touching that slimy object, or thinking he'd touched something, had set his stomach away again. Acid was chewing his gut and that perpetual bloody taste in his mouth was driving him round the bend. It had only been imagination, same as in that hotel. He'd simply imagined he'd touched against something cold and slimy; he'd even stopped at the side of the road, searched floor, seats, the entire bloody car with a torch but there was nothing. Imagination! He flicked an indicator and pulled into the right-hand lane of the dual carriageway, his foot reaching for the boards. Work or no work, tomorrow he would see a doctor. Cancelling the indicator he sat in the offside lane.

So Mr Richard Torrey was Bartley's chauffeur, and what else? Behind him a car flashed headlights in a request to pass. Daniels ignored it. A little further investigation wouldn't go amiss in that quarter; a drink in the Frying

Pan, a chat with Echo Sounder could turn up all sorts of interesting cards.

His rear mirror showing the impatient flash of lights, Daniels reluctantly steered the car to the inside lane, catching the irritated sound of a horn as a car raced past. Bloody speed merchant, he gazed at the disappearing tail lights; should he catch up, flash his warrant card and nick the bugger? No. He dismissed the idea. Let the local force earn their keep, there were too many coppers sitting on their idle arses, tucked in cars that never moved out of a lay-by! He coughed at the bitterness sticking to his throat, grimacing as it slid past his taste buds. Christ, that wasn't imagination, and the stench in his nostrils, it was getting worse. He opened the window again, closing it swiftly as the smell folded back on him like a fog.

'Bruce . . .'

Daniels's eyes shot to the mirror. The rear seat was empty. But of course it was bloody empty, what the hell else did he expect? Yet he could have sworn he heard . . . he pressed down on the accelerator, ignoring the definite judder of the steering. He'd be glad to get home.

'Bruce . . . Bruce . . .'

Again instinct lifted his glance, again the mirror showed nothing but empty seats. A copper's mind could play tricks the same as anybody else's. He breathed hard. That was all that whisper was, a trick of the mind.

He stared ahead at a ribbon of red tail lights stretched like a gigantic artery along the grey arm of the road.

'Bruce.'

The sound was no longer behind but seemed to come from beside him and it was no longer a whisper it was . . .

The car swerved drunkenly as his hands jerked and a tattoo of horn blasts ripped as he pulled back into lane.

'Bruce!'

It filled the car, a cloud of whispering sound.

'There is nothing and no one in this car but you.' Daniels repeated the phrase aloud, trying to revive his flagging reason.

'Bruce.'

The breathy edge that fused the sound into a whisper was gone. He had heard it clear and firm. Daniels shivered with spasmodic fear . . . an old remembered fear.

'There is nothing and no one in this car.'

'Bruce.'

The voice was stronger, refusing denial. It was the voice of a man, a voice he recognised. Fear jerked his head sideways. He was in the passenger seat. Jack Daniels . . . the father he had killed.

But his old man was dead and there was no such thing as ghosts! It was imagination. He'd let this stomach thing go on too long, he hadn't been well for months and now nature was taking a hand, forcing him to recognise the fact: yes, that was it . . . it was imagination . . .

'Bruce.'

His father was long dead, yet as Daniels stared at the figure beside him he knew it contained a reality. This was no imagining on his part, no projection of a tired mind, no mental aberration. The thing there on the seat, whether from heaven or hell, was real. He shuddered, road and car forgotten at the horror he was facing.

'Bruce,' it was loud, authoritative, 'wheer am ya? When I catch ya I'll 'ave the skin off yer arse, yoh bloody little bastard!'

Daniels tried desperately to retain a grip on reason but suddenly he was a lad again, cringing against the rage in that voice. He tried to pull the car over, to get out and run as he had always run. But his fingers were rigid, welded to the plastic circle of the steering wheel, his right foot cemented to the accelerator.

'Wheer was yoh?'

The tone had altered. The thing that had left the grave to search for him had found him. He watched the head turn towards him. Black hair plastered wetly into the bull neck, slime and oil streaking black fingers down a face half rotted away. Pale worms wriggled at the corners of staring lifeless eyes, burrowing into flesh turned green by corruption.

'I'll tell yer where yoh was . . .' the voice grated and a large mouldering hand lunged upwards, fastening about his wrists, waves of putrid stench rising from the decaying body as it swivelled towards him. Daniels wanted to be sick, to puke the fear of boyhood from his system.

'. . . paradin' yer prick in front o' them wenches . . .'

The half-eaten fingers tightened.

'. . . down along the canal . . .'

Daniels saw the other hand move and loosen the heavy buckled belt.

'. . . well that'll be the last thing yoh will feel like doin' when ah'm finished.'

Bloated lips pulled back in a vicious snarl of a grin, the rotted hand holding the leather belt lifted trailing slime-covered weeds, the belt that had often left him senseless, the belt that had killed his mother. The hand fastened about his wrist began to pull.

'No!' His other hand suddenly free Daniels smashed a closed fist towards the horror beside him, towards the face that was no longer that of Jack Daniels. Towards a figure that stared at him. A figure with a handsome laughing face that even as he stared changed to a bruised beaten pulp, one half falling away into a ragged-edged hole.

'All be ready?'

'Everything as you said.'

'Then it be time.' Martha Sim looked at the two women sitting with her in her small kitchen. 'I thank you for the candle, Rosie.'

'I can help, Martha, as I've done times afore.' Rosie Harper handed the other woman the thick white candle, one of the kind made from pure beeswax, made by the Harpers for generations and used only by the village church.

'You sure as Tom 'Arper knows the use of this, he knows the reason of my asking?'

Rosie Harper nodded as she met the eyes glistening like ripe blackberries. 'My Tom knows the truth of it. He laid his 'and upon it and said the words just as you told. After seeing him at service last Sunday he agreed that priest needed all the help that could be given, and I be of the same mind, you must let me stay, three be stronger than two.'

'It might be the power that plagues that lad will be stronger than that of Martha Sim. Should it prove so then there must be the two of you, you and my Hilda, to stand beside the priest, two of you to battle the evil that be draining away his life.'

Glancing at Martha's daughter, Rosie Harper's brow creased, her eyes asking that Hilda Sim demand she stay but the younger woman shook her head.

'Mother be right, Aunt Rosie. There has to be someone who can fight for the Reverend.'

'But you don't know what it is you be challenging, you don't know the powers of the dark side, what it is your mother be up against.'

'We none of us knows,' Martha said quietly. 'That be my reason for saying that you, Rosie Harper, must save your hand to place with that of my daughter should I fail.'

'But I be going to work with you.'

'No, Hilda.' Martha's grey head swung several times.

'But I've always helped, always, from being a child.'

'You be versed in the ways of the old ones, and that is why you must not be with me tonight. There must be them remaining to challenge after me should it be the will of the Almighty that my own efforts to protect the lad be not enough. The two of you must leave this house, you must not be here when that evil comes, it must not know there are others who possess the knowledge.'

'But, mother . . .'

'No buts!' Martha's voice was firm. 'Stay with the 'Arpers, watch and pray if you will but take no step towards this house afore the breaking of dawn light. Now go, for the moment be fast approaching.'

The two women gone, Martha moved about the silent room collecting the things she would use, and all the time her senses strained to the silence. It would come, the evil that stalked the young priest, it would come and it would use its powers to destroy. Nonsense, the lad had called her warning. She crossed to a cupboard, reaching out a plain earthenware bowl and several small bottles. To him the old ways were something to be laughed at as young people laughed off all things. They said the war had been won and everything begun again, everything modern, everything new. But it was not new, beneath the surface the world's ancient heart was beating still, and the ancient evils lived on.

A prayer silent on her lips she took the bowl into the garden. Filling it with water she drew fresh from the well she glanced at the moon. It was rising with a ring around it. Martha smiled. The powers of light were present. Lifting the bowl towards the bright orb she stood a moment then turned quickly as she heard the sound, a rustle at the hedge, the brush of something against the gate. An animal? Her fingers wet from water spilled from the bowl she turned indoors. No, it was no animal watching from the shadows.

Indoors she took the cord she always wore from about her neck, pouring a little of the water over the stone it held. Plain brown with an eye-shaped hole at its centre, the stone was the most powerful of all her talismans, her most potent protection, her most cogent guardian. The All Seeing Eye. Without it she was vulnerable, open to the same evil that plagued the priest. But if she hoped to save him then to him must go its protection.

Taking a stub of pencil from among the articles she had assembled she wrote on the stone in thin spidery strokes: 'From all evil PETER DARLEY protect' then laid it alongside the candle she had fashioned into the shape of a man. She had touched the sleeve of the priest as he rose to leave after visiting her here in this house but neither he nor Hilda knew of the hair she had plucked from it, the reddish-brown hair she now took from a tiny cotton-lined box and wrapped around the wax figure.

Taking a taper to the fire she held it at the centre of the glowing embers, the pure heart that burned away malignancy, then returning to the table she lit two smaller, slimmer candles before turning off the overhead light. Beyond the window the moon edged charcoal clouds with silver. Gazing for a moment she breathed deeply, reaching open hands towards the moon then bringing them back to her chest and taking the light into herself, the powerful light of the moon at its full, which alone was her protection against the struggle to come. Behind her the twin candle flames burned tall and straight, only by their burning would her powers be sanctioned. Now she must finish what she had begun, and before the moon waned Peter Darley's fate would be decided.

Turning back to the table she dipped the third finger of her left hand into the bowl, the finger of love. Sprinkling drops of water over the wax effigy she began to whisper.

'From the heart comes the love, from the water comes the cleansing, from the stone comes protection.'

Around the walls of the kitchen shadows moved, advancing then receding, like veiled figures that watched her every move; across the room the embers of the fire flared into sudden blue-tipped flame as if disturbed by a sharp draught. For a few seconds Martha paused, every nerve in her body flaring like the flames of the fire. It was not too late, she could stop now . . . but to stop was to abandon the young priest, to leave him in the clutches of an evil that wanted more than his body, an evil that would possess his very soul. From every corner it seemed the moving shadows took voice, whispering her name, whispering 'Go back.'

Finger trembling, keeping her eyes from the shadows that called, she picked up a smaller earthenware dish then sprinkled salt from it in a circle enclosing the stone and the waxen figure, intoning quietly.

'Water, blood of the earth, cleanse all evil from thee; salt, the pure body of the earth, surround and protect thee; together they keep thee, let no spirit of Darkness approach thee, nor evil assail thee.'

From each corner of the room the whisper of voices increased; the shadows grew in size, spreading and darkening, covering walls and ceiling, enclosing Martha and the table in a tenebrous dusky veil. Martha breathed slowly. The forces of evil were close. To show fear now would be to seal her own death warrant. Exchanging the dish for the twig of rowan she had collected as the first touch of a rising sun kissed its leaves, her whisper hardly audible, she held it above the candle flame.

'Servant of the Dark Lord, thy power be broken as this twig be broken.'

Snapping the twig into two pieces she threw it into the fire, her whole body tensing against reprisal. Would she be strong enough, would the powers passed to her through countless women stand against the powers of Satan or would she be wiped away by the breath of its coming? The shadows had halted, the whisperings stilled, but she felt the presence of evil all around. It would not give up the priest easily. She had to force it into the open, force it to reveal the face of evil, bring it to herself.

Opening each of three tiny bottles in turn she tipped one drop of their contents into the bowl of water. Eyes fixed steadily on the locked door she spoke firmly.

'Oil of Cypress call thee forth. Oil of Juniper command thy presence. Oil of Cinnamon compel thee to me.'

Touching the tip of one finger into the bowl she dabbed it to the centre of her forehead and spoke slowly.

'My mind bind thy mind, my will bind thy will. The Powers of Light reveal thee, the Power of the All High banish thee.'

With the last word hardly finished the voices that had stilled rose in a crescendo tearing the stillness apart, the shadows that had halted cavorted in a dance of fury, while the door that had been firmly locked crashed in upon itself.

Her entire body shaking, Martha Sim breathed the tangy aroma of spice. Turning towards the door a gasp broke from her throat as she saw, dark on dark, the figure. At its back the vivid moon showed silver-gold hair touching the collar, the sudden flare of candles catching hyacinth-blue eyes that smiled from a handsome face.

My mind bind thy mind . . .

The well-shaped mouth moved soundlessly, the words heard only inside Martha's head.

. . . my will defeat thy will.

Lifting one hand, the figure shimmering in the open doorway waved it towards the table; at the same moment, a blast of wind exploded over the table, sweeping the waxen figure into the deepest part of the fire.

My will defeat thy will!

The words laughed out, the hand swept towards her and as Martha fell backwards she saw the handsome smiling face change, half of it swollen and purple with bruises, the other half a blackened jagged-edged hole.

Chapter Seventeen

So much for that! Kate Mallory swung her large leather bag on to her shoulder as she walked down the steps of Darlaston police station. The freckle-faced cop who had answered her questions hadn't looked old enough to be out of school but he'd been polite, that at least she could say, but providing the public with information? Either that part of his training was yet to be given or else the part that taught him a hundred ways to say no had been too well learned!

At the last of the three well-scrubbed steps she delved into the bag, coming up with a new pack of Rothmans. Coffin nails, her editor called them, whenever she dared light up anywhere near him. Well, Sidney Webb could hammer in as many as he liked when fastening the lid on her, just so long as he slipped a lighter and a few packs inside!

'Detective Inspector Daniels is not at the station.'

That had been the answer when she had asked to see him. Kate drew on the cigarette.

'I don't have that information.'

That one had followed her asking if there had been any word from the Commons regarding the inspector's preventing that MP from possibly being injured.

'The inspector did not say . . . perhaps the sergeant might be able to furnish you with that information.'

That had been the end. All she had asked was when would the inspector be back at the station. Had the KGB really been dissolved or had they simply transferred to the Darlaston cop shop! Lord, it had been like talking to one of those speaking toys kids had these days, monotonously repetitive without really saying anything. And the sergeant? Forget that . . . she'd wasted enough time trying to get music from a broken fiddle!

But she had interviewed that MP, if you could call half a dozen snatched words as he was ushered into his car an interview. He had been full of praise for the quick-witted inspector. So where was the evidence of his gratitude?

Kate Mallory drew deeply on her cigarette, holding the smoke in her mouth.

Had the Honourable Member of Parliament forgotten so quickly . . . or had his thanks taken some tangible form? A form the public were not being told about?

Releasing the smoke in a grey cloud she smiled. There was one reporter on the *Star* would be keeping a closer eye on the brave inspector.

*

Peter Darley pushed wearily to his feet, the food he had gone through the motions of preparing forgotten. Grey shadows ringed his eyes like painted circles, sleep had long ago suffered the same fate as his appetite.

Sleep . . . he turned towards the window, his tired eyes reaching out towards the quiet rectory garden . . . how long now since he had slept through a night? He laughed, a hollow mirthless sound that didn't make it past his throat. How long since that thing had taken possession of him? And prayer, long hours of begging forgiveness that brought no relief from the guilt tearing him apart and no relief from the touch of evil, that touch which was becoming an obsession and driving every other wish and heed before it until like an opium addict he yearned for that which was slowly destroying him.

He glanced at his watch though he needed no mechanical aid, the coldness at the pit of his stomach telling him it was time for Mass. Crossing the hall that smelled of polish, he entered the small room that served as his study. Light streamed through small panes of bevelled glass. Though not as ancient as the church the rectory had seen a few centuries. From the desk he picked up a sheaf of handwritten notes. Smudges of ink erased words on the pages.

Ask and it shall be given . . .

He stared at the words. The mercy of a forgiving God, that was the theme he had taken for his sermon. But how could he preach to others that which was denied to him? All men were equal in the sight of God, all who came to Him in truth were forgiven. Yet how could he stand in the pulpit and preach that when he had not received such forgiveness; when almost daily he felt the presence of the obscene evil that was robbing him of his faith?

Yet how could he not preach? It would be easier to end his life. With the notes of his sermon in his hand he left the rectory.

It was a crisp early autumn morning, fields and hedges sparkled with an unexpected coating of hoar frost. That had been one of the delights of coming to a country parish, being able to watch the colour and spectacle of each changing season, but today he walked unseeing along the narrow lane that led to the church. Frost would prove no deterrent for the regular few who attended Mass every Sunday regardless of the state of the weather. But today there would be more than the widows in their Sunday hats, more than the Harpers and the Briers, reared in the tradition of worship; there would be those who had come not in the hope of the Lord but in the hope of seeing something a little more physical. These were the sensation seekers wanting to see for themselves the shaking hands and the young face prematurely aged with grey expressionless fear.

A fear of what?

He followed the turn of the lane, its high hedges closing the white sprayed fields from view. That of course was the winning question; turn up for service and you might just get to see the answer. The repressed half laugh in his throat was pure bitterness. People hadn't got time for God . . . it took every moment just to make a living these days; wasn't that what many of his parishioners told him when he made his pastoral visits? But give them the faintest whiff of possible scandal and they would travel for miles: and he knew it was scandal the people of Monkswell had decided must lie at the root of their young priest's problems . . . after all, what else could it be? Not money problems, because the church took care of that sort of thing, didn't it? That left only one other thing it could be . . . a woman.

Reaching the boundary wall of the church he rested a hand on the ancient lych gate. If it were only that simple his parishioners would have understood and sympathised . . . but how many would offer the hand of sympathy after being told their priest had made love in their church . . . and that before the high altar.

It needed no answer.

Tiredly, eyes averted from the grey stone walls, he walked towards the church, his footsteps crunching on frosty ground. Reaching the huge oak door he paused, a prayer for help on his lips. Away to his left a crow screeched.

The vestry was dark and cold. The Reverend Darley shivered as he slipped the embroidered vestment over his head, his hand shaking as he smoothed the robe over waist and hips. But the sudden snap of cold was not the sole cause of his shaking hands, that was almost permanent these days and especially so when he was in church.

It only ever happened in church, never anywhere else, as he had told Philip Bartley when arranging the scouts' camping weekend. That weekend had been good, he thought, as he blinked away tears of weariness; whatever the evil that had settled on him it had not manifested itself at all that weekend. It was as though he had been released from a long prison sentence, there was a sense of freedom, the almost physical lifting of a heavy weight from his body. He turned towards a fly-specked mirror hanging from age-blackened beams. The relief had been short lived, the circles under his eyes testifying to its return.

Beyond the door a murmur of voices ruffled the silence, the congregation assembling for Mass. The small organ, a gift of Elias Simmowe, an early Victorian benefactor, and converted now to electric power by Sam Maden, the local electrician cum general handyman, swelled into the opening bars of the first hymn, the following shuffle of sound telling him the congregation had risen to its collective feet.

It was time.

His empty stomach rolled convulsively, draining the last vestiges of grey from his face and endowing it with a deathly pallor.

It was time, time to face those watching, seeking eyes.

The sermon notes it had taken so much effort to write dropped from his nerveless fingers.

'Lord of all hopefulness, Lord of all joy.' The hymn spilled into the stillness of the vestry.

Lord of all hopefulness . . . that was the message of the hymn. With God there was always hope, but his hope had all but died, destroyed by the torment of the evil which invaded his body and the agony of knowing the constant rejection of prayer.

'Whose trust ever childlike no cares could destroy.' Voices lifted their paean of praise.

His thin shoulders bent into a half circle the priest covered his face with trembling hands. 'O Lord,' he sobbed softly like a child withdrawn from the one love he had always known, 'look this day with mercy on thy servant . . . forgive my sins . . .'

Deep at the base of his stomach a flicker of warmth sparked into life and with it Peter Darley breathed a long relief-filled breath. At last God had heard his desperation. Today in the church he had defiled he would know the full mercy of the Lord's forgiveness.

Breath ratling in his lungs he grasped the twisted iron circle of the medieval door handle, stepping out of the vestry and into procession behind the two men who would serve as altar attendants.

'Lord of all gentleness, Lord of all calm . . .' the hymn went on. Within the silent circle of his mind now came a calmness of spirit he had not felt in many days, the calm and contentment that came from knowing his prayers had at last been acknowledged. A surge of happiness washed over him, a great purifying tidal wave that left no doubt, no uncertainty in its wake: the sin of Peter Darley was being washed away. He raised his eyes, seeking the high altar. Eternal God, he prayed, a smile lifting the corners of his drawn mouth, who changeth not as men change, who though we be faithless, yet abidest faithful, increase our faith . . . He breathed again, deeply as before, carrying the delicate scent of the floral decorations into his lungs.

At the base of his stomach a flicker of life roared into a flame. No flower in those vases held the perfume suddenly filling his soul, a perfume heady with the scent of spice.

It smashed the prayer from his mouth with savage fury, his stomach seeming to cave in upon itself.

It was with him!

That terrible force that seduced him mind and body, that filled him with a lust he could not deny, was present with him now in a church filled with people eager for spectacle. But it couldn't be. God had listened to his prayers, he had felt the warm touch of forgiveness, felt the life reborn within him. But the warmth was not the touch of God; he dragged at the air, sucking in that malignant scent, feeling it feed the carnal fires already ablaze in his groin. He had been wrong, the touch that had brought the beginnings of happiness, of calm, was not the hand of the Lord . . . it was the hand of Anna. He shuddered violently, missing his step.

'Steady, Vicar.' Tom Harper had been watching the nuances of emotion chase across the young priest's face, happiness then uncertainty and now . . . the churchwarden leaned forwards, a hand under Peter Darley's elbow. 'Steady, lad,' he whispered, as the priest stumbled on. Poor young bugger, he thought, whatever the lad had done he didn't deserve the terror that sat tight across his young face.

*

The shipment had gone out. Philip Bartley leaned into the comfortable rear seat of the Rover. Clifton Mather could have no more grumbles. Grumbles! He stared into the passing darkness. What bloody cause did *he* have to grumble? It wouldn't be him caught with five million pounds worth of drugs in his hands, it wouldn't be Mather got caught with anything, be it drugs or the likes of that pretty rent boy who had climbed out of that basket, not while Deputy Commissioner James Connor was on his team.

But not all coppers were like Connor. Bartley felt a sharp tingle of concern tickle along his veins. Daniels was no patsy of Mather and Daniels was suspicious, of that he was sure; otherwise why that raid on the Leys unit? How had he got to know of that shipment . . . how had he got to know of the drugs at all? Somebody had talked out of turn, the big question was *who*? He'd find that out, but right now it would pay to find out what it would take to call off Daniels, every bloke had his price and the little policeman was no exception; and every bloke *took* his price and kept eyes and mouth closed or found himself dead . . . and the little policeman was no exception to that either.

'We need petrol.'

Bartley glanced at the back of the head of the man who spoke. He'd felt safer since hiring Richard Torrey, there had been no more imagined hitch-hikers; but imagination or otherwise he liked Torrey at his back even when they were not in the car, it paid to take precautions against more than hitch-hikers and if what he had said when they had talked at the Abbey was anywhere near the truth, then this man knew how to handle himself.

'I'll pull in at the next station.'

Bartley nodded. He couldn't fault Torrey for the tank being near to empty, it had been he himself who had ordered they drive straight back from Brackley yesterday without stopping anywhere. No more imaginings? So what had been in that bedroom the night of the birthday party, what was it had lain in that bed beside him, played fingers over his crotch until he'd risen like a stallion?

'Do you need anything from the kiosk?'

Shaking his head Philip Bartley watched the tall figure stride towards the tiny shop attached to the garage forecourt. Did he need anything? He might have said 'a priest' but seeing what was happening to Peter Darley that would do no good either!

Framed in the doorway, his figure in sharp relief against the background, Richard Torrey paused, pushing the receipt for petrol into a leather wallet. Watching him, Philip Bartley gasped as the yellow light played over dark hair turning it gold. It was a trick of the light, no more than that. Releasing breath in a long shaking stream he closed his eyes. He had to pull himself together, he was letting imagination get the better of him.

'Do you want to call anywhere?'

'No.' Bartley answered as Torrey settled back into the driver's seat.

'Then it's straight on to Monkswell?'

It was a whispered, smiling answer. His eyes jerking open, Philip Bartley felt his heart hammer against his ribs, blood pound like a road drill in his ears, and in his nostrils the faint fragrant echo of spice. Head turned waiting for his reply, the face watched him. A face half shot away.

He should have seen a medic months ago. Inspector Bruce Daniels grimaced at the pain lancing through him. The bloody acid from his gut had burned his brains away, got him to thinking he was seeing ghosts! It had been a trick of the mind, he had only thought he'd touched something slimy in that glove compartment, thought he'd seen the face of his father in the seat beside him, a face that changed even as it looked at him; but thoughts could put pictures in the mind, persuade the brain that what was merely illusion was real: and it had seemed real to him, so real it had him as terrified as he had been when a lad, so terrified he had struck out, leaving the car to career off the road. And now here he was with multiple injuries and a spinal condition that would keep him out of action for months. He should think himself lucky, the doctors had told him, how he hadn't been killed outright was a mystery to them. Mystery! He laughed, a cynical gurgle that never left his throat. He could tell them mystery, tell them of a figure there with him in that car, a man dead some thirty years, a man ready to beat him as he had beaten him all those years before, a heavy thick-set man covered in slime and weeds, his worm-eaten face changing to a handsome laughing one that suddenly became a purple bruised mask, half of it dropping away into a black gaping hole; he could tell them but he wouldn't, a hospital was bad enough to spend months in, the bloody madhouse would be worse! And they *would* think him out of his mind. Daniels drew a deep breath. He couldn't be sure he wasn't!

'They say you won't be home for months . . .'

Marjorie sounded relieved. And so was he. He almost smiled. Every cloud had its silver lining but it also had its black side, and the black side to his cloud was the fact that yet again promotion would pass him by. Yes, he could kiss that pipe-dream goodbye, a politician's gratitude wouldn't last long enough to be around when he left this hospital and he could hardly hope for it to be given while he was unable to fulfil his duties.

'. . . I'll come as often as I can . . .'

Christ, Marjorie had never talked as much! It was like a river going on and on, he couldn't stomach much more! Closing his eyes he let it wash over him allowing it no inroad on his thoughts.

What duties was Connor performing? How far was he up the arses of those men who had been at that party? Was he a flossie same as Mather, were they all perverts? That was one question he wouldn't spend time pondering, he'd seen for himself. Oh, they were all up to more than shirt lifting, he was convinced of that, and they could all end up behind bars, but to put them there he needed proof, same as he needed proof about Torrey and the tart from the canal and he wouldn't get that lying in a hospital bed.

He had burned his boats. Torrey watched the shadows dance on the ceiling of his room. He had relinquished the tenancy of his council house, consigned everything he had owned to the scrap heap and turned his back. It might almost have been as if he had died as well as Anna.

'Ye brought nothing into the world and ye shall take nothing from it.'

The words preached so often during his years at school spoke softly in his mind. So it had proved with Anna; naked as the day of its birth the body had been drawn from the canal. Whoever was responsible for the murder hadn't wanted the corpse recognised, hadn't wanted any claimants; and that was the way it probably would have turned out had the killer chosen some other town in which to dump the body. And what was he doing about it, what was he doing to bring that killer to justice? Nothing . . . he was doing nothing! He'd got himself an easy little number driving Philip Bartley. He'd changed his house in Dangerfield Lane for a cottage in the back of nowhere, how could he hope to find Anna's killer living like this? Or was agreeing to live here the excuse he had found himself, was it because he knew he stood no chance of finding the one responsible that he'd come so far from the scene and stayed? And if he went, what then? He'd no job to go to, no home to live in and a police inspector who was taking more than a casual interest in him. Now why was that?

Somewhere in the grounds of the Abbey an owl hooted and was answered in the same eerie vein. Turning his head Torrey stared towards the window whose curtains he didn't bother to draw. If there was anybody out there who got turned on by the sight of him sporting no more than a pair of pyjama bottoms then they were welcome to watch; now he watched the branches spread wide black patterns on a silver background.

Daniels had come to the house. His thoughts switched back. He'd asked a number of questions but though they were meant to be angled towards Anna he'd felt Daniels was after different game. But which particular animal was the man tracking, could it have been one of those present at that birthday bash? He'd watched the man's face the whole evening, watched frown deepen to scowl, distaste turn to disgust – then with the opening of that basket . . . Torrey smiled at the memory . . . Daniels's face had become a picture, the loathing he felt plain for everybody to see, only nobody had except him, the rest were all too occupied with the rise of Venus. Daniels had left then, at least he had been free to please himself while he, Torrey, had been forced to wait it out.

Outside the owls hooted again; one call following the other like an echo on the silence. Torrey closed his eyes.

That was the wrong word to use. He hadn't been forced to stay at that house any more than he was being forced to stay at this one, nobody forced Richard Torrey to do anything he didn't want to. The truth was as he'd realised before. Here he had found the excuse he needed, the excuse to do nothing about Anna's murder, here was not like being in the house they had shared together, here he wasn't constantly reminded of the things they'd done, of what they had meant to each other. But he, it seemed, had not meant as much to Anna. If he had, why had she left? Rolling on to his stomach he pressed his face into the pillow. Here he didn't have to face up to that question. But as sleep still refused to soothe, Torrey knew he was continuing to make excuses. No matter where he lived that was one thing that would stay with him, one question he would always have to face.

Chapter Eighteen

'The wine, Father,' Tom Harper prompted as he had throughout the service. Something was terribly wrong, something had Peter Darley in a hold he couldn't break. He looked at the milk-pale face, the eyes tortured by God only knew what. At the priest's left hand Tom's counterpart rang a tiny brass bell. 'The wine,' Tom Harper whispered again, 'you must elevate the wine!'

Again the brass bell sounded, three short tinkling notes. Deep in his private nightmare Peter Darley fought to respond. Dropping low to one knee he made his obeisance to the Holy Presence then rose and taking the silver chalice lifted it to level with his forehead, shuddering as metaphysical fingers moved against his groin, fanning across his stomach, touching his navel, each in turn tracing a breathtaking line downwards. It had begun the moment he took his place before the altar, the touching and the stroking. Even in his worst moments he had never thought the evil that followed him would manifest before a congregation, but it had and he was power-less against it.

As if knowing his thoughts and wanting to prove the rightness of them unreal hands cupped his testicles, tormenting the rock-hard flesh between his legs. Above his head the silver chalice rocked from the unstoppable surge of pleasure-filled agony, sending slops of dark red wine over the rim.

Tom Harper glanced across to the man officiating on the other side of the priest, a slight shake of his head halting an interceptive move. They couldn't take the chalice from the priest's hands, not in full view of the congregation. They would steer him through the giving of Holy Communion then tell the worshippers Father Darley was unwell and could not continue. He watched the priest lower the cup jerkily to the table, his breathing shallow. No one could argue the decision. From the organ loft strains of quiet music floated across the body of the church; strands of delicate colours from stained-glass windows streaked the pale light of a winter in the first throes of birth, tossing transparent ribbons about the shoulders of people moving towards the communion rail.

Across the remainder of the congregation kneeling in their pews, heads bent in silent prayer, a figure dressed in blue denims and loose jacket stared unblinking at the priest.

One by one the communicants knelt on the small embroidered hassocks lined at the foot of the well-polished rail, some with hands clasped in prayer, others watching the altar attendants prepare the bread and wine.

The unreal hands continued their touching, their stroking, as they had since the moment he had begun Mass.

'Ready, Peter?'

'Yes . . . yes, now . . . now . . . please now . . .' Yet it was not his altar attendant Peter Darley heard nor his altar attendant he was answering but a soft seductive voice.

'. . . don't leave . . . not any more . . . don't . . .' His hand clutched the base of his stomach.

'Father!' Tom Harper glanced nervously towards the waiting communicants. Had any of them heard . . . seen? 'Father?' He returned his attention to the priest, seeing the fine mist of sweat on the upper lip, the glaze blinding the eyes. 'Are you all right . . . would you rather we called a halt to the service?'

At the rear of the church the figure in blue watched with an unwavering hyacinth gaze.

'What?' Peter Darley blinked as though suddenly emerging into light. 'What was that, Tom?'

'You're not well, man,' Tom Harper answered, 'let me tell the congregation so now, they'll understand.'

'No!' The priest took the silver bowl of round wafers in his hand. 'I won't give in,' he murmured, moving towards the waiting line of worshippers, 'I won't let it win.'

'Receive the Body of Christ.'

He placed a thin wafer on the tongue of the first communicant.

At the back of the church the blue eyes lifted.

'Receive the . . .' Peter Darley faltered. Beneath his robes soft hands caressed his body. 'Receive . . .' the gentle rhythm dragged at his mind. At his elbow a slight push brought temporary sanity.

'Receive the Body of Christ.' He moved along the kneeling line but the hands were already back, the tip of a finger tracing over his testicles and along the rigid length of flesh. Around him the smell of damp stone mingled with incense but he smelt only the sweet sharp tang of spice.

In the rear pew golden eyebrows drew together in concentration.

'Receive . . . receive . . .'

Communion wafer in hand Peter Darley faltered, almost dropping the bowl, the touch against his genitals changing to the warm moistness of a mouth, the tracing finger to the tip of a tongue. Feel my mouth, Peter. The seductive voice was in his head. Feel it, Peter, your warm little cave you called it, your own little place of love. Feel it, Peter . . .

'Receive the Body . . .' Almost mindless of what he did, Peter Darley placed a wafer on the waiting tongue.

You liked it when I sucked you, Peter, when I took you in my mouth . . . The voice whispered velvet music, the finger tormented his flesh, stroking to the point of eruption then withdrawing at the last moment, extending the excruciating longing . . .

You can have that again, Peter, the soft wetness you've craved so long; you don't have to crave any more, it's here waiting for you . . .

Enveloped in the fog of passion the priest looked down at the man kneeling before him.

'Receive the Body . . .'

Cropped brown hair changed to shoulder-touching gold.

'Receive the Body . . .'

Old brown eyes adopted the brilliance of hyacinths.

It's here for you, Peter; you want it, don't you . . . you want it so very much . . .

Beneath the robes of Mass the priest's body danced to the music of his own destruction.

'Receive the Body.'

Kneeling before him, a man's lips parting to receive the Eucharist became full and moist, the tongue rested on perfect white teeth then curved outwards and upwards, its invitation explicit.

I want it too, Peter . . . The witchery sang in his mind corroding his will, consuming the last of his defences. I want to feel you in my mouth, now, Peter . . . now!

In the half shadows that clothed the rear of the ancient church the hyacinth eyes flared.

At the altar rail the priest shuddered and the bowl dropped, spilling its fragile contents over the scarlet carpet.

'Receive the Body.' It was half shout, half moan, Peter Darley slumping forward on to the communion rail, hands ripping away the long robes.

A single stream of sunlight entering a high window touched the head of the figure dressed in faded blue gilding the fair hair to deeper gold, its reflection adding flames to the brilliant hyacinth gaze that travelled the length of the nave to where the priest was being helped to stand, and as their eyes locked the seductive mouth curved into a slow smile. For a moment the handsome face watched the trembling priest, then half of it fell away into a black hole.

'You be sure you be feeling better, lad?' Tom Harper looked worriedly at the pale face of the priest. What in the world had got into him, what had made him do such a terrible thing? He'd never live this down, not in a hundred years he wouldn't, to say nothing of the man who'd been hit on the head by the falling communion bowl. It was his fault, he shuffled his feet, embarrassment plain in every move; he'd seen the lad were not well, he should have called off the Mass, wouldn't have made no difference no how putting it off for one week. It would have created far less of a stir than letting it proceed had done.

'Thank you, Tom, I'm perfectly recovered.'

'Well I still says you should get yourself along to Doctor Mellish, he would 'ave been at Mass 'ceptin' the lass over at Yew Tree Cottage went into labour earlier on this morning but he be sure to be home by now.'

'Yes.' Peter Darley's head stayed lowered. 'I will go to see Doctor Mellish.'

'I'll go with you.'

'No!' The priest answered quickly. 'I would like to be by myself for a little while, but thank you for the offer, Tom.'

'I knows what you means.' Tom Harper removed his

vestments, hanging them carefully in the tall cupboard that almost filled the small vestry. 'I'll mek sure there be no folk dallying outside awaiting on you coming out. But mind you does as you says and go see the doctor.'

The heavy door closing behind the other man, Peter Darley covered his face with his hands, his shoulders racking with long-drawn sobs. 'Why?' he cried aloud. 'Why do this to me?'

But he knew why, just as well as he knew who. But if he had done what had been asked of him, he would have had to leave his church, to upset the comfort of his own life; and that he had been too selfish to do.

You wanted jam on both sides of your bread, Peter.

Soft and seductive as before the velvety voice whispered in his mind but this time the reaction was one of revulsion. This was evil for the sake of evil. Vengeance could have been taken without despoiling the church. But he had already done that, he had already committed that sin, carnal and unforgivable.

You should have done what I asked, Peter. The voice in his mind became hard, condemning. But you wouldn't, you didn't want anyone to know, didn't want the villagers to see their priest in his true light.

It was true. In his mind's eye Peter Darley saw the door to his sitting room at the rectory fly open and a figure rush in, neck length golden hair ruffled from running, eyes the special blue of early hyacinths gleaming with anger.

'*Is something wrong?*' Darley had stood up, a sudden alarm chasing along his veins.

'*Not for me, not any more.*' Well-shaped lips had smiled

showing white, perfectly even teeth. *'I've left the Abbey, Peter. I've left Philip Bartley for good.'*

'But why, for what reason?'

'Why!' Anna's voice, light and musical, had risen several octaves. *'Why, cos the man's a bastard, a selfish jealous overbearing bastard!'*

Holding his face in his hands Peter Darley remembered the feeling of concern, knowing it had flashed across his eyes. *'Jealous?'* He had spoken just that one word.

Anna had flounced to the window. He remembered the relief of seeing the heavy drapes being drawn, at least no one could see in.

'Yes, jealous!' The answer had been flung across the room. *'Though why the bastard should be beats me, he has enough on the side himself.'*

The chenille cloth covering the table had felt so soft in his fingers. The priest's hand moved slightly as if feeling it now. He had looked at it as he'd asked, *'What do you mean?'*

Anna's answer had been fast and furious, eyes burning across at him like blue fire. *'Mean! What the hell do you think I mean? You are a priest, Peter, but you're no bloody saint and you're not blind either, you've seen them up there, the scout masters, the occasional office boy down for a weekend in the country, and don't pretend you don't know why they get invited. Philip Bartley's sexual appetite, like his business, is varied and well developed. He likes it often and in different packaging, but because I fancied a little extra he comes over strong, the bloody hypocrite!'*

'Anna, are you saying Philip found out that you are seeing . . . seeing another man?' Darley had pushed a hand through his hair, pushing it away from his forehead.

'Yes. Oh don't worry, Peter, it's not you, Philip hasn't any idea about you.'

Darley's face had twisted, looking for a moment as if he were about to throw up. 'Then there are others . . . I thought that Philip was the only . . . that there was just . . .' He had dropped heavily on to a chair beside the table.

'Of course there were only two.' Anna's voice had rung angrily, blind to the pain on the man's face.

'Don't lie.' Darley's shoulders slumped now as they had then. 'Don't lie, Anna, it doesn't help.'

'These others,' Anna had crossed to the table, fingers walking across the soft cloth, 'they didn't mean anything to me, they were a joke, a one-night stand, no more.'

'Your bit on the side, in fact.'

Anna had fingered the cloth making no answer.

'Who was it, Anna?' Darley seemed to see again the mustard chenille cloth. 'Who was the man Philip found you with?'

For a moment Anna had hesitated, then answered, 'Tom Shelley.'

'Tom Shelley!' Darley's head had snapped up. 'Tom Shelley from the village?'

Anna had nodded.

'But he . . . he's little more than fifteen! Anna . . . he's no more than a boy!'

'Old enough!' Anna's full lips had parted. 'He knew what it was all about.'

Darley's hands dropped and spread motionless on his knees, the voice in his mind going on relentlessly. 'So what did Philip say?'

'He said he had a reputation to keep up in Monkswell, my having it off with the odd scout was one thing but when it came to messing around with boys from the village it was something else again; he wasn't going to have his life here ruined by cheap shit that didn't have enough sense to know when to say no. That was when he told me to clear out. But my playing around wasn't the reason he threw me out, the real reason was jealousy. He fancied Tom Shelley but I'd got there first.'

'What do you intend to do now?'

'I'm going to stay here.' Anna had moved to stand beside him then, slender-fingered hands resting on his shoulders. 'It's all happened for the best, Peter, don't you see?' The golden head had come close to his, the moist tongue nuzzling an ear. 'I can stay here now, we can be together, the two of us . . .'

'No!' Darley jerked, remembering how he had brushed the hands away, scrambling to the opposite side of the table. 'No, Anna, you can't stay here.'

'Why not?' Anna had smiled the enticement of a lover. 'Think of it, Peter, no more quick rides in the church but long nights together in bed, in each other's arms . . . in each other's mouths . . .'

'No!' He had rushed to the ancient sideboard and dragged a box from a drawer. Flinging the handful of notes and coins across the table he had turned away, his words riding over his shoulder: 'Take it . . . take it and go!'

Peter Darley, consecrated priest of God! He stared into the shadowed stillness. A man full of Christian charity . . . until that charity had threatened his own well-being.

Pushing slowly to his feet he began to remove his robes.

'You should 'ave seen, Martha, eh Lord above! It was dreadful, simply dreadful.'

'I thank the Lord I weren't there.' Martha Sim shook her head. "Tis a blessing the Almighty laid on me this day even though I didn't go to that church and worship Him, a blessing I falls short of for I should 'ave warned . . .'

'You don't be to blame, mother,' Hilda Sim broke in quickly. 'You tried to warn him afore but he would have none of it.'

'Then I should have tried again, I should have gone on a'trying until I made him see sense.'

'I thinks you tried hard enough,' Rosie Harper said, taking a long sip from the tea Hilda had brewed. 'You almost got yourself killed a'trying.'

'I was wrong.' Martha stared at the flames reflecting on the brass firedogs her daughter kept brilliantly polished. 'I thought my powers alone would be strong enough but they wasn't. Whatever the presence that plagues Peter Darley draws its powers from a high source. I hadn't thought for it to be so powerful but that be a mistake I'll not be for making a second time.'

'A second time!' Rosie's cup hit the saucer with a clang. 'You don't means you be going to try fighting it a second time!'

Martha Sim's head moved slowly on her lined neck. 'I has to, ain't nobody else to fight for the lad and I won't see no devil take him.'

'You hear that, girl?' Rosie looked up as Hilda bustled in with hot buttered scones and a pot of bilberry jam balanced on a tray. 'Your mother be for trying again.'

Lowering the tray to the table Hilda handed the older woman a china plate, its rim banded with gold-tipped yellow tea roses. Her smile bland she asked, 'Mother be for trying what, Aunt Rosie?'

'Now don't you go coming the innocent with me, girl!' Rosie snorted. 'I've wiped your bottom as many times as your mother has, I knows you inside out, Hilda Sim, so don't go trying to fool me, you knows what it is I be talking of, your mother be for calling on the spirits, that's what her be for trying!'

'It be the only way, you has to fight fire with fire.'

'But there be fires and there be infernos,' Rosie answered hotly. 'And you knows well enough that power be one you stood no chance against, call it back and it be like to kill you.'

'And if I don't then it be like to kill the priest,' Martha answered quietly. 'You yourself have told what happened this morning in that church, you told of the terror on the lad's face, saw that evil bring him down. Who can tell what it might do next, what terrible thing it will force him to commit; I can't, Rosie Harper, and neither can you. But this I knows, either we fight that presence, send it back to the darkness it came from, or it will take Peter Darley, drag him into that pit from which there is no escape. Do you want that, Rosie? Can either of us live with that on our conscience? I don't know the channel it used to come here, but that it came to claim the priest body and soul, that I does know.'

'But you don't have powers enough to drive that demon away, that be proved already.'

'Not on her own she don't.' Hilda's smile remained bland. 'But next time she will not be on her own, I'll be with her, my powers will be joined with hers.'

'No!' Martha's head lifted sharply. 'I won't have you doing that, you must stay away . . . away from the house, away from me. I told you last time, you has to be here lessen I fails, and it must be that way again.'

Spreading a scone with jam Hilda bit into it, one finger brushing a crumb from the corner of her mouth before she replied.

'Either I stay with you, mother, put my powers beside yours, or there will be no more trying. By your own admission you alone be no match for whatever be riding Peter Darley's shadow, it needs more than that if it is to be banished, but both of us working together, we can do it.'

'Then I be with you as well.' Rosie was adamant. 'Three sets of hands be quicker than two, three tongues calling on the powers of good carry louder than two.'

'We will need candles same as before, will Tom be able . . .'

'I be able to supply candles of the kind you asks . . .'

The three women turned to look at Tom Harper standing in the doorway of the Sim kitchen.

'. . . but there'll be no call for them. I just come from the church. Peter Darley has 'anged himself.'

Chapter Nineteen

'When was this, Mrs Barnes?'

'Must 'ave been soon after Mass this morning, or so Rosie Harper tells me. Seems 'er Tom were last to speak wi' him, but why would a young lad like him go 'ang 'isself, it don't make no sense.'

'No, no sense at all.' His face paling visibly, Philip Bartley tried to still the trembling of his hands.

'Such a nice lad, always a smile and a kind word for everybody . . . why would he want to go do a thing like that?'

He knew why and he knew what, but to say so would have everybody think him crazy.

'Who can say what it is makes a man take so drastic a step? But the shock has you shaking like a leaf, I insist you go home and rest. Never mind food for me, I can manage for one day.' He wanted the place to himself, he could think better that way than by closing himself off in his room.

'I does admit Rosie Harper's news has me fair knocked for six.' The woman's tears streamed over ample cheeks.

'Then you do as I say, go home and rest.' Taking his housekeeper's elbow Philip Bartley steered her towards the kitchen and the rear entrance of the house, his own shaking absorbed by hers. At the door he watched the woman walk towards the cottage she shared with her husband. 'Mrs Barnes.' He waited as the housekeeper turned. 'Would you ask George to go round to the Harpers', tell Tom I would like a word with him?'

Christ, what in hell had got into Darley! Turning back into the empty kitchen he struck a fist against the door lintel. He'd been all right after dinner the other night, whatever it was had rattled him he was over it by the time he left the Abbey.

But *he* wasn't over it, he was shit scared. His hand still shaking, Philip Bartley poured himself a stiff measure of whisky. It was early in the day to turn to drink but it wasn't every day a friend topped himself. But what had made Darley so scared? Not ghosts, no man in his right mind would believe in the existence of ghosts, if that had been the case the Church could have dealt with it, they had the means of chasing phantoms; what did they call it, exorcism? Yes, had ghosts been Peter Darley's problem he would have had that institution handle it.

Swallowing a mouthful of whisky he paced restlessly about the room. It had to be something else, something that little shit of a prostitute had left behind, something Anna had dreamed up just in case . . . but what, and, more to the point, did it somehow include his own death?

*

'Can I ask how long you've known the deceased, sir?'

'I met Peter for the first time on coming to live at the Abbey, some four or five years ago. He asked if the scouts might use the top field for a weekend.'

It had been three days since the suicide and Philip Bartley, at least so far as the outside world was concerned, was his natural self.

'Was that as far as it went, you didn't . . . mix with the vicar?'

He had already answered questions put by the local constable. Bartley felt a ripple of irritation as he looked at the inspector brought in from Shrewsbury.

'If you mean did Peter and I socialise outside of his duties with the Church, then no. I saw him only in this house and then only on those occasions he called to discuss a camping event for the scouts or the guides.'

'But not in church . . . I take it you are not a church-goer?'

'Do I take it you are, Inspector?'

This one was dressed in no shabby tweed jacket, he was no Bruce Daniels but he was every bit as devious. Philip Bartley looked evenly at the policeman. Devious he might be but as smart arses go he'd met his match.

'On his visits here did the vicar ever seem upset, worried in any way?'

If his last reply, meant to be blasé, had made any impression at all it didn't show in the inspector's even tone. Bartley mentally commended the police officer.

'I did remark upon the fact he seemed a little overtired when he had dinner here last week; he put it down to working late on his sermon. It appeared it proved something of a chore, so much so he made a habit of putting off writing it until the last minute; you might call it a bad habit.'

'And was that his only one . . . bad habit, sir?'

It was quick, thrust like a rapier. Well done, Inspector! Philip Bartley smiled inwardly.

'I wouldn't know about that.' He answered smoothly. 'But in a place like Monkswell any other would be hard to keep hidden. It may be a small village but its inhabitants are far from stupid and none as I know of are blind; anyone worth his salt should be able to find the answer to that question!'

Rising to his feet the inspector nodded. 'Salt is a useful commodity, Mr Bartley, it not only flavours and preserves, it is known to kill slugs. And fortunately it is in plentiful supply! . . . Oh!' He turned before reaching the door. 'Tell me, sir, do you have any idea why the vicar would strip naked before going outside to hang himself?'

If it was aimed to surprise then the clever copper had his sights way off line! Philip Bartley looked coolly at both men turned to face him. 'I asked Tom Harper the same thing. He has lived all of his life in Monkswell and understands better than I the feelings of the villagers.'

'Feelings?' The police officer frowned.

'Yes.' Bartley nodded. 'I wanted to offer any help that might be needed with the funeral – expenses and the like – but I didn't want to tread on anybody's toes, so I asked

Tom to come to the house. Naturally we spoke of what had happened during morning service and I asked if Tom could guess the reasoning behind Peter's removing his clothes before taking his own life.'

'And what was Mr Harper's answer . . . if you don't mind my asking?'

Meeting the other man's eyes, Philip Bartley allowed the trace of a frown to nestle between his brows. 'Why would I mind, Inspector? I'm sure your *only* interest is in discovering the truth.' Hesitating a moment, seeing the barb strike, he went on. 'Tom had no ideas of his own as to why but said Rosie – Mrs Harper – and a friend of hers reckoned he removed his clothing rather than taint church vestments with the sin he was about to commit; they also thought he deliberately chose to end his life in the field opposite rather than kill himself on sacred ground. To me that seems perfectly feasible. You see, Inspector, even though I am no churchgoer I do know that suicide is considered a sin in the eyes of the Christian faith and to have it take place in the building or the grounds would require the act of re-consecration.'

'And you think the expense of that affected Darley's decision?'

The frown remaining light, sardonic; Philip Bartley shook his head. 'Not the expense, Inspector. Peter's concern would be the aftermath. I did not know him awfully well but it was well enough to realise he knew you can clear a mess from a carpet but it always leaves behind a stain. The church . . . his church . . . would have been re-consecrated but in the belief of the villagers it would always bear the mark of his sin. Like them, I believe Peter Darley did not want that.'

No, Darley hadn't wanted that. Seeing the two police-men out, Philip Bartley returned to the sitting room, dropping heavily into a chair. And *he* didn't want coppers nosing about. Tip over a stone and you might find a worm, tip over a second and you might find a whole bloody can of them!

'The evil were there in that church the mornin' of Peter Darley's last taking of a service, and it were there again today.'

'That don't seem right somehow, Martha.' Rosie Harper walked beside the figure she had lived alongside, child and woman, their steps as much in harmony as their minds. 'If it were the Reverend it wanted, and it were, seeing as it has plagued no other body, then it got what it come for and would have no need of remaining.'

'Yet remained it has!' Martha Sim answered doggedly. 'I felt it during that buryin' as surely as I felt it the night I called on the old powers. It be here in this village so sure as I be!'

'But for what?'

'To take another!'

'What be that you says?' Rosie Harper looked astounded.

Her footsteps never faltering, Martha followed the rest of the villagers as they left the sheltered spot beyond the wall of the churchyard, its newly dug grave encompassed with floral tributes.

'I says it be remaining so as to take another. Peter Darley don't be the only one it come for, he weren't alone in what he done.'

'Be you saying that there be another body in the village committed the same sacrilege, some other defiled the church?'

A little way ahead, Hilda Sim nodded goodbye to the Barneses as the couple turned off along the track that led to their cottage, then stood waiting for her mother to catch up to her.

'No, I don't be saying that,' Martha replied as they drew level. 'You has the powers same as me, Rosie Harper, you knows there was none other in the church when that act took place, and none ever seen the Reverend and that other one together save Enoch Summers and he would never speak of it to nobody 'ceptin' us two.'

'Then be it Enoch as you think that devil will claim next?'

No invitation needed between them, Rosie followed into the cottage, settling at the kitchen table as Hilda immediately set about the business of brewing tea.

'It won't be Enoch Summers will be touched nor none other as has spent their life in Monkswell.' Martha groaned softly as she settled into her own chair drawn close to the glowing fire. 'I'll say no more 'cepting this. It were none of us brought this evil among us. It rides on the shoulders of another and it clings tight. I fears there be more evil yet for it to feed on.'

Richard Torrey guided the Rover expertly along the narrow lanes, the trees interspersed between high hedges holding desperately to foliage deeply garbed in the colours of late autumn. There had been a covering of hoar frost the day that priest had hanged himself but it had melted quickly and there had been no more since. That wasn't the only thing there had been no more of! He dropped to first gear, nursing the hedge as a tractor trundled past. The police had carried out their investigation, 'There was no need of further enquiries.' Now where had he heard that one before?

Sliding smoothly through the gears he brought the car back to speed. Closing files seemed to be a trend growing in popularity, first Darlaston and now here; or was it a spread of that disease commonly called idleitis? Was it easier to close a case than to follow it up?

Pulling on to the A5 he pressed down on the accelerator, the wider road answering some inner urge. There had been no more word of Anna, nobody had been found to answer for the killing, and it seemed there would be no more word of that priest or why he died. But to be fair, in his case there had been no murder, no one had blasted his face with a shotgun, his had been suicide. The Coroner's verdict had been that he had taken his own life whilst the balance of his mind was disturbed. But Anna's death had been murder, what disturbed mind had blasted a shotgun into that attractive laughing face, what deranged brain had decided that verdict?

'I won't be needing the car until around six.' Philip Bartley smiled as they took the turning for Darlaston. 'Why not take it and have yourself a bit of fun, pick up a girl, or even two if you have the energy, and you should have, for there's nothing in Monkswell worth taking your trousers off for.'

Torrey glanced in the driving mirror. Bartley had lost whatever it was had him scared, in fact since that priest's death he had seemed a bundle of joy; strange that . . . they were friends and, close or not, Bartley might have shown a longer display of something other than relief . . . yes, come to think of it, that was the description that fitted Bartley exactly . . . the man was relieved. Over what? Turning into the yard of the large supermarket Bartley had built on the Leys, Torrey pulled into the parking space marked with his employer's name. Bartley had made himself into a big noise in a little town and intended everyone to hear the echo! The only trouble with echoes was they were sometimes heard by the wrong folk.

'Take it.' Bartley's smile was broad as he climbed from the back of the car. 'Take the motor, cruise around and find yourself a bit of local skirt then rip it off, have yourself an afternoon in bed!'

'I might do that.' Torrey forced an answering smile.

'Never mind the "might" man, go for it, remember . . . the kid that hesitates never gets a kick at the ball!'

Bartley hadn't hesitated. Torrey glanced after the other man entering through a side door of a shop so big his mother would never have believed it; the huge plate-glass windows covered with posters proclaiming fantastic savings on this and wonderful not-to-be-repeated offers on that. And this wasn't his only shop; from what he had heard when talking with assistants in the staff canteen he knew Bartley had the same going in every town in the Black Country. Nice! He slammed the door of the car shut. But even so you wouldn't think selling groceries alone would bring the profits Bartley needed to finance his comfy little lifestyle. Perhaps it wasn't only groceries. Torrey ran another glance over the building. There had also been talk in that canteen of a police raid not so very long ago and of a certain doctor being sent down. But not Bartley, he had not been there, knew nothing about it, so they said. Torrey turned away and headed for the town. Now that was one thing he would never buy from Bartley Supermarkets!

'What about a shot of you actually working one of the machines, Mr Connor?'

Deputy Commissioner James Connor coughed several times, trying to clear the taste from his throat before answering the woman journalist. All teeth and pencil! He swallowed the taste that had plagued him for days and spoilt his nights. Bloody paparazzi, they'd be there when he took a piss if he let 'em!

He forced a smile against the returning taste in his mouth. He knew where he'd like to shove the woman's pencil, the same place he'd shove the straggle of cameras strewn across the scrawny chest of the photographer she had with her.

He rubbed a hand beneath his nostrils; this stink had him all riled up, if only he could get rid of it. Across the heads of the crowd he caught the lift of a camera. He must be careful, the bloody newspapers caught everything and he couldn't afford to show his irritation in public. He had been browbeaten into agreeing to open this combined work experience and leisure centre. 'It would present a caring view of the force,' that PRO had said, 'show the police were interested in getting kids off the streets, we might even have a few PCs assigned to doing a stint alongside the kids.' Psychological bloody blackmail! He blew several short snuffling blasts of air through his nostrils, stopping abruptly as he caught the smile from the back of the small crowd. Bloody public relations officers! Didn't know their arse from their elbow.

'What about a shot of Mr Mather instead?' He turned away from the camera. 'It is his money built the place after all.' The suggestion didn't stand a hope in hell. He knew the bloody media only too well, they'd have their pound of flesh then come back for the bones.

'Not exactly true.' Clifton Mather shook his head, his expertly fashioned hair lifting slightly on a sudden breeze. 'The centre is a gift of Coton Enterprises and as their representative I am pleased to attend its opening, but in turn I am certain Coton Enterprises would agree I let the police take the heat!'

A ripple of laughter broke out from the gathered representatives of the press.

'You heard him, Mr Connor,' the young woman reporter was determined, 'so how about a little show up front?'

James Connor raised his hands in surrender, the move bringing another titter of approval from the watching crowd. Except from Kate Mallory. A prominent journalist with the *Star*, she had a daily diet of crap and the taste didn't impress her any more. She glanced at Mather, Managing Director of Coton, the largest pharmaceutical corporation in the world, and at the tall figure beside him – Maxwell Seton, Managing Director of Satel, ditto in the world of communications, both companies being constituent corporations of Coton Enterprises. She glanced across at another woman reporter now urging the Deputy Commissioner to pose, but her mind was elsewhere. Clifton Mather was head of Coton Pharmaceuticals, a busy man, arguably too busy to give time to a venue like this; but then so was Seton. So why were they opening a two-bit centre kids would give the go-by to once they realised no work equalled no pay? And why two, and both Managing Directors! Why such high-powered execs for a PR job any ordinary company manager could have done? Interesting! Kate Mallory's mental filing system clicked.

'So where shall I stand?' James Connor turned to the middle-aged man given the job of running the centre.

'If you're going near the machines then a pair of overalls might be more convincing and help to keep any dirt off your suit,' Bart Melia answered, signalling for a pair of overalls to be fetched.

That's right. Kate Mallory watched the parade file

into the centre. No dirt must be attached to the Deputy Commissioner, none that could be seen anyway!

'Are you all right, Connor, not coming down with flu, are you?' Clifton Mather had watched the other man's effort to clear his nose.

'No, it's just a bloody stink in the nostrils.' James Connor rubbed his nose again. 'Nothing to worry over, it's just a nuisance. I think it must be some sort of air freshener they used in the hotel I stayed in the night of that birthday bash; whatever it was, I can't seem to get rid of it.'

'Overalls, Mr Connor.'

Taking the garment from the centre supervisor, Connor balanced awkwardly on one leg and then the other, catching a young woman's attractive smile as he pulled the overalls up over his crotch. He smiled back at the figure now moved closer to the front of the assembled group. Nice eyes! Very nice, a rather fetching shade of blue.

Joining in the teasing applause as the Deputy Commissioner fastened the final button, Mather asked quietly, 'That other policeman at the birthday do, the man that left early, has there been any more from him?'

'No.'

Mather glanced quickly at the people standing nearest to them, this wasn't the best place he could have chosen to have a conversation regarding that evening. 'From what Philip Bartley tells me, the fellow is still in hospital, that car crash seems to have banged him up a bit.'

'Hmm,' Connor nodded. 'Seems he's liable to be there for some time.'

'And he's sent no one else to the place to sniff around?'

'No, and I don't think he will. Daniels suspects but will keep this one under his cap. He won't give it to anyone, he sees bringing in the suppliers as his ticket to the top.'

Running a hand over his hair Mather smoothed breeze-lifted drifts into place. 'All the same it will be running a bit of a risk putting the stuff through Bartley's place, that police inspector won't stay bedridden for ever.'

'Quite!' Following at their heels Maxwell Seton came with the rest into the smartly painted workshop. 'Bartley Supermarkets were useful while they lasted but that particular venue has reached the end of its usefulness. We shall have to search around for another outlet for our particular commodity.'

'But where?' Mather touched a hand to his grey silk tie.

'I don't know!' Seton snapped, immediately regretting the lapse as Kate Mallory's sharp glance came his way. 'Let's leave it 'til this bit of theatre is over!'

'If you would stand here.' The supervisor led the way to a large wooden bench, a circular saw half moored in its bed.

'Will this do?' Connor turned his best smile to the crowd but his eyes were for the attractive face now at the very front of the audience.

From the further edge Kate Mallory noted the direction of the Deputy Commissioner's eyes, and the flare of interest that had them momentarily hot. It might be beneficial to take a little more interest in Mr James Connor!

'That will do nicely, sir . . .'

Watching the young woman reporter fussily lining up

her photographer as Connor posed beside the large bench, Kate Mallory smiled to herself. They all went through that stage!

'. . . but why stop there, why not the real thing? Can't have the public accusing the police force of fraud, now can we?'

Listening to the laughter of the invited few, Kate Mallory raised a congratulatory eyebrow. The girl clearly wanted her money's worth. She would go far in the world of journalism. But it wasn't that world Connor wished the girl in right now. Kate's glance flicked to the star of the show. The look on the man's face told exactly what he thought of newspaper reporters *and* the public.

'How do I start this thing?' Connor cleared his throat. That smell, it wasn't unpleasant as smells went, in fact the slightly spicy aroma could be quite the opposite, but not in every breath you took! It was beginning to get unbearable.

Touching a button on the control box attached to a side of the large bench the supervisor brought lateral steel jaws clamping about the huge bole of wood already mounted in readiness for slicing.

'The red button turns on power to the bandsaw,' he explained each button in turn, 'the white operates forward motion of the wood to be cut, the green is for reverse.'

Connor smiled but only for the effect it would have on his audience; at this moment he could do more with visiting a dentist or a doctor and getting something to clear this God-awful smell from his nose than opening a bloody workshop!

'Right,' he drew a hand beneath his nostrils, 'now give me the important bit, how do I stop it?'

'The black button.' The supervisor pointed to the bottom button on the console as the crowd laughed at the Deputy Commissioner's quip. 'Ready when you are, sir.'

Pressing the red button, Connor sent a hum of power singing over the pristine workshop.

'Better stand back.' One hand rubbing again beneath his nose he dropped it quickly as a pair of hyacinth-blue eyes smiled from the front of the group. Christ, that smell was choking him! Taking a handkerchief he blew into it, laughing when the woman reporter asked was he wiping his hands of the ceremony. Lord, he had made it worse; the taste clung in his throat, so thick he wanted to gag! But he couldn't stop now, he had to go through with this. Any more bright ideas from the PROs, though, and they could stuff 'em up their arse!

Returning the handkerchief to his pocket he forced a smile. 'I'm very much a new boy at this, I'm likely to make one hell of a mess of it.'

Across the few feet of space the attractive face smiled. Reading the invitation behind it and making a mental note to accept, Connor touched the forward button. Placing both hands on the bole of wood, leaning a little way over it, he turned his head, flashing a further smile at the watching crowd.

'Nearly there . . .'

At the front of the spectators a slim figure took one

step forwards, a figure whose silver-gold hair gleamed with light from an overhead skylight, whose hyacinth-blue eyes laughed back from an attractive face; a face that suddenly fell in on itself, dropping away into a black gaping hole.

'Christ . . . Christ, oh Christ!' The woman journalist's scream ripped out over the whirr of machinery as Connor's head, gold braided cap in place, whirled past spattering her face with blood.

'Oh my God!' The supervisor shoved a fist against his teeth trying to hold back a surge of vomit that squeezed between his fingers.

Beside the broad-topped bench blood pumped from the stump of Connor's neck in bright red spurts, painting the white overalls with vivid splashes of scarlet.

Somewhere to the right a dull thud followed the woman's hysterical screaming. Turning towards it Kate Mallory felt her stomach heave as the severed head bounced off the wall to roll sideways across the floor.

'Christ Almighty!' Maxwell Seton stared stupefied at the truncated body, the snapped blade of the bandsaw still firmly fixed in its housing behind it. 'Dear Christ Almighty!'

Momentum from the force with which the broken blade had wrapped around Connor's neck now spun the headless body around, dismantled nerves jerking spasmodically, working the legs in a convulsive macabre dance of death, carrying it towards the horrified watchers.'

'Holy Mother of God!' The thin photographer, his anaemic pimply face now the colour of a week-old corpse, dropped his camera, the flash exploding in a brilliant surge of light.

Beside him, vomit gurgling from her throat, his colleague dropped in a dead faint.

Jesus! Kate Mallory swallowed the sour bile filling her mouth, her eyes fixed on the body of the Deputy Commissioner, on the arteries in its neck painting Picasso splurges on the grey mastic floor.

'You were right, Connor,' she breathed as the jerking became a twitch and the body of Connor slumped to the ground, 'for just about the first time in your life you were right. You have made one hell of a bloody mess!'

Chapter Twenty

The insistent ringing of a bell bringing Torrey to a halt, he stood watching the ambulance rushing along the street, traffic moving aside to give it free passage. An accident somewhere! He followed the vehicle with his eyes. Why the police escort? That wasn't usual, there was nobody in this town important enough to warrant a police escort except perhaps one of the Owens, or maybe old man Lloyd. Only the money-laden industrialists got that kind of VIP treatment and with their finances they would hardly call upon the services of the local ambulance station.

His interest already waning he turned the way he had been walking, following along Willenhall Street towards the Frying Pan. Did Echo Sounder still haunt the place?

Taking a pint of best bitter he glanced about the tap room. It wasn't yet half-past twelve and already the room was hung about with a veil of grey tobacco smoke; some of the factory workers who came here to eat their dinner of bread and cheese did so with a cigarette never more than inches from their mouth.

This was what Bartley had got himself away from, this and a lifetime of graft drawing steel; and he should forget this town too, forget all it had been, forget Anna. But doing what he should had never come easy to Richard Torrey.

A draught from the street door temporarily displacing the grey haze, he caught sight of a figure hunched over an almost empty glass. Ordering another pint of best he carried it across to the table.

'Anything new on the streets?' he asked, setting the ale in front of the man sitting with no company other than his own.

'Nothin' as I've 'eard of.'

'Then what about something not so new?'

'I ain't 'eard of that neither.'

The little man was playing awkward, or was he scared? Torrey took a drink from his glass.

'Having trouble with your ears? Then let's try your memory, I hope there's nothing wrong with that.'

'I remembers you!' Ferret eyes darted a quick glance at Torrey then dropped again to the several-days-old copy of the *Sporting Pink* newspaper folded in half lengthwise.

'Good.' Torrey looked slowly at the men in the tap room, none seemed interested in him. 'I bet a certain three blokes that drink in the Bird-in-Hand remember me as well. How long were they in hospital, Echo . . . and how many weeks would you like to spend with Sister Dora?'

'I don't know nothin' about no blokes as uses the Bird!'

Grabbing his dog-eared newspaper, Sounder made to move then dropped back to his chair as Torrey's hand fastened over his wrist.

'That doesn't matter.' Words falling like rocks, Torrey held on to the other man. 'It's not them I'm interested in; I want to know about a corpse fished from the canal some time back, a corpse with half a face.'

'I ain't 'eard . . .'

'Don't piss me about, Sounder!' Torrey's fingers tightened. 'Remember this isn't Daniels you're talking to; I don't have to go pussy-footing around and the only worry I have about breaking your scrawny neck is the dirt that will rub off on to my hands. One more thing you should remember if you want your singing career to go on . . . I don't like lies!'

Beneath the steel of Torrey's fingers, Echo Sounder felt the bones in his wrist crack, a little more pressure and they would break.

'It . . . it was a couple o' nights after you . . . after them blokes was duffed up in the yard of the Bird . . .' Echo Sounder snatched his hand away as the fingers slackened about his wrist but he knew better than to try to move from the table. Them blokes in the Bird had been big and hefty yet still stood little chance against this man, *he* would stand no chance at all. '. . . Inspector Daniels came in 'ere askin' questions about who it was who had laid 'em out.'

'And you told him?'

'I . . . I 'ad to, Torrey.' Nervousness drawing the ferret features even tighter, Echo Sounder pushed his hands beneath the table nursing them between his knees.

'I bet you did!' His answer pure acid, Torrey's eyes carried a red-light warning.

'You knows Daniels, 'e don't be jokin' when 'e threatens a bloke wi' Featherstone.'

'I know how he feels . . . I don't make jokes either and if I want to hear another man crack them I'll buy a ticket to the Birmingham Hippodrome!'

There was no mistaking the real meaning of the words. Sounder could already feel that arm across his throat, a hand cupping his chin.

'I told 'im only that you 'ad a stable in Dangerfield Lane, nothin' else, that be the truth of it.'

He'd wondered who'd fed Daniels that titbit. Torrey took a swallow of beer. But that was of no consequence, Daniels would have found that information at the Council offices, that was always supposing he could read a polling register!

'So what else did you two talk about . . . and, Sounder . . . don't say you didn't talk, everybody in Darlaston knows you are in Daniels's pocket.'

That wasn't the truth. Echo Sounder glanced at the glass of ale, his throat dry with nerves. Once that became common knowledge he could kiss his balls goodbye; but Torrey would tell. Unless he got what 'e wanted 'e would shout it from the Town 'All roof. Sounder swallowed hard.

'He, Daniels, asked about that new grocery place up on the Leys.'

'How cosy. Echo Sounder and the blues chatting about the price of bacon.' Torrey gleamed cynically. 'Yours won't be worth tuppence a pound when the local lads get wind of that one.'

Sounder's glance made a swift inventory of the tables round about though his head never lifted.

Bringing up one hand he grabbed his glass, draining off the remaining ale in one swallow then wiping the same hand over his mouth. 'It were no eatables Daniels was after finding out about,' he said quickly, 'least not the sort as be good for a body, but I tells you flat that be the last word I'll be saying on that; it might as well be you as does for me as them runners Bartley brought in, an' they will, sure as God med little apples, they will!'

Bartley? Torrey felt the hairs on the back of his neck stand like recruits new to a sergeant major's bark. What had he got to do with this? Did he know anything of Anna's murder?

Eyes glinting like iced seawater became glued to the hunch-shouldered man. Resting each side of his glass, Torrey's fingers clenched and unclenched with slow menacing promise.

'A broken neck can bring death quickly, Sounder,' he breathed, 'but that is only one way the commandos teach; there are other ways, each slow and each increasing in pain. The choice I leave to you.'

The same furtive glance once more checking they were not being watched and that no one was close enough to overhear, Sounder took no chances. Dropping his voice to a murmur he spoke rapidly, wanting either Torrey or himself out of the pub.

'It were a few days afore Daniels came askin' about that

shindig in the Bird, he came in askin' what I knowed of Bartley. There was a new 'orse . . .'

'Leave the lingo to the *Sporting Pink*,' Torrey broke in.

'. . . there was a stranger standin' next to the bar,' Sounder accepted the all too clear suggestion, 'Daniels wanted to know who 'e was and who was another come to join 'im. I said as they was fresh muscle brought in by Bartley, probably to safeguard a shipment brought to his place on the Leys.'

'Shipment!' Torrey frowned. 'What exactly?'

'I told you I ain't sayin'.'

'Think again!' Torrey's hand closed over Sounder's, crushing the grimy fingers.

Tears squeezing beneath lids closed against the sudden pain, Echo Sounder fought to keep the squeal from breaking between clenched lips. 'I ain't sure what it were but Daniels seen promotion ridin' on its back. But 'e were pipped at the post by Connor, it was 'im took the race and 'im got the prize.'

'Connor . . . James Connor, the new Deputy Police Commissioner?'

'The same.' Sounder rubbed the hand suddenly released.

Well, well! Richard Torrey smiled to himself. No wonder Daniels had a face like fourpence at that drinks party, it wasn't only Mather and Co. being pansies that had disagreed with him.

'So what was it the new muscle was protecting?' Pushing the full glass closer to the little man, Richard Torrey watched him grab it with both hands and take a long swallow. Sounder might take the chance of having his teeth kicked in but he was taking no risk of having the drink taken away before he had downed at least three quarters of it.

'I asked what was so important Bartley needed a couple of extra men?'

Wiping beer foam from his mouth and on to the leg of his shabby trousers, Sounder almost whimpered. 'You must 'ave read the papers, they covered that meetin' for days.'

He hadn't read any newspapers following Anna's death, he hadn't done anything for weeks since her disappearance except lie in the house and drink.

'Remind me!' he said tersely.

'Read it up at the library, they keeps back numbers of the newspapers, but this much I'll say: Maryjooarna don't be the only shit some folks likes to smoke, there be a number who likes their 'bacca stronger.'

He could make the man sing a little more, he could make him sing a whole bloody opera, but it would do no good. He was scared as hell, too scared to say more of Bartley's doings even supposing he knew more.

Once more in the street Torrey turned in the direction of the library. He would take Sounder's advice, he'd read just what it was had gone down at the Leys, and what it was had been snatched from Daniels's hands.

'God Almighty . . . ! Are you sure?'

'Sure?' Clifton Mather snapped. 'One could hardly

make a mistake of that sort. The blade broke, sliced his head clean off his neck, the whole place was covered with blood.'

'Lord . . . poor Connor!' Philip Bartley tipped off his wine in one gulp.

'Poor Connor, yes, but it's also poor us.' Mather toyed with the crystal glass holding his own untouched drink.

'How "us"?' Bartley reached for the bottle left by the wine waiter.

Mather frowned as Bartley filled his glass to the brim and immediately swallowed a good third of the rich claret. This wasn't good. Bartley was drinking too much and that could be very bad for a man's health, it could be quite lethal in fact . . . and the end could come quickly for anybody threatening the lucrative South American end of Coton Pharmaceuticals.

'Without Connor to take care there is no more interference from the likes of that police inspector . . . Daniel something or other . . . then business of one particular import could fold and that would cost us all a great deal of money, you no less than any of us, Bartley.'

'There are other coppers.'

'As you so succinctly put it, there are other coppers. But how many of them are in the position Connor held, and how many are as willing to play the game we run?'

His eyes slightly glazed, Bartley grinned. 'No man would turn down the money we pay.'

They money they paid! Clifton Mather eyed the grin. As Bartley inferred it was a fair amount, too much to include a man who would no longer be of use to Coton

Pharmaceuticals, and with his premises no longer involved that meant Bartley.

'Things will go on same as before,' Bartley went on, 'the only difference being Connor won't be there. Christ, poor Connor! Him and Darley both.'

'Darley . . . such a pleasant young man.' Mather picked up his own glass, twisting it between his fingers. 'Was there any reason you know of for his taking his own life?'

Bartley shrugged his shoulders. 'He hadn't looked well for some time, I remarked as much when he had dinner at the Abbey about a week before. I advised then he go see a doctor.'

'Seton and I advised Connor much the same when we talked at that youth centre place. You can't be too careful with all this flu going about and Connor showed all the symptoms, clearing his throat, snuffling, complaining of a smell he couldn't get out of his nose and a taste that clung to his mouth.'

All the symptoms! Bartley almost dropped the glass he was holding. Yes, it seemed Connor had them all right, just as Peter Darley had, but were they symptoms of the same malady?

'Did Connor say how long he'd had this smell in his nostrils?'

Mather sipped delicately at his wine, letting the bouquet of it linger on his palate until Bartley wanted to swipe the glass to the floor and shake the answer from between those perfectly capped teeth.

'As a matter of fact he did.' Mather nodded. 'He said it was the night of the Brackley drinks party . . . something in the hotel he stayed at, a cleanser for the bathroom so he thought, said it had a slight hint of spice about it. But I still think it more likely to have been the onset of flu.'

A constant smell in his nostrils, a slightly spicy tang! The same things Peter Darley had spoken of! Philip Bartley set the glass down with shaking fingers. The same symptoms, but not of flu. Both men had known Anna, both men had enjoyed a more than friendly relationship with Anna, now both men were dead!

Both men had known Anna . . . in every sense of the word . . . and so had he! Both men had been aware of that special lightly spiced aroma . . . and so had he! Now both men were dead . . . and he, was he to be the next, was it Anna somehow wreaking vengeance for murder . . . ?

Of course not! Sitting in the back of the Rover, Philip Bartley drew a long breath, holding it in his lungs, forcing himself to stay calm. There was no such thing as returning from the grave, once you were dead you were dead and that was it . . . finished! But the symptoms, if you could call them that, had been the same in each case . . . had! His brain caught at the word, pushing it to the front of his mind . . . had . . . that was it, he had experienced the same thing as Darley and Connor, but it had not stayed with him; he hadn't caught a whiff of that scent nor felt that touch for weeks, with him it had all been imagination. Letting go of the breath he closed his eyes, relief washing over him. Ghosts! He smiled. He'd be seeing bloody fairies next!

Glancing in the driving mirror, Richard Torrey saw

Bartley relax against the leather. What about Doc Walker, how relaxed was he? He didn't know Walker yet he couldn't help but feel sorry for the bloke, going down on his own, taking the full rap while others waltzed away; and Bartley had to be one of those others, his claim he knew nothing of drugs stuffed into giblet sacks tucked inside frozen poultry was almost as genuine as a five-bob note. Philip Bartley was not the man to have anything going on at the Leys for which he wasn't in on the receiving end. But he had got away with it, stayed in the clear while another man took the shit! Walker and Daniels, they'd both lost out, Walker serving ten in Featherstone and Daniels remaining as an inspector while Connor got the gold braid. It had all been there in back numbers of the *Star* and so had a piece about Daniels's accident, but of Anna's murder there had been nothing. What had he hoped would be there? Coming up toward Gailey traffic island he pressed the brake pedal, allowing cars coming from his right to pass. A full confession, a photo of the one responsible? A cynical laugh resting in his throat he sent the car forwards, taking a left exit. He had as much hope of that as Walker had of a nine-year reprieve.

Its headlights biting into the darkness, the car ate the road. Bartley had made no mention of Bruce Daniels's accident yet he must know, they had both been guests at that birthday 'do'. Was it deliberate or was Bartley another who had given reading newspapers the go-by? Hardly! Oncoming headlights blinding him as they rounded a bend in the road, Torrey cursed softly, glancing at the high-sided lorry as it roared past. So what other reason would Bartley have for making no mention of the inspector's car smash? He talked about plenty of other things as they drove.

'I was at the library this afternoon.' Bartley might not have known but he was going to know now.

Behind him Philip Bartley's eyes flipped open. 'The library! Couldn't you manage anything better, or was the local talent not to your liking?'

'You could say that, anyway I found the newspapers more interesting.'

'How can a man find anything more interesting than an afternoon roll in the hay? You seriously disappoint me, Torrey.'

'I found a piece about Daniels.'

'Daniels, the little policeman . . . what was interesting about him?'

Should he mention the drugs haul, wipe the smirk off Bartley's face? Deciding against, he went on, 'Nothing much unless you call wiping off a car and landing yourself in hospital interesting.'

'Daniels has had an accident . . . wasn't to his nose, was it? He was always poking it where it wasn't wanted; serve the toad right if he'd killed himself!'

Torrey felt a tingle of irritation trickle along his nerves. Bartley should be more careful, his true colours were showing. Glancing again at the figure in the rear of the car he kept the thought under control, saying evenly, 'I went to see him after I finished in the library.'

'Your life becomes more exciting by the minute!' Bartley laughed. 'What's next on your social calendar, a fascinating lecture on the sex life of the amoeba?'

The flicker of irritation prickled again. Why? Torrey wasn't sure, he only knew that since reading of that police raid his respect for Bartley had become zero. It seemed he'd kept his head down, done nothing to help Walker, shown no sympathy, just as he was showing none for Daniels.

'It wasn't fascinating visiting Daniels,' he ignored the sarcasm, 'but it was interesting and you might say it was his nose caused his smash up.'

Now *you're* being bloody sarcastic. Bartley's thoughts held reproof as he looked at the back of Torrey's head. But he said nothing, he didn't want any bad blood between them. He felt secure with Torrey, he didn't want him walking out.

Not bothered which way Bartley took his comments Torrey smiled. 'If it hadn't been for Daniels's nose he probably wouldn't have had a crack-up at all.'

'How do you make that out?'

'From what he told me. Seems he got a whiff of something in his hotel bathroom, got the smell lodged in his nose and couldn't get rid of it, it was even a taste on his tongue. It got on his nerves so much he left the hotel before dawn, said it got worse as he drove.'

And then there were four! The phrase he'd read years before crashed into Bartley's mind. Himself, Darley, Connor and Daniels all had had a smell lingering in the nostrils, all had a taste in the mouth, and now two of the four were dead. Coincidence? Like bloody hell it was coincidence!

'Did . . . did Daniels say anything else?'

Torrey glanced to the rear as they passed beneath an overhead light. Bartley's eyes were wide open and there was no trace of a smirk on his mouth, but there was fear on his face, stark readable fear!

'He started to but then changed his mind and I could understand why; talking of hallucinations, people that weren't there, it could have seen him out of the Sister Dora and signed into Burntwood before he had time to blink.'

Hallucinations . . . people that were not really there! Bartley clenched his teeth, holding the trembling of his lips. It was all too much of a muchness, all of them had been plagued and now two were dead . . . was Philip Bartley next?

Chapter Twenty-One

Echo Sounder had denied having any knowledge of Anna; all he would own to was having heard of a corpse being pulled from the canal. Torrey lay in his room staring at the ceiling. If the little nark did know more then he wasn't letting on regardless of what he, Torrey, had threatened and *that* was interesting.

Wind-tossed branches cast flickering patterns over the moonlit room but Torrey was blind to all except the picture in his mind, the picture of a smiling face with laughing hyacinth eyes. Did Sounder really know nothing? He should have knocked hell's eyes out of the little git! A few less teeth for a bit more information.

So supposing Sounder was holding back, what could scare him more than the beating he knew he could get; what . . . or who? Who in that town had enough clout to have Sounder peeing in his pants? That was a daft question. Torrey stared at the shifting patterns of darkness. Almost anybody with a fist and the bottle to use it would have Echo Sounder pissing himself! But Bartley . . . did he scare as easily? There was no reason to think him involved with Anna's death yet somehow the feeling that the man was niggled at the back of his mind.

From the trees encircling the Abbey an owl hooted, the sound carrying clear in the silence. Bartley! Torrey shifted restlessly. Sounder had as good as said he was running drugs, and not just marijuana; the newspaper report had heroin seized from his premises. Was he a murderer too? And if so, was he alone in it, had he held the gun that had killed Anna, had his finger pulled the trigger?

From the moonlit shadows of night the owl called again. In all the months they had lived together Anna had not ever once mentioned knowing Bartley; if they had met, had it been before or after the time spent in Dangerfield Lane?

A pulse in his throat began to throb. Before, after or during? Had they met during the time Anna had lived with him, during the time Anna had loved him? And Anna *had* loved him. The pulse beating harder, Torrey let out a soft moan. Anna had loved him, but Anna had also loved money and all the things money could buy . . . all the things Philip Bartley could buy and Richard Torrey could not!

Anger erupting from the empty chasms of his soul he pushed up from the bed. He didn't know if Anna had taken up with Bartley, there was no proof, no reason to torture himself with these thoughts; he could go on in that vein until he suspected every man in the country! He must get a hold on his emotions, come to terms with his loss.

He had a home, a decently paid job and a boss who asked no questions, he must not let his own stupid suppositions deprive him of that.

Drawing several deep breaths, forcing the beat in his throat to normal, he crossed to the window of his bed-room and looked out towards the small copse bordering the gardens of his cottage and the Barnes's. In a cloud-free sky a hunter's moon hung low gilding trees and lawns with gold-washed silver. Anna would have liked living here . . . but for how long? Resting a hand on the cool glass of the window pane he stared at the moonlit scene. How long would Anna have stayed hidden away in a backwater, however peaceful and beautiful, how long before the need for entertainment, the need for excitement became too strong . . . how long before Anna . . . ?

Dropping his hand he pushed the thought away but as he made to turn back to the bed he caught a sudden move-ment, a shadow at the edge of the trees. In that half second his mind was clear, his brain alert, every nerve in his body tingling, every sense sharp as a razor.

A burglar sizing up the Abbey, a breaking and entering merchant bent on a night's profit? Torrey slid aside from the window, a quick glance taking in the shadow sepa-rating itself from the line of trees. It wasn't the Abbey . . . the cheeky bastard was moving in the opposite direction . . . coming towards the cottages!

Ignoring his nakedness he moved rapidly, clearing the stairs and living room, coming to the kitchen door in seconds. He could leave the house from the rear, wait for the bastard to get close and take him before he knew what had hit him. The door made no sound as he drew it slowly open. Thank the saints George Barnes had oiled the hinges only last week! Silent as a wraith, every Army-taught instinct fully in play, he moved around to one side of the house, the overhang of the thatched roof casting long shadows across its walls. It should be only a matter of moments before that thief reached his target . . . and before he got a lot more than he'd ever hoped to get!

The breeze that had played among the branches to send patterns dancing across his ceiling now played cold fingers over his naked body, but Torrey felt nothing except the cold numbness he had felt when waiting to take out a terrorist, the same impersonal coldness that had been in him when he'd taken those three yobbos in the yard of the Bird-in-Hand, a coldness that held him ready to do the same thing now.

Breathing slow and even, hands loose yet ready, he waited. Where the hell was the thieving bastard, he should have been here by now! He could have shinned to an upper window. He could have, Torrey acknowledged mentally, but not without his hearing, he could hear a fly fart half a mile away! The man had to be on the ground, but why hadn't he made the break-in?

Bare feet making no sound on dew-soaked grass, Torrey slipped to where he could peer around the edge of the wall to see the whole of the front garden and the stretch of ground beyond to the copse.

What the hell was he doing? Torrey frowned as he looked at the figure standing now in the open just beyond the garden fence. Was the fellow daft as well as being a thief, didn't whoever it was realise the moon had him lit up like the fairy on a Christmas tree? Watching for several seconds he caught his breath as the figure turned its head, the light of the moon sparkling on pale gold hair that reached to the collar of a shirt tucked into jeans that hugged a pair of long slim legs. He held the breath tight in his chest as the head moved in a slow half circle to look directly at the corner of the wall that concealed him. It wasn't . . . ! Torrey's fingers jerked convulsively into tight balls. It couldn't be . . . !

Overhead the moon seemed to laugh at his perplexity, the brightness of it intensifying and throwing the face he stared at into clear relief, a face that smiled . . . Anna's face.

'Are you driving back to London tonight, Clifton?'

Accepting a heavy measure of brandy, Maxwell Seton sat back in his chair.

'What . . . ? Er . . . no, I'll check into a hotel somewhere.'

'Won't Bartley think that a bit off, you putting up in a hotel when there's plenty of room here at the Abbey?'

'Who gives a shit what Bartley thinks!'

Maxwell Seton looked up sharply, a frown pulling his well-shaped brows together. 'Are you all right, I mean you haven't been in your usual form all night; is anything wrong?'

'I'm all right.' Clifton Mather's nostrils flared as he sniffed several times. 'It's just that damned smell.'

'Smell?' Seton dragged air into his own nostrils, his

look of confusion deepening. 'Can't say I smell anything.'

'Well you wouldn't, would you, not with a goblet of French brandy stuck under your nose!'

Mather had arrived at Monkswell in a bad mood last evening and it hadn't got any better today. Maxwell Seton ignored the sharpness of the other man's answer. Why was that . . . had his latest boyfriend kissed him goodbye or p'raps told him he was getting too old to play his favourite party games? Forcing back the smile behind the thought he looked at the man standing against the stone Tudor fireplace. 'What does it smell like?'

'Like . . .' Mather's nostrils flared again, '. . . like perfume. I could smell it last night when we were having dinner. I thought one of those Women's Institute creatures must be wearing it . . . why the hell did I agree to meeting them!'

'Must have been strong if you can still smell it since neither of them has been at the house today; you're sure you are not imagining it, you know . . . a bit overtired? These things do happen.'

Was he imagining that smell? Clifton Mather turned his back to stare into the fire. Had he imagined that visitor to his room last night, imagined the smile as long fingers had slid the ancient bolt into place, locking the door, imagined the slim firm limbs as first shirt and then trousers had been slowly, teasingly dropped to the floor? Had he imagined the leap of his flesh as the handsome dark-haired figure had walked towards the bed? Had it simply been a projection of his mind that had that figure beside him in bed, had those long hands fondling his crotch, had that attractive full-lipped mouth close over his own, driving a tongue deep into it?

The spicy smell thickening with the memory, Clifton Mather coughed. Had it simply been his own imagining or had those eyes laughed back at him as the lips trailed down over his chest, and had that tongue probed his navel before going on, slowly tormenting, to nuzzle his erection? And was it his imagination that the light in the bedroom glistened on dark hair turning it to pale gold, that those brown eyes changed to hyacinth blue, that the mouth about to take his flesh became twisted and blackened, that the face that lifted to smile at him dropped away into a charred hole?

'Sorry about that, bloody phone never stops ringing, I sometimes think it would be better for it to be ripped out . . .'

'Look, Bartley . . .' Clifton Mather swung round as his host entered the gracious drawing room, '. . . I have to go back to London tonight, some business early in the morning.'

'What about the stuff coming in from South America?'

'We can talk about that later in the week.' Mather set his unfinished drink on an ornate side table. 'I'd best set off now if I want to get a wink of sleep at all before that business meeting.'

'Well, if you must I suppose you must.' Philip Bartley reached for the bell pull that would summon his house-keeper. 'I'll get Mrs Barnes have your things brought down.'

'I really don't think you should drive, you know.'

Maxwell Seton swallowed a generous mouthful of brandy before going on. 'Fast cars and brandy don't make good partners.'

'Then make sure you don't drive! You're the one who has been sucking the brandy bottle like an infant sucks the breast!'

'Is that the business you can't wait to get back to? Have you been missing a mouth sucking your bottle?'

'Shut your bloody mouth . . . !' Mather broke off as the housekeeper's knock announced her arrival, but his face remained dark with anger.

'Perhaps you should have Torrey drive you, I won't need him tomorrow, he can put up somewhere and drive back here in the morning.'

And tell you I didn't go back to London after all? Keeping the thought to himself Clifton Mather shook his head. 'No need for that, Bartley, I'm perfectly capable of driving.'

'Then I might as well return with you seeing as I don't fancy a train journey home.'

'You are sure you trust me?'

Cheeks slightly flushed, eyes bright with drink, Maxwell Seton grinned. 'Only as far as driving a car goes.'

'I'll ring you one day next week, Bartley.' Mather ignored the remark. 'Thanks for your hospitality, you must come out to our place soon, Francey would love to have you.'

In more ways than one, and the more diverse the way the better she likes the play! Rising from his chair Maxwell Seton smiled his apology as he asked the returning housekeeper to have his own overnight bag packed and brought down.

Sat in the lush comfort of the Jaguar, the Abbey lost in the bend of the lane, Maxwell Seton glanced at the man whose fingers clutched tensely on the wheel. Something had Mather rattled and it sure as hell wasn't any smell of perfume. Had something gone amiss with the shipment? No, he would have said had it been that. Was it the fact he intended cutting Bartley out of the syndicate? Hardly, Mather couldn't give a shit for Bartley and if the little grocer threatened trouble then no doubt he'd be dealt with in Mather's own special way. So if none of that was the worm in his gut, what was?

'It wasn't just the smell of perfume had you out of that house as though the devil were fondling your balls, and don't bother to say otherwise. So what is it, Mather, what's got you all riled up?'

'No, it wasn't the devil, but it was something equally unnerving.' Clifton Mather's voice shook. 'It . . . it was Anna.'

'Anna!' The effects of the brandy rapidly wearing off, Maxwell Seton stared at the handsome profile. Mather wasn't given to making up stories to while away a journey, so this . . . 'Don't be ridiculous, man!' he snapped. 'You know as well as I do that's impossible, Anna is . . .'

'Dead!' Mather's lips were tight with remembered fear. 'And the dead don't walk and they don't make love, but nevertheless it was Anna in my room last night, Anna's hands on my body, Anna's mouth on mine!'

'That can't be. You were overtired . . .'

'And a tired brain plays tricks on a man . . .' The Jaguar's tyres screeched as Mather took a corner too fast. '. . . I was imagining things, was I? Just as I imagined that smell?'

Speed pressing him back in his seat Maxwell Seton tried to answer without showing the apprehension rising fast inside him. 'Well, nobody else mentioned any smell . . .'

'So that makes me a nutcase . . .'

'I didn't say that.'

'But you meant it!' Mather blew short sharp breaths down his nose then rubbed a hand beneath his nostrils. 'Well, I don't care what the hell you believe or what you think, I *know*. I know it was Anna in my room last night, in my bed!'

Seton glanced nervously into the stream of light as powerful headlamps melted a path through the blackness of the narrow country road. 'How?' he asked. 'How do you know?'

'Christ, Seton, I'm not bloody soft in the head!' Mather's hand brushed beneath his nostrils. 'You know Bartley's hospitality as well as I do, I thought he'd had a couple of rent boys brought in for the night, one for each of us. I just had the bedside lamps on and at first the figure was in shadow but I could see enough to know that if yours were anything like mine then you wouldn't have been bothering overmuch about sleep, and by the time it was in that bed with me then neither was I.'

'There was no rent boy provided for me. I was alone all night.' Maxwell Seton watched the hand worrying the nostrils, perhaps he ought not to have elected to be Mather's passenger, the man was definitely overwrought.

'So why did Anna just come to me, you were as involved as the rest of us?'

'Because you were probably already asleep. It was simply a nightmare, there was no Anna, there was nothing in your room, you were dreaming. That's it, pure and simple.'

'There was nothing pure and nothing simple about Anna.' Mather coughed as a spicy aroma curled into his nose. 'That one was a bitch, an out and out conniving bloody bitch who got her desserts! And I wasn't dreaming; it was no nightmare, it was real. I didn't imagine that figure, the mouth trailing down over my chest or the tongue in my navel . . .'

Hearing the quiet roar as Mather's foot pressed harder on the accelerator Seton's apprehension turned to fear as the powerful car surged into the blackness.

'Be reasonable, Mather,' he tried placatingly, 'it's nothing to get het up about, we all have dreams when we've been without for a while. Desire takes a man at any time, even when he's asleep.'

'I tell you I wasn't bloody well asleep!' Wrenching hard on the wheel Mather ripped into a bend so fast his passenger was thrown against the door and hit his head on the side window. The knock leaving him dizzy, Maxwell Seton shook his head as he pushed upright in his seat. The first pub or hotel they came to, Mather and he would part company; it would be suicide to go on with the man in this state, and Maxwell Seton wasn't ready to die just yet.

'Am I asleep now . . . ?'

Clifton Mather's voice was almost a screech and the soft glow of the dashboard showed fingers white with tension.

'. . . Am I, Seton, am I asleep . . . ?'

With all trace of dizziness, all remnants of brandy cleared from his brain Maxwell Seton looked at the face fear had twisted into a mask. One wrong word and Mather would be over the edge.

'. . . Am I dreaming now?'

Lord, he'd be glad to be out of this car, Mather was out of his head. His own voice shaky, Maxwell Seton tried to sound amused.

'Of course not, of course you're not dreaming.'

'Then . . .' Mather snuffled, blowing and sniffing, and at the same time rubbing at his nostrils, '. . . then what's that?'

Mather jabbed a hand towards the windscreen. Following the way it pointed Seton saw the slim figure standing at the side of the road, one hand outstretched and the thumb raised. Relief etching every word, he smiled.

'It's a hitch-hiker, someone looking for a ride; why not stop? A fresh voice and all that, give us both a break to talk to someone new, eh Clifton?'

'You . . . you're sure it's just a hitcher?' Mather's foot hesitated over the brake.

'I'm certain,' Maxwell Seton's smile spread, 'and it's a pretty one, look at that hair, just the colour you like; hit the brake, Mather, I think we might both be lucky.'

Tyres screaming at the sudden demand the car slowed.

Ahead, the figure stepped into its path and then turned and in the beam of headlights an attractive face smiled.

'No!'

Already intent upon the long-legged figure, whose pale gold hair glinted in the beam of headlights, whose face smiled more than a promise of gratitude, Maxwell Seton was only half aware of the other man's cry; then, as it came again, he glanced at the stricken face.

'No . . . you're dead . . . you're dead, you bitch, you're dead . . . !'

Thrown back against the leather as Mather's foot jammed the accelerator hard down, Seton stared at the smiling figure standing in the centre of the road, stared at the face as one side of it crumpled into a gaping black hole.

Chapter Twenty-Two

It had been a trick of the light. Torrey walked slowly in the direction of the village. He had no reason to be going there, he didn't need anything . . . anything other than to get away from that cottage, to get his brain back into gear. He had seen that figure, it had stood there looking at him as bold as brass, making no attempt to hide, to evade being seen. Lit by a moon that bathed the whole area in brilliant silver light it had lifted a hand, beckoning to him as if it had known he stood there even though the lee of the cottage kept him unseen from the garden and the copse. Nor had the figure moved as he approached though he must have shouted that name. Only as he was almost there, almost within touching distance, had the hand lowered, had the smile on that face disappeared; only as he reached to take the figure in his arms had that one word whispered across the night: 'Ritchie . . .' Then it was gone, fading into the silver glow, blending into the moonlight like a breath of mist, and he had stood there like a child who had suddenly been deserted, not knowing whether to cry or scream, only knowing he wanted whatever had stood there beckoning to come back, to smile at him again, to speak to him, to hold him. He had stood there until the first spatter of raindrops on his body had become a cold shower, washing his senses clear of that hallucination.

And that was all it had been, an hallucination, a projection of his own longing. It had not been real, it had not been Anna, he had seen no figure come to stand at his fence.

'You be goin' to hear it for yourself, lad?'

Deep in his own thoughts, Torrey had been unaware of the man sitting watching his approach from the silent tractor. Now he frowned as he drew level with the field gate.

'It?'

'You mean you ain't 'eard the news?'

'I don't bother with the radio.' Torrey halted at the gate.

'This were no news on the wireless, lad, this be news from right 'ere in Monkswell, well, no more than a few mile away.'

Climbing from the tractor Tom Harper ambled to the gate, resting one elbow on it as he spoke.

'Ain't much left o' that there Jagooar, and as for they blokes . . .'

'Tom.' Torrey lifted a hand. 'I'm not with you . . . where the hell would a jaguar have come from? There isn't a zoo within sixty miles of Monkswell . . .'

'I b'aint talkin' o' that kind o' jagooar,' Tom Harper shook his head, 'it be that motor I be a'speakin' on, that big fancy thing as brought they visitors to the Abbey last Friday evenin'.'

Usually he enjoyed a chat with old Tom but not now. Torrey moved restlessly. Right now he wanted to be alone. Christ! He stopped himself. He sounded like his mother's favourite film star . . . Greta Garbo: I vant to be alone! The slight smile rising in his mind acting like a sedative on his nerves he looked at the older man. So the car had probably had a puncture, even something as mundane as that made news in Monkswell! Asking as much he watched the greying head shake again.

'B'ain't nothin' so simple lad, that motor be more like a concertina so young Bobby Howes tells it, he be constable over at Bowton. T'were him found it turned on its roof in the ditch a'side o' the road.'

Bartley had said he wouldn't be needed; those men were staying the whole weekend and he wouldn't be needed. Torrey recalled the instruction clearly.

'When did Constable Howes discover the accident?'

'Can't rightly tell.' The older man scratched a finger across his scalp. 'But it must 'ave been as 'e were mekin his way to the station . . . it be a fair trek on that bike o' his from his 'ome over to Bowton . . . so it couldn't 'ave bin much after five this mornin'.'

That meant they must have left last night. But he hadn't heard the car, though that was nothing to go by, Jaguar motors moved almost as silently as the cat they were named after.

The real mystery was why, why cut the weekend short, why leave so suddenly? They hadn't come here to enjoy the view, of that he felt sure. He thought again of the two men he had seen arrive at the lovely old house, two men he had seen before at a house equally lovely, a house in Brackley. Could Bartley have other partners besides Doc Walker, other partners involved in his dirty little racket, partners such as Mather and Seton? Was that why they had come here, and did it have anything to do with their unscheduled departure?

'One o' they blokes be dead . . .' Tom Harper went on, '. . . an' t'other be in a bad way, bones broken and Lord knows what else. Took 'em to the cottage 'ospital over Bowton way, the one they took live were mumblin' summat about a woman but young Bobby Howes reckons there were no woman in that car and seein' 'ow it were bashed in 'e reckons nobody could 'ave walked away from it. Be strange, eh lad!'

'The man was probably rambling, you know how it is when you have a bump to the head.'

'No, I don't know 'ow it is.' Tom Harper hauled himself back on to his tractor. 'Nor does I want to, Torrey lad, not if I 'as to get concertina'd in no motor I don't. Folk were never meant to go racin' around the country-side in them things, they must be nuthin' but death traps to my way o' thinkin', what be wrong with a good 'oss and trap? You tell me that eh, you tell me that!'

There was nothing wrong with a horse and trap, no more than there was anything wrong with a horse and plough . . . but try telling that to old Tom! Raising a hand as the tractor coughed into life, Torrey turned back the way he had come.

He was as pleasant as a boil on the arse!

Kate Mallory stood outside the Sister Dora Hospital staring at the traffic whizzing along the Wednesbury Road. Inspector Bruce Daniels's mouth had closed tighter than a mussel shell when she had asked about his accident, but even that had seemed loose compared to when she had questioned him about Deputy Commissioner Connor. He resented that man's promotion, it had needed no words to tell her that. The look in Daniels's eyes had been enough. Well, you couldn't blame him for that, he'd served in the police force a good number of years and his record was good if not exactly star filled.

Leaving through the gateless entrance, Kate walked the several yards to the bus stop. What did reporters have to do to get issued with a car . . . or even paid enough to buy their own?

But there was more than resentment behind Inspector Daniels's closed mouth. Climbing on to the bus that laboured to a halt she glanced along the rows of seats. Never a one empty when you want it. Slight irritation tickling her nerves she grasped the large handbag slung over one shoulder then hauled herself to the upper deck, the already moving vehicle tipping her from side to side as she scrambled to the one seat empty at the back.

So if not merely resentment then what? Settled in her seat, Kate rummaged in the bottom of the vast bag.

'Ya could 'ave paid downstairs, save a man 'avin' to trawl all the way up 'ere.'

'And you could pack the job in if it's too much for you!' Kate's brown eyes flashed as she held out a pound coin.

'Sharp, ain't we?' The conductor's sallow gaze avoided Kate's as he punched a ticket, thrusting it at her with several bronze coins.

'Sharp enough to know the fare from the Sister Dora to the Bull Stake is fifty pence not ninety pence.' She clinked the coins, holding them on her outstretched palm.

His sullen face colouring, the conductor made a pretence of checking the change he had given as assenting murmurs rose from among the other passengers.

'A mistake be easy med!' What served for an apology squeezed between angry lips, the missing coins slapped into Kate's hand.

'The mistake being yours if you think I'm not up to your games!' An old hand with folk she felt to be cheating, Kate was not deterred by the sullen attitude but was prepared to give back in the same vein.

The man's boots clanging on the treads of the metal staircase she turned to watch the passing houses but her mind was already playing with the facts of that interview. She had tried every trick in her particular book to get Daniels to open up but he was wily, skilful at playing the ball back to her. He should be playing for the Wolves, Kate smiled to herself, he'd make a great winger.

She'd brought up the subject of Connor's death, watching for the reaction, but Daniels had shown none other than the usual shake of the head and expressions of sympathy. But that sympathy had been superficial, of course she couldn't say why, there was nothing she could set down in hard print, just that cold gut feeling that there was more to Daniels and Connor than met the eye. Then there was Mather and that other one, Maxwell Seton, representatives of Coton Enterprises. They had both been at that centre and Connor had seemed more than a little wound up as he'd stood talking with them. The bus pulling on to the Bull Stake, Kate followed the other passengers down the stairs, standing for a moment on the pavement. Those two were not residents of the town nor had she seen them before the opening of the leisure centre, but if they had been previous visitors then there was one man who would know. Crossing the street she turned the corner, heading towards the Frying Pan.

Echo Sounder would be thirsty right around now.

Now there were two! Philip Bartley sat hunched in the rear seat of the Rover, his eyes on the hands twisting together in his lap. Seton had been conscious despite the medication the doctors had given him, conscious and terrified. For almost the entire ten minutes the nursing staff had allowed for the visit Seton had babbled on about a hitch-hiker, a hitch-hiker who had smiled as it stepped into the path of the oncoming car, smiled as half of its face fell away.

It was almost the same as had happened to him that night he'd stopped to pick up a hitch-hiker standing in the rain, a hitch-hiker who hadn't really been there. What was it Seton had mumbled? '*It smiled as the car burst into flames, it smiled at me as I rolled free, it was still smiling as Mather was enveloped in fire, and as I tried to shout to tell it to help Mather its face . . . half of its face dropped away . . . then the whole figure just melted . . . it melted away . . . faded into the flames . . . just faded . . .*'

Half a face, and that scent! Bartley trembled at the thoughts rushing through his mind. Darley, Connor and Mather, all of them had been plagued by that spicy aroma just as he had, all had talked of hallucinations, of seeing figures that were not really there, just as he had seen; Darley and Mather had felt the touch of hands and mouth the same as he had felt them. Christ Almighty, what was it? Whatever it was it was no hallucination, and whatever it was it was after them all. Seton and himself were the only two left!

They had all joined in, they had all taken their sport, all taken their turn in . . . but not Peter Darley, not the priest, he had not been one of the gang of four so why had he been driven to take his own life?

His glance on the driving mirror Richard Torrey watched the play of emotions on the other man's face. He had said nothing of the condition of the man in hospital but something had put the wind up Bartley. Watching now he saw question precede fear, uncertainty feed fear and answers aggravate fear, but always there was fear. For what? Of what?

Behind him Philip Bartley's lips moved in silent rhythm with the thoughts pounding his brain.

It had all been usual enough to begin with. At the Abbey the four of them, Mather, Seton, Connor and

himself, had discussed the business of bringing in a shipment of drugs from South America. It was to follow
the same route as before, finally being distributed to the
dealers via frozen poultry, the profit shared as always: four
ways even. That over, they had gone from the study to the
drawing room and he had dismissed the Barneses for
the night. He had been helping the others to their particular tipple when they had been joined by Anna.

Bartley's fingers worried together. He had said to remain upstairs but since when had Anna taken orders! She
was dressed in hip-hugging blue satin trousers with a top
that cleaved to the slender body, her pale gold hair curled
just free of the shoulders, and her fantastic blue eyes had
smiled at each in turn. But Mather's had not smiled back,
they had smouldered, burned with a look Bartley had seen
before. He should have ended it then, marched Anna back
upstairs to the bedroom and locked the door. He should
have put an end to a lot of things that night but instead
he'd gone along with them.

Anna had laughed, a light teasing laugh, as Mather had
touched a hand to that silver-gold hair, trailing it to stroke
the tightly clad bottom. Glass in hand, glossy red lips
parted, Anna had whirled away from him, swaying seductively to the music on the stereo.

That had been the start of it . . . Christ, why hadn't he
finished it then!

Catching the sound of trembling breath Torrey
glanced again into the mirror. Something was worrying
the shit out of Bartley!

'Dance . . .' Mather had said. Fingers twisting tortuously,

Philip Bartley watched the pictures in his mind, watched the glances that had shot from Mather to Seton and then to Connor, watched Anna's lithe body sway, sinuous as a beautiful serpent, those lovely eyes inviting. 'Dance,' Mather had said again, 'dance for us, Anna.'

For some time Anna had ignored the request. Moving from one man to the other, allowing each a brief torment-ing touch of that slender body, blue eyes glistening, full lips parted in sensuous provocation, all the time knowing its effect on those that watched.

Then Seton had put that one record on. Lord, he could hear it now, the sultry tones of Matt Monroe. It had seemed to add to the fire he saw in Mather's eyes, the heat in his voice as he'd called, 'Dance, you little tease, dance for your money.' With that he'd thrown several banknotes into the centre of the floor, calling for the others to pay their tribute to the attractive figure lifting its glass to him.

That glass! Anna had brought it to be filled, then moving back to the centre of the room had lifted it again, this time pouring it over the bodice of the satin top, the wetness of it moulding to the shape beneath.

'Is this what you want to buy, Clifton?' The voice had been liquid velvet washing over Mather like a tropical storm. 'Is this what your money is for?'

He had seen the tremor rip through Mather. Bartley screwed his eyelids hard down but the picture remained painted indelibly on his memory. He had seen the desire flame in the eyes of the others as Mather had leaped forward, snatching at the wine-soaked top and ripping it away to expose the smooth flesh beneath.

'No,' Mather had almost groaned, 'it's to buy this, to buy a little strip tease, we want to see you dance naked.'

Anna had laughed and turned away. But the fire in Mather had been too strong, burned too fiercely to be quenched by a laugh or the turn of a back. Grabbing both shoulders he had held that slender figure against him, calling the others to strip away the silken trousers, the brief silk pants beneath. It had turned into a free for all, three of them grasping at the cloth and ripping it away; and when Anna was finally naked Mather had no longer wanted to watch a dance. Half carrying the protesting Anna he had flung the slight figure face down across a low table, instructing his eager partners to tear the silk fabric into strips, binding hands and ankles to the legs of the table. Then, as Anna had cried out, he had calmly removed his own clothing. Drooling with excitement he had knelt between those widely parted legs, laughing as he pushed between them. The others had done the same, each in turn had taken Anna, pushing into that slender body, vying with each other to see who could last the longest; and he, what had he done? His own flesh rampant with that same desire, lust a craving fed by what he saw, he too had raped Anna. But once had not been enough, not enough for any of them. Passion, greed, craving, call it what you will, they had each raped that whimpering terrified figure again, raped then left it tied to the table while they drank!

Christ, that was enough to bring anyone back from the grave, enough to make them defy the laws of heaven or hell to take their revenge.

And it *was* Anna. Despite all he had told himself he truly believed that. Only when in the company of Anna had he ever smelled that particular perfume, that pleasant hint of spice . . . and they had all smelled it recently . . . long after Anna's death.

Seton and Connor had finally untied the bonds that held their prisoner. Released, Anna had stumbled from the room but not before vowing the newspapers would have the whole sordid story the very next day.

Bartley opened his eyes as the Rover's tyres crunched the gravel leading up to the Abbey.

Himself, Connor and Maxwell Seton had stopped smiling. They had lost their heads, what they had done was wrong and they were sorry, they would pay . . .

Her expert make-up streaked by tears, Anna had flung back that yes, they would pay, in a way that would hurt far more than parting with their money, the world was going to know what they had done. Only Mather had continued to smile as the threats poured out. The heat in his eyes extinguished they glinted now with new flame, a cold calculating flame. Picking up the telephone as Anna had stumbled from the room he had spoken into it quietly before replacing it. '*All taken care of, gentlemen,*' he had told them, replenishing each glass with brandy then raising his own. Smiling broadly he had given the toast: '*To organisation.*' The next morning Anna had disappeared, resurfacing in a canal in Darlaston with half of that attractive face blown away by a shotgun.

*

323

Inspector Bruce Daniels looked at the tall figure sitting beside his hospital bed once more. Torrey looked different somehow. He was still the same man who had given a burial to that water lily they'd pulled from the canal, the only man to come forward for that corpse with half a face. The need to kill was still there but buried a little deeper in his eyes, over-ridden by questions. Like that woman's eyes, that reporter from the *Star* who'd come to visit the other afternoon. Visit! He swallowed hard. Come to poke her bloody nose, more like. But he'd told her nothing, Bartley and his arse-poking friends would be *his* kill, and what went for Kate Mallory went for Richard Torrey.

'It was nothing,' he answered now, his mind still on the question of why was Torrey here again, what was he truly after? 'I told you before, I was overtired, a full day's work, then a long drive down to Coventry and driving back after only a couple of hours sleep; it would be too much for any bloke.'

'Why did you drive back so soon, why not wait until morning?'

Torrey glanced at the young nurse, her uniform rustling as she came to stand at the other side of the bed.

'Will I wait in the corridor?'

'No need.' The nurse smiled back as she took Daniels's wrist in one hand, the other holding a watch pinned to a high breast. 'Matron has finished her rounds so Sister says you can stay awhile.' Recording the pulse rate on a chart hung at the foot of the bed she smiled again. 'Visitors are not normally allowed out of visiting hours, you must have charmed her.'

Watching her move briskly on to the next bed, a pert cap nestling atop shining auburn hair caught neatly beneath it, Bruce Daniels stifled a sigh. The girl was pretty, more than that she was always ready with a smile and a snippet of news from the outside world; she would be good for a man both in and out of bed. As Marjorie had been once . . . once, like a thousand years ago!

'Why did you drive back that night? It wasn't just a smell of perfume, there was something else, what was it?'

Tell what had happened and have Torrey label him a crackpot, a loony of the first water!

'What's your interest?' The inspector looked sharply at his visitor. 'Why should you bother what time I left that hotel, or why?'

'I'm not bothered, it's simply that a couple of Philip Bartley's associates did the same thing a few days back, left the Abbey late Saturday night when they were supposed to be staying for a long weekend; as for interest, I find it curious that one of them spoke of an hallucination the same as you did.'

That had his attention! Torrey saw the flicker cross the other man's eyes. It was the same flicker that had crossed them the first time he had visited, a flicker of fear. Now what was it would scare the piss out of Daniels? He'd lay two to one it was the same thing had Maxwell Seton jumping at every shadow.

'Who?' Daniels's fingers tightened over the edge of the sheet. 'Who are you talking about, what bloody hallucination?'

Easing his position on the hard-seated wooden chair

— comfort was the last word in their design, in fact it probably didn't appear in the design at all — Torrey shook his head. 'I'm no police inspector but I'm no fool, Daniels. I tell you, you tell me, a deal? Make up your mind before that ward Sister changes hers and has me out of here.'

There couldn't be any connection! Torrey was lying! Nobody knew what had happened all those years ago, nobody knew of the lad that had killed his own father. But what if they did; he'd often picked and worried before he'd dragged out the truth from a suspect, like a sparrow drags a worm from the ground, so why not someone else? What was to say some bloody smart Herbert somewhere hadn't found out the truth about him? He had already missed out on promotions; if that murder of his father became known he would miss out on the rest of his life. But Torrey had to be satisfied . . . though he didn't have to know it all.

'First you give me a name.' Inspector Bruce Daniels was giving nothing for nothing.

'Does the name Maxwell Seton hold any interest?'

'Wasn't he at that "do" in Coventry? Mr Bloody Clever thought he knew it all?'

Torrey sat silent, his face giving nothing away.

'You've got a deal, Torrey, but you'd better stick to it, remember I ain't in this hospital for good, and one more thing it will be in your interest to remember: spew it over the town and I'll see you get sent down. I 'appen to be a dab hand at finding reasons blokes should be put away; reasons such as leaving other blokes half-dead in the yard of the Bird-in-Hand or maybe helping Bartley shift his dirty goods.'

'You don't frighten me, Daniels . . .' Torrey watched the nurse patter along the ward, nice legs! '. . . so don't go sending your temperature up by trying, you wouldn't live to see any charge stick and you know it . . . so why not get on with it.'

Fingers clutching again at the sheet, Daniels swallowed hard as if the words were already stuck in his throat.

'I woke up, it must 'ave been around two. Bile was burning away my gut, drink doesn't suit any more, it aggravates whatever it is is wrong, I think I've got a bloody ulcer the way it goes on. Any road up, I woke and that smell was in my nostrils and in my mouth. Christ, Torrey, you must 'ave smelt it . . .' he shook his head remembering, '. . . no, no you couldn't 'ave, you stayed at that house . . . anyway it was thick in my throat. I had to get up to take a stomach tablet and thought that since I was out of bed brushing my teeth might clear the taste from my tongue. It . . . it was while I was getting the pack of BiSoDol from my overnight bag I thought I heard something . . . something trying to break in. I checked the window even though I knew my room was several floors from the ground and the window had an iron grille, but just to make certain nobody had already been hidden in there prior to my returning I checked the wardrobe and bathroom. I even looked under the bed but there was nothing.'

'That isn't what you said last time I was here.' Catching the eye of the ward Sister, Torrey flashed his best smile. Another two minutes and he'd have the lot.

'I told you . . .'

'So tell me again!' That Sister was definitely making for him.

Daniels's hand clutched the sheet, screwing it into tiny ripples of white. 'It . . . it was while I was in the bathroom, I thought I heard a voice, no more than a whisper, but the bathroom was empty except for me. I reckoned it must have been the central heating, them pipes make funny noises sometimes, but it came again, soft and soundless yet I heard it. I looked round from the hand basin and I saw . . . I thought I saw . . . just for a moment I thought I saw a figure. I tell you, Torrey, it was nothing, you don't see things clear when you are half asleep.'

Half asleep . . . with your guts on fire! Daniels was losing it if he thought that one would wash.

'This figure,' Torrey asked, 'what did it look like?'

'There wasn't really any figure!' Daniels's fingers screwed into the bedclothes. 'I only thought.'

'So humour me, pretend.' Aware that the woman in the pale grey uniform, a wide metal-buckled belt circling her waist, was fast approaching along the ward, Torrey knew this would be the last chance he would have of getting Daniels to talk; if he didn't hear it all now he never would.

'It stood about five eight,' Daniels too glanced at the ward Sister, his words coming quickly so she would not hear, 'attractive looking, slender with hair that touched to the collar, pale hair . . . like gold overlaid with silver though the figure seemed no older than, say, twenty-two or twenty-three; but it was the eyes I remember most, bright they were, like two bright blue jewels.'

Torrey felt his stomach tighten. The description was one he could have given himself, one that fitted the figure he'd seen outside the cottage.

'Name?' He pushed the word through the slit that a second before had been his throat.

'None.' Daniels shook his head. 'It didn't say its name.'

He didn't need it. Torrey glanced up as the nurse came to the bedside. He didn't need to hear the name, he knew it already. Anna!

Chapter Twenty-Three

So Daniels had seen it too! Torrey guided the car along the busy Wednesbury Road. The inspector had seen what he himself had seen . . . and what was that? A shadow . . . a trick of light, it could be nothing else. But that trace of perfume, the smell lodged in Daniels's nose and throat, hadn't that same faint aroma of spice washed over him that night in his own house, the night he'd dealt with those three yobbos in the Bird-in-Hand?

But that was understandable. He touched the brake, slowing as he approached a set of traffic lights. The trace of Anna was bound to have lingered. But Anna had been gone from the house for weeks and no trace of perfume lingered that long!

One thought negating the other he sent the car forwards as the traffic light flipped to green.

For himself he could accept it . . . if he accepted that the dead could return, which he didn't . . . but why Daniels, where did he fit in all of this? He'd looked sick as he'd spoken of seeing a figure, sick and scared as hell, almost as scared as Philip Bartley had looked the evening he'd ordered they drive past a hitch-hiker when there had been no hitch-hiker on the road, as scared as he'd looked yesterday when coming out of that cottage hospital. Tom Harper had said Seton had mumbled something about a third person being in the car when it rolled over. Had there been someone besides Seton and Mather in the car, had that someone been a hitch-hiker? Or was it Anna?

This was getting out of hand! Turning the car towards the rear of the supermarket he parked in a space painted with Bartley's name. He was imagining Anna with every bloke he came into contact with! But Anna was dead, he'd seen the body! Leaving the car he walked towards the building. There could be no connection . . . but tomorrow he would go visit Maxwell Seton . . . just to be friendly!

Another visitor to the Abbey. Torrey halted, watching his employer walk with a younger, more slender figure. Bartley certainly liked company, any company so long as it was young and willing. Like that dark-haired lovely he'd brought down with him last weekend, and the redhead he'd fondled all the way home the weekend before that. But the visitors he brought from the Midlands never got invited a second time; for Bartley, it seemed old playmates were the past . . . let's get on with the new.

This one was new. He caught the turn of the head as the new paramour looked at Bartley. This one hadn't been brought here in the Rover, leastways not by him; Bartley must have got his confidence back, he must be driving himself again. That would mean goodbye job! Oh well, there was always the dole, or maybe Daniels would put him on the same unofficial payroll he had Echo Sounder on, give him a job as coppers' nark! He might also scoop top prize on Littlewoods, both alternatives having about as much chance as the other, although the Pools had the slight edge!

So why had Bartley sent for him? He didn't seem in any hurry to be disturbed. Standing at the edge of the patio Torrey hesitated as the figure touched a hand to Bartley's arm, the head tilting slightly back to look into his face.

Maggie Barnes should have said Bartley had somebody with him. He turned towards the house. He'd wait in the kitchen 'til he was sent for. As he half turned away a soft laugh had him look back to face the garden in time to see a pair of slender arms curve about the other man's neck, a trim body press close into his, short fair hair catching the evening light as one mouth lifted to the other.

Christ, what a way to get your kicks! Bartley wanted a bloody audience now; well, he could look elsewhere for that!

Anger rising swiftly, Torrey looked away. There was more than one kind of pervert in the world, Bartley was well in among them, but what he did was of no matter to Richard Torrey . . . so long as he wasn't asked to play . . . or to watch.

'Torrey!' Philip Bartley's breath was heavy as he came into the kitchen. 'Torrey, why the hell didn't you come as

I asked, if I hadn't managed to see you turn back into the house . . .'

'I didn't think you would want to be disturbed.'

Catching the look that went as quickly as it came to his housekeeper's face, Philip Bartley frowned. 'I wouldn't have bloody well sent for you if I hadn't wanted to be disturbed. Come into the study, there's something I want you to do.'

Don't ask if it's anything your little playmates might do! Torrey's thoughts tingled as he followed the other man. We wouldn't want Maggie Barnes finding you with a broken back!

Slipping into the mahogany captain's chair behind a heavy desk Bartley opened a drawer, taking out a cash box and counting out twenty five-pound notes.

'I want you to go into Upwater. Hire a car there, give any name but your own or mine, then pick up Maxwell Seton from the hospital in Bowton and drive him to London. He is booked into a private nursing home there.'

'A car?' Torrey questioned. 'Wouldn't an ambulance be better seeing the man was injured in a car crash?'

'I suggested a private ambulance but that would mean having medical staff travel with him and Seton absolutely refused that, said he'd been fussed over and messed around with quite enough, a quiet transfer with himself and a driver was all he wanted. I know it must seem a bit cloak and dagger having you go all the way to Upwater but Seton is a very prominent businessman and as such values all the privacy he can get, and should the press get wind of his transfer he won't be allowed much of that, you understand?'

He understood. Torrey took the money, folding it into his pocket. Seton didn't want the press involved, but it wasn't the car accident that was worrying him, it was more likely to be whatever it was had brought him and Mather to this house in the first place.

'There's already been enough publicity. Unfortunately Mather's death couldn't be kept from the press, but there's no need for Seton to be harassed any further.'

Returning the cash box to the drawer, Bartley added, 'You'd best take a taxi to Bowton to make it seem you are just visiting the hospital, then get another into Upwater; we don't want the Rover seen there, too many bloody nosy folk around.'

Meeting the bland look, Torrey nodded. If the man wanted to play dodge the journalist why should he argue, his pay was the same whether he drove Bartley's or a hired car.

'What did you mean back there in the kitchen when you said you thought I wouldn't want to be disturbed?'

The question coming as he reached the door, Torrey glanced behind him. 'Just that,' he said non-committally. 'You seemed pretty occupied with your companion so I guessed whatever it was you wanted me for could wait.'

'Companion?' Bartley frowned. 'What the hell are you talking about?'

He wasn't going to deny it, surely Bartley couldn't expect him to believe he hadn't seen him with his new interest!

His look cynical as it rested on the other man, Torrey smiled coldly. 'You want that kept secret too. Well, don't let it worry you, I'm sure we can all be relied upon to keep our mouths shut.'

Philip Bartley's hand came down sharp on the desk. 'Torrey, I'll ask you again, what are you talking about?'

'The dish, the one with the legs, the one hanging on to your arm, the one who made sure I saw you kissing.'

Slamming the desk drawer shut, Bartley shook his head. 'Seems you're the one needing medical staff! Go on like that, Torrey, and they'll have you in a strait jacket!'

'You don't have to lie, Mr Bartley, makes no difference to me how many visitors you have here . . . or their trade! I just drive your car and that's the way it stays.'

'No, wait!' Bartley was on his feet. 'You really mean it, don't you . . . you really think there was someone with me in the garden?'

'No, I don't *think*, I *know* you had someone with you, I'm not blind and neither am I losing my mind. But, like I say, your business be your business . . .'

'Wait!' Bartley's voice trembled. 'This . . . this other person, what . . . what did it look like?'

It! Some description! Bartley changed his lovers as often as he changed his shirts but to speak of one of them as 'it'! His cynicism becoming contempt, Torrey stared evenly across the desk. 'Like I said, a dish, certainly it looked that way from where I was standing; good legs, trim hips, short hair just touching the shoulders, looked a nice colour too, especially as the sun touched it.'

'Colour?' Philip Bartley's question was hoarse, his eyes staring as they fixed on Torrey. 'What . . . what colour was it?'

'You don't need me to tell you that!' Tired of the other man's horseplay, Torrey swung open the door, throwing his words behind him as he strode from the room: 'It was golden . . . pale gold!'

That doctor had been right, Seton shouldn't even be out of bed let alone travelling in the back seat of a car. Glancing in the mirror at the figure bundled in a blanket, Torrey remembered the short out-of-patience snap of the woman doctor as he had half lifted Maxwell Seton into the Rover: *It is madness, it's likely to do him even more damage.* But Seton had signed his own discharge and nobody could argue with that. Though when he reminded the doctor of that it hadn't mollified the woman any; just the reverse, it seemed to add to her already irate temper. Just like a woman . . . Torrey smiled to himself . . . couldn't stand not having everything her own way. Yet fair was fair, he thought as he flicked the indicator to the right, easing the car among the traffic scurrying out along the busier trunk road, the woman was concerned for Seton's health. But it was more than the mending of broken bones giving concern to Maxwell Seton. Torrey looked again into the mirror as the man behind mumbled, his head jerking rapidly from side to side.

He had paid that visit to the hospital, saying he was there on behalf of Bartley. He had stayed an hour, an hour which had told him Seton was balanced on a knife edge, one tip and it would slit his throat.

Returning his attention to the road, Torrey let the

thoughts roam free in his mind. *'It laughed,'* Seton had mumbled as the sedative administered by one of the nurses had begun to take effect. *'It laughed as Mather burned. I didn't know . . . I didn't know . . . it was Mather's doing, he set the dogs loose . . . I didn't kill . . .'* The drug had taken him then but even in sleep the man had moaned, his eyes beneath closed lids darting here and there like terrified sheep.

Terrified was the only word. Torrey glanced again at the rear seat. Something had Seton almost out of his mind. *'I didn't kill . . .'* The words returned, raising the tiny hairs on the back of Torrey's neck. Was murder the reason for the man's fears, had he been somehow involved with a killing?

'. . . attractive looking, slender with hair that touched to the collar, pale hair . . . like gold overlaid with silver . . . but it was the eyes I remember most . . . like two bright blue jewels.'

Torrey felt the blood freeze in his veins as the words of Inspector Bruce Daniels danced in his head. They matched the figure he had seen with Bartley in the grounds of the Abbey, matched what he'd seen for himself that night outside the cottage, and matched what Seton had mumbled as he drifted into that drugged sleep. And each description fitted Anna!

Fingers gripping the wheel of the car he stared at the tail lights of a lorry as it roared past.

'I didn't kill . . . it was Mather's doing.'

Mather and Seton, they were both involved in somebody's death and they were both associates of Philip Bartley. Was that association more than simply commercial business? Was Bartley too an accessory to murder?

His foot pressed the pedal, shooting the car forwards and cutting dangerously close to the lorry as it sped around it, but Torrey was oblivious of the enraged blare of a horn or the driver's two fingers held to the windscreen in a prostitute's farewell.

Had they known Anna, had Anna been at the Abbey . . . was it Anna's death Seton had mumbled about?

Tomorrow he would be back at Monkswell. Tomorrow Philip Bartley would be answering a few questions or it would be Philip Bartley being taken to a private nursing home.

'I tell you that were no accident.' Martha Sim looked at the man sitting opposite her in the tiny room of her cottage. 'I hears what you says, Tom 'Arper, but still I tells you it were no accident took that car from the road, no accident rolled it on to its roof afore setting it to blaze. It were the hand of the Dark One done all o' that, it were him sent his minion to bring his own to him, it was the time of reward.'

'You can't be sure o' that, Martha, they just be visitors to the Abbey . . .'

'Can't be sure!' Martha's blackberry eyes glistened. 'Can't be sure! I be sure enough to tell you the one died in the flames don't be the only one will pay that price, the Dark One don't be satisfied so easy. No, Tom 'Arper, there be others bearing his mark. That one were not the first nor will 'e be the last.'

'You said as 'ow there was one, one not belonging to

the village . . . was it him you was meanin', was it that fancy fellow that had been a visitin' up at the Abbey?'

'It weren't him.' The berry-bright eyes shifted to the woman sitting beside Tom. 'There be another yet.'

'Another!' Rosie Harper's ruddy cheeks paled. 'I thought . . . I 'oped when I 'eard . . .'

'We all did, Aunt Rosie.' Hilda Sim touched the hand of the woman who had always been as a second mother to her. 'We all 'oped it would be over and the evil gone from the village, but mother feels its presence too strong. It be 'ere for somebody else yet and it won't go without what it come for.'

'But who be the somebody?' Rosie directed the question at Martha.

'It be one that bides in Monkswell though it be not the place of his birth. I see the sign of death on his brow and the shadow of evil smiles at his shoulder. His days number less than you 'ave fingers but before his taking there will be one other, one who at this minute is facing the servant of the Lord of Darkness.'

'Oh dear God!' Rosie Harper crossed herself, her hand shaking as it reached for her husband's.

'Be there nothing you can do, Martha . . . I brought fresh candles.'

'It'll tek more'n candles, Tom 'Arper.' Martha shook her grey-streaked head. 'And my powers by themselves be no match for what stalks Monkswell.'

'But you and my Rosie . . .'

'Don't still be enough.' Martha cut him short. 'The evil that carried off young Peter Darley be the same as took that visitor to the Abbey; it be strong, Tom, too strong for Rosie and me. It swept me aside like a leaf in a storm, it could have killed me as easy as swatting a fly and I don't know why it didn't, I only knows that alone we be no match for it.'

'Alone?' Rosie Harper's hand clenched tight about the gnarled old fingers of her husband. 'Be you saying there be somebody as can 'elp, somebody as can drive this devil back to where it come from?'

Swivelling her glance to the fire Martha Sim stared into its glowing depths, her words coming quietly.

'The powers told me of one . . . one who don't believe in the ancient ways, one who 'olds no faith. 'E alone can stand before the forces of darkness, 'e alone can break the 'old of the Evil One.'

'Then we 'ave to ask 'im!'

Martha's hand swung again, a sad smile touching the wrinkled corners of her mouth.

'I fear the answer, Tom. Folk from the big cities, they've long since left the old ways behind, they believe nothing they can't see nor 'old in their 'and. Their gods be money and possessions, and the force of Right be for them that which brings the most profit.'

'Tom be right none the less, Martha.' Rosie Harper spoke softly though anxiety still echoed in her voice. 'Whoever this one be the powers spoke to you of, he 'as to be told of what be going on, we 'ave to ask 'im to 'elp rid the village of fear, to banish the evil that's come to Monkswell.'

'The powers . . .' Tom Harper leaned forwards his

rheumy old eyes holding to Martha's face, '. . . did they tell who this one they spoke of was, did they give a name?'

Looking up slowly, the firelight turning her eyes to black flame, Martha Sim nodded.

'Yes, Tom, the powers of Light gave a name, the name they spoke of was Torrey . . . Richard Torrey.'

Chapter Twenty-Four

'Leave me alone . . . I paid you well . . . we all paid you.'

Manoeuvring between a stream of lorries Torrey had not glanced at his passenger for several minutes, now as the man's mumblings became more of a moan he looked again into the mirror, a puzzled frown settling between his dark brows. Seton had thrown off the blanket and was crouched in the corner of the seat, one arm held protectively across his face, the other, encased in plaster, held to his chest.

'Please . . . it wasn't me, it was Mather . . .'

Behind him Maxwell Seton whimpered like a frightened child, his hand pushing at empty air. Something was playing havoc with him, but what? Torrey's glance swept the road. He couldn't stop the car here; to come to a standstill would be suicide, those trucks would grind them to scrap metal before they could pull up.

'. . . I didn't . . . I didn't send the dogs in . . .'

Dogs! Torrey's frown deepened as he watched the road

for a layby or at least a gap in the verge where he could
beach the car.

'. . . no . . . you're wrong . . . you're wrong . . .'

His voice rising hysterically Seton's arms flailed. Was
it the sedative that doctor had given him before they left,
was the medication having an adverse effect on his system,
causing him to have nightmares? Some bloody nightmare!
Torrey struggled with the steering as Seton's plastered
arm caught him across the shoulders, knocking him
forwards over the wheel.

'Seton . . .' He shouted as the angry blare of a lorry's
horn cut through the night '. . . Seton, what the hell's the
matter with you? You'll have us under a bloody truck!'

He could have saved his breath. Torrey grunted, struggling to keep the car on an even keel, ignoring the flash of
lights from the driver at his rear. If he didn't find a place
to pull in soon they'd both be in plaster . . . or in boxes!

'Seton!' He called again, the name dying on his lips as
he caught the faint whiff of perfume. That perfume!
Nostrils flared, teeth clamped hard together, he tried not
to breathe, not to smell that delicate hint of spice, to tell
himself it was his imagination.

'. . . I didn't want you killed . . .'

Torrey's glance flicked to the man sitting behind him.
Christ, it wasn't true! It was a trick of the lights flashing
from the car a few yards back. His foot hovered over the
brake pedal; he could bring that bastard to a stop and
shove his indicators so far up his arse they'd light his eyes
up!

'. . . it was Mather . . .' Seton was crying now, his voice

trembling with sobs. '. . . Connor and Bartley . . . we told him not to . . .'

Bartley! Torrey's lungs exploded in a gasp then sucked hungrily at the fragranced air. He hadn't been far wrong in thinking Seton had been involved in a murder, a murder it seemed Mather, Connor and Bartley all knew about.

'. . . he said it had to be done . . .'

Oblivious now to the blare of horn and the flashing of headlights, Torrey stared in the mirror at the scene behind. Seton's face was hidden, hidden behind a swathe of pale gold hair, a long-fingered hand rested on one shoulder, a slender figure in a blue top, long legs encased in tight-fitting jeans, lay half across Seton's crouching body.

It couldn't be . . . it was impossible! Torrey's nerves jarred. There was nobody in the car save himself and Seton! So what were his eyes showing him? And that perfume, he'd smelled it that night in the house in Dangerfield Lane and again the night he'd seen that figure outside the cottage. It was the same, elusive . . . memorable, the hint of fragrance Bruce Daniels had spoken of, the same aroma that had filled the church as he had tried to help that young priest . . . the perfume worn by Anna!

'. . . no . . . get away . . . get away . . .'

The cry nothing short of an agonised scream Maxwell Seton grabbed at the door handle, twisting it downwards. God Almighty, one more second and he'd have the door open! The realisation jerking his thoughts back to the present, Torrey flung a hand over the back of his seat in an attempt to grab the screaming man, but the plastered arm jabbed it away.

'Seton . . . Seton, for Christ's sake!'

No, not for Christ's sake, Ritchie, but for mine.

The words, accompanied by a soft silken laugh, seemed to whisper in his mind and as he twisted to glance across his shoulder the pale-gold head turned, the face of Anna smiling back at him.

'Anna!' There was no fear in the cry that forced itself from his throat only a deep longing, a starving yearning need for something lost too long.

'. . . I didn't kill you . . . get away . . . get away . . .'

Caught by the wind rushing past the speeding car the door snatched itself from Seton's grasp, swinging wide back on its hinges.

The sudden draught of night air sweeping the interior acted like cold water on Torrey's senses. Shouting Seton's name he grabbed again for the man's wrist but the heavily plastered arm swung upwards, catching him full in the face.

How many more bloody questions? Christ, they'd already asked enough to start their own television quiz programme! Ask Me Another . . . that would be an apt title . . . or Inspector Smartarse Investigates. Every bone in his body aching, Torrey looked at the man sitting across from him, saw his rough tweed jacket frayed at the cuffs. Like Daniels, this man's clobber had seen better days, so much for police pay . . . remind me never to go for a copper's job!

'So tell me again, Mr Torrey, exactly what happened?'

He hadn't made such a good job of hiding what he felt — that the cops were making a balls-up of the whole thing — so now Inspector Smartarse was getting his own back, going through the whole business again.

'I've told you three times already!' Torrey gritted through lips badly swollen from that blow from Seton's plastered arm. 'You know, they run night classes for slow learners!'

Inspector John Sumner of the West Mercia Police could afford the smile. The longer this twat dished the sarcasm the longer he'd sit in this interview room and to hell with what that doctor had said about rest.

'Thanks for the information,' he answered pleasantly. 'P'raps you'd be good enough to give me the name of the place you attended.'

Touché! His mouth too painful to smile, Torrey paid the tribute inwardly.

'When you're ready, Mr Torrey.'

'Is it too much to ask for a cup of tea?'

Obvious pleasure resonating in his words the inspector nodded at the uniformed constable standing just inside the closed door as he answered. 'Not too much at all. Oh, and Constable, Mr Torrey might like a straw with that.'

Careful, Inspector! Torrey's veins iced. Even the brass has to go home some time and you could just find a lethal surprise waiting for you one dark and dismal night!

'Shall we get on with it, or do you still want to play match the quip?'

'Not the game I prefer but my choice can wait, so let's go for yours.' Torrey nodded as a polystyrene cup of tepid tea was set on the table in front of him and the same constable settled with a tape-recorder. Tired now but with anger keeping his mind sharp, he recounted the happening in the car, finishing with, 'Mr Seton must have been reacting to the drugs the hospital gave him.'

'And that's all that happened, there was nothing else?'

'What else could there be?' Torrey stared evenly at the police inspector. What else but some sort of bloody apparition; but tell that to the cops and they'd have the men in white suits here quicker than an old man could fart.

'You tell me.' The inspector leaned back in his chair, his whole attitude one of 'I can wait'.

'Look.' Exasperation lacing his voice Torrey pushed the cup of tea to one side. 'I've told you what went down. Seton was restless, he started to thrash about. I tried talking to him, to quiet him until I could find a lay-by and p'raps get a medic out to look at him. But that did no good and he got slowly worse, flailing his arms about until a time or two I almost lost control of the car. Try pulling in a couple of the lorries that were alongside, ask them if I'm telling the truth.'

'No one says you're not, Mr Torrey, we're merely trying to establish the facts.'

'The fact is I've had it up to the teeth with your bloody questions . . .'

'Then the quicker you answer, the quicker it will all be over. Do go on, Mr Torrey.'

Get this one in the yard of the Bird-in-Hand and he'd never walk out of it! Torrey felt the deadness rise from the core of him, the same cold impersonality he had been taught to apply to the killing of an enemy.

'The talking did no good . . .' He tried pushing the feeling back. The man was doing his job but, Christ, he'd better tread gently. '. . . Seton got steadily more and more violent, throwing himself about . . .'

'But the man was injured, he'd only recently been involved in a serious car accident.'

'Don't ask me how he found the strength.' Torrey heard the doubt. 'All I know is what I saw.'

'And what did you see?'

For a moment there was no sound in the small bare room. The constable looked up waiting for the answer.

'I saw his hand on the door handle. I shouted for him to leave it alone and when he ignored me I made a grab for his wrist . . . that was when he jabbed me in the face with his plastered arm and flung himself out of the car . . . right in front of a twenty-ton lorry!'

Pushing back his chair the inspector stood up.

'Thank you for your statement, Mr Torrey. If you will just sign it the constable will arrange for a car to drive you to a hotel . . . Oh and by the way,' he turned at the door, a bland smile on his face, 'be sure not to leave the contact address you gave without first informing us.'

The same bloody goddamn ritual! Torrey kicked his own chair backwards. He'd gone through it all before when those coppers had called to ask about a corpse dragged out of the canal. The whole thing was a carbon copy of the other – did they get a list of questions that had to be learned parrot-fashion or were they all morons? Anything else they wanted to know they could ask in Monkswell, that was where he would be . . . asking questions of his own.

Echo Sounder hadn't quite lived up to expectation. Kate Mallory hitched her over-large bag higher on her shoulder. He hadn't wanted to tell her anything: 'Nuthin' to say to the bloody *Star*.' But that had changed with the appearance of a pint of best and a whisky chaser. There had been a few stares as she had walked into the smoke-filled tap room of the Frying Pan, a woman venturing into the hallowed precincts of a man's preserve. But that hadn't troubled Kate Mallory, she was impervious to stares and well able to hold her own in the insult stakes. Sounder had been sitting at a table in a corner facing the bar and the door, a place conducive to seeing everyone who came and went without being conspicuous. She had gone straight over to him, hooking out a vacant chair with one foot and sitting down without the invite she knew would never be given.

'Ya be wastin' ya time, I don't talk to no bloody reporters.'

Kate smiled, remembering her answer. 'Now isn't that strange, it doesn't sound a bit like the piece appearing in this evening's edition: "Tipster sounds off in pub . . . echoes all over town." It won't take the local colour long to sort out who that is, will it? And *once they do you'll give no more tips, racing or otherwise.'*

The look that had flickered beneath those hooded eyes had resembled a cobra about to strike. Kate turned along Willenhall Road towards the town centre. But Echo Sounder's look meant nothing and she had continued to question. There had been no piece ready for print but Sounder couldn't know that and it was the not knowing that had loosened his tongue. Even so, he had said as little as possible.

He didn't know a Clifton Mather or a Maxwell Seton, if they didn't drink in the Frying Pan then he wouldn't know them. Kate had smiled at that. Anything this little shit didn't know hadn't happened.

'And Doc Walker?'

Thrown unexpectedly it had caught the weedy little man off guard, the look that flashed across his ferret-sharp features telling her he had the whole story of that police raid, and much else besides, printed on his brain in capital letters.

She had opened a pack of Rothmans, offering it across the table, and Sounder's greedy eyes had glittered as he saw the corners of two ten-pound notes folded among the cigarettes. That was the money saved towards the suit she had drooled over in Marston's shop window. Oh well! P'raps next year! She checked her watch as the clock of St Lawrence church chimed two. She should have reported in a couple of hours ago, Scotty would be fuming . . . but then when did her editor do anything other than fume? Deciding it was as well to be hanged for a sheep as for a lamb she turned in the direction of Alma Street.

'I ain't tellin' you shit about Doc Walker,' Sounder had said but as she had closed the pack of cigarettes, returning them pointedly to her large open-topped bag, he had grabbed his pint glass, muttering into it.

'Ya wants to know about 'im and the other two ya'll needs talk to Philip Bartley.'

'He won't even give me the time of day and you know it; you'll have to do better than that if I'm to wipe out the copy set for tonight's paper.'

It was an unsound gamble and if he'd chosen to take her up on it that would have been it: Kate Mallory reports . . . nothing! But he hadn't taken the bet, Echo Sounder would wager on most things but not his own neck.

'It's still going on, isn't it?' She had taken the Rothmans from her bag, stroking one finger absently over the blue and white packet. *'Putting Walker away didn't finish it.'*

'I don't know what goes on . . .'

'Not true, Echo, but this is: either you tell me what I want to know or tonight will find you plastered all over the next edition of the Star *and tomorrow will see you floating in the canal wearing rope bracelets and a wire necklace!'*

'All I seen was the two runners Bartley brought in . . .'

'No racing jargon, please, I'm allergic.'

Sounder had glanced up at that, greed and venom mixed in his shifty eyes. *'Two men,'* he'd gone on, his gaze retreating to the depths of his glass, *'strangers, 'adn't never been seen in 'ere afore that night, reckon they was fetched in to guard whatever it was bein' brought into Bartley's place.'*

'You mean the drugs Inspector Daniels has told me about?'

She hadn't so much as blinked, the lie slipping from her tongue like cream.

'Daniels would never . . .'

'Spill the beans? But he did, and why not . . .' she had eased the top of the cigarette packet open slightly, just showing the edge of the folded notes, '. . . his little parade was rained off so he had nothing to lose.'

Emotions chasing across his narrow features like the race horses he was so fond of watching, Echo Sounder had grabbed the whisky chaser, throwing it into his mouth and swallowing noisily. He couldn't be sure she was telling the truth but he was sure of the winner of the three thirty at Haydock . . . and twenty quid on that would see him nicely over the next few months.

Kate could have quoted his thoughts verbatim, instead she had eased her chair backwards and gathered her bag.

"'Old on!" The shifty eyes had swept the tap room without lifting. 'It be truth when I tells you I don't know the form over at Bartley's place, I ain't not never been there so 'ow could I?'

He had paused there and through Kate's inner nose was twitching she nodded calmly.

'Of course you couldn't, Echo, it was stupid of me to think you might.'

'I said I d'ain't know the form, not I couldn't put somebody else your way.'

Kate Mallory smiled to herself as she approached the newly built supermarket rising like a large red boil out of the flat empty heath. The twenty pounds had worked. Echo had given her a name, now all she had to do was find the face it fitted.

Chapter Twenty-Five

'Ritchie . . .'

The sound swam in his brain, a soft tender breathing of his name whispered as it always was when Anna . . .

'Ritchie . . .'

Whispered though it was, it snatched the veil of sleep from Torrey's brain. Wide awake now he stared at the first flimsy shadows of early evening slipping silently into his bedroom. He hadn't meant to rest, he had meant to confront Bartley as soon as he got to Monkswell. A groan breaking from him, he rose and went into the bathroom, splashing his face with ice-cold water. It was as well he was awake, that dream . . .

'Ritchie.'

With the towel pressed to his face he stood perfectly still. He wasn't dreaming now, nor was he imagining things. He *had* heard that voice whisper his name . . . and the voice was Anna's!

'I was coming home, Ritchie, coming to you.'

The towel falling from suddenly nerveless fingers Torrey wanted to turn to face whatever it was he knew stood behind him but he couldn't; facing terrorists was one thing, but this . . .

'I loved you, Ritchie.'

Breath blocking his throat, Torrey wrestled with the emotions racing through him: desire, need and common sense, the first telling him not to argue with what was happening, the second urging him to take what was necessary to satisfy that hunger, the last saying don't be a bloody fool.

'I wanted to come back, come back to you, Ritchie, but they wouldn't let me . . .'

Hands moved slowly over his naked hips, lips pressed to his spine, a delicate spicy fragrance filled the air.

'You were the one, Ritchie, you were the only man I ever loved . . .'

Tremors raced along, burning every nerve end as the touch of a moist tongue traced his backbone.

'. . . you know that don't you, my love . . .?'

Torrey listened to the breathy whisper brushing against his cheek, head and shoulders arching backwards, breath locked in his lungs as soft unseen hands stroked over his hips and down into his groin. God, he wanted this . . . wanted Anna!

'. . . I was wrong to leave you . . .'

The musical voice whispered on, the touch stroking between his legs, caressing the mounds of swollen flesh, the stiffened column jerking against his stomach.

'. . . but I'll never leave you again.'

The words a song in his heart, Torrey gasped as the moist tongue transferred to his chest and trailed slowly, tortuously down, setting his whole being on fire as it nuzzled the tip of his erect manhood.

This couldn't be happening, Anna was dead and what he heard, what he was feeling, wasn't real. Desperately his brain tried to reassert command of his senses, to break the hold that had mind and body prisoner, but the flames of desire shooting from his groin had already reached their zenith and with a loud groan he erupted. Gulping in a deep breath he reached for the head pressed to the base of his stomach, sinking to his knees as his hands closed on empty air.

It was perfectly natural. It had taken minutes to pull himself together, to accept the fact that he was alone in the cottage, that he had been alone all along. What had happened to him happened to other men, he'd seen it often while in the Army; starve your body too long and it will find its own nourishment. That was what had happened just now. He had woken with the need for sex; that was it, pure and simple, his own body had done the rest. Standing under the shower he tried to dispel the strong feeling of self-disgust that swept him. He should have been strong enough, he shouldn't let desire . . . any sort of desire . . . override common sense. But that voice, that touch; Christ, he could have sworn they were real! Sworn it had been Anna there in the bathroom, Anna that had touched him, made love to him.

But Anna was dead, nothing could alter that. He lifted his face, letting the spray of hot water play over his closed eyes. Anna was dead . . . and the dead didn't return.

No, the dead didn't return. Dressed, Torrey caught up the jacket he had flung across a chair. But the dead could haunt a man, the memory of them plaguing his mind until he was ready to believe anything. But it needed no trick of the imagination to remind him of Anna, or of a corpse dragged from that canal.

Leaving the cottage he stood staring across the little garden at the expanse of open ground bordered in the distance by a line of trees, half expecting, totally wanting, to see the figure he had seen a few nights ago. Over towards the church a crow called loudly as it flew low across the sky, breaking the moment. Christ, when would it be broken for good! Torrey turned away. When would he stop imagining Anna at every turn? But he knew when: when he had the answer.

Walking slowly in the direction of the lovely old Abbey he let his thoughts run free. Daniels, Mather and Seton. They had experienced much the same as he, the smell of perfume, the touching, the whispering . . . so what was it plaguing *their* minds?

'I wanted to come back, come back to you, Ritchie, but they wouldn't let me . . .'

The words that had whispered in his mind whispered again. Who were 'they'? It was too late to ask Mather or Seton, like Anna they were dead; but Bartley . . . Bartley was still alive.

*

'I were just on my way to your place but I sees you wouldn't 'a bin there.'

Deep among his own thoughts, Torrey had been unaware of the older man approaching. Stopping now he smiled at the leathery face of Tom Harper.

'Evening, Tom.'

'Evenin', lad. Like I says, I was a'coming over to see you.'

'Anything I can do, Tom, for you or for Rosie, you need only to name it.'

Tom Harper looked at the man who had come to live in the village. He was well liked by the folk here, always a smile, pleasant enough to speak with and willing to give a hand when asked, but scratch the surface and you'd find bonded steel. Richard Torrey was a man he'd rather have as an ally than an enemy.

'T'weren't me nor my Rosie a' wantin' anythin' of ya, lad, but Martha Sim. Her be askin' if you'd be so good as to go visit her at Cobweb Cottage.'

'Martha Sim.' Torrey looked puzzled. 'Any idea what she wants, Tom?'

'T'ain't for me to say, lad. Martha Sim be best at tellin' her business; all I knows is her asked would I come for ya and I come, I can't tell no more.'

That in itself rang a flawed bell. Torrey watched the other man scratch a finger beneath his cap. He wouldn't call Tom Harper a liar but then again he wouldn't say the man was telling the whole truth and nothing but the truth.

Hiding the smile that rose behind the thought, Torrey nodded. 'I'm on my way to see Mr Bartley right now but tell Martha I'll look in at her place on my way back.'

Tom Harper's gaze lifted to the flock of geese flying in vee formation to their evening roost. 'Won't do no good.'

'What do you mean? She asked to see me, didn't she?'

The rheumy eyes smiled as they returned to Torrey's face. 'Ar lad, Martha asked to see ya.'

'So where's the problem?'

'It don't lie at Cobweb Cottage.'

He liked Tom Harper and at any other time the old man's habit of going all around the Wrekin to say something would have amused Torrey, but right now his patience balanced on a tightrope. Trying to keep it from slipping he glanced towards the stately old house, its brickwork gleaming in the lowering sun.

'Look, Tom, I have to see Mr Bartley . . .'

'I told ya, it won't do no good.'

'What!' The tightrope quivered. 'What won't do no good?'

'You goin' up to yon house.'

'Why?' Torrey's voice cracked with impatience.

Scratching his head once more, Tom Harper answered agreeably, 'Be a waste o' time, Torrey lad, seein' as 'ow Philip Bartley don't be at the Abbey.'

'Not at the Abbey,' Torrey frowned, 'then where?'

'I can't be a tellin' o' that, all I knows for sure be what I 'eard from George Barnes onny yesterday. Seems after you left from talkin' to Bartley the man 'ad some kind o' turn, thought there was somebody other than hisself in the room with 'im, some woman so it seemed, for 'e kep on callin' 'er Anna.'

Anna! Torrey's whole being lurched violently. He had been right to suppose Bartley had known Anna, that meant the others too, they had to be the ones behind the killing.

'I wanted to come back . . . they wouldn't let me . . .'

A cold dispassionate calm settled over him as the words drifted into his mind sheathing the anger, replacing it with a frozen determination, a cold lethal desire to kill.

'They wouldn't let me!'

Anna's attractive face smiled, the lithe beautiful body dancing across his inner vision.

Seton and Mather were gone, those he could not kill; but Bartley . . . Bartley would die at his hands! Quietly, his lips hardly moving, he asked, 'What did George Barnes tell you?'

'T'were a strange carry on an' no mistake.' Tom settled his cap back in place as he answered. 'Maggie Barnes were doin' a bit o' tidyin' in the kitchen and 'eard Bartley a' shoutin'. Sounded like 'e were cryin', her said, then when her 'eard things bein' throwed about her went to see if 'e were all right, that were when her seen 'im pushin' at summat as weren't there, tellin' it to go away an' leave 'im alone, that it weren't 'im had done it. But what "it" was Maggie d'ain't find out for soon as 'er spoke to 'im he screamed for George to pack 'im an overnight bag and then phone for a taxi. That were it, 'e left soon as the car arrived. Maggie said it were funny though, there'd been nobody savin' you, Bartley and 'erself in that room but for a time after it smelled of perfume, slightly spicy, tangy, but definitely perfume, and it were a perfume she 'adn't never smelled in the 'ouse before.'

It was as if every letter was being chiselled into his brain. Bartley and his fancy friends had murdered Anna. Was it Anna's ghost that wanted revenge? No, he wouldn't have that, ghosts were for kids' stories or for fools who knew no better than to believe such crap . . . but that perfume, they had all smelled it, and they weren't all fools!

'Where did Bartley go?'

Tom Harper had watched that impassive face. There was something sinister beneath the rigid set of it, something eating at the heart of Richard Torrey. Martha Sim were right, it were something that would destroy the man sooner than let go.

'George said as he 'eard Bartley mumble summat about a 'otel but couldn't say where. Summat must 'ave unsettled 'im good an' proper forrim to go leavin' his own 'ouse for to stop in some 'otel, that be all I can say.'

The desire to avenge Anna, the desire to avenge himself for the loss of a loved one no less strong, Torrey knew satisfaction would have to wait. But he would have it, yes by God, he would watch Philip Bartley die!

Kate Mallory walked slowly along the aisles of Bartley Supermarkets, stopping every now and then to read a label on a can or deposit a package into a metal basket, the handle cutting painfully into the soft flesh of one arm. She didn't need any of the things she selected but choosing them provided cover while she looked for one special item.

But it wasn't on any of the shelves, just as she had been told it wouldn't be. Running a glance once more over the selection marked 'Baking' she took a small bag of self-raising flour and put it with the other items in the basket, then proceeded to the nearest till, smiling at the woman cashier as she paid.

She had spoken with the man Echo Sounder had mentioned. but not at the supermarket, that would have been too dicey. She sighed, hauling herself on to the bus along with a bevy of other women all loaded with bulging shopping baskets and most trailing a string of kids who snivelled for some treat or other the housekeeping hadn't stretched to. And her own housekeeping would be strained next month too, seeing it had cost her another quid for Sounder to arrange a meeting and a couple of tenners to get the bloke to talk.

Paying for her ticket she squeezed her shoulder bag between herself and the window, excluding it from the prying fingers of a child ignored by its mother.

Amos Hodgkin had once owned a grocer's shop on Pinfold Street but with the coming of the supermarket the business had gone downhill until at last it had closed altogether. The blame for that Amos had placed directly on 'that bloody no good Bartley'. Not without some reason. Kate stared resolutely out of the window, ignoring the child's constant chatter.

But no longer owning a business did not mean Amos Hodgkin was no longer a businessman. '*You want information, then you pays for it,*' he had told her flatly. And paid she had: one fiver not enough she had held out the other. It wasn't only Hodgkin had a head for business, but he wouldn't get the rest 'til he'd coughed.

He'd got himself taken on in the warehouse helping to unload the lorries bringing supplies from various parts of the country then feeding them into the store whenever they were needed. It was the supply of flour that had caught his attention. Unlike the usual stuff it came in a small white-painted van with fancy brown lettering. 'Valeton Mill, the finest of fine flour' Only Valeton flour never reached the shop itself. The delivery van was always met by Bartley himself and the half-dozen boxes shut away in a side room. He hadn't asked any of his workmates the reason; whatever made Bartley lock that flour away he'd find out about it in his own way. That was when he'd begun to check the shelves and found this particular brand of flour was never offered for sale. Then on the lead up to Christmas of last year he'd been asked to work an extra shift, fill in for a man who'd gone sick. Left alone to sort the items needed for next day he'd picked the lock of that side room and taken a good hard look at the small one-pound packets in each box. And fine flour they weren't, in fact if they were any sort of flour then he'd never been no grocer.

'*So what was in the packets?*' Kate had asked.

'*Felt like flour.*' Amos Hodgkin had frowned, clearly puzzled. '*But it didn't have the smell of wheat nor of any grain I*

*could name, yet it did have a smell, a sharp acrid tang that stung the
nostrils. No, either them bags don't hold flour or my name ain't Amos
Hodgkin and I have a birth certificate that says it is.'*

'Can you get me one of those bags?'

He had smiled at that, shaking his head. *'I ain't taking no
risk like that but I can get you some more information and hope to God
it puts bloody Philip Bartley where he put me, out of business.'*

Reaching the Bull Stake the bus came to a halt, women
and children jostling to be off first. Being in no such hurry
Kate waited, stepping off the platform after the last of
them.

The second time they met, Amos Hodgkin had looked
around to make certain no one else was listening. Sitting
in the locally termed 'spitters', the cheapest seats in the
ABC cinema, Kate had remained silent as the attendant
had shone her torch between the rows of seats. Had the
venue been Hodgkin's choice or was it Sounder's way of
having the last laugh? He had waited while a couple
squeezed past. Kate could still feel a twinge from where
the man's foot had come down heavily on hers before he'd
flopped into a seat beside her own. Hodgkin had become
even more reluctant than before, casting several glances at
the man and his companion before his words squeezed
between closed teeth.

*'That van comes every two months, regular as clockwork and always
round about the same time, eleven o'clock in the morning. Judging by
what's gone before I puts the next delivery at that time day after
tomorrow.'*

The Pearl and Dean advertisements had begun then
and Amos Hodgkin's mouth clamped tight. A few more

minutes and the second house would begin. She could sit through another showing of Schwarzenegger gunning his way through *Terminator* while Linda Hamilton raced across the screen in an ongoing battle with a creature from her future . . . but then again she couldn't, that was too much to ask! She had scrambled her way along a row of avid watchers, their mumbled expletives of the kind that would put the most hardened Hollywood gangsters to shame.

Both Sounder and Hodgkin had been prepared to play ball for a price. Kate hitched her huge bag more comfortably on one shoulder, grasping a brown paper carrier bag of groceries with her other hand. It remained to be seen whether the next man would play at all.

Chapter Twenty-Six

Bartley was not at the Abbey! He could go after him now but where to look? He could be in any hotel anywhere . . . But tomorrow he would be in his office, that man allowed nothing to come between him and his business. Nodding to Tom Harper, Torrey turned back towards the lane that led to the Sims' cottage. He had waited this long, one more night would make no difference. Following the older man he did not see the figure that watched from beyond the tree line, a figure whose attractive face hardened, its hyacinth eyes glinting like blue ice, a figure that glided silently behind.

Almost as old as the Abbey, Cobweb Cottage, like its illustrious neighbour, appeared to have changed little. Of course there must have been a measure of rebuilding over such a span of time, Torrey reasoned, looking at the ancient thatched roof and half-timbered walls reflecting the amber gold sunset, but it had been done with a skilful hand and loving heart. Following through the white-painted gate he felt a sudden calm, it was almost as if this house held the key to peace. Then the feeling was gone and a tingling touched his spine. He had had those feelings before when his commando unit was in the field, and always it had proved to be the enemy watching . . . waiting. Turning sharply he scanned the lane and fields beyond the hedge. There was no one there. Cursing himself for being a fool he ducked his head to enter the low doorway . . . while in the lane the same watching figure smiled.

'I thanks you for giving the time to come, Mr Torrey.'

Martha Sim's soft Shropshire brogue welcomed him into an interior every bit as pretty and peaceful as the exterior of Cobweb Cottage had promised. Glancing briefly at her daughter he shook his head as the woman offered a chair.

'Thanks, but if you don't mind I'd like to make this short; no offence but I'm not up to socialising right now.'

'We knows of the bump you took in that there motor and realises your bones be sore . . .'

'How do you know? It hasn't had time to reach the local newspapers yet!'

Martha Sim's lined face smiled. 'Let it be enough to say we knows, knows that Seton fellow were terrified out of his wits afore he hit you in the face with an arm encased in plaster, that he said it weren't him, weren't him sent the dogs in . . .'

Torrey's eyebrows pulled together as he stared at the old woman. How could she possibly know . . . know the very words Seton had spoken?

'. . . he said it were not him wanted the killing done,'

Martha's eyes watched the effect of her words play across Torrey's bruised face, 'that it was Mather. Do I need to tell you more, tell you of the slender figure with pale-golden hair that lay across your passenger in that back seat, tell you of a perfume you remember well, tell you of the face you also remember, one that turned to smile at you as Maxwell Seton throwed himself out of the motor beneath the wheels of a truck?'

'No.' Dazed by what he heard, Torrey shook his head. 'No, there's no need to say any more except to tell me why I'm here, why you asked Tom Harper to bring me.'

'Before I tells you that I be asking have you any objection to Rosie, Tom or my Hilda being present?'

'Why should I have?' Torrey's laugh was pleasant enough. 'It seems they already know all I know myself.'

'They knows more'n that, Mr Torrey, much, much more.'

'In that case say what you have to; like I told you, no offence, but I'm not yet up to socialising.'

Settling back into her chair, Martha Sim's blackberry eyes rested on her visitor. 'You don't deny that presence in the motor car, a presence that has visited you yourself, the last time nobbut an hour since.'

His look giving answer she continued.

'It be the presence of one you loved, one that died a while gone; deny it if you will but in your heart you knows Martha Sim speaks true. The one you love deserted you and though you searched there was no trace, not until you visited a morgue and found a body with a tiny mermaid tattoo, a body with half a face. That loved one be returned, Mr Torrey, but there be no love in its coming; it seeks revenge, already it has taken vengeance but it don't be finished yet. Four men are dead of that vengeance and another be yet to die, one you plans to kill yourself . . . but you won't . . .'

'That's where you're wrong!' Torrey swung away, blazing fire behind his eyes. 'I don't know what hocus pocus you've used to get your information but I wouldn't rely too heavily on your source, it hasn't got *everything* right.'

'You'll have proof that don't be so afore another day be passed.' Martha's glance followed the man striding to her door. 'And when you have, you think on this. The fifth man to die will satisfy that vengeance but that don't be the all of what be wanted. There be evil in its coming, a dark unspeakable evil, an evil that seeks to claim you, Mr Torrey. You'll have the proof of what I tells you and when you do, Martha Sim will be your only aid, only she and you together can hope to stand against evil which intends to take you down into hell along of itself. Mark me, that presence be here to claim more than revenge, it intends to take you with it.'

Kate Mallory stood outside the neat little semi-detached in Michael Road. Branching off the lower end of Wolverhampton Street it was far enough from the town centre to be thought of as quiet, that was if any part of Darlaston could be given that description.

It had taken more than a bit of doing to pacify Scotty. 'Wasting bloody time,' her editor had scowled, then sent her off to cover the retirement 'do' of a manager at the Station Street works of Precision Grinding; what would Scotty say when he found out she had given that assignment the go-by?

But it was too late to worry over that now. As her grandmother would say, 'You've chosen your cake, me wench, now you eat it.'

Kate hoped she wouldn't choke on the crumbs! Going along the well-swept garden path she knocked on the door. A quick phone call while at the office had told her Inspector Daniels had been discharged, only thing now was would he see her?

'You'd best come in, Miss Mallory.'

Daniels's wife dropped a fearful glance to the hall carpet as Kate's feet passed over it, then cast a mortified look at her beloved cushions as she showed her into the living room.

'I'll make some tea. Do you take sugar?'

His face sour as his wife left the room Daniels whispered, 'I don't know why you're here but whatever you want it's yours if you put your bottom on one of those cushions.'

'Done!' Kate grinned, giving an extra wriggle as she settled.

Returning his thanks to her enquiry after his health Bruce Daniels watched his wife's face blanch as she returned with a tray. Poor Marjorie, it must feel like a heart attack, seeing her precious cushions actually being sat on.

'I see what you mean about the cushions,' Kate said as the other woman left them alone.

'I couldn't resist it. I had to see them sat on just once in my life.'

'Send in fools where angels fear to tread.'

'Angels and police inspectors.'

'Fortunately for this angel she gets to leave after a while, she won't be the one called upon to pay the piper!' Kate observed drily.

'I always knew I should have gone to church more often . . . too late now, you reckon?'

The man had actually made a stab at humour! She took the tea Marjorie Daniels had poured, passing a cup across the polished glass coffee table.

'So, what is it this time?'

So much for the camaraderie! Kate swallowed hard. Daniels was her only way into Bartley's warehouse, but would he open the door . . . or slam it in her face?

Returning her cup to the tray she launched quickly into her story, telling of her meeting with Echo Sounder and of bribing Amos Hodgkin, finishing with, 'You know Bartley was in on that drugs deal, the one you should have been given credit for busting; well, I think he's playing the same game, I think those bags don't hold flour. I think they hold heroin.'

'You think.' Inspector Bruce Daniels gave no hint of what was racing through his mind. If this woman proved right he was sure of a Chief Inspector's desk, but if he went barging into Bartley's and she was wrong then he'd be well up shit alley.

'It has to be that.' Kate Mallory leaned forwards, her face alight with the prospect of a scoop. 'Why else have boxes of flour locked away in a special room?'

'There could be another reason.'

'Such as what? It isn't an order from Buckingham Palace, those boxes don't have "by appointment" stamped on them, so what else makes them so special?'

It sounded feasible enough and he'd always had it in his gut that Bartley knew all about Doc Walker's little trick of stuffing drugs up the arses of frozen chickens.

Kate held her breath. Let him agree, *please* let him agree; get this one and she could be on her way to working for one of the nationals.

Reaching into a pocket of his cardigan, Daniels slipped a tablet from a blue and yellow box then popped it on to his tongue. He had an ulcer, they had told him while in hospital. 'It will need surgery as soon as you have recovered.' They'd have a bloody long wait! He replaced the box, all the time watching the woman sitting opposite. Oh to hell . . . he was already half-way up shit alley!

'Who have you told about this?' His eyes watched every nuance cross her face.

'Nobody.'

'Then don't. I signed back to active duty this morning, I'll be at that supermarket tomorrow at eleven . . .'

'And I'll . . .'

'You'll stay away!'

Walking back along Michael Road, Kate Mallory smiled. 'Like hell I will, Inspector,' she murmured, 'like hell I will.'

*

He had slept late. Richard Torrey cursed the slow-moving line of lorries impeding his progress along the A5. He had promised himself he would be at that supermarket by this time, that Bartley would already be dead.

'. . . *another yet to die, one you plans to kill yourself but you won't . . .*'

Torrey's hands tightened on the wheel. Martha Sim and the others were nice enough folk but they were wrong if they thought that mumbo jumbo cut any ice with him. First he would wring the truth from Bartley and then . . . the rest was simple, he would break the man's neck; after that Martha Sim's words might well prove true, hell would be his next destination. Thirty minutes later he guided the car through Darlaston's narrow streets as the St Lawrence church clock sounded eleven.

Bartley had to be there . . . he *would* be there. Shooting along Alma Street he turned into the yard of the supermarket, parking the Rover in its usual place. Climbing out he glanced around. Everything seemed normal: there were a couple of lorries at the warehouse being unloaded, a white van with the logo 'Valeton Mill, the finest of fine flour' alongside them. Everything was as usual, so why did he have this feeling that it wasn't?

Slipping the car keys into his pocket he had almost reached the warehouse when a uniformed police sergeant stepped around the side of the parked van.

'Excuse me, sir, might I ask where you are going?'

'Well it isn't the bloody park!' The words spat like bullets.

'No, sir.' Unperturbed the sergeant stared back. 'Then where?'

Slowly, giving each word a stinging emphasis, Torrey answered through clenched teeth.

'I am going to Mr Bartley's private office and before you ask, yes, I'm going through the warehouse and up the back stairs, the way I always go.'

'But not today, Mr Torrey.'

Turning to the voice behind, Torrey made no effort to disguise his irritation.

'I knew something was about to spoil my day and now I see what it is!'

'Got in your way, have we?'

'You could say that.' The north pole a hothouse compared to his look, Torrey smiled. 'But it's nothing I can't move.'

Making to step past Daniels he was confronted by the burly figure of the sergeant, backed now by two more uniformed men.

'Will you move us first, sir, or does the inspector take precedence?'

It was said with a smile but the meaning was understandable, he'd have to go through a clutch of coppers before getting to the stairs. For a moment he was tempted, he could take them out before they knew he'd moved, a kick to the balls, a knee in the back, a side chop to the throat, they could be deader than a doornail in seconds; but these men had done nothing to him, he had no score to settle with them, his quarry was Bartley.

Mistaking hesitation for capitulation the sergeant moved forwards a few steps.

'If you wouldn't mind waiting outside, sir.'

'Torrey,' Daniels said as the sergeant stepped forwards again, 'I wouldn't bother trying the stairs in the store, we've got that covered too!'

Why hadn't she thought of it before! Kate Mallory smiled at the simplicity of it all. Her landlady had an evening job, two hours Monday to Saturday cleaning the staff canteen at Bartley's supermarket. It couldn't have worked out better if heaven itself had planned it. Today was her land-lady's day for visiting Birmingham's rag market and that meant she wouldn't be home before 4 p.m. The pink and white check overall had slipped easily over her tan tweed suit, while Mrs Price's faded green everyday coat hid both. A blue paisley-patterned head square tied turban fashion hid her sherry-coloured hair, leaving two of the other woman's steel curlers showing above her brow. The whole effect was finished off by clumpy shoes and a large shop-ping bag. Not even her own mother would have known her. But would any of the other assistants question her? That thought had bothered her as she had walked through a door marked 'Female Staff Only', but when she had emerged resplendent in Mrs Price's overall, the name 'Bartley's' worked across the top pocket, nobody had given her a second glance.

First she must ascertain whether that van had arrived. Holding a sheet of typewritten paper prominently in one hand, deliberately shuffling her feet, she walked outside and around the building to the warehouse.

'I 'aves to give this to 'Odgkin,' she scowled as a police constable blocked her way, 'I don't 'and this to 'im then the shelves don't get restocked an' I finishes up wi' me bleedin' stamps licked on!'

'It's all right, Constable, let the lady do her job.'

'I should bleedin' well think so an' all!' Kate glared at the sergeant. 'Get a woman the sack playin' yer daft games, seen too many of them gangster pictures, that be your trouble, yer thinks everybody be a bloody criminal!'

'Not you, luv,' the sergeant winked over her head to the young constable, 'you be much too pretty to be a criminal.'

Still mumbling Kate shuffled deeper into the warehouse. Let the coppers have their little laugh . . . she could wait for hers.

Amos Hodgkin had almost given the game away by gasping with surprise when he realised who it was handing him the sheet of paper, but Kate's swift step on his foot turned it into a yelp.

'Sorry,' she said loudly, 'it be them bleedin' coppers, they 'as me all of a work!' Then when Hodgkin had taken the sheet and was looking down a list of items she had typed herself, she added, 'They says to tell yer they wants these straight away.'

Running a finger down the list he turned towards a pile of boxes stacked one on top of another. Appearing to check the list he moved slowly, increasing the distance between them and the watching constable.

'We don't 'ave none of this.' He pointed to the order for flour.

'But the van . . .' Kate whispered, disappointment clogging her throat.

'It was delivered,' Hodgkin murmured, 'but it ain't been put in that room. Bartley 'ad it took straight up to 'is office.' Then louder, 'Tell 'em I'll get the stuff brought in as soon as I'm allowed, 'til then they'll 'ave to manage best they can.'

'Manager ain't gonna like that,' Kate answered.

'Then 'e can tek it up wi' them.' Hodgkin nodded significantly towards the policeman standing inside the door.

'Why the 'ell be they 'ere, that's what I'd like to know, bloody coppers . . . you finds 'em everywhere, gets where a draught couldn't get!' Grumbling loudly, Kate shuffled back towards the store.

Chapter Twenty-Seven

Unnoticed by those in the canteen, all of them interested in the latest theory as to why the police were in the store, Kate took a buttered scone and a cup of tea, balancing them on a tray as she shuffled out. Bartley too must take a break; anyway, it was the only way she could think of getting into that office.

Following her nose she shuffled along a corridor, keeping up the pretence she had adopted earlier; it had stood her in good stead then and it might again.

'Mr Bartley was already here when I arrived.'

'Is that usual?'

A deep voice. Daniels! Kate cursed inwardly. Of all the luck. But she'd got this far and if a fight was what it took to get her the rest of the way then she was ready. Using her hip, she pushed the open door a little wider, muttering as she shuffled into the room.

'All that bleedin' way, why don't 'e go to the canteen same as other folk?'

'Hold up!' Inspector Bruce Daniels glanced at the tray. 'Where do you be going with that?'

'Where the 'ell do yer think?' Kate kept her head low on her chest. 'It be fer the gaffer but why 'e can't 'ave it down the canteen . . .'

'Mr Bartley is . . . isn't ready for his tea yet, you . . . you'll have to take it back.'

Kate turned her back on Daniels, and keeping her voice asperic she answered the smartly dressed fair-haired girl sitting at a desk, 'Oh ar! Tek it back, is it, an' who'll fetch it when 'is lordship do be ready? Who else but this skivvy, no thought for nobody, that be some folk!'

'I'm sorry . . .'

'How long has he been locked in there?' Daniels broke in, interest in her already waning. Kate could think of no way of remaining in the office. If ever the devil helped his own she could do with that help right now.

'The key?' he snapped.

Near to tears the secretary looked up. 'I don't have one.'

Daniels slapped a hand hard down on the desk. 'Don't mess me around, get the key.'

'I don't have one, that's the truth. Mr Bartley never allows anyone a key to his private office.'

The devil *did* help his own. Kate almost whooped with relief as the girl burst into tears. Turning back she banged the tray on to the desk, putting her arms around the sobbing girl.

'That be just like a man, frighten the life out of a wench. It be the onny bleedin' thing they be good at!'

'I don't have the key, honestly I don't.'

'O' course yer don't, luv,' Kate kept her head bent over the girl, 'tek no notice of 'im, the bleedin' bully!'

This wouldn't last long. Kate reached for the cup, pushing it into the girl's hands. Daniels would have her thrown out any second now. That was when they heard it, a low drawn-out cry of sheer terror.

Shoving the cup back at Kate the secretary screamed and Daniels swung towards the inner office.

'Christ, what was that?'

Clinging to Kate the girl pressed her face into the overall splashed across with tea. 'It . . . it's Mr Bartley, he . . . he's been crying out like that for the last hour. I asked if there was anything wrong but he wouldn't answer.'

'Well there's something not right, that much is certain.'

The cry coming again Daniels banged a fist on the door, calling Bartley's name.

'Keep away, keep away . . . I tell you it wasn't my fault, I didn't do it, it was Mather . . .'

Mather, Managing Director of Coton Pharmaceuticals! He'd been at the opening of that centre, him and Maxwell Seton, they had talked with James Connor, and now Bartley was babbling on about him. Kate's ears pricked. This could be even better than she'd hoped.

'. . . it wasn't me, I never ordered no murder . . .'

'Break it down!' Daniels ordered the constable who rushed in, alarmed by the girl's scream. Then when that proved futile he shouted at him 'to get a bloody axe!'

Holding the trembling girl, Kate kept her face averted. This was no time to push her luck.

'Mather did it . . .' Bartley's moans seeped past the

closed door. '. . . he ordered you killed and Connor . . . Connor covered up, they were in it together . . . Seton and me, we never wanted any murder.'

Seton. Now where had she just seen that name? Kate Mallory racked her brain. It was in the editor's office. Scotty had taken a phone call, writing the name Maxwell Seton as he'd answered. Then he'd yelled for Glover, telling him Seton was dead and to get the story.

Curiouser and curiouser! Kate's mental filing system clicked open. Connor was dead, his head sliced from his shoulders; Mather was dead, burned to death in a blazing car; and now Maxwell Seton had joined his name to the list. All accidents? Maybe . . . maybe not!

'No, you won't get me, you got the others but you won't get me . . .'

The cry coming once more the inspector leaned across the desk, his voice brittle with urgency as he spoke to the girl hiding her face against Kate.

'You said there was no one in there with him.'

'He was alone when I arrived and no one has gone in since, I've been here all the time and . . .'

'Then who's he talkin' to . . . himself?'

Daniels's bark made no improvement to the secretary's nerves. Her painted fingernails sharp against Kate's arm she answered tremulously, 'There . . . there's only been the man who carried in those boxes. I stood in the office with Mr Bartley while he counted them. Then he dismissed me, he was alone . . . there's been nobody since.'

Boxes! Inspector Bruce Daniels straightened. Boxes

carried straight into his private office . . . the door locked
. . . drugs? P'raps not, but it had to be something shady or
why lock the door? But if Bartley was alone, as the girl
maintained, then who was he talking to?

'No . . . no, please . . . don't touch me, don't touch
me . . . !'

More scream than moan it was followed by a crash and
the sound of breaking glass.

Standing beside the Rover, Torrey looked skywards as the
crash of glass resounded over the yard, his eyes fastening
on the large plate-glass window where a chair stuck half
in, half out of a gaping hole.

Somewhere to his right a woman screamed as a figure
pushed the chair, sending it toppling to the ground. But
Torrey's stare remained on the figure climbing out
through the hole left by the chair, shards of shattered glass
drawing crimson streaks across hands and face.

Bartley! He didn't need to glance sidewards to know the
young constable set to keep an eye on him was taken
up with the woman, who had fainted. Using the fast-
gathering crowd as cover he moved quickly behind the
lorries parked in front of the warehouse. That young
copper's arse was going to smart from the kicking his
inspector would give it but that was his problem.

The warehouse was empty, workmen and coppers
having joined the watchers outside, but safe was always
one up on sorry! Making no sound he passed quickly

through the warehouse and into the store, walking straight to the door he knew led to the office quarters. Bartley wasn't going to get away.

Taking the stairs two at a time and the corridor at a run he burst into the room. Ignoring Daniels's shout he placed one foot directly against the lock of Bartley's door, one short sharp jab splintering it free.

'Stay out of there . . .'

But Torrey was already in and across to the window.

Freeing herself from the secretary's clutch, Kate Mallory edged towards the broken doorway. Daniels was bawling at the newcomer: 'Get out, Torrey, and leave this to the police.' But he ought to try singing another tune for that one was having no effect.

Torrey . . . where did he fit into the puzzle? Kate's well-ordered brain filed the name under 'to be investigated'.

Turning towards the constable who chose that moment to bring in the axe, the inspector's eye fell on Kate. 'Get them women out of here!'

'All right, all right, you've no need to shove, bloody coppers throwin' your weight about!' Kate kept up her pretence as she was escorted from the room. Thank you, Inspector, she thought, there might be more to see from outside.

Spears of glass ripping at his jacket, Torrey reached through the gaping hole. 'Bartley . . .' he called, 'Bartley, don't be a fool!'

Balanced on the narrow ledge abutting the rear wall of the building, Bartley turned his head, a look of absolute terror flashing over his face as he saw Torrey.

'. . . I know you,' he muttered, eyes rolling with fear, 'I know you, you bloody bitch! Mather was right, you deserved what you got, Anna, you deserved to die!'

Out of his own mouth! Bartley had condemned himself. His hand closing on the other man's jacket, Torrey knew he could hold him, p'raps long enough for the fire engine he could hear clanging along the street to get here.

But he didn't want Bartley rescued, he wanted him dead, he wanted to feel him die; it was a desire so strong it ripped at him. He'd been trained to put such emotions aside, he should not allow desire . . . any kind of desire . . . to override common sense and common sense said he couldn't take Bartley without them both crashing to the ground.

'Leave it, sir, trying to grab him will only scare the man more than he is already . . . leave it to us, sir.'

'You heard him, Torrey, leave it or does it take a couple of truncheons to convince you?'

Bruce Daniels grimaced, a sudden whiff of perfume wafting beneath his nose.

'I told you . . .' He whirled towards where the two women had stood . . . but the perfume he could smell had not been worn by either of them. It was the perfume he had smelled in that hotel bathroom, the one that had plagued him before he'd smashed the car into the hedge. Not again; Christ, not again!

Half out of the window Richard Torrey caught the same elusive fragrance and an attractive face laughed at him from the depths of memory. At that same time Bartley screamed again and Torrey's fingers parted. Free of the grasp that held him, the scream following all the way, Philip Bartley crashed to the concrete seventy feet below, a brown paper package spilling white powder across his chest like a drift of freshly fallen snow.

'. . . *Four men are dead . . . another be yet to die, one you plans to kill yourself . . .*'

Martha Sim's words buzzed like wasps in his mind. But he hadn't killed Philip Bartley! Bruce Daniels's warning not to leave Darlaston already dust in his brain, Torrey pushed the Rover into gear.

He'd had hold of Bartley's jacket, he could have dragged him back, a few seconds of pressure to the neck and the man would have been dead, instead he had opened his hand.

But he hadn't opened his hand! Bartley had turned to look at him, his mouth drooling, his eyes those of a crazy man, and at that moment he had smelled that perfume and his hand . . . he *had* felt his fingers being prised apart, felt his grip broken by something stronger than himself. At first he'd thought it all in his mind. It had been the blues hauling him back from the window, that had broken his hold! At least he'd told himself that until he'd climbed into Bartley's car. Then he'd glanced up at the window of that office, seen the figure smiling down at him, a figure with collar-length pale-gold hair, a figure with half a face!

Swinging the car out of the supermarket yard and on down Alma Street he paid no attention to the slim young woman, sherry-coloured hair bobbing as she tottered along in three-inch stilletos, a large shopping bag in one hand.

Kate Mallory watched the car as it sped past. Now where was the gallant Mr Torrey off to? And going there as if the devil and all his demons were in pursuit. He had not noticed her and if he had he wouldn't have recognised her as the woman who had been standing with Bartley's secretary. For that matter neither would Daniels. Her landlady's coat, overall and head square tucked with her clumpy shoes into the shopping bag, the steel curlers gone and her hair combed through, Kate Mallory had walked from the store.

She was footloose but that didn't mean she was fancy free. Very soon now Inspector Bruce Daniels would place a ban on any publication, he'd come up with some crap about first having to establish the facts. Well, Inspector, you do your establishing . . . me? I've got an editor to see.

Her heels tapping on the pavement, Kate Mallory smiled to herself.

Chapter Twenty-Eight

'Get out of the bloody way!'

Torrey barely looked at the figure standing at the edge of the town, one thumb raised as the Rover sped towards it. Any other time Bartley was not in the car he would have stopped, it did no harm to give a hitch-hiker a lift. But not today, today he was in no mood to play the Good Samaritan.

Coming up to the junction with the A5 he slowed, the glance he lifted to the rear-view mirror automatic. Some way behind, the hitch-hiker began to walk towards the car.

'Find somebody else, mate!' Torrey snapped as if the figure could hear what he said, then sent the car forwards into the mainstream traffic.

Why the hell had he come back? Garaging the car he glanced at the graceful old Abbey. There was nothing for him here, no job now Bartley was dead, this place would be the same as any other, empty without Anna.

Anna! He turned, walking slowly towards the cottage

that had gone with the post of chauffeur. Had it been real, that face he'd seen at Bartley's window, had his fingers really been prised loose of that jacket, or had it all been some sort of delusion?

But Bartley was dead and *that* was no delusion, the bastard was dead and he had failed.

'. . . *one you plans to kill yourself but you won't . . .*'

The truth of the words stung his brain. After all the self-promises he'd made he'd failed, and worse . . . he'd failed Anna! Bartley had died but not by his hand, and it wasn't suicide; despite what any future Coroner's court might rule he was certain Philip Bartley had not thrown himself off that ledge. Torrey saw again the look on the other man's face as he'd turned his head. Bartley had been terrified, and by what? Had he seen the same figure, seen the smiling face fall away into a jagged black hole, had the same something that had prised his own fingers apart reached for Bartley . . . pushed him off that building? Delusion or not he had failed and now he had to live with that. But not here. He stared at the cottage for several moments. There were few things inside that belonged to him, just a couple of changes of clothes he'd bought while in Monkswell. Glancing across to the copse bordering the open fields he drank in the russets and orange-golds of the leaves. A week or so and they would be gone, snatched from the world by winter . . . just as Anna had been snatched away from him.

It was here, in this house!

Standing just inside the door, Torrey remained stock

still, the small hairs on the back of his neck standing upright.

It was here . . . waiting.

Every nerve tense, every sense alert, he glanced about the tiny sitting room. Everything was as he'd left it, nothing had been moved and there was no sound, only the air was different.

Spiced with a faint hint of lemon, a fragrance filled the room.

'. . . it seeks revenge . . .'

Much as he did not believe, did not *want* to believe, the memory of Martha Sim's quietly spoken words brought a chill to his spine. But that very word negated the whole theory; if what he'd seen and felt were anything at all of Anna then it wouldn't be after revenge.

'. . . there be evil in its coming . . . it intends to take you with it . . .'

Rubbish. He pushed the thought away. Carry on like that and he'd be next to top himself. Crossing to a dresser tucked into an alcove beside the inglenook fireplace he drew out an envelope. Writing Bartley's name on it he slipped the car keys inside. Turning to place the sealed packet on the table in the centre of the room his hand froze in mid air.

'Ritchie . . . !'

Soft as a hushed whisper it seeped into his dazed mind. Across the room a slender figure stood, eyes vivid as a summer sky as they smiled at him.

'It's over, Ritchie . . . !'

The smiling mouth made no movement.

'They've all gone, now we can be together . . .'

'Anna?' It took every effort of will to speak, an inn
sense telling him that what he saw was a fabrication, an
illusion, but with the question the slender figure raised its
arms towards him.

'Your Anna.' The eyes became smoky, the smile inti-
mate. 'Your own Anna, Ritchie.'

The envelope fell suddenly from his hand, the clat-
tering as the keys hit the table snapping his brain.

'I don't know what I'm looking at,' he grated, 'but
illusion or fantasy I know it's not Anna.'

'Look at me, Ritchie . . .' The figure glided closer. 'Look
at this body, the body you held so often in your bed . . .
this mouth you kissed. We can be together again . . . come
with me, my love.'

'No!' Anger, frustration and pain echoed in the kick he
aimed at a chair, sending it crashing against the wall.
'There is no Anna!'

'We will be together, Ritchie . . .'

Only feet away the eyes gleamed enticingly, '. . . you
and me, together for always.'

Across in the copse a dog fox barked and suddenly
Torrey saw the stupidity of what he was doing. He was
talking to a bloody shadow!

'Be together for always!' He laughed, a cynical despair-
ing laugh that got no further than his throat. That bubble
had burst weeks ago!

'You be in the same boat as we be, lad. We thought as 'ow
we'd be 'ere in Monkswell for the rest of our lives but

ow . . .' George Barnes shrugged his shoulders. 'Seems it might be a job sweepin' a foundry floor somewhere; who'd a thought it, eh lad, who'd a thought Bartley would 'ave tumbled from a winder?'

Bartley had not fallen from a window, nor from that ledge . . . not accidentally. Torrey nodded sympathetically while the thought was acid in his veins.

'Be the wife I worries over,' George Barnes continued, ''er'll miss this place.'

'We all will, George.' That was a lie if ever there was one. Torrey turned to where his own cottage stood. He wanted only to leave . . . so why hadn't he?

Bidding the other man goodnight he walked quickly across the ground between the houses, paying no mind to the scene about him. Closing the door of the cottage behind him he breathed deeply, a slight fragrance in the air bringing a smile to his lips. This was why he hadn't left Monkswell, this was where Anna was, this was where he must stay.

Almost immediately the caressing began, the touch of hands cupping his face, the brush of a mouth against his own. Closing his eyes he gave himself up to it; this was what he wanted, this was all that mattered.

'Ritchie . . .'

Soft as silken gauze it whispered. Against his ear or in his mind he didn't care, just so long as the loving went on.

'Soon, Ritchie . . .'

The voice laughed, a soft, deep, throat-locked laugh, unseen fingers tracing down the front of him.

'But first you must eat . . . eat, my love and then . . . then we will make love.'

Slowly, wanting nothing but the touch of those hands, those lips on his own, Torrey walked mindlessly into the kitchen.

'Hurry, my love.'

With the soft whisper the scented air seemed to thicken, filling his mouth, his nostrils, drugging his brain until only one thought remained: Anna.

'Now, Ritchie . . . come to me now.'

It was low, seeping seductively into every crevice of his mind. Torrey's fingers closed on the large kitchen knife. Across the room a golden-haired figure watched him, attractive full mouth smiling, hyacinth eyes smouldering, holding him in a grip of velvet steel.

'I love you, Ritchie . . . I love you.'

The knife lifted to his throat, Torrey stared at the smiling face as he pressed the blade into his flesh.

The time had come. Martha Sim stared into the fire that for once seemed to send no heat into her tiny living room.

The evil that had come to Monkswell was growing impatient, soon now it must claim the last of its victims. But even knowing all she did, all the ancient powers had shown her, she knew she could do nothing on her own. The hunted must turn hunter, only that way could the minion of the Dark One be defeated.

But he had not come to Cobweb Cottage, Richard Torrey had not sought her help. She had knelt in the church, prayed to the good Lord for help, prayed Torrey would see what she saw, the evil behind the smile; but to no avail, he had not come.

Low in the grate a flame spurted suddenly, its blue tip turning to ebony as it shot outwards into a room that was instantly ice cold.

Her lips moving in silent prayer, her fingers closing over the stone worn about her neck, she waited. It was almost here, the reckoning she had known would come; tonight evil would claim its own.

Sitting opposite, Hilda Sim felt a fear she had never known before. She had done all her mother had asked, the precautions were complete, but were they sufficient? She had the same beliefs, the same trust in the old ways. They had helped the people of Monkswell in times of illness and worry, but this . . .

A sudden sharp kick to the door startling her, she gasped.

'Open it and then you must leave.'

'No, Mother, I'll stay . . .'

'You can't and that you knows well.' Martha's lined face lifted to her daughter. 'In you be the Light, you be the one to carry it once I be gone, to you will be given the powers that rest in me; that can't be put to risk. Once that door be opened you goes to Rosie 'Arper an' there you stays 'til this night be done . . .'

It would do no good to argue, they had discussed her staying, talked of it for hours but her mother would not relent. Taking her coat from the peg, Hilda opened the door.

'Mr Torrey!'

Blood staining his shirt, Torrey stumbled into the room.

'Mr Torrey, whatever 'as happened?'

Over her head, Martha's glance was fixed on the open doorway.

'Go, wench,' she ordered quietly, 'do as you be bid, leave now.'

'But shouldn't I . . . ?'

'There be no place for you 'ere this night, remember what it be I told you.'

Leaving go of Torrey's arm, Hilda nodded. 'God bless.' She looked at her mother one more time. 'God bless,' she whispered again as she left.

'I know now that what you said was true.' Taking the cloth the old woman held out to him, Torrey held it to the side of his neck. 'I suppose I realised it from the first, but I couldn't face up to it, face up to the fact that it was no love that was haunting me, that there never had been any love. How could there be, what love brings a man to cutting his own throat? I almost did it too!' He threw back his head, his mouth sucking in a deep draught of air then releasing it in a long whoosh of self-deprecation. 'Who would have thought that, eh? Richard Torrey cutting his own throat, and for what? A bloody ghost!'

'But you didn't.'

'No.' He lowered the cloth, looking at the crimson stain. 'But it was purely a case of luck, I already had the blade biting into the flesh . . . if that church bell hadn't rung when it did . . .'

Martha took the cloth. Seeing the cut to the side of his neck was shallow and the blood staunched she laid it aside. 'That were no luck,' she said quietly, 'that bell were rung to send you 'ere, that also you knows to be no coincidence or why else would you be in this house?'

Why had he come? He hadn't set out to come here; that bell had rung, the clear sound cutting through the trance-like hold on his brain, the sting of the knife jolting him back to his senses and he'd rushed out of the house.

'You be 'ere cos deep inside you knows this be the one place you can find what be needed, the strength to fight off that which seeks to kill you, to take you with it into darkness.'

'I don't believe that mumbo jumbo.'

'You d'ain't believe the one you loved held no real love in return, but you found the truth of it minutes ago in your kitchen.' Martha's berry-bright eyes flashed. 'The same truth you knows in your 'eart, one that tells you the 'ands that fondles your body, the mouth that kisses your lips and the voice that whispers beside you in your bed be not real, be not sound and touch of love but of evil, an evil that will not rest, will not leave until you be dead. There be this night and this night only can Martha Sim help, refuse an' you damns yourself.' Lowering herself to her chair she motioned Torrey to sit. 'The priest,' she went on speaking quietly, 'young Peter Darley, he were hounded until he did what you almost did half an hour since; he chose suicide as the way of ridding himself of torment. Bartley and them others, Connor, Mather and Seton, t'were no accident took them, they were the food of its revenge. Oh yes, I knows of their doings same as I knows that revenge be not slaked, it 'ungers yet, it 'ungers for you.'

'And Daniels?' Torrey's eyes reflected doubt. 'How do you explain his part in all of this? He had the same experiences as myself, as Bartley and the others, yet he isn't dead.'

For a moment Martha stared deep into the fire, then quietly as before answered, 'You cried out, "I want them dead, Anna, I want them dead." Daniels thought to hold you in that town until he could solve a case involving Philip Bartley, but the dark powers could not allow that. It would have kept you from Monkswell, and also the evil that needed you to bring it here; so Daniels met with an accident severe enough not to kill him but to keep him out of the way until what you had asked were done.'

'Are you saying I'm in some way responsible for Peter Darley . . . ?'

'You were the means, no more than that. You be the channel by which the Dark One sent his servant and you be the only channel by which it can be sent back. Believe me, unless you do as I tells you, you will die, and p'raps others along of you. You be askin' of yourself if this presence that comes more and more often, that takes away your senses, be the Anna you loved? The answer be in your 'eart, search it deep afore you decides.'

Peter Darley, Clifton Mather, Maxwell Seton, James Connor and Philip Bartley, all dead! Torrey drew a deep breath. Martha Sim had proved correct so far, should he believe her when she said others might also die? Or was the fear beginning to niggle the back of his mind a fear for his own skin? He didn't need to search for the answer to that one, he had been trained to face death in whatever shape or form, but he had also been trained to protect. Meeting the blackberry gaze, he nodded.

Chapter Twenty-Nine

'Be you ready, lad?'

As Torrey nodded, Martha glanced at the several articles set out across the table. She had failed to save the
life of Peter Darley, would Richard Torrey reap the same
fate?

Lighting the candles Tom Harper had provided she
removed the strangely shaped stone from her neck.
Writing on it with the stub of pencil: 'From all evil
RICHARD TORREY protect', she slipped it over his head.

Following the ritual exactly as before she lifted both
hands to the window and as the light of the moon filled
it she breathed deeply, drawing the silver purity of its glow
inside herself. Turning back to the table she dipped the
third finger of her left hand into the water she herself had
drawn and sprinkled drops of it over the man standing
beside her.

'From the heart comes the love, from the water comes
the cleansing, from the stone comes protection.'

Beyond the door a sound of rustling began, a brushing as of dried leaves. Torrey turned towards it but Martha moved quickly. Exchanging the water for salt she looked at him, a strange intensity in her black eyes.

'Once the salt be spread take care not to step outside of it, it can only protect if you stays within its circle.' Taking a handful she pivoted slowly, laying a ring of salt about them both as she recited.

'Water, blood of the earth, cleanse all evil; salt, the pure body of the earth, surround and protect; together they keep us, let no spirit of Darkness approach nor evil assail.'

Returning the bowl to the table she drew a long breath. Tonight she could lose not only her life but her very soul. The ancient powers had protected her on that previous night but the evil that had manifested had only played with her, brushing her aside as if she were of no more danger to itself than a fly. Tonight would be different, what it wanted was here in this room and it would allow nothing to prevent the taking; only the words whispered to her at her mother's passing, the great words of power, only by speaking those could she hope for salvation. They were words she had revealed to no one, neither Rosie Harper nor Hilda, words that even deep in her heart she trembled to think of. But this night they must be said, for no other way could this man or herself be saved from the pit of hell.

'Once I speaks the words there can be no going back,' she looked again at Torrey, 'you must say now if it be as your mind be changed.'

Should he take the chance offered and go? The Army

had prepared him for all events, all events save hocus pocus! But those deaths . . . there were too many too soon for each to have been an accident. Yet how could he believe that Anna . . . ? Nodding his head once more he swallowed hard. There was only one way to find out.

Beside him the frail old woman breathed deeply as if gathering the strength to go on. Touching her breast with the sign of the cross she began to speak, the words falling clearly into the soft hush.

'Ephas Metahim, Frugatiui Appellavi . . .'

The words seemed to ring, rolling back from the shadows as if with a life of their own.

'. . . Adonai, King of Kings, Lord of Light, send forth thy servant Michael, greatest of High Angels, Keeper of the Gates, that he might vanquish that evil which is amongst us.'

In the same fraction of a second it took for the last consonant to leave Martha's lips a great peal of thunder shook the room, a noise like that of a thousand aircraft fractured the silence; then it was back, a grinding pulverising silence that seemed to crush the brain, to drag the mind inside out. Despite himself Torrey gasped.

Outside, the quiet rustling grew louder, the door rattling on its hinges.

'Netsah.' Her voice trembling, Martha began again. 'Keeper of the Sword, High Lord, Holder of the Ten Wisdoms, I call . . .'

'No!'

No more than a whisper yet somehow filling the room with sound it came from the doorway. His glance drawn towards it, Torrey felt the roof of his mouth go dry. From the shadowed recess a darker shadow began to move; separating, forming and reforming, whorls of darkness rolled and coiled about each other. Slowly it floated, in a grotesque symmetry, and as he watched, Torrey knew it was more than shadow, that somehow it possessed a life of its own, that it watched through hidden eyes and what it watched was him.

'No . . .'

With the sound-filled whisper the coils of darkness began to move. First an outline, no more than shadow on shadow, then a tenebrous silhouette of blue-black opalescence, finally it began to take on shape.

'The Keeper of the Gates cannot answer, his fiery sword is sheathed, the words of power have no strength against the greatest of all Lords, the Prince of Darkness.'

Staring at the dense floating shadow, hearing the whisper from the shadows, Torrey heard the old woman's frightened gasp. Whatever it was she had hoped to conjure it didn't seem to be that floating cloud!

Martha Sim's trembling sob was drowned beneath a grating laugh that echoed from the walls of her tiny home.

Its blackness now so dense it stood clearly outlined on its sister shadows, the transformation of shape on shape continued; body, arms, legs and finally a head.

What the hell was it? Torrey frowned. There was no such thing as magic, black or white; this whole business was a fake, a charade. Martha Sim had somehow set him up. Half turning he glanced at her, seeing her lift both gnarled hands towards the floating shape.

'Aieth Gadol Leolamus . . .'

The words stopped abruptly as the mist-formed figure erupted into a mass of flame, the brilliance of it bathing the room with a light that smarted against Torrey's eyes before coalescing, becoming once more a figure, but now a figure fashioned of living flame, a great red-gold aura encircling the head.

'In Nomine Satanus.'

An incandescent hand lifted, reaching towards the old woman.

'In Nomine Satanus.'

The words, softly spoken a moment before, now crashed into the room like the clashing of cymbals. For a second the hand hovered before Martha's face, while eyes that glowed like pools of molten lava smiled at Torrey, then a finger of flame brushed the lined brow and Martha Sim dropped like a stone.

The figure floated before Torrey.

'You called upon the Great One, the Lord of Darkness.'

Each word, wrapped in flame, hurled itself at Torrey, the heat of them searing his flesh. It wants me to flinch! All the strength of his commando training coming into force he stared defiantly at the flame-encircled face. That obscenity could terrify an old woman, he breathed the calm slow breath of experience, now see what it could do against a man! It wanted him to shit himself with fear. Watching flames leap as the hand moved, Torrey smelled the acrid odour of singed flesh. Chances of doing just that were thousands to one, and none in his favour!

'Is that all your so-called Great One can do?'

His glance holding to those fiery eyes, Torrey pointed to the woman lying crumpled on the ground.

'No, Ritchie, he can do much more than that.'

The arm lowered, becoming one with the body of dancing flame, the movement filling the room with an exotic fragrance, a delicate mixture of blossom touched with lemon and spice. Its eyes holding Torrey's to the last moment, the flame-born figure faded, a milky vaporous mist forming from where it had floated. Slowly as before the mist formed and reformed, drifting, spreading then coming together until a few feet from him it hovered, a tenuous spindrift column.

'So what am I supposed to do now, scream, make a run for it? Or p'raps I should just drop dead with fright, same as the woman!' Arrogance his defence, Torrey laughed, 'If that's the best the Prince of Darkness has up his sleeve . . .'

'You always were impatient, Ritchie, but like I told you, he can do more than that.'

For several seconds the column of mist hung, the glow of firelight from the grate shimmering through it; then, as at the start, it began to separate. Arms . . . legs . . . Torrey watched the transformation . . . a lithe slender body and finally a head, a head with a covering of pale-gold hair curling into the nape of the neck.

A figure clothed in faded jeans and denim jacket, hyacinth-blue eyes laughing back from the mist-formed face.

'This is what the Great One can do . . .'

The attractive face smiled.

'. . . He can give me back to you, Ritchie, we can be together again, together for eternity.'

That was what he had wanted, waited for, wanted all the time while Anna had been with Bartley and the rest of them. Now he was to be the reward, the payment for murder by revenge.

'No, Anna, if you are Anna.' He looked directly into those brilliant eyes. 'I don't want you any more.'

Across the narrow space the eyes lost their laughter. Hard and cold they spurted blue flame, the smiling mouth twisting.

'You called me, you shouted my name.'

'And you answered. You used me, Anna, used me to kill five men, men you gave yourself to, men you could have left any time you wished. But they had what you wanted, they had money, or at least four of them did. They could give you the things Richard Torrey couldn't give, all he had to give you was love, the same as Peter Darley. That priest did you no harm, Anna, yet still he was driven to take his own life. You did that, or should I say the evil you've become did that.'

'You saw me, Ritchie . . .'

The filmy figure floated nearer, halting at the edge of the salt ring.

'. . . you saw my face in that morgue, you saw what they did to me.'

'Yes, I saw and I see you now and I tell you again I don't

want you. When I shouted those words I was in agony and if I have to roast in hell to atone for them then so be it . . . but it will be alone.'

'No, Ritchie . . .'

Like a serpent's tongue the words flicked from a mouth suddenly pulled downwards, half of the attractive face falling away into a hole, its jagged edge scorched and blackened, one hyacinth-blue eye staring back at Torrey, the words a menacing hiss.

'I came not only for my killers, I came for you . . .'

One vaporous arm lifted and despite himself Torrey stepped backwards, his foot catching against the woman slumped at his feet.

'. . . I came for you, Ritchie,' the grotesque mouth twisted in a horrifying smile, 'I won't leave without you.'

'Use the words.' Martha Sim struggled to her feet. 'It be too strong for me, lad, but with the words you can banish it.'

'I don't know the words!'

Torrey threw a protective arm across the old woman as a spume of blue flame reached for her.

'They'll be given you.' Martha gasped. 'Listen, keep your mind to what the powers tell, then speak the words they give.'

This was madness! Torrey watched the floating horror. Sheer bloody tripe! This thing wasn't real!

'I knows what you thinks,' Martha answered his thoughts. 'But that figure you sees plain, its voice you hears plain, an' that you can't be denyin'. Now you hear *me* plain: you an' you only can send it back to where it belongs. Listen to what speaks inside you.'

Tongues of scarlet-tipped black flame licked around the ring of salt, tasting, seeking, feeling for a way in.

'Now, lad,' Martha urged, 'now, afore it be too late!'

How? He watched the disfigured face, the figure that seemed so real advance and recoil as it neared the salt. How could this thing be Anna, the Anna he had loved would never harm him. Almost as though the thought had been spoken aloud the charred hole came together, healing before his fascinated stare until the attractive face smiled at him from beyond the salt circle.

'Come with me.' The full mouth smiled, the whisper seductive, full of promise. 'Come with me, Ritchie, we can be together.'

'Together in hell is where you'll be.' Steady now on her feet Martha Sim stepped in front of Torrey, her arms spread as if to defend him. Drawing one breath she faced the smiling entity, her voice rising clear despite the tremor of fear.

'Sar ha-Olam, High Angel of the Presence . . .'

At the very first syllable the features contorted, the grisly blackened mouth opening in a scream of rage, the vaporous shape twisting into a sinuous spiral, a huge serpentine column of undulating grey mist that arched above the circle, tongues of black flame licking down towards the old woman.

'. . . Metatron, Highest of the High . . .'

A scream like pale thunder bounced from wall to wall

whilst from the coiling helix of mist the ghastly face stared. Eyes spitting jets of ebony flame, a long serpentine tongue flicked towards Martha.

Without realising he had moved, Torrey snatched the woman clear. Whatever it was floating there in front of them, it meant Martha Sim no good, it meant neither of them any good. Daft as it seemed, daft as every part of him said it was, he had to do something. But the commandos had taught him nothing of the way to handle a bloody column of mist!

Wary now, the amorphous shape floated around the protecting salt ring, its fiery eyes never leaving Torrey.

Christ, what the hell could he do? Rotating, matching the filmy mass movement for movement, he wrestled with the unbelief rocking his brain. He knew it was all in his mind, put there by an old woman's mumbo jumbo, but no matter what he himself believed that bloody monstrosity had half killed Martha Sim once tonight and the next attempt might well see the job through.

'Anna.' He hadn't thought to speak, to say anything, but the word came without his help. Beyond the circle the floating column stood still then slowly changed to the figure he knew so well.

'Anna,' he said again and the attractive face smiled, wide blue eyes stroking his face.

But that thing smiling at him wasn't Anna. It was as if only now the full realisation hit him. Placing Martha behind him he breathed deep. The next couple of minutes would see this thing gone or himself a candidate for the funny farm.

'No, not Anna.' His voice rang around the tiny sitting room. 'That was a name I gave to someone I thought I loved but that's no longer the case.'

Behind him Martha Sim touched a reassuring hand to his shoulder as he went on.

'I have no special words of power, I can only say what I feel in plain everyday language, but every word will be the truth. I don't know what it was caused me to think I loved you, I only know now it was a mistake. You had no real love for anyone but yourself, you took what you could from me and from the men you killed. But that wasn't enough, was it? A man's life is not enough to satisfy you, you want his soul along with it. Well, you can have mine, it's no more than I deserve, but it will be exchanged for that of the priest!'

A few feet away the vaporous figure shimmered, the light of the dying fire reflecting red on the grey spindrift body, the mouth losing its smile.

The words already present in his mind, Torrey looked deep into eyes that glinted like hard blue stones.

'Anna, the power of the Most High God commands you, release the soul of Peter Darley.'

From the window a burst of brilliant moonlight streamed into the room, encircling the figure that writhed and twisted, its grotesque mouth screaming in soundless agony.

Blinding radiance gleamed pale gold, ranging through the spectrum to ivory, silver and finally a whiteness of an intensity that burned. Unable to look at it, Torrey folded Martha in his arms, burying his face in her grey-threaded hair, a prayer for help on his lips, help that would take Anna from the world and from his life.

Kate Mallory lit a cigarette and leaned comfortably against the pillows of her bed, blowing a series of short drifts of lavender smoke through pursed lips.

Why hadn't she seen it when it was as big as the nose on Gérard Depardieu's face?

She drew on the cigarette again, holding the smoke behind her teeth. First there had been James Connor, Deputy Commissioner of police. Next Clifton Mather, pharmaceuticals had been his game. Then had come Maxwell Seton, the dapper banker who saw himself as God's gift to women . . . or maybe not women!

Pulling deeply she inhaled smoke low into her lungs, feeling the bite of nicotine.

Finally there had been Philip Bartley. All dead but all connected somehow. Daniels would say nothing even if he knew. He'd got what he wanted, Bartley's body had been covered with white powder, that burst bag still clutched in his hand . . . yes, Bruce Daniels had his drug peddler . . . and Kate Mallory? She had her story but it wasn't the whole story. Little Katie had smelled a rat and now it was staring her in the face.

Mather had died in a car fire not far from Monskwell, Seton had rolled from a car and been crushed to death by a lorry on that self same road, and Bartley lived at Monkswell! But Philip Bartley did not drive himself.

With smoke trickling between her teeth, Kate Mallory

smiled. Richard Torrey had been the odious grocer's chauffeur . . . and Richard Torrey wasn't dead!

Extinguishing the cigarette she hauled herself along the landing to the bathroom, the smell of her landlady's cooking wafting up the stairs. That was one thing could be said in favour of the late Mr Bartley, he allowed his staff to buy at a generous discount and her landlady bought plenty. She had been lucky finding this place; leaving the small town of Birtley in the North East she had never hoped to find a body as kind as the mother she had helped bury, but that was exactly what she had found here. Annie Price was more like a second mother than she was a landlady.

Bathed and dressed, her damp hair shining like polished amber, she ate the generous helping of double-yolked egg and bacon fried crispy the way she liked it; she would have to exercise if she wasn't going to finish up a modern day Billie Bunter . . .

'They'm still goin' on about it over at the supermarket.' Annie Price refilled both cups with steaming hot tea. 'Nobody seems to know whether the place will be shut down altogether or mebbe's bought by another firm, but if they does then that firm won't be Asda, they 'ad a place 'ere but closed it a couple of years back . . . eeh! It be a worry for folk and no coddin', what with 'alf the town lookin' for jobs as it is.'

No, it was no joke. Kate swallowed a mouthful of tea. Like Birtley, Darlaston was suffering under the yoke of an industrial depression that had many parts of the country in its claws.

'There will be somebody who'll buy it,' she smiled at the worried face. 'It's certain the store won't be closed for good, it's about the only place left to shop in Darlaston.'

'That be no lie neither!' Annie returned the heavy pewter teapot to the tray that held a pretty tea caddy. 'D'ain't do no good for this town Bartley building that place, put just about everybody else out of business, little blokes stood no chance against 'em.'

Little blokes like Amos Hodgkin? Leaving the table, Kate heaved her bag to her shoulder calling goodbye to the still muttering Annie as she left the house. But little pins could still prick and Amos Hodgkin had been sharp enough to burst Philip Bartley's balloon.

But what of Bartley's chauffeur? That was the man who interested her. If what Inspector Bruce Daniels had told her could be taken as truth then Mr Richard Torrey was back in Darlaston.

Daniels had owed her a favour after she let him in on the titbit Amos Hodgkin had given her . . . given her! Kate gave a snort of disgust, she'd paid plenty for that but at least Scotty had reimbursed her. Her editor had been delighted with her copy and not stingy with his praises, but if her plan worked out there might be more still to come. The question was . . . where to find Torrey?

He was out of a job . . . he would have to sign on for benefit . . . first place first! Having reached Katherine's Cross, Kate turned left into Pinfold Street. And first would be the dole office.

*

'According to what I read in the *Star* you saw as much as I did.' Almost bumping into her as he had left the dole office, Torrey had refused the offer of a drink in the Frying Pan. Echo Sounder and the rest of the low life in this town would know soon enough of his talking with this woman without his sitting under their noses. He could have refused to talk to her, he could still get up off this park bench, turn his back and tell her to go to hell . . . but that was a place he'd almost gone to himself and he didn't like the residents . . . but he did like Kate Mallory; she was no beauty but there was a genuineness about her that appealed to him.

'I saw . . . yes.' Kate nodded, her sherry-coloured hair glinting in the afternoon light. 'But what I saw didn't show why . . . why Philip Bartley crawled out on to that ledge . . . why he screamed in fear before he threw himself off.'

Had he thrown himself off? Torrey seemed to feel again his own fingers being prised apart, being torn loose from that jacket . . . or had something pushed him off?

'The man was terrified, you can't deny that.'

Torrey kept silent. He couldn't deny it but that didn't mean he had to talk about it.

'. . . and I have a feeling it was terror caused Maxwell Seton to throw himself from that car . . .'

'Who said he threw himself?'

Rummaging deep in her bag Kate found the cherished Rothmans. She had struck the first chord, now for the overture.

'Nobody said,' she opened the packet, 'but a smart girl puts two and two together. Seton was badly injured, his arm in plaster. The last thing he would willingly do was dance a jig in the back of that car, yet you say that is exactly what he did before rolling out to fall under a lorry. Anybody in the pain he must have been in wouldn't flutter an eyelid if he didn't have to, so it must have been something extreme that drove him to wrestle open that door and heave himself out. So why not tell me, Mr Torrey?'

'You've had your story.' Torrey shook his head. 'There's no more to tell.'

But there was! Kate offered the cigarettes, smiling as he muttered they were killers. That was what Scotty said but she enjoyed them and it was her life after all.

'I think there is, Mr Torrey.' She blew a thin stream of smoke into the crisp air. 'And what's more I don't think you will ever be really over it until you tell someone the whole story.'

'And that someone should be you . . . is that the way you hope to get your next story?'

Watching his shoulders slump, hands between his knees, Kate admitted to herself that had been her intention exactly, but now . . . ! Now there was something that said he had gone through enough.

'And if I promise there will be no story, that not a word will be printed, could you trust me enough to share what's still inside you?'

Did he want to share what still haunted him, did he want to talk about it to her or to anybody? Torrey stared at his hands held together between his knees. But then if he spat it out then p'raps it really would be over.

'Print one word and I'll deny it.' He looked up at the

face watching him, a face with a slightly out of line mouth that made it interesting. 'I'll sue the *Star* for defamation and anything else a solicitor can think of.'

Kate blew a stream of smoke, staining the air lavender-grey.

'You have my word,' she said as he dropped his head again.

Slowly at first, then the words coming so fast they tripped over one another as they left his lips, Torrey told the whole story.

'The most unbelievable part . . .' he shook his head as at last he lifted it to look at her, 'the part you'd have to laugh at if it weren't so bloody pathetic you wanted to cry . . . the most unbelievable part was that I, Torrey, a commando who served with the toughest of the tough, fell for such a little tart . . . !'

'It's not that unusual.' Kate spoke for the first time in minutes.

'No.' Torrey laughed, a self-condemning painful laugh. 'But I really believed she loved me. Lord only knows what went wrong.'

'And it was Anna . . . or Anna's ghost, you believe was behind all those deaths. Yet it didn't kill Daniels . . . why . . . why would it let him live?'

'I wondered that myself.' Torrey straightened, stretching his legs out in front of him. 'It took Martha Sim to spell it out. I had said I wanted Anna's killers dead and that spirit or whatever it was latched on to that, but it could only work through me and if Daniels had me sent down for laying out those three men in the yard of the

Bird-in-Hand then I couldn't have gone to Monkswell or been chauffeur to Philip Bartley.'

It all fit so nicely. Kate lit another cigarette. Pity she couldn't print it . . . but she wouldn't, there was something about Torrey she felt deserved her loyalty . . . and her friendship? Kate smiled to herself, yes, she would like to give him that too.